Time to
Say Goodbye

Rosie
GOODWIN
Time to
Say Goodbye

ZAFFRE

First published in Great Britain in 2020
This edition published in 2020 by
ZAFFRE
80–81 Wimpole St, London W1G 9RE

A CIP catalogue record for this book is
available from the British Library.

Hardback ISBN: 978–1–83877–022–8
Paperback ISBN: 978–1–83877–023–5

Also available as an ebook

1 3 5 7 9 10 8 6 4 2

Typeset by Palimpsest Book Production Limited, Falkirk, Stirlingshire
Printed and bound in Great Britain by Clays Ltd, Elcograf S.p.A.

Zaffre is an imprint of Bonnier Books UK
www.bonnierbooks.co.uk

This one is for my wonderful children,
Donna, Sarah, Christian and Aaron.

You're my world xxxxxxxxx

Saturday's child works hard for a living

Prologue

November 1930

Sunday Branning smiled as she stood at the window of Treetops and watched her daughter Lavinia – or Livvy, as she was affectionately known – gallop down the drive on her horse. Livvy adored horses and riding, just like her father, who had once again built up a reputation for being the finest stud breeder in the Midlands. It had taken years to rebuild his stables after the Great War, but somehow, he had managed it, and once again people were coming from far and wide for his horses. Sunday could well remember how heartbroken Tom had been when she had written to tell him that his stock had been taken for war horses after he had left to fight in the Great War. He had raised many of them from foals and knew that it was unlikely any of them would survive. It was to his credit that through sheer hard work he had got his business up and running profitably again once he had returned.

It was just as well, for following the stock market crash the year before, money was tight for most people and businesses were closing daily. Treetops was an expensive house to run and now they no longer ran it as a children's home, Sunday was constantly trying to find little ways of saving money.

Once Livvy had disappeared from sight, Sunday returned to her desk, where she had been writing out invitations for her sixtieth birthday party, which she'd be holding in two weeks' time.

Sixty! She sighed as she thought back over her life. It hadn't started so well – she had been left on the steps of the Union Workhouse as a newborn – but things had improved when she had finally been reunited with her birth mother. And then there was Tom, the love of her life. She still adored him as much as she had on the day she had married him, if not more. As if thoughts of him had conjured him from thin air, he suddenly stuck his head round the door and gave her a cheeky wink.

'All right, sweetheart? Hope you're not working too hard?'

Sunday laughed as she waved him away. 'Oh, be off with you and let me get this done.'

He grinned and blew her a kiss, and once he was gone, she tried to concentrate on the job in hand again. It was hard to believe she was this old, but then she supposed age caught up with everyone in the end and Tom had always assured her she didn't look it. Glancing towards the mirror, she stroked her fair hair as if to convince herself that he was speaking the truth. It was streaked with grey at the temples now, but her eyes were still a clear, bright blue, and apart from a few lines around them and her mouth, her face was still attractive. Livvy took after her in looks, with her fair colouring, whereas Tom's son, Ben, was dark, and as he had matured had become the double of his father. And then there was their adored Kathy, who at nearly twelve was the double of her mother, Kitty. Sunday and Tom

2

had brought Kitty up from a baby and had loved her as their own, until she left them at sixteen to join her birth mother in London. Once there, Kitty had become the darling of the music halls – but her pretty face and vulnerable nature had made her a target for an unscrupulous man. When she had finally returned to Treetops, she was heartbroken and hiding a secret. She tragically died giving birth to an illegitimate daughter, and it had come as no surprise to anyone when Sunday and Tom had adopted her baby too.

Smiling, Sunday turned her attention back to the invitations – but she had barely started to write again when the door burst open and Cissie Jenkins, her long-term friend, burst unceremoniously into the room, all of aflutter.

'You'd best come straight away, pet,' Cissie gasped, holding her hand to the stitch in her side. 'My George says Tom has had a fall in the paddock. I've sent Ben off for Dr Lewis.'

Whereas time had been kind to Sunday, Cissie looked her age and had grown portly with the years. Their friendship had started when they were both children incarcerated in the Union Workhouse, and had withstood the test of time until now they were more like sisters than friends, and Sunday loved her unconditionally.

The colour drained from Sunday's cheeks and she stood up so abruptly that she almost overturned the chair. 'A fall . . .? Is it bad?'

Cissie shook her head. 'I've no idea, you'd best come and see.'

Side by side the two women rushed through the house and, once they had emerged into the stable yard, they turned as one and began to race towards the group at the back of the stables, where Tom trained the horses.

3

'Was it Storm he fell from?' Sunday asked breathlessly, and when Cissie nodded she bit her lip. Hadn't she told him that she didn't think Storm was ready to be ridden yet? He was a beautiful young stallion and admittedly from brilliant stock, but had proved very difficult to train.

They rounded the corner to see Storm tossing his head, snorting and pawing the ground at the other side of the paddock, while George leaned over Tom, who was lying motionless on the ground.

Sunday was glad of the new calf-length skirts that were fashionable now as she sped towards them.

'Don't try and move him,' George warned as she dropped to her knees beside them.

She showed no sign of hearing him as she focused her attention on her husband and gently lifted his hand.

'Oh, Tom, *why* didn't you wait for another couple of weeks before you tried to ride him?' she whispered.

'He's out cold,' George said unnecessarily. 'Best not touch him till the doctor gets here in case he's broken anythin'. We might make things worse.' Then, turning to his wife, he said, 'Run an' fetch a blanket to cover him, would yer, love?'

Cissie set off straight away; the late autumn air was cold. Luckily the cottage she and George lived in was close by and she was back, huffing and puffing, in minutes. George had barely had time to cover Tom with the blanket when they heard the sound of horses' hooves followed by that of an engine and Ben and the doctor arrived back at the same time.

As Ben leapt nimbly from his horse, the young doctor climbed out of his car and hurried towards them, clutching a large black leather bag.

Dr Lewis was a nice young man, fresh out of medical school,

who had recently taken over the practice when Sunday's family doctor retired.

'Is he conscious?' he asked, as he too fell to his knees beside Tom.

Sunday shook her head fearfully, still holding tight to her husband's hand. 'N-no, he isn't.'

The doctor nodded as he hastily took a stethoscope from his bag. 'Could you all stand back please and give me some space?'

His face was grim as he bent to listen to Tom's heart, then very gently he lifted Tom's head. It lolled to one side and Sunday's heart began to pound so loudly she was sure they would hear it.

The doctor sat back on his heels for a moment then shook his head as he looked at Sunday and told her gravely, 'I'm so sorry, Mrs Branning. I'm afraid he's gone. It looks like he broke his neck in the fall; death would have been instantaneous. He wouldn't have felt anything.'

'*No-ooo!*' Sunday's head wagged from side to side in denial and Cissie started to cry, while George and Ben stood so still they might have been turned to stone.

'B-but he *can't* be dead . . .' Sunday began to shake Tom's hand and Cissie leaned down and gently drew her to her feet.

'Come away, pet,' she muttered through her tears. 'There's no more you can do here. The men will do what needs to be done.'

Sunday suddenly uncharacteristically lashed out, almost sending Cissie flying. 'So, what *do* I do then?' she cried in an anguished voice. 'Just leave him lying there?' Then, turning to George and Ben, she ordered in a voice quite unlike hers, 'Get a door from the stables and carry him inside. I refuse to leave him lying out here!'

5

The men instantly went to do her bidding, as Sunday turned and staggered back towards the house. At that minute, Livvy appeared on her horse at the end of the drive and she drew her mount to a halt, just as Cissie and her mother were about to go in by the front door.

'What's wrong with you two?' she asked, as she stared at Cissie's tear-stained face.

'Let Cissie take your horse round to the stables and come into the drawing room,' Sunday said. 'I need to tell you something,'

With a deep frown Livvy dismounted and did as she was told.

'What's happened, Mum?' she asked only a few moments later, as they entered the drawing room. She knew it was something bad. One look at her mother's lint-white face and shaking hands told her that.

'I . . . it's your father . . .' Sunday gulped deep in her throat and forced herself to go on. 'I . . . I'm afraid he had a fall from Storm and he's . . .' She found that she couldn't say the terrible word. But she had said enough and Livvy's pretty face crumpled.

'Y-you mean he's *dead*?'

When Sunday slowly nodded, Livvy broke into sobs and dropped onto the nearest chair as her mother rushed over and gathered her into her arms. Sunday was in deep shock and, somehow, she couldn't take it in. Just a few minutes ago all had been right with her world but now she knew it would never be the same again.

The day of the funeral dawned dark and dismal. Going in search of Sunday, Cissie found her standing by the window in the drawing room, staring out across the lawns. Approaching her quietly, she laid her arm gently across her shoulders. Sunday smiled – a sad smile that didn't reach her eyes. 'I was just picturing Tom and me down there on the lawn on the evening of our wedding day, dancing in the moonlight,' she said huskily. As yet she hadn't shed a single tear since the terrible day Tom had died, but Cissie knew her well enough to know that when they did finally come, they would be hard to stop.

'It were a grand day, all right,' Cissie said, in a wobbly voice. 'I can still see you both now with all the lanterns that were strung in the trees and the moon shinin' down on you. You looked like a fairy princess in your beautiful gown and Tom looked like the happiest man on earth. It's a precious memory that no one can ever take away from you; you must hang on to that.'

And then they saw the black hearse approaching down the drive, coming to collect Tom, who had been lying in the day room in his coffin. She said sadly, 'Come on, pet, it's almost time to go.'

Without a word, Sunday turned and followed her from the room.

It was with relief some hours later that Cissie escorted the last of the mourners to the front door, leaving only the solicitor who had stayed to read Tom's will to the family.

Sunday was waiting for him in the drawing room along with Ben, Livvy and Kathy.

Cissie turned towards Mr Dixon and, without a word, led him into the room, then left, closing the door quietly behind her.

'Before I begin, may I offer my condolences to you all?' Mr Dixon said quietly, as he rummaged in his briefcase and produced Tom's will. 'Mr Branning was a true gentleman and I know he will be sorely missed by all that knew him. I have never seen so many people attend a funeral before. But now, down to business.'

He cleared his throat and began. 'This is the last will and testament of Thomas Branning. It is all very straightforward, short and to the point, but should you have any questions, please feel free to interrupt me.'

Ben leaned forward in his seat.

'To Cissie and George Jenkins, my long-term friends, I leave the cottage in the grounds in which they have resided for many years, with my thanks for their friendship, loyalty and support. To my only son, Ben, I leave my gold Hunter pocket watch. To my two beautiful daughters I leave all my love always. Treetops, the business, and all the rest of my worldly goods I leave to my beloved wife, Sunday Branning.'

Ben looked shocked as he leaned even further forward in his chair. 'But surely there's some mistake,' he said as colour rose in his cheeks. 'Isn't it customary for the eldest son to inherit?'

Mr Dixon shook his head. 'In years gone by it would have been,' he answered. 'But times are changing, and it is quite usual now for the first person in a marriage to pass away to leave what they own to their spouse.'

Ben's lips set in a grim line and, without a word, he rose and marched from the room. No one seemed to notice. Livvy and Kathy were too busy crying, and Sunday seemed trapped in a world of her own.

Chapter One

'I thought we might all go to the carnival next Saturday,' Cissie suggested, as she folded the clothes she had fetched in from the line outside.

Sunday was peeling potatoes for dinner at the sink. She shrugged. 'Hm, we'll see.'

Cissie sighed. So much had changed since Tom's death five years before. And not just at Treetops. Change was afoot in the town too. Council housing was springing up to house the poor who had been forced to live in the Union Workhouse, which was now closed, much to Sunday's delight. She had no happy memories of the place, although once she was grown, she had worked tirelessly with the board of governors to ensure that the living conditions for the residents were vastly improved.

Now that Treetops was no longer run as a children's home, Cissie and Sunday did most of the work about the house themselves. There was no longer a need for hired staff, but although Sunday did more than her share, she had never really got over the death of her husband and rarely smiled anymore. Most of the rooms had been closed up, as it was too expensive to light fires in them all, and the furniture inside was swathed in dust sheets. Cissie often felt sad as she thought back to days gone by when the house had been full of children and their laughter had echoed along the corridors, but she was made of stern stuff and there was no point in living in the past. She did her best to get on with things.

Livvy was doing a secretarial course and working at a solicitor's office in the town, and Kathy had started her nursing training and was working at the General Hospital in Manor Court Road. When she wasn't at the hospital, she would still help out in the stables and ride whenever she could. In fact, she never seemed to stop, as Cissie had once remarked to Sunday.

'Ah well, you know what they say,' Sunday had replied with a smile. 'Saturday's child works hard for a living.'

Cissie had her own thoughts on that. For some time, she'd been concerned that Kathy was getting just a little too close to Ben for comfort. They had been brought up as family and Cissie feared nothing good could come of it. Admittedly they were not blood related, but Kathy was not yet seventeen, and he was well into his forties! The thought of the scandal a relationship between them would cause, and how upset Sunday would be, made Cissie shudder. Not that she dared to voice her opinion. Kathy could be feisty – like her mother Kitty had been before her – and Cissie was all too aware that should she say anything Kathy would probably snap at her and tell her to mind her own business.

Since Tom's death, Ben had taken over the household accounts and was now responsible for paying the bills. In addition, he and George tended the grounds and ran the stud business, which was thankfully still thriving. It was just as well, for the money that Sunday's mother had left her was long spent. Sunday's mother – the late Lady Lavinia Huntley – and her second husband, had gone to live in the South of France to enjoy their twilight years together in the sun, and had sadly passed away within months of each other the year before. That had been yet another heartache for Sunday to bear, for once reunited with the mother she had never known she had as a child, they had forged a strong bond. Sunday had taken her passing badly.

But now Cissie was determined that it was time for Sunday to face the world again. The way she saw it, she couldn't grieve forever, so she went on, 'I thought if we went to watch the carnival, we might do a little shopping when it was over. I can't remember when you last had a new dress and they're so easy to buy off the peg now. The days of havin' to be measured an' go for all them fittin's are well an' truly over, an' to my mind that's no bad thing. So, what do you think? I could do wi' a day out, to be honest. It feels like it's all work at the minute an' yer know the old sayin' – all work an' no play . . .'

Sunday glanced at her friend's face and sighed resignedly. Cissie had been her rock and she supposed it would be selfish to refuse her. 'I'll think about it,' she answered quietly and, satisfied, Cissie nodded.

'Well, we had a rare good time at the last one, didn't we?' she chuckled as she remembered, and hefted the wash basket to the side of the heavy wooden ironing board. 'It's hard to believe that it's been five years already since the town had the first one. And all that money it raised for the hospital, eh? Why, it must have been just before Tom—'

She stopped abruptly and colour burned her cheeks as she realised what she had been about to say – but if Sunday had

11

noticed, she gave no sign, and carried on peeling the potatoes. Cissie meanwhile hastily reached up to remove the bare light bulb that dangled from the ceiling, and plugged the iron into it, thanking the lord for the electricity they now had. It seemed a world ago since she had been forced to do the ironing with flat irons. She could do it in half the time now.

She had just started when Ben strode into the kitchen. As usual he was frowning. Cissie often found it hard to remember the fun-loving boy he had been before he had marched away to war. Like many young men who had been fortunate enough to come home, he had seen things on the battlefield that would haunt him forever. In addition to this, his face and one arm were badly scarred, a fact he had never really come to terms with. At that time, he had been convinced that no one would ever love him looking as he did, but then he had married Maggie. They had been blissfully happy, until she had died in childbirth just a few years after they were wed. The child, a baby boy, had died with her and he had never quite got over it. Now his father's death seemed to have added to his depression. Cissie knew he had been expecting to inherit Treetops and that he felt resentful because he hadn't, although she hadn't said as much to Sunday, who still seemed to find it hard enough to just get through each day, so Cissie had no intention of adding to her worries. But she was determined to do something about that now. To her mind, Sunday had grieved for quite long enough and now it was time to try to bring her back into the real world.

'I was just sayin' that I thought it would be nice if we all took some time off to go to the carnival next Saturday,' Cissie told Ben, as he helped himself to a cup of tea from the big brown teapot standing on the range. 'Do you fancy comin'?'

Ben snorted as he threw himself onto a chair. 'And why would

I want to do that? I've horses to look after and accounts to keep. Besides, Blaze is due to have her foal anytime. I need to be here.'

'Hm!' Cissie sniffed disapprovingly, but she didn't push it. Ben could be as stubborn as a mule when he had a mind to be, and she knew she'd have been wasting her breath.

That evening, after Kathy and Livvy had both got home from work and they were all sitting together at the kitchen table, Cissie raised the subject again.

'Well, I'd *love* to go,' Livvy said immediately.

'Hm . . . I think I'd best stay here with Ben, just in case Blaze needs us,' Kathy said.

Cissie sighed.

Livvy meanwhile was looking hopefully at her mother. Like Cissie, she felt that it was time for her to get out and about again. It had been hard for her and Kathy to lose their father too, but over the last few years their mother had been so locked in her own grief that sometimes the girls felt they had lost her as well. The only time she ever ventured out was to attend meetings at the town hall about the new housing that was being built in and around the town.

'So, shall we go then, Mum?' Livvy asked pointedly, and Sunday sighed, knowing when she was beaten.

'I suppose so, if you *really* want to.'

'*I do!*' Livvy declared joyously.

Cissie beamed with satisfaction.

On Saturday, they set off for Nuneaton in George's motor car, and were soon wandering amongst the throngs of people lining the streets, waiting for the carnival to start. Luckily it was a fine, sunny day and when the first float appeared everybody began to cheer. Once again, all money raised would go to the General Hospital, and for the next hour they stood cheering and throwing pennies into the fundraisers' buckets, as the gay carnival floats passed by. Dotted in between them were marching bands, dancers, clowns and horses, and the air rang with the sound of laughter.

The last of the floats was just passing them when Sunday noticed Livvy speaking to a very attractive young man. Her heart did a little flutter. Livvy had shown no interest in courting as yet – but perhaps things were about to change?

Hurrying over to them, she introduced herself, 'Hello, I'm Livvy's mother.'

He quickly removed his cap and gave her a disarming smile, showing a set of straight, white teeth. She noticed his hair was dark, with a tendency to curl, and he had lovely blue eyes.

'How do you do, Mrs Branning?' He gave a courteous little bow. 'I'm David Deacon.'

'*Dr* David Deacon,' Livvy chipped in, with a grin. 'He works at the hospital with Kathy.'

'Only *junior* doctor.' He laughed. 'And is Kathy not here with you today?'

When Sunday shook her head, she thought she detected a look of disappointment flash in his eyes. 'Oh well, do give her my regards when you get home, and enjoy the rest of your day,' he said politely, and, lifting his hat, he disappeared off into the crowds.

'What a charming young man,' Sunday commented, as she watched him go.

'I reckon he's sweet on our Kathy,' Livvy told her, with a grin.

'Really? Then I wonder why she has never mentioned him?'

Livvy shrugged. 'I don't think she's interested, which is a shame because he's a really nice chap.' Then putting David Deacon from her mind, she turned her attention back to the carnival procession.

When the last of the gaily decorated floats had passed, they followed the crowds to Riversley Park where the town mayor would choose the winner. Then Livvy insisted on trying her hand at the coconut shy and some of the other stalls set up there. She even had a go on the carousel, laughing as the brightly painted horses rode up and down. Next it was the hall of mirrors, which had them all in fits of giggles, and then they were off to see the bearded lady. After that they treated themselves to toffee apples and candy flosses, before taking turns on the hoopla stall. When they had finished, Livvy insisted on going to see the strong man and having a go on the large swingboats, which made her feel slightly sick.

'Phew, I reckon I might pop off an' have a pint wi' Sam Arnold at the Wheatsheaf in Abbey Street afore we set off fer home,' George said eventually.

He was worn out, and suddenly realising that the time was going on, Cissie nodded. 'You do that, luv. Me an' Sunday an' Livvy have got a bit o' shoppin' to do, so we'll meet you by the Co-op in a couple of hours, eh?'

'Sounds good to me.' George straightened his cap and set off, whistling merrily. It wasn't often that he got to have any time off and he intended to make the most of every minute.

Meanwhile the women headed back to the town centre, where they spent a time wandering amongst the stalls in the market before heading for the dress shops.

'Ooh, look at this one.' Cissie held up a sky-blue dress. It had a dropped waist with a mid-calf skirt and padded shoulders, long sleeves and tiny pearl buttons all down the front. 'This would suit you a treat wi' your colourin', Sunday. An' it's your size, an' all. Why don't you try it on?'

Sunday looked at it doubtfully. It was very pretty, admittedly, and much more up to date than most of the clothes in her wardrobe, but she rarely left Treetops to go anywhere to wear it, as she pointed out to Cissie.

'Rubbish!' Cissie snorted. 'You go to your council meetin's an' this would be just right for them.'

And so, very reluctantly, Sunday took it into the fitting room, where the owner of the shop helped her put it on. Staring at herself in the mirror once it was on, she did have to admit it looked very nice. In fact, she realised in that moment how much she had let herself go. She'd taken little interest in her appearance since she had lost Tom, and tended to wear practical, dark colours – but the soft blue of the dress seemed to lift her spirits.

'Are you sure it's not too young a style for me?' she asked Cissie worriedly, when she came out of the fitting room to show it to her. 'I am sixty-five, you know. I don't want to walk about looking like mutton dressed as lamb.'

Livvy giggled. 'Of course, it's not too young for you,' both she and Cissie assured her. 'And actually, Mum, I think you look really good for your age, although you could do with doing something with your hair. That style is really out of fashion now.'

'Really?' Sunday's hand rose to her hair which was pulled back into a severe bun at the back of her head. 'In that case I'll take the dress and we'll make the hairdresser's the next stop.'

Luckily, they found a hair salon that was able to fit her in without an appointment, which was just as well because Sunday

16

knew that if she had time to think about having her hair chopped off, she might well change her mind. Tom had always loved her hair long, but styles were changing.

'So, what would you like?' the young hairdresser asked as she brushed Sunday's long hair and smiled at her in the mirror.

Sunday gulped and Livvy piped up, 'Let's go for the Greta Garbo look. Shoulder length, then it won't be too much of a shock all at once. Smooth on top, parted to one side and curly all around the bottom.'

The young woman nodded, and Sunday closed her eyes as she felt the girl make the first cut. Her hair fell to the floor in long strands and it wasn't until sometime later, when she was told to open her eyes, that Sunday dared to take a peek in the mirror.

Her breath caught in her throat as she viewed the transform-ation, and when she turned her head from side to side, she hardly recognised herself and felt curiously light-headed.

'It looks *wonderful*!' Livvy clapped her hands with delight.

'It certainly does,' Cissie said approvingly. 'It's knocked years off yer. In fact, I might have mine done.'

Sunday was quietly pleased, and after paying the hairdresser and leaving her a generous tip, she followed Cissie and Livvy from the salon.

'Well, much as I don't want to, I reckon we ought to be headin' off to meet George else we'll have no dinner tonight. If I can drag him out o' the Wheatsheaf, that is,' Cissie said glumly.

They hurried along Stratford Street and turned left into Abbey Street, weaving their way through the stallholders who were busy packing up their wares. George was waiting for them outside the Co-op as promised and he whistled through his teeth when he saw Sunday.

17

'You look a treat,' he told her as he opened the car door for her, and for the first time in a very long while, Sunday really smiled. Perhaps it was time to start getting more involved with the family again. She could never bring her beloved Tom back but at least she still had them, and they were all very precious to her.

Chapter Two

A few days later Sunday entered the study to dust it only to find Ben sitting at the desk with the accounts book open in front of him.

'Oh sorry,' she apologised. 'I thought you were over at the stables; I didn't mean to disturb you.'

'It's all right.' He snapped the book shut and took it to the safe. 'I'd just finished anyway.'

'Actually, I've been meaning to have a word with you,' Sunday said, seizing the opportunity now that they had a few moments alone. 'I've realised that I've been rather selfish leaving so much on your shoulders since your father died and I think it's time I started pulling my weight a bit more.'

When he raised his eyebrows, she hurried on. 'I could at least take over doing the business accounts again. You and George have more than enough to do outside in the stables.'

Much to her surprise he slammed the safe door shut and shook his head. 'Are you not happy with the job I've been doing then?'

'Of course I am,' Sunday assured him hastily. 'But . . .'

'I *like* doing the accounts and with no disrespect intended I know far better than you what the stables are making. Blaze's new foal is a little beauty. He'll fetch a fine price when he's a bit older, but then you wouldn't really expect anything else with his pedigree.' Storm, the horse that Tom had fallen from, was the foal's father and had turned into an excellent stud. People from miles around brought their mares to be covered by him. It was ironic, when Sunday came to think of it. Following Tom's fatal accident, George and Ben had been all for shooting the horse, but it had been Sunday who had pointed out that the accident hadn't really been the animal's fault. He had just been young and wild, and Tom should have known that he wasn't tame enough to be saddle-trained. So, he had been allowed to live and was now earning them a large portion of their income.

'The thing is, if you take over doing the accounts again, I shall have to tell you every time we have a customer,' Ben pointed out. 'It's so much easier if I just do it myself, and all the bills have always been paid on time, haven't they? I give Cissie the housekeeping money every Friday morning as regular as clockwork, so what's the problem?'

Feeling somewhat patronised, Sunday shook her head. She had truly felt it was time for her to become more involved in the business again but then she was also aware that Ben, as he had quite rightly pointed out, *had* done a good job of keeping things going and she didn't want to offend him. 'There isn't a problem,' she admitted. 'I just thought . . . But anyway, if you're quite sure you're happy to continue as we are?'

'I am,' he said abruptly and, turning about, he stalked from the room.

Sunday frowned. *Well, I made a right mess of that*, she thought glumly. When she and Tom had first received the letter, quite some time after their marriage, informing them that Ben was Tom's illegitimate son from another relationship, it had caused a rift in their marriage for a while and Sunday had felt a little jealous of the child. But not for long. Whatever Tom had done was not Ben's fault and by the time she tearfully waved him off to war, she had thought their relationship was back where it always had been, and for her part, she still loved him as much as she always had. But when he returned, traumatised by what he had seen and the scars he had sustained, she had felt a rift between them once again. He had grown even colder towards her since the death of his wife and father. And the discovery that Tom had left the house to her had only seemed to deepen the problem.

She feared Ben had never really come to terms with the fact that he was the result of an affair his father had had before his marriage to Sunday, even though Tom had had Ben's name changed to his and had proudly welcomed him into the family and openly recognised him as his son. Now she realised that if she forced Ben to let her take control of the business again, he would resent her even more. For the time being, she decided, it would be best to leave things as they were. With a sigh she got on with the dusting.

That evening as they all sat at dinner, Kathy said casually, 'David Deacon asked if he might come over on Sunday and take one of the horses out for a ride with me. His family in Yorkshire have horses and he misses riding so I didn't think you'd mind?'

'Isn't that the nice young doctor I met on the day of the carnival?' Sunday asked as her heart beat faster. He was such a pleasant young man and although Kathy was still very young it would be lovely to see her fall in love. Up to now she hadn't seemed interested in much at all except her nursing career and spending what little spare time she had in the stables with Ben. 'Of course I don't mind,' she ended quickly. 'It will be nice to see him again.'

Livvy rose from the table at that moment, saying, 'Sorry but you'll have to excuse me, I'm going roller skating with some of the girls from work this evening and I'm supposed to be meeting them in an hour. I shall be late if I don't get my skates on . . . excuse the pun!'

Sunday smiled as her daughter hurried away to get ready. Livvy had just started to spread her wings a little and go out with her friends, and although it worried Sunday slightly she was also keen to encourage her to be independent. In 1930 the Palace Cinema in the town had been turned into a skating rink and Livvy had been a regular there ever since. In fact, Sunday had heard she was now a very good skater. She wished Kathy had more of a social life too. After all, she was virtually grown up now and with Livvy just a few months younger Sunday supposed she should prepare herself for the fact they might each meet a nice young man soon.

'I should get on as well.' Ben wiped his mouth on a napkin and rose. 'I've got the vet coming first thing to look at one of the mares who has a nasty cut on her side so I shall be getting an early night when I've settled the horses.'

'I'll come and help you,' Kathy offered, rising and following him quickly from the room.

Glancing at Cissie, who was busily loading a tray with dirty pots, Sunday saw her raise her eyebrows, and frowned. 'And what is that look for?' she asked, bemused.

Cissie shrugged. 'I suppose I was just thinkin' it were about time Kathy got out an' about a bit more wi' people her own age instead of spending all her spare time wi' Ben,' she answered.

'But what are you implying, Cissie? Didn't you hear her say her friend is coming to go riding with her at the weekend? That's a start, surely? And anyway, why *shouldn't* she spend time with Ben? You know she's always hero-worshipped him since she was knee-high to a grasshopper.'

'She might have done but with the age gap between 'em bein' so great I don't think it'd be healthy if she got a crush on him,' Cissie replied.

'B-but she would *never* look at Ben that way, surely? They've been brought up as family.'

'They might have been brought up as such but actually they ain't related by blood, are they? An' stranger things happen.' Cissie sailed from the room without another word, leaving Sunday to stare after her in consternation.

In the stables Ben began to fork fresh straw into the stalls before bringing the horses in from the fields as Kathy swung on the half door watching him.

'So, who's this young man you've invited over then?' he asked, without taking his eyes off what he was doing.

Kathy sniffed. 'Oh, just a doctor I work with. He's very nice and loves horses so I'm sure he'll be in his element here.'

'Hm, and do I sniff a romance in the air?' It was funny, Ben thought, somewhere along the way and without him even noticing, Kathy had turned from a little girl into a very attractive young woman.

'Of course not,' Kathy scoffed. 'He's just a good friend; I'm sure you'll like him. But I'll go and start to bring the horses in now, shall I?'

He nodded and leaning on the pitchfork he watched her thoughtfully as she crossed the yard to the field beyond, where the horses were grazing. As usual, when she wasn't wearing her nurse's uniform, she was dressed in jodhpurs and an old jumper, but he realised with a little shock that the clothes couldn't hide the fact that she had a very tidy figure. Very tidy indeed, he thought. It occurred to him then Kathy was now the image of her mother Kitty at that age and he felt a stab of pain in his heart. Kitty had been so beautiful, and Ben had adored her.

As his thoughts turned back to Sunday, he scowled. She'd started to take a bit of interest in things all of a sudden and had offered to take over the accounts again. Well, she could think on. That was his job now and he had no intention of letting her interfere. It was bad enough that his father had left the house and the business to her instead of him. He'd been so certain that when Tom died he would inherit the lot, and it still rankled that he hadn't. As far as he was concerned, he didn't feel that Sunday had ever loved him as much as she loved Kathy and Livvy – but one day he'd make her wish that she had, if it was the last thing he did. By God he would.

With his lips set in a grim line Ben stabbed another forkful of hay and got on with what he was doing.

Chapter Three

'Crikey you're an early bird,' Kathy exclaimed as Sunday showed David into the kitchen where she was enjoying a cup of tea early on Saturday morning. 'I didn't expect you till later. I haven't been up long.'

'Kathy, really, you'll make your visitor feel unwelcome,' Sunday scolded as she ushered the young man towards the chair next to Kathy's at the table. Then she fetched another cup and poured a cup of tea out for him.

'There's a bacon sarnie here for you, an' all, if you fancy one?' Cissie offered from where she was standing over the stove.

'Oh, not half,' David answered with a cheeky grin. 'I can't remember the last time I had one. I get porridge in my lodging house if I'm lucky. Thank you very much.'

Sunday felt herself warming to him as she spooned sugar into his tea from the large pressed sugar bowl on the table. He was such a nice young man and quite handsome too. She'd be very happy to see a romance develop between him and Kathy. Her thoughts flitted back to what Cissie had insinuated about Kathy being besotted with Ben, but she dismissed the idea immediately. Ben was well over twice her age and as far as she knew had never shown any interest in the girl, or any other since Maggie had died, for that matter. Turning her attention back to David she said cheerily, 'So Kathy tells me you're from Yorkshire, David. How do you find it living in the Midlands?'

He grinned as Cissie placed a doorstep bacon sandwich in front of him. 'Not too bad, though it's very different to where I lived,' he said as he took a big bite and sighed with pleasure. 'My parents own a farm and we have quite a few horses. That's what I miss the most – not being able to saddle up and go for a gallop across the moors whenever I feel like it. I think my dad hoped that I'd take over from him eventually so it must have been a big disappointment when I chose to become a doctor – although in fairness neither of my parents ever tried to talk me out of it. They said I must do whatever made me happy and supported me all through medical school. Truthfully, my brother was always much more suited to farming than me so I've no doubt things will work out for the best in the end.'

Sunday smiled at him approvingly. 'They sound like wonderful people.'

'They are,' he agreed as he bit into the sandwich again. 'And I just wish I could get back to see them more often. I never dreamed when I started out just how many hours doctors have to work. And nurses too, of course,' he added hastily with a cheeky wink at Kathy.

Eventually, after another cup of tea and finishing his sandwich, which he assured Cissie was the best he had tasted since leaving home, he and Kathy headed off to the stable block, leaving Sunday with a broad smile on her face.

'Isn't he just the loveliest young man?' she said to Cissie.

Her friend snorted. 'Yes, he is, I have to agree. But I wouldn't go buildin' me hopes up for a romance if I were you,' she warned. 'Seems to me he's the one wi' the fancy fer Kathy. She don't seem much interested in him.'

'*Yet!*' Sunday insisted doggedly. 'Just give things time.'

Cissie shook her head but said nothing, although she had an awful feeling that Sunday might end up being disappointed. Why, it seemed as if she was almost planning their wedding in her head already, but it wasn't her place to tell her. What would be would be!

'Ah, Ben, this is my friend David that I told you about,' Kathy said when they reached the stables. 'I thought he might be able to take Bracken out for a gallop, what do you think?'

'Suit yourself.' Ben inclined his head as he continued to brush down a beautiful dapple-grey mare. 'Bear in mind he's feisty though,' he warned.

'Oh, that should be fine,' David assured him. 'I'm quite an experienced rider.'

'Good, he's one of our best studs an' I don't want him injured,' Ben said sulkily.

Kathy frowned as she led David along the walkway in the stables to where Bracken was stabled next to Bramble, her own horse. In no time at all they had the horses saddled and Kathy mounted hers and trotted from the stables with David close behind.

'Sorry for Ben's rude behaviour back there,' she apologised. 'I'm afraid he's grown to be rather antisocial. He doesn't get out much, you see!'

David grinned and waved her apologies aside airily. 'Don't worry about that. I came to see you, not him.' And then he gently dug his heels into the horse's side and he was off like the wind, leaving Kathy to follow with a slight frown on her face.

Three hours later, after they had brushed the horses down and settled them back in the stables, they arrived back in the kitchen, bright-eyed and exhilarated from their ride.

'David, you must stay for lunch,' Sunday coaxed. 'Cissie has made one of her delicious steak and kidney pies. Unless you have to be somewhere else, of course?'

'I'd love to stay,' he answered quickly. 'It isn't often I get a day off so I may as well make the most of it.'

Lunch, which they ate around the kitchen table, was a light-hearted affair. Everyone was in a good mood, apart from Ben who remained silent.

'That was as good as my mother makes,' David told Cissie when he had eaten second helpings. 'I'm so full I don't even feel like moving.'

'Then don't,' Sunday said quickly. 'Stay and keep Kathy company. Or why don't you both go out somewhere?'

'*Mum!*' Kathy blushed. 'I'm sure David has better things to do than try to keep me entertained.'

'Actually, I don't,' he piped up. 'In fact, I was going to ask if you fancied going to the cinema. They usually show a film on Saturday afternoon although I've no idea what it will be.'

At this point Ben rose from the table and left the room with a face like thunder, while Kathy silently cursed Sunday. She was so blatantly matchmaking that the poor girl was almost squirming with embarrassment.

'Well I was, er . . . planning to—'

'*What?*' Sunday butted in. 'Whatever you had planned surely you can do it another time? David here is far from home. The poor chap needs a bit of company.'

'In that case I'd best get changed,' Kathy muttered, feeling as if she really didn't have much choice as she picked a bit of straw out of her dark, tousled hair. The brisk ride had made her cheeks glow and David thought she looked beautiful.

All the way up the stairs, Kathy fumed. *Goodness knows what's got into Mum*, she thought to herself. *It's almost as if she's trying to marry me off and it's quite embarrassing. I shall certainly be having words with her!*

Fifteen minutes later she was back downstairs looking neat and tidy in a mid-calf-length skirt and a long-sleeved blouse with ruffles down the front.

'You look lovely, darling,' Sunday told her as Kathy reached for her coat and scowled at her.

'She certainly does,' David agreed, his eyes openly admiring.

Kathy squirmed. 'Right, I should be back for tea,' she informed Sunday as she ushered David towards the door.

'All right, and will David be coming back with you?' Sunday asked hopefully.

'No, he won't! I'm sure he has things to do,' Kathy ground out and before another word could be said she almost pushed him through the door.

'Hold on,' David gasped as he ran to keep up with her. 'You didn't even give me a chance to thank the ladies for lunch. They'll think I'm very rude and ungrateful.'

'Huh! I doubt that very much,' Kathy snorted in disgust. 'Mum seems to think the sun shines out of your backside and I must apologise for her behaviour. Why, it was almost as if she was trying to marry us off.' Her cheeks were crimson with embarrassment.

He shocked her then when he grinned and replied, 'Would that really be such a bad thing?'

'Oh, don't be so stupid,' she snapped. 'We barely know each other.'

'You're quite right and we never will if we don't get to spend some time together; so, what do you say? We could start going out a bit more.'

Kathy was squirming again now and wishing the ground would open up and swallow her.

'Well I, er . . . It's very nice of you and I'm flattered but the truth is I rather like to spend what little spare time I have around the horses. Although we can still be friends, of course,' she ended hastily. She didn't want to hurt his feelings.

He shrugged and looked slightly disappointed, but then smiling again he took her arm and they clambered into his car. Kathy was truly delightful, and he wasn't going to give up on her yet, not by a long shot!

Chapter Four

January 1936

When Sunday came down to the kitchen on a cold and frosty morning in January to find Cissie sniffing into a large, white handkerchief, she was instantly concerned.

'Why, Cissie, love, whatever's the matter?' Hurrying over to her friend she put her arm about her shoulders.

'It's just been on the wireless. King George has passed away at Sandringham House in Norfolk,' Cissie sniffed. 'May God bless his soul.'

'Well, he had been suffering from a chronic bronchial complaint,' Sunday pointed out. 'But I'm still very sad to hear it. I dare say Prince Edward will succeed him now.'

'Huh! He shouldn't be allowed to,' Cissie said indignantly as she mopped at her tears. She was a great royalist and loved everything about the royal family, apart from Prince Edward, it appeared. 'He's messin' around wi' that American, Wallis Simpson, an' her a married woman, an' all. It ain't right!'

Sunday grinned ruefully. 'Perhaps he'll end their affair

now that he knows he's going to be king?' she suggested tactfully.

Cissie shrugged as she mopped at her teary cheeks. 'We'll see, won't we? But now I'd better get the breakfast on the go. Kathy an' Livvy will be down any minute an' I don't want 'em to be late for work.'

Ben and George had already been in and made themselves a pot of tea before heading off to the stables but Cissie knew that they too would be in shortly wanting to be fed, so she hurried over to the stove and soon the smell of sizzling bacon filled the kitchen.

It was hard to believe that they were already well into January, Cissie thought as she expertly flipped the bacon. Christmas and the New Year seemed to have passed in the blink of an eye. It hadn't been the happiest of holidays. Livvy had come down with a severe cold the week before Christmas and had spent most of the time in bed coughing and spluttering, bless her. Ben had spent the majority of his time in the stables or in his room and Kathy had had to work, so it had been just herself, Sunday and George for most of the time and Cissie had been secretly pleased when it was all over. She had hoped that her children, who were now all grown and flown the nest, might visit, but they were taken up with their own families and their own lives in different parts of the country. And now to hear that the poor king had passed away . . . Well, it certainly wasn't the best start to 1936 as far as she was concerned. But soon the room was full of the family all eager for their breakfast so Cissie pushed the sad thoughts from her mind and got on with things.

The following day Cissie was incensed to read in the newspaper that the new King Edward had broken royal protocol by watching the proclamation of his own accession to the throne from a window of St James's Palace, in the company of the still-married Mrs Simpson.

'He won't last as king fer five minutes if he carries on like this, you just mark my words!' she ranted to George and Sunday, who were enjoying a mid-morning cup of tea with her. 'Why, it's disgraceful behaviour. Lord knows what the dear old king would think of it!'

'But times are changing, Cissie,' Sunday pointed out, but Cissie was having none of it and shook her head vigorously.

'They may well be fer the likes of us, but you expect royalty to set a better example.'

In the end George and Sunday smiled at each other and let her rant on. As George quite rightly pointed out, 'There ain't no use doin' any other when our Cissie has a bee in her bonnet.'

The following week Livvy came home from the office all excited. 'Some of the girls at work were saying that a chap called Billy Butlin is opening a holiday camp in Skegness in April and we thought we might go for a week in the summer, if that's all right with you, Mum?'

It would be Livvy's first holiday on her own without either herself or her mother to chaperone her and Sunday's first instinct was to refuse to let her go but then she knew that wouldn't be fair. Livvy was a sensible girl and should be allowed to grow up so she forced a smile and told her, 'It would do you good. Why don't you ask Kathy if she can book some time off to go with you?'

The girls had always holidayed in the South of France with Sunday's mother, until she had passed away, and Sunday thought a break would do them good.

'Huh! I doubt she'd do that.' Livvy pinched a scone from

33

the rack Cissie had just taken from the oven and promptly had her knuckles rapped with a wooden spoon. 'All she ever does is work nowadays.'

Sunday sighed. Both her girls were very attractive yet neither of them had shown any interest in walking out with a young man or marriage as yet. Admittedly Livvy had gone on more than a few dates but nothing had ever come of it, and Kathy was still on very friendly terms with the handsome Dr Deacon. He was clearly besotted with Kathy, but it seemed his feelings were not returned. But then they were still both very young and had plenty of time so Sunday wasn't complaining; she loved having them at home, but she worried about how they would fare if anything happened to her. After all, no one lived forever so it would give her peace of mind to know that they were happy and settled before her time came.

The following morning Cissie was washing up when she heard Bill Dewhurst's coal lorry pull into the yard, so she hastily wiped her hands on her apron and went out to greet him.

'Mornin', Bill. Dump the order in the coal shed, would yer, then come into the kitchen an' I'll have a nice cup o' tea waitin'.'

He doffed his sooty cap, and she scuttled back inside to put the kettle on, and minutes later he joined her. Normally Cissie and Bill enjoyed a nice gossip, but she noticed that this morning he seemed slightly edgy, so after a time she asked, 'What's up then, Bill? Has the cat got yer tongue this mornin'?'

He smiled, his teeth appearing snow white in his coal-black face. 'I, er . . . were just wonderin' if Ben were about,' he said, clearly feeling ill at ease. 'Only he ain't paid me fer the last lot o' coal I delivered yet so I thought he might settle up this mornin'.'

Cissie looked astounded. 'He's taken a horse to the black-smith's to be shod, but never fear, just as soon as he comes in, I'll tell him to drop it off to yer. It must 'ave slipped his mind.'

'Thanks, Cissie,' He seemed to relax a little then and went on to tell her what his wife Betty had been up to. 'She's joined the Women's Institute an' it seems to have given her a new lease o' life.' He chuckled. 'I wonder you don't go along to one of their meetin's, Ciss. I reckon you'd enjoy it.'

Cissie grinned. 'To be honest, Bill, it's just comin' home to me that I ain't as young as I used to be an' it takes me all me time to keep this place goin' now. Between you an' me, although Sunday does more than her share, I've been thinkin' o' suggestin' gettin' someone in part-time to do some of the cookin'. I have to be in the kitchen for half six every mornin' to get 'em all fed afore they go to work an' it'd be lovely to have a lie-in now an' again.'

They carried on chatting for another ten minutes but eventually Bill glanced at the clock and told her regretfully, 'I should be goin' then, Ciss. The coal won't deliver itself, will it? Ta-ra fer now, love.'

With that he went off whistling merrily, leaving Cissie to get on with her chores.

Later, when she and Sunday were folding the washing, Cissie remembered what Bill had told her.

'Bill Dewhurst mentioned earlier that he ain't been paid fer a couple o' months. Yer'd perhaps better mention it to Ben.'

'I shall,' Sunday promised, looking puzzled. As far as she knew Ben had always been prompt at paying the tradesmen and the household bills. But then they had been very busy in the stables for the last few weeks, so it had probably just slipped his mind.

'The other thing I wanted to talk to yer about,' Cissie said, looking slightly nervous, 'was about perhaps gettin' someone from the village in to do a bit o' the cookin'.'

Sunday instantly looked guilty and horrified. 'Oh, Cissie, I'm so sorry. Is it getting too much for you? I should have noticed.'

Cissie flapped her hand and grinned. 'O' course it ain't too much, it's just that none of us are gettin' any younger an' this is a big place for me an' you to keep goin'. I just thought it would take a bit o' work off us.'

'I'll advertise for someone straight away,' Sunday promised. 'Although it's not so easy to get help nowadays. Since the war ended more and more women have jobs outside of the home. I suppose it comes from them doing the men's jobs while they were away at war,' she suggested.

Cissie's head bobbed in agreement. 'You're right, but just someone part-time would do, an' there ain't no rush. There's still a bit o' work left in me yet.'

Later in the morning when the men came in for their tea break Sunday mentioned the outstanding coal bill to Ben and was dismayed when she saw a dull-red colour creep up his neck.

'So, are you suggesting that I deliberately didn't pay him?' he asked irritably.

'Of course not! I know how busy you've been,' Sunday answered quickly. 'I was just jogging your memory, that's all. I can get the money out of the safe and pay him myself if you're too busy to,' she offered.

'There'll be no need for that. I'm going into town this afternoon, so I'll call in at the coal yard and pay him then!'

'All right, there's no need to get so angry.'

Ben scowled and strode out of the kitchen without even waiting for his coffee as Sunday gazed at Cissie perplexed, wondering what she had said wrong.

Chapter Five

Once he was back in the stables Ben stood fuming. Sunday had shown no interest in anything since his father had died so why should she suddenly start now? His thoughts were interrupted when Kathy cantered into the yard on her horse and hopped lightly down from the saddle. Despite the bitter cold, she was dressed as usual in her old jodhpurs and a thin shirt that showed off her figure, and Ben found himself staring at her.

'Hello there.' She smiled at him as she led the horse into her stall and began to unsaddle her. 'I was meaning to tell you that David will be over again this Saturday for a ride. Is that all right?'

He shrugged. David had been a regular visitor for some weeks now and he wondered why she even bothered to ask. The horses weren't his after all – or the house if it came to that, thanks to his father leaving everything to Sunday instead of to him. But then he supposed he shouldn't have expected anything else. Looking back to the time when Sunday and Tom had discovered that he was Tom's child, it had taken Sunday a long time to accept that her husband had a child by another woman. It didn't matter to him that she had tried every day since she had finally accepted him to make amends. He'd forgotten all the times Sunday had rushed to his room when he was caught in the grip of a nightmare after he first returned from the war, and all the times she had sat by his bed whispering soothing words and holding his hand until the sun came up. As far as he was concerned, since Kathy and Livvy had come along, they had always been her favourites, and this only added to his feeling of resentment.

'So . . . you've been seeing this David for some time now, haven't you? Is it serious between you?'

Kathy looked mildly surprised at the question; Ben didn't usually show any interest in what she did. Then she threw her head back and laughed. 'Of course it isn't,' she told him. 'David is a really nice man and I think a great deal of him but only as a friend . . .'

When she quickly looked away and flushed, Ben frowned. 'Ah! So, is there someone else you have your eye on?'

'Might be.' Kathy sniffed. She was saved from having to say more when Cissie appeared carrying a mug of coffee.

'Here you are, grumpy,' Cissie said, pushing it towards Ben and sloshing some of the contents onto the sawdust on the floor in the process. 'You were so busy snappin' Sunday's head off back there in the kitchen that you stormed off wi'out this.'

'Oh . . . er, thanks,' he said, taking the mug from her.

Cissie wagged a plump finger at him. 'There weren't no need fer that,' she scolded. 'Sunday's been good to you an' you'd do well to remember it.'

'Oh yes, and aren't I good to her?' Ben growled. 'It's mainly *me* who keeps this business going, in case you hadn't noticed.'

'I ain't even goin' to stand here an' listen to you when you're in this argumentative mood,' Cissie told him with a glare. 'I really don't know what gets into you just lately, me lad!' And with that she turned on her heel and flounced back across the yard. Ben narrowed his eyes and watched her go, and sensing that all was not well, Kathy scuttled after her leaving him to wallow in his self-pity.

Early in June, Livvy set off for Billy Butlin's new holiday camp in Skegness with two of her older friends from work, who had promised Sunday they would look after her, for a whole week's holiday.

'It's quite close to the beach, according to the brochure,' she informed her mother excitedly as Sunday helped her pack her case.

'Just make sure you enjoy it and have a good rest,' Sunday urged. Livvy was such a hard-working girl she deserved a holiday. 'I just wish you were going somewhere a little more exotic where you were guaranteed the sun.'

'Huh, there's nothing wrong with Skeggy,' Livvy replied. 'And from the sounds of the place there will be lots to do even if it rains. I just wish I could have persuaded Kathy to come with me.'

'I wish you could have too – she works far too hard,' Sunday agreed, closing the clasps, and following behind as Livvy humped the case down the stairs. Ben was waiting outside the front door to run her to the train station to meet her friends, so after giving her mother and Cissie a swift hug she got in the car, waving wildly from the window as it drove off.

'Oh, to be young again, eh?' Cissie sighed before pottering away, and Sunday could only nod in agreement.

The summer seemed to pass in the blink of an eye and by the end of it, Sunday was convinced that Kathy and David were becoming a couple, although Kathy still stoutly denied it. But why else would he visit on a weekly basis? And why would she go to the pictures and out for meals with him? Sunday mused. It was clear David was besotted with Kathy, and Sunday could only assume Kathy was playing hard to get. Even so she had high hopes that something would come of it in time and she always went out of her way to welcome him. After all, he was far from home, which was why Sunday suggested to Cissie one weekend in mid-September, 'I was thinking of inviting Verity and Edgar for dinner one evening and I thought it might be nice to ask David too – if he could get away from the hospital, of course. What do you think?'

'I think it's a grand idea,' Cissie agreed. Sunday and the Locketts had been friends for as long as she could remember, although Sunday hadn't seen quite so much of them since she had lost Tom. Edgar had been the vicar at Chilvers Coton Parish Church, until he had retired the year before and now he and his wife, Verity, had left the sprawling vicarage that had been their home for many years and were living happily in a little cottage in Attleborough. 'Why don't you ask David when he has a night off?' she suggested. 'I dare say Verity and Edgar could come most any evening now that he's retired.' It was nice to hear Sunday planning social events again.

'Mm, you could be right. I'll do that and you and George must join us too.'

'Oh, you know my George ain't much of a one fer standin' on ceremony,' Cissie pointed out. 'An' besides, I'm still tired from me weekend away. I'll do the cookin' for you instead.'

Sunday smiled at her affectionately. Some weeks before Cissie

41

and George had caught the train to London to watch the International Lawn Tennis Challenge at Wimbledon, then they had stayed an extra day in a very nice hotel in the city to do some sightseeing before catching the train home again. Cissie had thoroughly enjoyed it, especially when Great Britain had won, but she was a home bird and had been glad to get back and had no intentions of going away again anytime soon.

Now Sunday sighed guiltily. Despite Cissie requesting some help some months before and Sunday promising she would advertise she hadn't got around to it as yet but now she promised herself that she would. She had thought of asking Ben to do it, but she didn't want to pressure him because he was so busy in the stables. On top of that he seemed to be in a permanent bad mood lately and sometimes she and Cissie felt as if they were walking on eggshells trying not to say anything that might upset him.

'That doesn't seem fair,' Sunday pointed out glumly. 'I'm just putting extra work on you.'

'I don't mind,' Cissie assured her as she shuffled the newspaper on the table and then as something caught her eye, she snatched it up and frowned. 'Would you just look at that,' she said angrily, stabbing a finger at a picture of King Edward and Wallis Simpson. 'He's *still* walkin' out wi' that married woman, bold as bloody brass!'

Sunday refrained from smiling. She didn't want to upset Cissie further.

'I tell yer, the prime minister'll have somethin' to say about this soon if he carries on the way he is.' Cissie sniffed indignantly. 'Just what example is he settin' to the nation, eh?'

Sunday didn't even bother to comment. Cissie was clearly very against the king seeing his lady friend and she knew there was nothing she could say that would make her change her mind.

It was almost a week later before David could accept Sunday's invitation and he turned up shortly before the Locketts, bearing a bottle of very good wine and looking neat as a new pin and very handsome.

'My contribution to the evening,' he told Sunday as he gave her an affectionate peck on the cheek. But his gaze was on Kathy who had just appeared on the stairs and Sunday noticed how his eyes lit up. She watched closely for Kathy's reaction but was disappointed to see that she greeted him no differently to any other visitor.

Delicious smells were issuing from the kitchen as Sunday ushered the two young people into the day room while she hurried away to help Cissie put the finishing touches to the meal. They had decided to do a straightforward roast dinner. Cissie was the first to admit that she wasn't any good at what she termed 'fancy cooking' and Sunday smiled as she entered the kitchen. The vegetables were cooking on the range and Cissie was just removing a sizzling joint of roast beef from the oven.

'You might not like to do anything fancy, but you can certainly do a wonderful roast,' she praised and Cissie's chest puffed with pride.

Once Verity and Edgar had arrived and joined David and Kathy in the day room, Sunday went down to the cellar to fetch some more wine. She would only need one bottle as Livvy was out with friends and Ben had declined the invitation to join them. It had been a long time since she had ventured down there but Tom had always kept it well stocked, so she was surprised to see that most of the wine racks were now empty. Ben was in charge of ordering whatever they needed, but they didn't drink much anymore, so she couldn't imagine where it could have gone. She selected a bottle from what was there and, pushing this puzzle to the back of her mind, went back upstairs.

They had a very enjoyable evening and once they had finished, Kathy left the room to show David – who was on call early the next morning – out.

'What a lovely young man,' Verity commented. 'And he's clearly very smitten with your Kathy. Do you think we might be hearing wedding bells soon?'

Sunday sighed. 'I certainly think we could if it were up to David but I'm not so sure about Kathy,' she admitted. 'The poor chap has made it more than clear how he feels about her and he's a regular visitor here, but Kathy doesn't seem to want their relationship to go beyond friendship.'

'Ah well, friendship is a good start.' Ever the matchmaker, Verity grinned.

Sunday sincerely hoped that her friend might be right. Nothing would make her happier than to see Kathy settled with a good man – Livvy too if it came to that. But still, she consoled herself, they were both still very young and she could live in hope. Both girls were far too beautiful to stay single forever!

Chapter Six

Shortly after waving David away, Kathy made her way to the stables to find Ben there bedding down the horses. George had already left to join Cissie in their cottage.

'Oh, I thought George was seeing to them this evening and you were having an early night,' she said in surprise.

'I was, but I changed me mind,' he muttered, keeping his eye on the horse he was rubbing down.

'So why didn't you come and join us for dinner then?'

He glanced up, taking in her shining hair and bright eyes. 'I dare say I didn't want to sit and watch you swooning over your fancy man,' he muttered.

Kathy's heart began to hammer. Ben must be blind if he hadn't realised by now how she felt about him. There was a big age gap between them, and she was sure he just viewed her as his little sister, but that made no difference to how she felt about him. Her voice was ragged as she said, 'How many times do I have to tell you? David is *not* my fancy man . . . If you must know my feelings lie elsewhere . . .' Her voice trailed away.

Ben narrowed his eyes at her. 'Oh yes . . . and is it anyone I know?'

'Oh, you're just . . . just *so* . . .' She turned away blindly with tears in her eyes but before she could reach the door, he had caught her arm and swung her towards him. Looking into her face he saw all she felt for him shining in her eyes and he grinned as the feelings she had kept from him for so long gushed out of her like water from a dam.

'I only let David keep coming because Mum seems intent on marrying me and Livvy off and it makes her happy!' she choked. 'But you *must* know that it's *you* I want? It's *always* been you – I've tried not to feel this way, but I can't help myself!'

She and Livvy were Sunday's little treasures. How would Sunday feel if he were to take her precious girl down? Ben wondered, his jealousy eating away at him. It would probably be them who inherited the house one day and the way he saw it, it wasn't fair! He didn't love Kathy, but he had been noticing for some time what an attractive young woman she had grown into and he was only a man after all! His bodily needs were usually satisfied by a certain lady who lived on the outskirts of the village but here was Kathy offering herself to him on a plate and what better way of getting revenge on his stepmother?

'L-let me go, Ben,' Kathy sniffed, deeply embarrassed now that she had declared her feelings. But if anything, his grip on her arm tightened, and she wished the ground would just open up and swallow her.

'You do realise that I'm old enough to be your father, don't you?'

She nodded as a solitary tear slid down her cheek. Then she lifted her chin defiantly. 'So what if you are?' She stared at him. 'I find young men my own age boring and immature, if you must know.'

'And what about these?' He lifted his fingers to touch the scars on his face. 'Most women would find me repulsive.'

She shook her head, making her beautiful hair dance on her shoulders. 'No, *no*,' she denied. 'You're . . . Well, they just make you look more . . . interesting. You're actually very handsome.' She had always thought of him as a hero and now without doubt he knew she would be like putty in his hands.

Tilting her chin with his free hand, he stared down into her flushed face and smiled as he suggested gently, 'Shall we go up into the hayloft to talk?' And it was as simple as that. She followed him meekly up the rickety ladder like a lamb to the slaughter.

When he silently undid the buttons on her dress she stood woodenly, her lips trembling and her face a mask of embarrassment, but she made no attempt to stop him. This was what she had always dreamed of. She could see his outline by the light of the moon that shone through the small, grimy window in the roof and when he began to hastily undress, she quickly looked away. As a nurse, she had seen many naked men, but this was entirely different.

He drew her down onto the straw and when his hand found her breast and started to tease her nipple she gasped with pleasure as she experienced feelings she had never known existed. Soon she was naked, and as his hands roved across her soft flesh she groaned with anticipation. She knew what she was doing was wrong; Sunday had always drummed into both her and Livvy that they should never allow a man to go too far with them before they had a ring on their finger. But this was Ben, the man she had loved all her life and it felt right. Her mother would be horrified if she were ever to find out what was happening between them, but his soft feather kisses were leaving a trail of fire across her flat stomach and when she felt his hand slip between her legs she sighed with pleasure as his fingers slid inside her. Then he parted her legs and climbed on top of her and as he penetrated her, she gasped and closed her eyes tight as he began to buck on top of her.

Sometime later, as she lay with her head on his bare chest listening to his heartbeat, she smiled with satisfaction. After all the years she had worshipped him he was finally hers, all hers, and she was his. Surely he'd have to marry her now and make her dreams come true? She wouldn't allow herself to think what her mother would say about such a thing – she was determined that nothing should spoil the moment, it was just too special. It was the first time she had ever given herself to a man and she was wondering what all the hoo-hah the young nurses at work talked of was all about. She had enjoyed the foreplay and the closeness, admittedly, but the act itself had been rather painful and over very quickly. Perhaps sex was like a good wine, and improved with time?

However, while she was quite happy to lie there in the after-glow of their loving, Ben seemed to have other ideas and, rising abruptly, he told her curtly, 'You'd best get dressed. They'll be wondering where you are over at the house.'

She stood up quickly and began to throw her clothes on as colour burned into her cheeks. Suddenly it felt as if Ben couldn't get rid of her quickly enough.

'D-did you never guess how I felt about you?' she asked softly, hoping to recapture the moment as she struggled with the buttons on her dress and tried to untangle the bits of straw from her thick, dark hair.

'Why should I have?' His voice was abrupt, and she felt hurt.

'S-so, what happens now?'

He scowled as he snapped his braces into place and raked his fingers through his thatch of hair. 'Nothing happens. We go on as before, of course,' he answered tersely. 'Do you really think your mother would accept anything else? We've been brought up as older brother and little sister.'

'I know, but we're not, though, are we? So why *shouldn't* we make a life together?'

'*Whoa* there,' he exclaimed, holding his hand up as if to ward her off, much as he might have done to one of the horses. 'We'd be best to keep this to ourselves.'

Tears welled in Kathy's eyes as she absorbed the pain of his words. 'But *surely* what just happened between us meant *something* to you?' There was a catch in her voice, but it did nothing to soften him, and he turned away and headed for the loft hatch.

Kathy had no choice but to scramble after him. As she descended the ladder the sweet smell of hay and horseflesh met her, but Ben was already striding towards the door.

'Sh-shall I come over and see you here when I get back from the hospital tomorrow?' she asked hopefully.

'You come to the stables every night,' he pointed out and then he was gone, his boots striking the cobblestones in the stable yard.

She stood quite still, until she heard him enter the house and only then did she allow the tears she had held back to fall. *But it wasn't over yet*, she silently vowed. Now that he finally knew how she felt about him she would make him love her too if it was the last thing she did!

When Kathy came down to breakfast the next morning, all prim and proper in her nurse's uniform, Ben was sitting drinking tea. The second she appeared he hastily drained his cup and strode from the room without giving her so much as a second look.

'Somebody got outta bed the wrong side this morning,' Cissie commented wryly, cocking her head towards the door. 'I really don't know what gets into him lately. But now what do yer fancy fer breakfast? There's some porridge, or I could do yer some bacon an' eggs?'

'I, er . . . I'm not hungry thanks, Cissie,' Kathy said, her cheeks flaming. 'In fact, I think I'm late so I'd better be off. Bye for now.' And with that she was gone like a bullet from a gun, leaving Cissie to shake her head.

The nights were beginning to draw in and it was already getting dark when Kathy returned from her shift that evening. As she had been about to leave the hospital an emergency had been admitted and she and David had both stayed behind to help deal with it so they were much later than they should have been. David had given her a lift home in his car, which was his pride and joy. They were supposed to have been going to the picture house, but Kathy had pleaded a headache, so after giving him a peck on the cheek she got out of the car and watched his car lights disappear down the drive before entering the house.

'Oh, you're earlier than I expected – what happened to the pictures?' Sunday greeted her. 'We've kept your dinner warm in the oven, everyone else has eaten.'

'Our plans changed, *so sorry* for ruining your evening,' Kathy snapped as she flung her cape over the back of a chair. 'We had an emergency appendix case come in just as me and David were about to leave so we stopped to help get him ready for theatre.'

Sunday glanced across her shoulder as she carried Kathy's dinner to the table. 'Is that why you decided not to go to the pictures after all?'

'I have a headache, so he's gone home for an early night.'

Kathy didn't really have much of an appetite, but she supposed she should at least make an effort to eat something if Cissie had gone to the trouble of cooking it for her. Her thoughts had been on Ben and what had happened between them last night all day and as if she could read her mind, Sunday told her, 'Ben is over at the stables. Midnight's foal is due any time, so I dare say he'll be spending most of his time with her now till it arrives, and Livvy has gone out with her friends from work.'

'Mm.' Kathy mumbled as she attacked the chop on her plate. It had dried up considerably and was as tough as old boots, but she forced a mouthful down.

'Jamie and Flora came to see me today,' Sunday rambled on. 'Apparently Constance is pregnant. It'll be their first grandchild.' She beamed happily. 'So that makes me almost a great-grand-mother!' Jamie was another person who Sunday had brought up since he was a small child and she was very close to him and his wife who lived in a small cottage in Hartshill village.

'That's nice.' Kathy tried another mouthful, sure that she would need a new set of teeth if she tried to eat it all. Eventually she gave up and apologised, 'Sorry, Mum, I'm afraid with this headache I'm not really very hungry.'

Instantly concerned, Sunday whipped her plate away. 'It is a bit shrivelled,' she admitted. 'How about I make you a nice sandwich instead?'

When Kathy shook her head, she sighed. 'Then if you're not feeling grand get yourself upstairs to bed and I'll bring you a cup of tea and a nice hot-water bottle.'

Kathy smiled tiredly. 'Thanks, but there's no need to fuss. I think I'll get changed and go and see if Ben needs a hand. The fresh air might help clear my head.'

Sunday nodded as Kathy left the room before turning her attention to the dirty pots in the sink as yet another lonely night stretched ahead of her. Cissie and George had already gone home to their cottage. Livvy wouldn't be in till late if Sunday knew her, and once Kathy was with Ben and the horses, it was doubtful she would be back any time soon. She paused with her hands deep in the soapy water as she gazed towards the window.

'Oh, Tom, I miss you *so* much,' she whispered to the empty room, then blinking away tears she forced herself to continue with what she was doing.

Chapter Seven

Just as Sunday had predicted, Kathy found Ben in Midnight's stall. He was tenderly stroking her silky mane and talking soothingly to her as she restlessly pawed at the ground. It was clear that it wouldn't be long before her foal was born, and she knew that Ben had high hopes for it. Both the mare and the stud had pedigrees as long as her arm, so Ben was expecting the foal to be something very special. If it was it would be worth a great deal of money.

He suddenly seemed to sense her presence and straightening he inclined his head as she slipped into the stall with him.

'How is she doing?'

He shrugged. 'She shouldn't be long now.'

An awkward silence stretched between them, until Kathy said quietly, 'It's a wonder George hasn't stayed to help you.'

'He wanted to, but I told him to get off home to Cissie. There's no point in us both sittin' up all night.'

She nodded and, before she could stop herself, she blurted out, 'I've been thinking about you all day.'

He felt a momentary pang of guilt as he looked at her face but then he hardened his heart as he thought of Sunday. Very soon now his revenge would be complete, and he would hurt her as much as Tom had hurt him when he had chosen to leave Treetops and the business to his wife rather than his only son.

I bet he wouldn't have done that if I hadn't been illegitimate, he thought, and again resentment coursed through his veins like iced water.

Midnight tossed her head then, interrupting his thoughts, and he warned Kathy, 'You'd better get on the other side of the door, she's close and she could kick out.'

Kathy hastily did as she was told. She knew how unpredictable mares could be when they were giving birth and she didn't want to get kicked. Ben meanwhile had hurried around to the back of the animal and after lifting her tail he smiled with satisfaction.

'That's a good girl,' he crooned as a gush of water flooded out of her. 'Nearly there now.'

It never failed to touch Kathy when she saw how tender he could be with the horses, and she made a silent vow that, somehow, she would make him love her as much as he did the animals.

Twenty minutes later, after a lot of help from Tom, Midnight gave birth to a coal-black foal.

'It's a little filly,' Tom said triumphantly as he lifted a handful of straw and began to wipe her before stepping aside so the mother could wash her. 'I was hoping for a colt but she's a little beauty all the same. She'll be worth a small fortune in a few years' time.'

He watched as the filly struggled drunkenly to her feet and wobbled towards her mother. Satisfied that all was well now, Ben dried his hands and left the mother and baby to bond, joining Kathy on the other side of the stall.

'She's just beautiful,' Kathy whispered as she looked at the foal, transfixed.

Ben nodded in agreement and they stood side by side admiring the new arrival for a moment.

'Right, I may as well turn in now that's done,' Ben suddenly said, and he turned and left without another word.

Watching him, Kathy had to blink away the tears and compose herself before she dared go back into the house. It was as if the night before had never happened, but she wasn't ready to give up on him yet – not by a long shot!

'Off out with young Steven again, are you, darling?' Sunday asked Livvy innocently a few evenings later. 'That's the second night this week you've seen him, isn't it?' Steven was the son of one the partners at the law firm in town where Livvy worked and much in demand with young ladies from what little bit of gossip she had heard. Perhaps he would be the one to steal her heart?

Livvy giggled as she eyed her mother in the dressing table mirror. 'Oh, *Mum*, you're such a matchmaker. I could almost think you can't wait to get rid of me!'

'*Of course* I don't want to get rid of you,' Sunday denied. 'But I *would* like to see you happily settled before anything happens to me. I'm not getting any younger after all!'

'I'm far too young to think of settling down with anyone just yet. And that's *quite* enough of that silly sort of talk,' Livvy responded heatedly.

'Oh, I wasn't inferring that I was going to croak it tomorrow.' Sunday grinned. 'But I would like to see any grandchildren you might present me with before I do.'

Deeply annoyed, Livvy tossed her head. She hated it when her mother spoke like that and couldn't bear to think of a time when she might not be around. She knew only too well that her mother had never been quite the same since the death of her father but that was emotional rather than physical and Livvy hoped that time would be a great healer.

'I'm not even prepared to talk about it anymore,' Livvy said sullenly and rising from the stool she flounced out of the room, saying over her shoulder, 'Don't bother waiting up for me. I shall probably be in late.'

Sunday listened to Livvy clumping down the stairs followed by the sound of the front door slamming before crossing to the window. She was just in time to see a car, driven by a very striking-looking young man, pull up outside just as Livvy appeared and hopped in beside him. She watched as the car roared down the drive before turning and making her way downstairs. Kathy was working a late shift at the hospital and it looked like another lonely evening lay ahead of her.

She was surprised to find Ben drinking tea and smoking at the kitchen table. Since his father had died, he had taken to spending most of his time in his bedroom when he wasn't working either in the stables or in the gardens and when she entered the room he instantly stood up, stubbed his cigarette out in the ashtray and turned towards the back door.

'Don't go, Ben.' Her voice stayed him, and he turned slowly to scowl at her.

'Did you want something?'

'No . . . but it isn't often we get a minute alone nowadays.' She smiled at him. 'I thought we could have a chat while I join you for a cup of tea. Is there any left in the pot?'

He grudgingly sat back down as he nodded and when she had poured herself a cup, she joined him at the table.

He seemed reluctant to even look at her so after a moment she asked softly, 'Is something bothering you, Ben?'

'*No!* Should it be?'

Sunday sighed. She knew he was still grieving for his father, but didn't he realise she was grieving for Tom too? If only he would talk to her they could comfort each other. The atmosphere between them was so thick she could have cut it with a knife, but she didn't know how to change it.

'If there was anything worrying you, you know I'm always here for you,' she said tentatively, but once again he rose from his seat and, this time, he had no intention of sitting back down.

'Look, I have work to do,' he said curtly, and without another word he left the room, slamming the door resoundingly behind him.

'*Damn woman!*' he muttered to himself as he headed towards the stables; yet he couldn't help but feel a small stab of guilt. He immediately hardened his heart and a little smile played around his lips as he thought of what he was about to do. He would be away from this place for good soon and suddenly it couldn't come quickly enough and then Sunday would have all the time in the world to spoil her darling girls!

His thoughts returned to Kathy. In truth he'd thought of little else since the night they had laid together and he had battled with his conscience, but that was behind him now. She would be just another means of getting revenge on Sunday before he left. And after all, it had been *her* who had almost thrown herself at him. Thinking of her taut young body made him harden and he rubbed the bulge in his trousers. Grinning, he entered the stables and began to settle the horses in their stalls. Maybe he'd wait up for her to get back.

Much later as he was relaxing in his bedroom, Ben heard a car door slam when Kathy returned from her shift and, hurrying to the window, he watched her climb out of David's car. He had obviously given her a lift home but thankfully he pulled away as soon as Kathy entered the house. Slipping from his room he hurried down the stairs in time to see her hanging her cape on the coat stand in the hallway.

'Oh . . . hello, Ben.' She had thought everyone would be in bed and looked mildly surprised to see him.

She looked tired and slightly nervous as she peered at him. He had been avoiding her like the plague ever since the night she had told him of her feelings for him but now he was smiling.

'I thought I heard you come in. Come through to the kitchen. I'll make you a cup of cocoa. Your mother is in bed.'

She followed him silently into the kitchen and once he had switched the light on and placed some milk to heat on the hob, he walked across to her and began to unfasten the pins that held her cap in place.

'I . . . I don't understand,' she whispered, but there was no time to say any more before he kissed her roughly on the mouth.

When they finally broke apart her eyes were shining. 'Does this mean you don't regret what happened between us?' she dared to ask eventually. He hurried over to the stove and lifted the milk off the hob, then soundlessly took her hand and led her up the stairs to his room.

Once inside, his hand fumbled at the buttons on her uniform and, once he had undressed her and laid her on the bed, she gave herself to him willingly. She had dreamed of this since she had been a little girl and for now no one else in the world mattered but him.

Chapter Eight

'Have you seen the papers this mornin'?' Cissie asked Sunday when she entered the kitchen one cold and blustery morning in October with George close behind her. He did love his cup of tea before he started work.

'No, I haven't.' Sunday yawned. She had barely had time to wake up let alone read the papers.

'That Wallis Simpson has divorced her husband, Ernest.' Cissie shook her head in disgust. 'Didn't I tell yer she had designs on the king?'

Sunday smiled as George winked at her with an amused grin on his face. 'She may well have but the prime minister has already told him that he will not be allowed to marry her while he's king,' she pointed out.

'Huh! The man is smitten,' Cissie snorted. 'This won't be the end of it, you mark my words.'

Cissie was proved right when in December, witnessed by his three brothers – the Duke of York, the Duke of Gloucester and the Duke of Kent – the king signed an instrument of abdication at Fort Belvedere. Prince Albert, the Duke of York, then became King George VI.

'It's disgraceful,' Cissie raged. 'The whole country must be up in arms about it! An' to make matters worse he's cleared off to Austria wi' that Wallis Simpson. You just mark my words they'll be wed before yer know it.'

'Actually, I think it's quite romantic,' Sunday said. 'He must love her very much to give up the throne for her, and times are changing, Cissie.'

'They may well be but not fer the better,' Cissie grumbled as she expertly flipped the sausages she was frying. Then she remembered something and changed the subject. 'By the way, when I went into the butcher's yesterday, he mentioned that the bill hasn't been paid this month. I got the same in the grocer's.'

Sunday frowned as she fetched some knives and forks and began to lay the table. 'Oh dear, Ben must have forgotten to settle them up. Perhaps I should talk to him again about letting me take over the household expenses. He's been so busy with the stables I bet he forgot all about it.'

'That's all very well but I don't mind tellin' yer I was embarrassed,' Cissie huffed. 'There were a queue o' people behind me an' all. What must they have thought of us?'

'Don't worry, I'll mention it to him when he comes in for breakfast,' Sunday promised. 'And if he hasn't got time to go into town and pay the bills, I'll do it. I have a meeting with the councillors anyway later this afternoon about the new phase of council houses they're planning to build so it wouldn't be any trouble.'

'Hm, well just see as yer do,' Cissie said grumpily. 'I've never known us to be in the red before in all the years we've lived 'ere!'

Kathy breezed into the kitchen then, looking bright-eyed and happy, and for now the topic of the unpaid bills was dropped.

Sunday ushered her to the table with a smile. It was lovely to see her looking so happy and as David was still a regular visitor to the house Sunday secretly hoped that it was because their relationship was developing. Kathy certainly showed all the signs of being in love, but Sunday had had enough young women in this house to know that asking about it would just cause Kathy to clam up, so she would have to wait and see and let nature take its course.

As it turned out it was mid-morning before Sunday managed to have a moment alone with Ben. One of the horses had sprained a leg and Ben was spending a lot of time with him so he had missed breakfast.

Cissie was working in the wash house tackling a pile of dirty sheets when he eventually came into the kitchen to grab a hot drink and she instantly asked, 'How is Thunder? Any better?'

Ben nodded curtly as he seated himself at the table. 'The vet thinks he'll be fine. We just have to make sure he rests it. We can't afford to lose him, he's one of our best studs.' Ben had bred him and had a huge soft spot for the creature, but then he was fond of all the horses. In fact, Sunday sometimes wondered, particularly lately, if he didn't prefer the company of them to people.

She quickly made him a sandwich and a pot of tea and as it was mashing, she suddenly remembered the conversation she'd had with Cissie that morning and said tentatively, 'Oh, Cissie told me that both the butcher and the grocer are waiting for payment.' When he scowled, she hurried on, 'Don't worry about it. I know how busy you've been, but I thought I could pay them this afternoon if you give me the money. I have to go into town anyway. It wouldn't be any trouble.'

'I'll see to it,' he answered, his voice sullen. 'I have to go into town an' all so I'll do it then.'

She opened her mouth to object but then thought better of it and clamped it shut again. Ben was so temperamental these days she was in constant fear of upsetting him. For some time, she'd been thinking of suggesting she should have a look at the bank statements, but she had been too afraid of upsetting him. Her solicitor, who had also been a close friend of Tom's, had suggested that she and Ben should have a joint account shortly after Tom's death, but she had been so deep in grief back then that once it was set up, she had been more than happy to leave everything to Ben. But he had always kept a certain amount of cash in the safe to pay the bills and she couldn't see why he wouldn't just give her the money and let her pay them. As she removed the tea cosy and stirred the tea in the pot, she glanced at him to gauge his mood and seeing the frown on his face decided to leave suggesting it until he was in a better mood. *If he ever was*, she thought!

Before they knew it, Christmas was racing towards them and Cissie said one afternoon, 'I reckon I'll ask Ben to go into town an' pick us up a Christmas tree next market day. It's only three weeks away now, it'll come round afore we know it!'

'Good idea, I might ask him if I can go with him to get some of my Christmas shopping done,' Sunday agreed. So that evening, as they all sat at dinner, she put it to him.

He shrugged as he bit into one of Cissie's delicious steak and kidney pies. 'If that's what you want,' he answered sulkily and Cissie and Sunday exchanged a glance.

Cissie left immediately after dinner with a plateful of food for George, after Sunday and the girls assured her they would see to the washing-up. George had been confined to bed back at the cottage with what had started as a heavy cold but had swiftly turned to bronchitis and they were all concerned about him. It meant that for now Ben was running the stables single-handed, apart from when Kathy could help him on her days off, and he looked tired.

'Why don't you get yourself an early night?' Sunday suggested, but he merely glared at her.

Sunday flushed but didn't push it. She had only been trying to be kind, but she was getting used to having her head bitten off by him. Sometimes she felt as if she couldn't do right for doing wrong.

'I'll come over and help you settle the horses,' Kathy volunteered.

Livvy was happy to help too and piped up, 'Yes, you do that and me and Mum can do the dishes.'

So, while Kathy and Ben hurried over to the stables, Sunday and her youngest began to clear the table.

'I don't know what gets into our Ben lately,' Sunday confided glumly as she piled the dirty dishes into the deep, stone sink.

'I know what you mean.' Livvy was keen to get the jobs out of the way as she had a date that night with one of the junior partners from her work. She had soon tired of Steven and was now on to her next beau.

Sunday was again hoping something would come of their dating as Harry Townsend was a very personable young man indeed, although she wasn't holding her breath. Livvy breezed from one young man to another and seemed to be quite happy to be footloose and fancy-free.

'It'll all change when she meets the right one,' Cissie had told Sunday when she'd shared her hopes with her. 'Some young bloke will come along when you least expect it an' bowl her off her feet an' I guarantee she'll be wed in no time. Meantime, let her enjoy herself. You're only young once, ain't yer?'

'You're not wrong there,' Sunday had agreed wryly. The bitterly cold wet weather had suddenly made her feel every year of her age. 'That's why I'd like to see both the girls settled. I've always imagined them walking down the aisle in a froth of satin and lace on their father's arm.' Tears pricked at the back of her eyes because that could never happen now. 'And I'd like to see Ben meet a nice girl too, but he doesn't seem interested,' she added.

'Hm.' Cissie had pursed her lips. 'Ben don't seem much interested in anythin' anymore from what I can make of it, 'cept the horses, o' course. I can't believe how much he's changed since his dad passed on.'

'I know what you mean.' Sunday had sighed as she wondered what she could do to reach him.

Over in the stables Kathy almost pounced on Ben, and planted a kiss on his lips the second he shut the door behind them. 'I've been wanting to do that all night,' she admitted with a twinkle in her eye, but Ben gently held her away from him.

'Hm, well we've animals that need seeing to,' he told her grumpily and she pouted.

'I never know where I stand with you,' she complained. 'We've been seeing each other like this for weeks now. When can we tell everyone that we're a couple? We have nothing to be ashamed of!'

Often she felt that their relationship was very one-sided. Ben had never once told her that he loved her whereas she told him all the time.

He scowled. 'I'm quite sure the rest of the family will not approve,' he pointed out yet again. 'We've been brought up as family and I think your mum will be shocked.'

'*So?*' She tossed her head defiantly. 'It's not up to my mum who I fall in love with, is it? She'll just have to get used to the idea.'

'Let's see how things go for a time,' Ben responded, then he went about his business as if she wasn't even there, leaving her to quietly fume.

Chapter Nine

Sunday spent an uneventful and quiet Christmas and New Year at home with her family. Cissie and George had gone to spend it with their youngest daughter and her family who lived in a small village on the outskirts of Leicester. George was still far from well following a severe dose of bronchitis and as a result the majority of the stable work was still falling to Ben, although in fairness he never complained. As Sunday ruefully commented to Livvy, it seemed the only time he was happy was when he was with the horses. For the rest of the time he was still walking about like a bear with a sore head. In fact, she was becoming increasingly concerned about him but the closer she tried to get to him the further away he seemed to push her, until eventually she just kept her distance.

And then on a wet and windy morning towards the end of January he didn't come down for breakfast. At first, she thought he was over in the stables so when Kathy and Livvy had left for work she hurried over there, only to find there was no sign of him.

'It's unlike Ben to lie in,' she commented to Cissie when she raced back into the kitchen out of the blistering rain. 'I hope he's not ill.'

'Pour yourself a cuppa an' I'll pop up an' give him a knock,' Cissie volunteered.

Minutes later she barged back into the kitchen, her face as white as chalk. 'He ain't there,' she panted breathlessly.

'What do you mean?' Bemused, Sunday stared at her.

'Just what I say – he ain't there. His bed ain't been slept in an' all his stuff has gone out o' the wardrobe.'

Sunday shook her head. 'So where is he then?'

'Beats me,' Cissie answered. 'Did you see him last night?'

Sunday tried to think. 'Not after nine o' clock. I had a slight headache, so I had an early night and he was in the kitchen when I went up.'

'He must have gone off sometime in the night then, when we were all abed.'

The two women stared at each other, confused.

'But why would he just go off like that? Th-this is his home,' Sunday stammered, then as a thought occurred to her she said hopefully, 'Perhaps he's taken himself off on a little holiday. God knows he deserves one.'

'Huh! I doubt that. He'd have told us if that was what 'e were plannin'.' Cissie shook her head, setting her chins wobbling. 'We can hardly get him to go into town let alone take a holiday.'

Their conversation was stopped from going any further when the sound of Bill Dewhurst's coal wagon drew into the yard and Cissie bustled away to put the kettle on. She knew he he'd be glad of a hot drink today with the weather being as it was.

When Bill had emptied the sacks of coal into the coal store he rapped on the door and came into the kitchen, looking ill at ease as he removed his cap.

'Morning, ladies.'

Cissie ushered him to the table and the reason for his discomfort soon became clear when he said, 'I hope yer don't mind me askin', Mrs Brannin', but do yer reckon yer could settle yer bill today? There's eight months owin' now wi' the load I've dropped today.'

Sunday's eyes stretched wide as she stared at him in shock. '*What*? . . . But Ben should have paid you. He promised me he would!'

Bill shrugged, looking mightily embarrassed as he took a swig of the hot tea Cissie had placed in front of him, nearly scalding his throat. 'I know, missus, but he just kept sayin' he'd settle up next time an' I didn't want to cause no fuss, what wi' you bein' such good customers.'

'Oh, Bill, I'm *so* sorry!' Sunday was mortified. She had always prided herself on her bills being paid on time and now more than ever she wished that she had insisted she take over the household accounts again. But Ben had been so against it, insisting that he could manage.

'I shall go and get some money and pay you immediately,' she told him, hurrying out of the door. Once inside the office, she swung aside the picture that hid the safe and gasped when she saw that the door to it was slightly open. Worse still, it was completely empty! Her hand rose to her throat as she stared at it in shock. But it couldn't be, the stables had been doing well, so where was all the money? Yet even as she stared at the empty safe a terrible thought was taking hold of her. Ben was gone and so was the money. Surely he wouldn't have taken it? Yet what other explanation could there be? And then it dawned on her. Ben must have paid all the money into the bank. Pulling herself together with an effort she made her way back to the kitchen to tell Bill in a shaky voice, 'I'm so sorry, Bill. I can't put my hands on the money right now but please leave your bill and I'll come into town and settle up with you just as soon as possible. And I'm *so* sorry.' She was finding it hard to force a smile and not panic, but somehow she managed it.

'No problem at all, pet,' he assured her with a smile, sensing how awkward she was feeling. She was a lovely lady and the last thing he wanted to do was upset her, which was why he had left the unpaid bill as long as he had. 'Ben's probably just been so busy he forgot all about it.'

'Yes . . . yes that's what it'll be.' Sunday was so embarrassed she could barely look him in the eye and as soon as he'd gone, she told Cissie in a wobbly voice, 'Th-the safe was open and the money's gone, Cissie.'

Cissie paused and narrowed her eyes. 'What do yer mean, it's *gone*? He always kept enough back each week in the safe to pay for the bills an' any emergencies that might crop up.'

Sunday nodded as she wrung her hands together. 'I know.' Her tongue flicked out to lick her suddenly dry lips. It was clear what they were both thinking but neither of them wanted to put it into words. 'Are you quite sure Ben hasn't left a message for us?'

'I didn't see one but let's go an' check.' Cissie dried her hands on her coarse work apron and hurried away to Ben's room with Sunday close on her heels. Between them they systematically searched the room but apart from the furniture it was as if Ben had never lived there.

'What are we going to do?' Sunday asked in a tremulous voice.

Cissie straightened and shook her head. 'Well, from where I'm standin' there's only one thing yer can do. You need to get into town an' check the bank account an' if he's taken the money out, you'll have to ring Mr Dixon.'

Mr Dixon had been Sunday's solicitor for many years, as well as being a close personal friend. When Tom was alive, he had always advised him on any financial matters as well as keeping track of how the stud business was doing. Each month, Tom had submitted a list of his takings to him and at one time Mr Dixon had invested a certain amount of the profit for him in stocks and shares. Now that Sunday came to think of it, she realised that they hadn't seen him for some months, but she knew that Cissie was right. She would have to contact him for advice to see how much money was left tied up for them. But first she would check how much money was in the bank.

'I'll ring him straight away and ask him to come out to see me,' Sunday agreed and hurrying down to the hall she lifted the phone and rang his office in Bond Gate.

'He's out at the minute but his secretary assured me she would pass on my message and get him to come as soon as possible. But what do we do now?' she asked Cissie as she came back into the kitchen.

'We wait,' Cissie said, her lips set in a straight grim line. 'Meanwhile I'd best get George to run you into town. You need to get some money out of the bank to pay Bill and he'll have to see to the horses an' all if Ben's cleared off.'

'But he still isn't well,' Sunday objected.

'No, he ain't, but I doubt the horses will care about that,' Cissie answered as she hurried away to find him.

Two hours later Sunday returned from town and as she entered the kitchen her chalk-white face told its own tale.

'He's cleaned you out, ain't he?' Cissie said softly and Sunday nodded, still too deep in shock to answer.

When the girls returned that evening and Sunday told them what had happened, Sunday was shocked at Kathy's reaction. Livvy was understandably upset but the colour drained out of Kathy's cheeks and she was frantic.

'What do you mean – he's *gone*?'

Her mother shrugged helplessly. 'Just that. He didn't come down for breakfast and when Cissie went up to see if he was all right, she found his room empty.'

Kathy plonked down on the nearest chair and began to cry. 'But he wouldn't just go off like that . . . he *wouldn't*!'

'But he bloody well has! An' the young bugger has emptied the bank account an' all,' Cissie snapped unsympathetically as she began to dish up the meal, not that anyone had much appetite. Ben's disappearance seemed to have taken the wind right out of all of their sails, but she had noticed that there seemed to be more to Kathy's upset than the fact that Ben could well have left them destitute

'Ah well, at least Mr Dixon should still have a sizeable amount of money tied up for us and the stables are doing well so we'll still have an income,' Sunday said, trying to be optimistic. She couldn't allow herself to believe that Ben would just disappear with all their money, she couldn't!

As soon as the meal was over Kathy disappeared to her room where she sobbed into her pillow inconsolably. She couldn't countenance her life without Ben; she adored him and he was her whole world. *But he'll come back*, she comforted herself. *He loves me, he must do!*

Sunday was up early the next morning. There was no point in lying in bed for she'd hardly slept a wink all night. Cissie was already downstairs in the kitchen as was Kathy who shocked her mother when she informed her that she wouldn't be going in to work that day. Sunday had never known her have a single day off before, but she didn't say anything. She had too much else to worry about.

At just after nine o'clock the postman came whistling down the drive and Sunday went into the hall to fetch the mail. Ever since Tom had died Ben had always fetched the mail leaving anything that was addressed to her on the hall table, so it felt strange to be sorting through it herself.

There was a letter from a councillor inviting her to a meeting about the next lot of social housing they were planning to build and a letter from Verity inviting her to afternoon tea the following week. The third envelope looked very official, but she had no idea what it might contain. She took it into the day room and ripped it open.

Suddenly the floor seemed to rush up to greet her as her eyes flicked down the page and she had to read it over again to make herself believe what was written there.

Arrears on Mortgage . . . £187 . . . to be paid immediately . . . bailiffs will be appointed if said arrears are not redeemed in full . . .

She shook her head, her face a mask of dismay. There had to be a mistake. There was no mortgage on Treetops, nor had there been for many years!

Chapter Ten

'What do you make of this?' Sunday asked, dashing into the kitchen and thrusting the letter into Cissie's hand.

Cissie read it quickly before passing it to George who scratched his head. 'But this house hasn't had a mortgage on it in all the years I've lived here,' he said bewildered.

'*Quite!*' Sunday was angry now. 'So there's clearly been a terrible mistake. I shall go into the bank this very day and give them a piece of my mind!'

She had no time to say more for at that moment the doorbell rang and Cissie went to answer it. 'It's Mr Dixon,' she informed Sunday when she came back. 'I've shown him into the day room so make sure as you take that with you to show him.'

Sunday nodded and with the letter clutched in her hand she went to join their visitor, while Cissie set about preparing a tray of tea for them.

'William, thank you *so* much for coming so quickly,' she greeted him. 'I'm afraid I desperately need your advice . . .' She hurried on to tell him about Ben's disappearance, the empty safe and bank account, then she handed him the letter. By the time he had finished reading it he was frowning.

'I'm afraid this doesn't look like a mistake to me,' he told her worriedly. 'Are you quite sure Tom didn't take out a mortgage on the place before he died?'

'No, of course he didn't. Tom would never have done something like that without consulting me! And anyway, there was no need to. The stables are doing well and with what you have invested in stocks and shares for us we're very financially comfortable.'

She was so wound up that she failed to notice the look of dismay that flitted across his face before he stood abruptly. 'I'm going to go back into town immediately and try to get to the bottom of this,' he informed her. 'Try not to worry, my dear. I shall be back as soon as I possibly can.'

He left just as Cissie was carrying the tray into the room and frowning she asked, 'Where's he off to in such a rush? Anyone would think 'is tail were on fire the way he dashed out.'

'He's gone to the bank to try to get to the bottom of this mortgage business.'

'Oh, then in that case we'd better drink this, it's a shame fer it to go to waste,' Cissie said stoically and Sunday gave a weak smile for the first time that morning. The world might be crashing about her ears but dear Cissie would never refuse a cuppa!

Upstairs Kathy was prowling up and down her room like a caged animal with tears pouring down her cheeks. How could Ben do this to her? If he had only told her that he needed to get away, *surely* she should have known that she would have gone with him? She would have followed him to the ends of the earth if need be. But then, she tried to console herself, he would come back! Of course he would. Hadn't she shown him how much she loved him? Nodding, she swiped the tears away with the back of her hand. All she had to do now was wait and soon he would be back where he belonged.

It was almost lunchtime when Mr Dixon returned, and Sunday knew from the grim look on his face that he was the bearer of bad news. She ushered him into the day room, it was the only room that had a fire in, and he strode towards it and stared down into the flames for a moment as if trying to pluck up the courage to speak to her. Eventually he turned and sighed before gesturing her towards a chair.

'I think you'd better sit down,' he told her, his voice grave. 'I'm afraid that what I'm going to tell you is going to come as a terrible shock.' Suddenly he wished that he were a million miles away. Sunday had gone through so much and now he was going to bring what was left of her world tumbling about her ears. 'The thing is, my dear . . .' He swallowed, making his Adam's apple bob up and down his throat. 'The letter you received from the bank this morning was correct. There is a mortgage on Treetops and the payments are greatly in arrears.'

Her head wagged from side to side in denial. 'N-no, there can't be. I've never mortgaged the property. Why would I?' The stricken look on her face made him want to run but he stood his ground. The sooner this unpleasant business was out in the open the better.

'It was Ben that took out the mortgage on it.'

Her eyes stretched so wide he feared they might pop out of their sockets. 'B-but he couldn't have. The house is in my name and I never signed anything.'

'No, but after Tom died you gave Ben a letter saying that he would be in charge of all your finances until further notice. It was he that took the mortgage out. And that isn't the worst of it, I'm afraid. He also told me to cash in all the stocks and shares that Tom had invested in. He said that was what you wanted and when I told him that I would come and talk to you about it he got quite shirty and told me that you weren't receiving visitors – any visitors – and that he was acting on your instructions.'

Sunday suddenly understood why William hadn't been to see her for some time and she felt sick. 'So where does that leave me now?' she asked with a tremor in her voice.

He spread his hands, feeling helpless. 'Well, unfortunately . . . you are now in debt to the bank. Ben has taken all your cash and so . . .' He gulped, hating what he was going to say. 'All you have left is the business. My advice to you would be to sell the house and the business to clear your debts. Hopefully you will have enough left to buy a small cottage somewhere but until I've had time to look properly at your finances, I can't even promise that.'

'*Sell* Treetops!' Sunday was stunned. 'B-but I can't do that. This is my home. The house my mother left to me!'

'I know, my dear.' Mr Dixon looked almost as upset as Sunday felt and had Ben been there, he would have derived great pleasure from wringing his neck! 'I'm so very sorry,' he went on in a gentle voice. 'But let me get an agent to come out and view the property and value it. Meantime I shall add up exactly what you owe, and we'll take it from there. Would you like me to do that?'

Sunday nodded numbly. She just couldn't take it all in; it was her worst nightmare come true and there wasn't a single thing she could do about it.

Mr Dixon left shortly after. In truth he couldn't get away quickly enough and he knew he would never forget the stricken look on Sunday's face for as long as he lived. The poor woman. As if she hadn't had enough to put up with losing Tom. And now this – it just didn't bear thinking about!

Minutes later Sunday stumbled into the kitchen and told Cissie what the solicitor had said. Cissie dropped heavily onto a chair, but then, as always, her spirit roused her from her despair and she told her dearest friend, 'We'll get through this, pet. We're not beaten yet. Me an' George have a bit put away fer us retirement and I'm sure the girls will pitch in some o' their wages to keep the house runnin' till Mr Dixon's sorted somethin' out. One good thing is we own our cottage thanks to you an' Tom so you'll not be wi'out a roof over yer heads. Let's face it, this great old place was gettin' a bit too much fer us to manage anyway an' though it'll be a bit of a squeeze at our place we'll get by one way or another.'

'Oh, Cissie . . . what would I do without you?' Sunday sobbed and suddenly she was in her friend's arms and she clung to her like a drowning man might cling to a raft.

The next day an agent came to value the house and contents and soon after Mr Dixon returned.

'I have collated all your debts,' he told her gravely, 'and unfortunately Treetops will have to be sold to meet them. However, I noticed as I drove in that there is a small lodge at the entrance and I wondered, if you sold the estate but kept that, how you would feel about living there?'

Sunday blinked. The lodge, or the gatehouse as it was sometimes referred to, was a pretty little dwelling built just to one side of the entrance gates to the estate. It had arched stone windows and a little turreted roof and had not been occupied for many years. She couldn't even really remember what it was like inside, although she knew that it did have three bedrooms, which would accommodate herself and the girls. And it would be a way of staying close to her beloved Treetops.

'I suppose it is a possibility,' she said uncertainly. 'But the girls and I would have to go and have a proper look inside it. It's probably fallen into disrepair after being empty for so long.'

'Well, if you did decide to do that the good news is that there would be a certain amount of money left. Enough for you to live frugally on for a few years at least.'

'I'll go and look this evening, just as soon as the girls return from work and I shall let you know tomorrow. But what happens then?'

The kindly man sighed. 'I would advise that you put Treetops on the market as soon as possible,' he said solemnly. 'I can instruct the agent to do that for you if you wish?'

Sunday nodded miserably, she really didn't have much choice.

Chapter Eleven

'Live in the *lodge*!' Both Kathy and Livvy looked horrified when their mother put the idea to them that evening.

'If we do that at least we wouldn't have to pay out for somewhere else to buy or rent. Then any money we did have left could go towards making the lodge comfortable, and living expenses,' Sunday pointed out. 'Admittedly Cissie has offered to let us all go to live with her, but I wouldn't feel right doing that. She and George deserve their own space and this way we would still have a measure of independence, at least.'

'I can see the sense in that,' Kathy admitted miserably. She was still reeling from shock at what Ben had done and the way he had abandoned her, but Livvy's chin jutted angrily.

'But *Treetops* is our *home*!' she spat angrily as burning tears spurted unchecked from her eyes. 'I grew up here and I can't bear the thought of leaving it! It is our legacy, our grandmother lived here, and all our childhood memories were made here!'

'None of us *wants* to go, darling,' Sunday said quietly. 'But I'm afraid we have no choice. Ben has taken every penny we had, and we have to live somewhere.'

'Then let's walk down there and take a look at the place.'

Kathy's face was glum. 'Though it's dark so we'll have to take torches. There's no electric in there, is there?'

'I can't remember if your father had it put in when we had Treetops done,' Sunday admitted. 'But we'll take torches just in case.'

They wrapped up warmly and armed with torches set off down the tree-lined drive in the bitterly cold evening. The wind was howling, and a fine drizzle was falling so by the time they reached the lodge they were all soaked through and feeling thoroughly miserable.

Sunday fumbled in her pocket for the key but at first the lock resisted all efforts to open it. 'It must have rusted up,' Sunday told them but eventually she managed to turn it and the door creaked open. They stepped into a small sitting room, dismayed to find that it was almost as cold inside as it was out, and the whole place smelled damp and musty. The one good thing was that as Sunday shone the torch around the walls, she spotted a light switch and when she flipped it on the room was flooded with light from a bare light bulb that dangled from the ceiling.

'That's something at least,' she muttered as she stared around in despair. Old pieces of furniture covered in layers of dust were dotted about and thick cobwebs hung from the beams on the ceiling like intricately woven lace.

'When me and your father first came here an old gentleman and his wife lived here,' she remembered sadly. 'I can't remember their names now and sadly they both died soon after and the place has stood empty ever since.'

'I-it's *disgusting*!' Livvy spluttered as tears coursed down her cheeks. 'We can't possibly live in this . . . *this slum*!'

Kathy said nothing but just stood there looking thoroughly

miserable. *How could Ben have reduced us to this?* she wondered as her heart broke afresh.

Sunday walked around the room, looking into corners. 'I'm afraid we don't have much choice.' Her voice was firm. 'And I'm sure it's not as bad as it looks. I think it's damp because there hasn't been any heat in here for a long time. A few good fires should sort that, and a lick of paint will make it look different.'

Livvy looked horrified. 'But how can you even *consider* living in a place like this after being brought up in Treetops?'

Sunday turned to stare at her, her face stern. 'Believe me, my girl, I've lived in far worse places when I was a girl,' she told her shortly. 'Don't forget I was brought up in the workhouse! This is a palace compared to what that place was back then.' As always when her back was against the wall, Sunday's indomitable spirit had come to the fore. She had shed her tears over losing Treetops and now it was time to look to the future and ensure that her girls at least had a roof over their heads, even if it was only a humble one.

Livvy's hands clenched into fists of rage. 'Ben should be *punished* for what he's done to us,' she ground out through clenched teeth. 'Have you reported him to the police? He can't be far away, and he must still have all or at least most of the money he's stolen!'

'I shan't be doing that,' Sunday answered coldly. 'I've already had this discussion with Mr Dixon.'

'But why not?' Livvy was outraged. 'He *deserves* to be punished.'

'He was your father's son. And no matter what he's done, he's family,' Sunday said simply and Livvy saw from the look on her face that she would not be swayed from this decision, so turning about she stormed off into the night leaving Kathy and Sunday to investigate the rest of the lodge.

'It's very dirty but I think a good clean and some paint would make it look very different,' she told Cissie the next morning.

'Me an' George can help you do that,' Cissie said. 'But just remember the offer of movin' in wi' us still stands.' Secretly she was almost as outraged at Ben's betrayal as Livvy was. Now she just wished she had heeded the signs before he got away with it. They had all been there as clear as the nose on her face when she looked back – the unpaid bills, his refusal to let Sunday have anything to do with finances – but never in her wildest dreams had she ever believed that he would be capable of such deception. Admittedly he had made it clear how disappointed he was that he hadn't inherited the house after his father's death, but to do this!

'Come on, we'll go for a walk down there now an' see what needs doin',' she offered kindly. Seeing Sunday, who was so kind and who had done so much good for so many young people in her life, so upset almost broke Cissie's heart.

George was now running the stables single-handed again, so the two women walked down the drive to the lodge and let themselves in. If anything, the place looked even more dismal in the cold light of day but Cissie put a cheerful face on as she said, 'Hm, this could be quite cosy wi' a bit o' work. Old Reggie an' his missus were always happy enough here. I'll get my George to go into town an' pick some paint up later on an' we'll make a start on it as soon as you like.' Looking slightly embarrassed then, she fumbled in her apron pocket and produced a small wad of bank notes, which she pressed into Sunday's hand.

'But . . . wh-what's this?'

'It's enough to tide you over an' pay a few bills till Treetops is sold.'

When Sunday opened her mouth to protest, Cissie shook her head. 'Now don't be daft!' she scolded. 'It's thanks to you an' Tom that we were able to save this *an'* have a roof over our heads may I add. Look on it as a loan if yer must but just take it. We've still got more than enough fer us needs an' if friends can't help each other when the chips are down, then it's a sad world.'

The tears flowed fast again as Sunday's chin drooped to her chest and she began to cry. 'Th-thank you, Cissie,' she said in a wobbly voice and then Cissie's arms were about her and they clung tight to each other.

Cissie eventually pushed her away and said bossily, 'Come on then, there's no point in cryin' over spilt milk. It's time we were getting' on wi' things if we're to make this place into a home again.' And she marched away as Sunday watched her go, thinking whatever else had befallen her, she was truly lucky to have such a wonderful friend.

Two days later, Mr Dixon informed her that Treetops was now officially on the market. Kathy seemed too wrapped up in misery to care but Livvy was still outraged at the thought of having to leave her childhood home.

'It's just not *fair!*' she ranted to Cissie in the kitchen one evening after work.

Cissie shrugged. 'That's one thing you'll discover as yer get a bit older, pet,' she said wryly. 'Life ain't always fair an' yer just have to take what it throws at yer an' get on wi' things.'

But deep down she truly empathised with the girl. She knew how much she loved her home and wished heartily that things could have been different.

Early in February, Mr Dixon visited again, but this time he hoped with what they would consider good news.

'I got to thinking,' he explained as he and Sunday sat in the day room at Treetops. 'A very good friend of mine who lives in Yorkshire lost his wife some two years ago and he's staying with me at present. As it happens, he has shares in some of the local businesses here and he mentioned last night over dinner that he was thinking of moving. The house he owns holds too many memories now that his wife is gone, apparently, and he wants a fresh start. He's already sold his place so he and his grandson, who lives at home with him, are looking for a suitable place here. I mentioned Treetops to him, and he said it sounded just like what he is looking for. So . . . I was wondering – he goes home the day after tomorrow. Would you like to show him around here before he leaves to see if it would be suitable for them?'

Suddenly the prospect of seeing someone else living in Treetops was very real and Sunday gulped. But then she nodded. She was looking far from her usual tidy self as she and Cissie had been busy in the lodge painting and she appeared to have got more on herself than on the walls.

'Yes, I could do that,' she forced herself to say with a weak smile. 'Do you think eleven o'clock in the morning would suit him?'

'I'm sure it would,' Mr Dixon assured her. 'And don't worry, he's aware of the price and doesn't think it's unreasonable. His name is John Willerby – he's a very nice chap and I'm sure you'll like him.'

Long after he had gone Sunday sat staring dully into space wondering what her beloved Tom would make of all this. She was sure that he would have been heartbroken but what was done was done and all she could do now was try to get on with things to the best of her ability.

Chapter Twelve

At precisely eleven o'clock the next morning a smart automobile pulled up outside Treetops and a very presentable gentleman stepped out and stood for a few seconds surveying the front of the property as Sunday peeped at him through the snow-white lace curtains. He was very tall and distinguished-looking with thick, silvery grey hair and a small, neatly trimmed beard. Sunday thought he might be about the same age as herself, but she didn't have long to think on it because within seconds he had rung the doorbell and after hastily checking her hair in the tall, gilt mirror in the hallway she hurried to answer it.

She had made an effort with her appearance today and with her hair twisted into a neat French roll on the back of her head and wearing the smart two-piece blue costume that matched the colour of her eyes, she looked every inch the lady of the manor as she greeted him.

'How do you do. You must be Mr Willerby?'

His eyes were openly admiring as he shook her hand warmly and she noticed that they were kind and friendly with a twinkle in them. For some reason she had convinced herself that she wasn't going to like him. He was possibly about to be the new owner of her home, after all, but she found it very difficult not to.

'Welcome to Treetops, Mr Willerby. Do come in.'

As he stepped past her into the hall he smiled. 'Why, this is quite charming,' he said appreciatively, and she found herself smiling back.

'Thank you. Perhaps we should start upstairs and work our way down?' she suggested. 'Then when you have seen the house, George, a dear friend of mine who has lived here with his wife for many years, will show you around the stables and let you see the horses.'

'That would be wonderful, thank you.'

She took his hat and hung it on the coat rack and they made their way upstairs. Almost two hours later Cissie brought a tray of tea into the day room and, while Sunday poured for them both, he told her, 'The house is just what I'm looking for, Mrs Branning. I shall go and see the agent who is in charge of the sale directly I leave here. And I understand from our mutual friend Mr Dixon that we will be neighbours?'

'Yes.' Sunday frowned as she concentrated on straining the tea into the cups. It suddenly all felt very real. 'My daughters and I will be living in the lodge by the gates, but I assure you you'll have no interference from us.'

'I shall be highly delighted to have you as a neighbour,' he assured her with a grin. 'And you will be very welcome to interfere any time you wish.'

'So?' Cissie asked her the second he had left.

Sunday smiled, a sad smile that didn't quite reach her eyes.

'It appears that the property is sold, Cissie, so soon, hopefully, I shall be be debt-free and be able to pay you back as well. And I have to say Mr Willerby does seem to be a very nice gentleman.'

Cissie grinned and nudged her with her arm, 'Ah, he's a bit of all right an' all, ain't he?' she laughed. 'Cor, all that lovely silver hair! A bit different to my George wi' his monk's cut, bless him.'

Sunday smiled back, but the smile soon faded and she became solemn. 'Now I just have to tell the girls,' she fretted. 'And I have an idea they're not going to be too pleased at all to hear that their home has been sold!'

Cissie became solemn too as she nodded in agreement.

As it happened, Kathy showed little reaction to the news at all. She didn't seem to have any interest in anything, even the horses, since Ben had gone, but Livvy was a different kettle of fish altogether and flew into a tantrum.

'This is *all* Ben's fault; how *could* he do this to us?' she raged as tears flooded down her cheeks. She had been praying for a miracle that would prevent them having to leave but now it seemed that it was inevitable.

Sunday tried to wrap her arms about her but Livvy slapped them away and, turning, she fled to her room vowing she would never forgive him for what he had done, *never*!

One evening towards the end of February John Willerby paid Sunday another visit. Kathy let him in and sullen-faced showed him into the day room where Sunday was sitting beside the fire reading. Livvy had gone to the pictures to watch *Fire Over*

England starring Vivien Leigh – one of her favourite actresses – and Laurence Olivier, and so Sunday had expected to spend a quiet evening alone. Kathy was no company anymore and crept about the house like a ghost when she wasn't locked away in her room or working.

'Ah, Mr Willerby, do come in.' Sunday quickly put her book down and rose to meet him, looking mildly surprised.

'I do apologise for calling in unannounced,' he said, taking his hat off. 'But I was here on business and just wished to tell you that the solicitor who is handling the sale of the house thinks all the paperwork should be completed within the next couple of weeks. Of course, if you haven't got the lodge quite ready to move in to by then there is no rush whatsoever. I also wanted to say please take whatever furniture you wish. I shall be bringing certain pieces of my own anyway so I'm sure I shall have far too much.'

'That's very generous of you, thank you.' It had been agreed that he would buy the house and all its contents but seeing as the furniture that had been left in the lodge was not salvageable it would take a great weight off her mind knowing that she would not have to rush out to scout around for second-hand pieces. *Not that I will take advantage of his good nature*, she told herself. Much of the furniture in the house would be far too big and grand to fit into the lodge anyway but she would be grateful for the beds and some smaller pieces.

'Please also take all of your pots and pans,' he went on. 'My cook and maid will be coming with me so they will be bringing anything they need from the other house. I would also be very grateful if you would tell Mr and Mrs Jenkins that should they wish to continue their posts here, be it full-time or part-time, I would be most grateful. This house is rather too large for one maid to manage on her own so I'm sure she would welcome the help.'

William Dixon had told him of Sunday's plight, and he felt heartsore for her.

Sunday's pride was at the fore now and she felt utterly humiliated, but she forced a smile before saying, 'I shall be sure to pass on your message. Would you like a drink, Mr Willerby? Perhaps a brandy or a cup of tea or coffee?'

'Thank you, but no. I have no wish to take up any more of your time. I just thought that as I was in the vicinity I would pop in and bring you up to date. And please . . . call me John.'

Sunday flushed. She could never picture herself addressing him as such so she merely inclined her head, her back straight.

'Thank you and please let me know the date you wish to move in.'

'I shall. Goodbye for now, Mrs Branning.' And with that he turned and left, leaving Sunday all of a dither. Suddenly it all seemed heartbreakingly real. Very soon now she would be forced to leave the home where she and Tom had known such happiness and the pain she felt as she contemplated it was almost physical.

When she passed on Mr Willerby's message to Cissie the next morning her friend paused and narrowed her eyes.

'Hm . . . I dare say George would be happy to still be involved with the horses even if it's only part-time,' she mused. 'Him an' your Tom bred some of 'em an' raised 'em from tiny foals so I know he's very fond of 'em. An' me . . . well, I suppose if I ain't got to do the cookin' anymore I'd consider helpin' with the cleanin' part-time. I'll have to give it some thought, but it was good of him to ask. I suppose we have to think ourselves lucky that if this has got to happen then at least it's a nice gentleman who's buyin' the place. But if as he says the move is imminent then I reckon we should start gettin' some o' the stuff you want to take down to the lodge. It's all ready now. George finished whitewashin' the last bedroom last night an' it looks a treat.'

'I'd never have managed it without you and George,' Sunday said quietly as tears burned at the back of her eyes. 'You'll never know how grateful I am to you both, Cissie.'

Embarrassed, Cissie flapped her hand at her. 'Eh, get away wi' yer! Look at all you've done fer me an' George over the years. Now come on, we'll have a walk round and decide what yer want to take. George can move it in the trap.'

As they walked about the house Sunday felt as if her heart was breaking. Each and every piece of furniture had been chosen either by herself or her mother and, until now, she hadn't realised how hard it was going to be to leave everything behind. Between them they chose a number of smaller pieces that would look well in the lodge and shortly after lunchtime George came and began to load them onto the cart, while the old pony they used to pull it stood contentedly nuzzling on a nose bag.

When they arrived at what was to be her new home, Sunday looked about. They had all spent every spare minute on it and now that it had been scrubbed from top to bottom and given a new coat of paint it looked entirely different. George had burned all the old furniture on a bonfire and had even swept the chimney so at least they would be cosy there. Even so, Sunday's heart was heavy as they began to carry the furniture in and position it where she wanted it. It was going to be very hard to see someone else in the home that she loved, but Ben's betrayal had ensured that it could be no other way and, in that moment, she almost hated him.

Chapter Thirteen

Livvy flew into a rage again when Sunday informed her that the move was imminent.

'If only you'd reported Ben to the police and told them what he'd done they might have caught him by now and we might have got our money back!' she stormed at her mother, as if everything that had happened was her fault.

'I'm sorry, darling. I know how hard this is for you, but I couldn't do that.' Sunday reached out to her but Livvy backed away, her lovely blue eyes blazing in her pale face. 'Your father would turn in his grave if I did that. He is your brother, remember,' Sunday pointed out, but Livvy was inconsolable. She loved her home and the thought of losing it was like a knife in her heart.

'I'll *never* forgive him for what he's done to us!' she snapped, and turning on her heel she slammed out of the room.

Kathy was sitting at the table, her eyes dull and Sunday looked at her imploringly. '*You* understand why I can't report him, don't you?'

Kathy shrugged. Her whole world had fallen apart when Ben left but that wasn't the only thing that was troubling her. She had now missed two of her courses and for the last few mornings she'd had to dash to the bathroom to be sick the second she lifted her feet over the side of the bed. Being a nurse, she was only too aware of what it could mean, and she was terrified. Her mother had so much to cope with at present, so how would she feel if she were to tell her that on top of everything else, she was also going to have to cope with the shame of having an illegitimate grandchild as well?

She pushed the thought away. *Perhaps it's just the upset that has caused all this*, she tried to persuade herself, but the niggling doubt was there in the back of her mind all the time now.

'Kathy . . . did you hear me?' Her mother's voice jerked Kathy's thoughts back to the present.

'Yes . . . I heard you, but it will be all right. Ben will come back, you'll see.' She had to hold on to that thought otherwise she would go mad.

'Right then!' Cissie stood back and rubbed her hands together with a satisfied smile.

It was early in March and she and Sunday had just spent the morning hanging curtains in the lodge. Cissie had found them stored in a trunk in the attic in Treetops and, now that she had cut them down to size and laboriously stitched them to fit the windows, they looked grand. They were chintz in shades of pink and red with pretty roses all over them and they made the rooms feel warm and cosy. The fires they had been lighting daily had dispersed the damp and now the three bedrooms each boasted a bed, a small wardrobe, a chest of drawers and a washstand complete with jugs and bowls.

'They look lovely. You've done a wonderful job on them,

Cissie,' Sunday answered gratefully. But as pretty as the place now looked, she knew that actually living there was going to be a massive lifestyle change for herself and the girls. They were all used to the convenience of an indoor bathroom for a start and she dreaded to think how they would cope with just a jug and bowl to wash in, let alone a tin bath!

As if she could read her thoughts, Cissie patted her arm. 'You'll get used to it,' she told her. 'An' it's still bigger than my cottage.' She was now in the process of making the beds and, hoping to take Sunday's mind off things, she told her, 'My George reckons this civil war in Spain could affect us eventually.'

'Really?' Sunday frowned. 'I don't see how something that's happening all that way away could.'

'Well, George ain't usually wrong,' Cissie said glumly, then changing the subject she tucked the last blanket in and said, 'I reckon that's about it. There's just yours an' the girls' clothes to come now. We could perhaps get them to start bringing them here this evenin'. Saturday will be here afore yer know it.'

Saturday was the day they had agreed John Willerby, his grandson and his staff would all move into Treetops and Sunday was alternately looking forward to it and dreading it. Half of her just wanted the move to be over, while the other half wondered how she would bear it.

'Hm, I suppose we'd better head back and get some lunch on the go now then,' Sunday said as she straightened the eiderdown on her bed. In the bedrooms she and Cissie had scrubbed the floorboards to within an inch of their lives and laid down rugs that they'd also found in the attic back at the house. Some of them were a little threadbare but they certainly softened the rooms and made it more comfortable underfoot. Since living at Treetops Sunday had rarely ventured into the attics but when she did, she had discovered that it was like an Aladdin's cave.

Now as they set off on the windy walk back along the drive, Sunday pulled her coat collar up and asked Cissie, 'Do you think Kathy is all right? She looks so pale and since Ben has been gone, she rarely speaks unless she's spoken to. She just gets up, goes to work then comes home and goes to bed. She isn't eating properly either and I'm getting really worried about her.'

Cissie kept her eyes straight ahead as she answered cautiously, 'Well, she always were the closest to Ben, weren't she? She's bound to feel it.' In truth she'd had her suspicions about what might be wrong with Kathy for the last couple of weeks but with all that Sunday had on her plate at present she hadn't dared to voice them. Best let them get into the lodge first and then face each problem as it came.

That night Sunday, Kathy and Livvy took their clothes down to the lodge, although Livvy complained bitterly all the way.

'I can't *believe* we've been reduced to this level,' she ranted miserably. 'Ben has a lot to answer for. I just hope he never knows a day's peace after what he's done! My friends must all be laughing at us.' She rammed her clothes into the wardrobe and dropped onto the edge of the bed in a sulk.

Up until this point Sunday had been as patient as a saint but now she turned on Livvy with her eyes flashing fire. 'If your friends can laugh at what's happened to us then they're not true friends!' she snapped. 'And furthermore, instead of feeling sorry for yourself all the time, my girl, you should give a thought to how hard me, Cissie and George have worked to make this place comfortable for you. It's difficult I know but at least we're not being turfed out onto the streets!'

Livvy instantly looked shamefaced and rising she crossed to her mother and put her arms about her waist. 'Sorry, Mum. I deserved that, didn't I?'

Sunday sighed as she pushed a lock of hair from her eyes, suddenly feeling very old and worn out. 'Just try and make the best of it,' she advised and went downstairs to put some of the paperwork she had fetched from the house away in the little escritoire she had brought from the day room. It had been her mother's and she hadn't been able to bear to leave it.

Thank goodness you aren't here to see what's happened, Mother. It would have broken your heart as it's breaking mine, she thought as she ran her hand across the intricately inset rosewood lid.

The following Friday was spent transporting the pots and pans, crockery, cutlery and all the last-minute items they wanted to take to the lodge and by teatime they had finished and moved in.

'I'll just walk back up to Treetops and make sure everywhere is tidy for Mr Willerby, while the girls put the rest of the things away,' Sunday told Cissie.

Cissie said nothing. The house was as neat as a new pin as Sunday was well aware but Cissie rightly guessed that she probably just wanted to say her goodbyes to the place. All her happy memories had been made there and Cissie could only imagine how hard it was going to be for her seeing someone else living in what she would always consider her home.

'I'll just go an' check on George while you go in,' she said tactfully at the top of the drive. 'I'll be back shortly, pet.'

Sunday nodded and climbing the steps she walked into the

hall. It felt strangely empty, but she was remembering a time when it had rung with the sound of children's laughter. She only had to close her eyes and she could picture the many children she had loved and cared for racing up and down the corridor when it had been too cold for them to go out to play. She made her way upstairs and stood in the doorway of the room she had shared with Tom. They had been little more than children themselves when they had come here as newlyweds and here, they had grown old together. She crossed to the window and again she could picture them dancing on the lawn in the moonlight on their wedding day. They had been so young and so in love, with their whole lives stretching out ahead of them. Where had the time gone?

Systematically she worked her way through each room seeing in her mind's eye each of the many children that she and Tom had cared for over the years, and by the time she went down the stairs again her cheeks were wet.

Cissie was waiting quietly in the hall for her and, without a word, she wrapped her arms around her and let her cry on her shoulder.

'That's it, pet, you let it all out,' she muttered soothingly, and it was some minutes before she realised that she too was crying. It was the end of an era.

Chapter Fourteen

The smell of a cottage pie and vegetables cooking wafted around the lodge later that day as Sunday went to the bottom of the stairs and called the girls for their meal. They had spent most of the afternoon putting their clothes away and settling into their rooms, but Sunday was greeted with silence from Livvy's room.

'I wonder if she's dozed off,' Sunday said to Kathy as she came down the stairs.

'I'll go and give her door a knock.'

Kathy turned and climbed the stairs again but when she tapped on Livvy's door the girl shouted, 'Go away! I'm not hungry!'

With a frown Kathy opened the door and barged into the room. 'So, what's wrong with you?' she demanded. In truth she was just as upset as the others at having to leave her home, but she didn't see how feeling sorry for herself was going to help anything.

Livvy was curled into a ball on her bed crying into her pillow and for a moment Kathy felt sorry for her but she hardened her heart and snapped, 'Mum has spent all afternoon cooking this dinner for us. The least you could do is come down and eat it! Lying there and feeling sorry for yourself isn't going to get us anywhere. We just have to get on with things and think ourselves lucky. At least we still have a roof over our heads!'

For a moment Livvy didn't respond but eventually she reluctantly swung her legs over the side of the bed and swiped the tears from her cheeks with the back of her hand. 'I know you're right,' she sniffed. 'But I'm going to miss Treetops so much. It's been our home all our lives.'

Kathy nodded in agreement. 'Yes it has, but just think how much worse this must be for Mum. She and Dad lived there all their married lives.'

Livvy scowled. She knew Kathy was right. 'I think the hardest thing for her must be having to come to terms with Ben's betrayal.' She shook her head. 'How could he do this to us? Just go off like that with almost every penny we had.'

Kathy gulped. Even now she couldn't believe that he wouldn't come back. He had to!

Once downstairs the girls tried to eat the meal, but the food seemed to stick in their throats.

'We must be a laughing stock in town,' Livvy suddenly commented bitterly as she pushed the food about her plate. 'Fancy being known as the owners of a big posh house like Treetops and then being reduced to living in this!'

'You should think yourself lucky we're not reduced to living on the streets,' Sunday reminded her and Livvy's eyes widened with shock. It was so unlike her mother to snap at any of them.

'I . . . I'm sorry.' She lowered her eyes in shame, then pushing back her chair she rose from the table. 'I'll do the washing-up,' she told them, hoping to atone for her thoughtlessness.

101

Sunday meantime bowed her head and once the girls had left the room, she finally let the torrent of tears that had been building inside her gush down her cheeks. This was the start of a new life for all of them and, somehow, they were just going to have to come to terms with it – unless a miracle happened, and she doubted very much that that would come about.

On Saturday large wagons and vans pulled into the driveway laden with Mr Willerby's possessions and Sunday peeped through the lace curtains to watch them pass. Cissie was there with her sharing a pot of tea and she peeped over her friend's shoulder.

'Looks like he's got a lot o' stuff,' she commented.

'I wonder if I should go along and offer to help?' Sunday said but Cissie shook her head.

'You'll do no such thing. You might have been reduced to living here in the lodge but you ain't a servant,' she stated indignantly. 'Anyway, be the looks of it he's got more than enough helpers. Let 'em get on wi' it, that's what I say. Least till I turn in for me first shift there tomorrow anyway!'

Sunday smiled wryly. Cissie had been her rock throughout the difficult times yet again and she really didn't know what she would have done without her. At that moment Mr Willerby appeared through the gates driving his motor car, a handsome young man sitting beside him.

'That must be his grandson,' Sunday murmured. 'He's a good-looking young chap, isn't he?'

Livvy peeped over her shoulder then with a toss of her head

she flounced from the room. She for one certainly wasn't going to help anyone settle into what she felt was still her home!

Cissie went back to work at Treetops the next morning although now she would only be doing part-time hours. Mr Willerby had brought his own cook so Cissie had agreed to help the maid with the cleaning and she had to admit he had been more than generous with her rate of pay. It had also been agreed that George would continue to work in the stables with Mr Willerby's grandson and the young groom that Mr Willerby had employed. After all, as he quite rightly pointed out, George knew the horses better than anyone. He had even agreed to Kathy and Livvy keeping their horses there free of charge, so all in all none of them could deny that he had been more than generous.

'I must say he's got some nice stuff,' Cissie informed Sunday as they sat drinking coffee at the lodge following her first day in Mr Willerby's employ. 'Though in fairness he ain't moved much of what you left out o' the way. An' Mrs Gay, the cook, is a lovely old soul an' so is Edith, the maid. They've both been with him for years.'

'And what about the grandson?' Sunday questioned curiously.

'Ah, I ain't properly met him yet,' Cissie admitted. 'But he seemed friendly enough. He were just leavin' to go into town an' order food for the horses as I got there. He seems to know his stuff when it comes to horses, so I reckon he'll do well takin' over the stables.'

Sunday nodded. It was still hard for her to accept that someone else was living in the home where she and Tom had known such happiness, and harder still to think of someone else running the business that Tom had so painstakingly built up, but then she had to grudgingly admit that at least Mr Willerby seemed very kind and friendly. The solicitor had brought her good news as well. It seemed that following the sale of the house, all the debts had been paid and there was still a tidy sum left over, which would at least alleviate any immediate financial worries.

'So, all in all I reckon things are lookin' up again,' Cissie said optimistically as she drained her cup. Then as something else occurred to her she frowned. 'Though I've noticed Kathy ain't been lookin' too grand lately,' she commented.

Sunday nodded in agreement as she poured her friend out another cup of coffee. 'I've noticed too,' she admitted worriedly. 'She's right off her food and I'm sure she's lost a bit of weight, but then it's hardly surprising really, is it? She was so close to Ben and with everything that's happened it's no wonder she's looking peaky.'

As she pushed the cup across the table Cissie scowled as she began to spoon in sugar. 'Hm, yer probably right but I'd keep an eye on her all the same, if I were you. Perhaps suggest she gets herself off to the doctor's fer a check-up?'

'I'll give her another few days for everything to settle down and then if she looks no better, I will,' Sunday promised, and the two women lapsed into silence as they enjoyed the rest of their break.

'Aw well, I have to say today's gone far better than I thought it would,' George admitted that evening when he joined Cissie in their cottage after he had finished work. 'Mr Willerby seems a nice enough chap an' Billy Harper, the young groom he's employed, is a pleasure to work wi'. He ain't got that much experience of workin' with horses as yet but he's keen as mustard to learn an' that's everythin'.'

'Then as I said to Sunday things might be lookin' up fer everybody now, wi' a bit o' luck.' Cissie carried a large steak and kidney pie to the table and paused to say, 'I'd still like to get me hands on Ben though! I swear I'd throttle him wi' me bare hands if I could!'

'I understand what yer sayin' but yer know what they say, pet. What goes round comes round,' George reminded her as he lifted his knife and fork and licked his lips in anticipation. There was no one could turn out a pie like his Cissie! 'He'll get his comeuppance, you just mark my words. Now, get some o' that pie on me plate afore I faint wi' hunger.'

With an affectionate smile Cissie did as she was told.

Across in the stables, Livvy was stroking her horse. She had got changed immediately she got home from work and hurried to check that her little mare was all right. Just as her mother had assured her, she found that Willow was quite happy, but then she should have known that George would make sure of that. If asked, Livvy would have been forced to admit that she was nowhere near as mad about riding as Kathy was anymore, but she'd had Willow for some years now and she was very fond of her, so it went sorely against Livvy's pride that she was now being housed in a stable that no longer belonged to her family.

'There's a good girl,' she crooned as she removed a carrot

from her pocket and fed it to the animal as she stroked her silky mane.

'Ah, hello there, you must be Kathy?'

Livvy started as a voice came from directly behind her and, whirling about, she found herself face to face with a very attractive young man. His hair was thick and dark with a tendency to curl and his eyes were the bluest she had ever seen. He was tall and muscular and dressed in very old clothes.

'Oh, hello. You must be Billy,' she answered, assuming he was the groom George was training. 'And no, I'm Livvy, Kathy's younger sister.'

'Ah, well I'm not Billy either,' he told her with an amused twinkle in his eye. 'I'm Giles Willerby, the new owner's grandson.'

The smile instantly slid from Livvy's face and she deliberately ignored his outstretched hand.

Jumped-up snob, she fumed to herself, *who did he think he was? Was he trying to rub salt into the wound? Just because he and his grandfather now owned her home!*

She fed Willow another carrot before turning abruptly to tell him primly, 'It's very good of your grandfather to allow me and Kathy to keep our horses here, but have no fear, as soon as we can find somewhere else to stable them, we will.'

He frowned. 'But why would you want to do that? They're perfectly content where they are.'

She raised her chin and sniffed. 'But they would be, wouldn't they? They've been born and raised here. But of course, now that we no longer *own* the place, I wouldn't *dream* of imposing on your good nature for any longer than I have to!' And with that she gave a toss of her head and strode past him without so much as glancing in his direction.

Giles watched her go with a bemused expression on his face.

All he could hope was that her sister might be a little friendlier than her. They certainly hadn't got off to the best of starts, though he couldn't for the life of him think what he might have said to offend her. *But then that was women for you*, he thought with a shrug, putting her from his mind as he got on with his work.

Chapter Fifteen

Early in April Kathy emerged from the toilet in the nurses' staff room at the hospital and leaning heavily on the edge of the sink she stared at her pale face in the small mirror above it. She looked, as Cissie would say, like death warmed up and she felt it too. And now she could no longer deny what she had feared. She had missed her third course and without any doctor confirming it she knew that she was carrying a child – Ben's child.

Fear gripped her as she thought of the effect this was going to have on her life. Matron would insist she resign the moment she found out and her mother . . . What would her mother say? On top of everything else she'd had to endure over the last months she would be presenting her with an illegitimate grandchild. Just for a moment panic overwhelmed her and she wondered if she should visit a certain lady who lived on the outskirts of the town, but she dismissed that thought almost immediately. The woman was well known for helping young ladies get rid of unwanted babies but only the year before a girl had been admitted to the hospital after visiting her and it had cost her her life when she had haemorrhaged and bled to death. It had been terrible for Kathy and the staff to have to stand helplessly by and watch the girl die and she knew she would never forget it for as long as she lived.

Sadly, there had been no evidence for the police to link the death to the woman who was responsible and as far as Kathy knew she was still performing the illegal abortions. But no matter what happened, she decided, she would not be one of her victims. She was carrying Ben's child and despite what he had done she still loved him. And of course she knew that she herself had been illegitimate before Sunday and Tom had adopted her and, after all the children her mother had helped, Kathy knew that if her mother ever found out she'd aborted a child, she would never forgive her.

Her mind went on to thoughts of David and despite the warmth she shivered. He still visited the lodge at least once a week and she still went out with him occasionally. He had been kindness itself to the family since they had left Treetops and she was aware that her mother was expecting them to announce their engagement any time soon. Up to now it had suited Kathy to let her think that – it was better than have her mother keep rambling on about how it was time she and Livvy thought about settling down. How would he take the news? They had never shared more than a perfunctory kiss, but he would be devastated at her betrayal. Still, that couldn't be helped now. She must decide what she was going to do, because it was obvious she wouldn't be able to keep the terrible secret for much longer. The dire morning sickness she had been suffering meant that she had lost weight, but even so, already the waistbands on her skirts were becoming uncomfortably tight and when she had glimpsed herself in the mirror the night before as she got out of the tin bath her slightly swollen stomach had looked out of proportion with the rest of her now skinny frame, which she had thought rather strange, as to her reckoning she could only be a little over three months pregnant. Surely the baby shouldn't be showing this early? Perhaps she could go away? Tell her mother that she was being sent to work in another hospital for a time? But no, Sunday would want to visit her if she was going to be away from home for any length of time so that wouldn't work. Panic gripped her then. What *was* she going to tell her mother? It would be a big enough blow for her to discover that she was about to be presented with an illegitimate grandchild but if she were ever to find out who its father was . . .

Her thoughts were interrupted when the door swung open and one of the other nurses strolled in.

'All right, Kathy. Ooh, if I don't get to the toilet soon, I'm sure I'm goin' to wee meself.'

Kathy managed a weak smile as the girl shot off into one of the cubicles and after hastily washing and drying her hands she went back to work, not that it would be easy to concentrate.

For Kathy, April passed in a blur of worry. Outside the world seemed to be coming back to life after a long, cold winter. The tender green buds on the trees were unfurling, primroses and daffodils were blooming but Kathy barely noticed them.

And then things finally came out into the open one evening two weeks later when Kathy got home from work hot and flustered and decided to take a bath. Unlike back in the big house there was no indoor bathroom at the lodge, so they had to bathe the old-fashioned way in a tin bath that was brought in from the wash house and filled with hot water from the copper. It was a lengthy process but strangely they all seemed to find it quite relaxing to lie in a warm bath in front of the fire. Usually the others disappeared to give each other privacy but on this particular night Sunday was out visiting Cissie when

110

Kathy got home and Livvy was over at the stables. So, after filling the bath she undressed and sank into the hot water. She was just climbing out when without warning Sunday appeared through the back door.

'Oh, sorry, darling, I didn't know you were . . .' Her voice trailed away as she stared at her daughter's slightly swollen stomach and the colour drained from her face as she asked falteringly, 'Is there something you need to tell me, Kathy?' Her voice came out as a squeak and Kathy blushed furiously as she grabbed a towel and hastily wrapped it around herself.

They stood silently surveying each other for a moment and it was Kathy who finally broke the silence when she said quietly, 'I was trying to think how to tell you, really I was. I . . . I'm *so* sorry, Mum.'

Sunday pulled herself together with an enormous effort and forced a smile, although she was crying inside. 'These things happen, darling. You're not the first and I dare say you won't be the last girl who lets their feelings run away with themselves before they've got a ring on their finger. Have you told David yet? I'm sure he'll be thrilled. It's more than obvious that he loves you. It will just mean that you'll have to get married a little sooner than you'd planned.'

Kathy was so shocked that her eyes bulged. '*D-David?*' she spluttered. 'No . . . I haven't told him and I'm not going to.'

Sunday looked confused as she placed the wicker basket full of vegetables she had just lifted from Cissie's garden on the table. 'But of course he'll have to know. It isn't something that you'll be able to hide for much longer, is it?'

'But you don't understand.' Kathy shook her head. 'I don't want to tell him . . . and there will be no wedding!'

'Now come along,' Sunday said coaxingly. 'He deserves to

111

know. We all know that he'd marry you like a shot if you'd only say the word. Let's face it, you could do a lot worse. He's a doctor with a wonderful career in front of him and he's clearly mad about you. What more could you ask for?'

'But I don't love him,' Kathy said dully as tears leaked from the corners of her eyes and rolled down her cheeks. And then, before Sunday could say another word, she clutched the towel even more tightly about her and left the room, leaving Sunday standing there looking stunned.

'It's a pity she didn't think of that before she allowed him to make love to her,' she muttered with a shake of her head. 'And what will become of her and the baby now if she refuses to marry him?' When no answer to her question was forthcoming, she sat staring into space in silence save for the ticking of the old grandfather clock that they had brought from Treetops, which now ticked away the hours and minutes in the small entrance hall.

It was late the following afternoon as Kathy was about to finish her shift when David caught up with her in the foyer of the hospital. 'Ah, here you are,' he greeted her. 'I've been looking for you all day. I thought we might go to the pictures this evening. Do you fancy it?'

Knowing how much she was about to hurt him, Kathy lowered her eyes. 'Actually . . . I've got a bit of a headache,' she muttered. And then mustering every ounce of courage she had she gently took his elbow and drew him into a corner, where they couldn't be observed. 'To be honest I've been meaning to have a word with you for some time now . . .'

Seeing the look on her face his smile faded and he had the horrible feeling that he was about to hear something that he wasn't going to like.

'The thing is,' she rushed on before her nerve failed her. 'I don't think we should see each other anymore. Only at work, of course. Our relationship isn't going anywhere and—'

'But that's down to you!' he said angrily. 'You must know by now that I love you, Kathy? I'd marry you tomorrow if you'd have me.'

It almost broke her heart when she glanced up to see the confusion and hurt on his face, but she was determined now. 'I'm so sorry,' she said gently. 'But I don't love you, David.'

'But you *could* if you'd only let yourself,' he argued. He loved her far too much to let her go without a fight.

She shook her head, knowing now that it was time to be honest with him. 'I think you should know that I'm . . . I'm going to have a baby.'

'*You're what?*' He stepped back as if she had physically struck him and without waiting for him to say a word she turned and quietly walked away, leaving him standing there feeling as if his whole world had come crashing down about his ears.

Chapter Sixteen

'So, I think it's time we had a talk . . . don't you?' Sunday dabbed at her mouth with a crisp, white napkin. She and Kathy were eating their evening meal alone as Livvy – who still had no idea what was going on – had gone skating with her friends from work.

It had been two weeks since Sunday had discovered that Kathy was going to have a child and she had not mentioned it once – not that she'd had much opportunity to. Kathy had been avoiding her like the plague, locking herself away in her room when she wasn't at work, and despite the lodge being small they had barely been in the same room together for longer than a few minutes. She had been hoping that Kathy would tell her what was going on, but as she had made no attempt to, Sunday had decided that as they had the house to themselves it was the ideal time to discuss the situation.

'What do you want to talk about?' Kathy's face was blank as she pushed the food about her plate.

'I would have thought, given the circumstances, that was fairly obvious.'

Kathy shrugged. She had known this was coming and, in a way, it was a relief to get it all out in the open. 'There's not much to say really. I'm going to have a baby – end of story,' she said bluntly. 'But if you want me to leave—'

'Of course I don't want you to leave!' Sunday interrupted, horrified. 'I just need to know what you . . . and David are going to do about it. I notice he hasn't been around for a couple of weeks?'

'We've finished. We're not seeing each other anymore,' Kathy informed her, and Sunday looked shocked.

'*Finished?* Do you mean to tell me he won't stand by you? Why . . . that's *awful*. I can't believe he—' ·

'*Mum*, if you must know it was *me* that ended it. It . . . it isn't his baby.' There, it was said, and Kathy was glad it was out in the open at last. Not that she had any intention of telling Sunday who the father was – not ever. 'So now you know, I repeat, do you want me to leave?'

Sunday's shoulders sagged but she slowly shook her head. 'No, but if the baby isn't David's then whose is it?'

'I'm afraid I can't tell you that.'

'Is it some other doctor from the hospital? Or perhaps you've got yourself involved with a married man who can't stand by you. Is that it?'

'As I said, I can't tell you.'

Sunday sat back for a moment trying to digest this news, but then she shrugged. 'In that case *we* shall care for the baby,' she said firmly. Kathy had been foolish, just as her mother before her had been, but Sunday loved her far too much to turn her back on her. As she thought back to the night Kathy had been born and her mother and twin brother had died, she prayed history wasn't about to repeat itself.

'You do realise that if I stay there will be gossip?' Kathy warned.

'So?' Sunday's eyes flashed. 'You know what my mother always used to say, "While the gossips are talking about you, they're leaving some other poor devil alone." And after what's happened to us recently, what do I care? I've no doubt they've had a field day, but it isn't so bad living here, is it?'

In truth, things were working out far better than she had hoped. Mr Willerby was a true gentleman. He had even invited her to tea on a couple of occasions, but as yet she hadn't been able to bring herself to enter what she still thought of as her home as a guest. The only thing that did trouble her was Livvy's attitude towards Giles Willerby. She appeared to hate him – and his grandfather, come to that – with a vengeance, but then Sunday supposed she would have felt the same about anyone who had bought her former home. She was still angry at Ben too, which Sunday thought was pointless. What was done was done. There could be no going back so she just wished Livvy would try and get on with things and accept their new life. And now suddenly there was to be another little person joining their family and come what may Sunday was determined to make the best of it.

Cissie showed no surprise at all the next day when Sunday confided to her about Kathy's forthcoming baby.

'I've had me suspicions fer a while,' she admitted. 'But the way yer have to look at it, it ain't the end o' the world. She ain't the first to find 'erself in this position an' she certainly won't be the last! Is the baby David's?'

Sunday sighed as she gazed towards the window. 'She says it isn't. To be honest, she won't even discuss it so we may never know.'

'Aw well, there's enough of us to look after the little soul,' Cissie responded matter-of-factly and Sunday could have hugged her. Cissie was never judgemental, which was just one of the many things she loved about her.

A month later, Kathy was working on one of the wards when a young student nurse approached her to tell her, 'Nurse Branning, Matron would like to see you in her office.'

Kathy's heart sank. She had been expecting this for a while now. It was getting harder by the day to disguise her swollen stomach, so after tucking the blankets about the patient in the bed and giving the girl a smile, she straightened, rubbed her hands down her apron and with her chin held high headed for Matron's office.

'Ah . . . Nurse Branning.' Matron looked mildly embarrassed. She was a middle-aged woman who was known to be firm but fair and Kathy had nothing but respect for her. 'I, er . . . don't quite know how to broach this,' she said haltingly. 'But I was wondering . . . is there anything you would like to talk to me about?'

Kathy took a deep breath. This was it then, the end of her nursing career, for now at least, yet she was almost relieved to get everything out into the open.

'There is actually,' she admitted. 'I was going to come and see you anyway to tell you that I'm expecting a baby, round about the end of September.'

'I see.' Matron steepled her fingers and tapped away at her bottom lip as if she was wondering how to respond. Kathy Branning was developing into one of her finest nurses and she would be greatly missed. But she had no option but to dismiss her. What example would it set to the other nurses if she allowed her to stay on? A young, unmarried, pregnant woman? It was common knowledge that, until quite recently, she and young Dr Deacon had been seeing each other. Now that she came to think about it, they seemed to have been avoiding each other recently and she briefly wondered if the baby was his, not that it was any of her business, of course, she silently reminded herself. What the nurses did in their spare time was up to them up to a point, but she did have the reputation of the hospital to consider and gossip like this would spread like wildfire once Kathy's condition became common knowledge.

'It's all right, Matron,' Kathy said suddenly. She almost felt sorry for the woman, knowing what a predicament she was putting her in. 'I am quite happy to resign my position as of today.'

Matron had to stifle a sigh of relief. She had been dreading having to dismiss the young woman. 'Then your resignation is accepted, nurse,' she said stiffly, and then on a kinder note, 'but I do hope you will consider coming back in the future? You are a good nurse and it would be a great shame to see your talent go to waste.'

'Thank you, Matron.' Kathy rose from her seat and after inclining her head she turned and left the woman's office with as much dignity as she could muster, although inside she was crying. Outside the door she leaned heavily against the wall for a moment.

Oh, Ben, where are you? she wondered. *You should be here to see your baby born!*

At that moment, David hurried round the corner holding some patient notes. When he spotted Kathy, he paused for just a second, nodded and hurried on his way.

She watched him go. They had deliberately kept out of each

other's way since she had told him about the baby, and she had been mildly surprised to find that she missed him. They had always got on well and, while she didn't have any romantic feelings for him, she had enjoyed his company. Rumour had it that he had recently been seen out with one of the other nurses and Kathy had scolded herself when she discovered that she actually felt a little jealous. But it was done now. With a sigh she went to collect her things from the staff room before making her way home.

Thankfully no one there was judging her. Even Livvy had taken the news of the baby well and seemed to be looking forward to having a little niece or nephew to spoil. At that moment she felt the child inside her move and her hand instinctively dropped protectively to her stomach. She was halfway through her pregnancy already and she suddenly realised with a little jolt that as yet she hadn't got a single thing ready for the baby. *But I will now that I don't have to work*, she promised herself, and in a slightly better frame of mind she hurried away.

Back at the lodge Sunday had just put the kettle on for a morning tea break when there was a tap at the door and, on opening it, she found John Willerby standing on the step with his hat in his hand.

'Ah, Mr Willerby, won't you come in?' She held the door wide for him to step past her.

He grinned. 'How many times do I have to tell you, it's John?' There was a sparkle in his eye, and she felt herself blush.

'Sorry I just . . .' She shrugged. 'I suppose we do know each other well enough to be on first name terms now so John it is, and you must call me Sunday.'

'It would be my pleasure.'

'Good, then would you like to join me for tea? I was just about to make a pot, as it happens.'

He gave a gracious little bow and followed her into the kitchen just as the kettle on the hob began to sing. 'Now *that* is what I call timing.'

She smiled as she spooned tea leaves into the pot and tipped the boiling water over them before placing the tea cosy over it and leaving it to mash.

'And to what do I owe the pleasure of this visit?' She ushered him towards a chair and sat down opposite him, suddenly noticing that he seemed rather ill at ease.

'The thing is . . . I, er . . . I don't quite know how to put this, so I'll just come straight out with it. Have you noticed that Giles and Livvy are not getting on? I wondered if he had perhaps done something to offend her? He swore he hadn't when I asked him, but they seem to be at each other's throats every time they meet.'

Sunday looked very uncomfortable as she fiddled with the fringe on the chenille tablecloth. 'In fairness I rather think this has more to do with Livvy than Giles,' she admitted. On the few occasions she had spoken to the young man he had always been very polite.

When John raised a questioning eyebrow she rushed on, 'I think it's because . . . Treetops was Livvy's home from the day she was born and she loves every inch of the place so I'm afraid she rather resents seeing someone else living there.'

'I see.' He stroked his chin thoughtfully and sighed. 'Then I'm afraid there isn't a lot you or I can do to improve the situation, is there? Apart from hope that she comes to terms with things in time, that is. But I would like her to know, and

120

yourself and Kathy of course, that you are all more than welcome to visit any time you like. Speaking of which, I'd greatly enjoy it if you'd come to dinner next Thursday evening. Mr Dixon and his wife are coming, and I do so hate being the odd one out. You'd be doing me an enormous favour if you agreed to come, if only to make up the numbers.'

'Then in that case I accept,' Sunday agreed with a smile. It would be the first time she'd been in the house since they'd moved out, but she couldn't avoid it forever. And John had been so kind, it felt rude to keep refusing his invitations.

Chapter Seventeen

'I don't know, it makes yer wonder what the world is comin' to,' Cissie grumbled as she sat in the small garden of the lodge with Sunday one sunny Sunday afternoon in early August browsing through the newspaper. It was a beautiful day with white powder-puff clouds floating across a clear, blue sky. She worked five mornings a week now at Treetops and often came over for a chat with Sunday in the afternoons. 'It's made a mockery o' the monarchy since Edward married that American, Wallis Simpson.'

Sunday smiled. They had heard nothing else since the month before when the marriage had taken place in France. 'An' now my George reckons trouble is brewin' abroad. He says he won't be surprised if it don't end in a war.'

'Surely not,' Sunday answered with a worried frown. It wasn't the first time George had prophesied war. 'How could the trouble abroad possibly affect us?'

Cissie shrugged. 'I've no idea, but that's what my George reckons an' he's usually pretty up on world affairs. He reads every newspaper he can get his hands on from cover to cover every single night.'

Just then Kathy waddled into the garden holding her back.

She still had about another seven weeks before she was due, but she was so enormous that Sunday was on edge. Especially every time she thought back to what had happened to Kathy's mother.

'Phew, this heat is killing me,' Kathy complained as she flopped heavily onto a chair beside them and swatted a wasp away. 'And just look at my ankles,' she groaned. 'They're like balloons.'

'Hm, yer should be restin' wi' yer feet up,' Cissie scolded. 'An' lookin' at the size of yer I'll eat me hat if yer go another seven weeks. Are yer quite sure yer've got yer dates right?'

'I think so.' Kathy gratefully took the glass of lemonade her mother was holding out to her and after taking a long drink she asked, 'So how did the dinner with Mr Willerby go last night? I must have been asleep when you came in because I didn't hear you.'

'It went very well,' Sunday admitted. She'd been to Treetops for dinner on a few occasions over the last few months and was now thoroughly enjoying John's company. He was very easy to get on with and she sensed that, like her, he was lonely following the death of his wife. He had confided that he and his wife had brought Giles up since he was ten years old when John's son and his young wife had both been killed in a driving accident and that had confirmed to her what a truly lovely man he was, for he was clearly very proud and fond of his grandson. It was nice to have someone to discuss things with, she'd decided, and she and John were comfortable in each other's company now.

Just then Livvy marched over in her riding gear with a face as dark as thunder.

'Oh dear, what's wrong now?' Sunday asked, noting her daughter's stormy face.

'It's that arrogant *beast* up at Treetops,' Livvy raged. They immediately knew she was talking about Giles. She never had a good word to say about the poor chap. 'Can you *believe* he just asked me if I wanted to have Willow shod along with the other horses George and Billy are taking to the blacksmith's tomorrow? Just who the bloody hell does he think he is? I'm quite able to pay for my own horse's shoes! We're not *paupers!*'

'He was probably just trying to be kind knowing that you'd most likely be at work,' her mother pointed out but Livvy was having none of it.

'Huh! He needn't *bother*,' she stormed, her pretty face twisted with fury. 'It's bad enough that he's taken over *our* stables without him being condescending!' She turned and slammed indoors without even waiting for an answer and Sunday shook her head.

'I've given up hoping those two will ever be friends,' she said sadly and Cissie nodded in agreement.

'I reckon yer right there. But in fairness, it's down to Livvy. Giles ain't a bad young chap if she'd only give him a chance.'

'There's not much hope of that happening now,' Sunday agreed glumly as Kathy hauled herself to her feet.

'I think I'll go and put my feet up for a while,' she informed them and once she'd gone Sunday shook her head again.

'I wish this birth was over,' she admitted worriedly. 'I keep thinking . . .'

'I know *exactly* what yer thinkin' an' yer can stop that nonsense straight away,' Cissie scolded, waggling a finger at her. 'Yer thinkin' o' what happened when she was born, ain't yer? But it'll be different for her, you'll see!'

'Hm, let's just hope you're right.' Sunday pursed her lips and stared across the lawn, trying to think of something else because the thought of losing Kathy was just too much to bear.

Early that evening, Livvy ventured across to the stables again. Now that Kathy was so huge, she had taken over the care of her horse too and she wanted to get them fed and settled as she had a date that evening with a young man she had met from the village. As she approached, she was surprised to see the vet's car parked outside and quickening her pace she entered the stable block and stood for a moment as her eyes adjusted to the light. After being out in the brilliant sunshine it seemed very gloomy in there.

'All you can do is watch her carefully and if nothing has happened by the morning ring me again and I'll come back out,' she heard the vet say.

Curiosity drew her towards the stall where he was talking to Giles.

'I'll do that, thank you.'

She saw that Giles looked worried as he tried to calm one of the mares who was due to have her foal any time.

'Is there a problem?' she asked as the vet nodded to her and strode past her.

Giles glanced up. 'There is actually, this one is having trouble I reckon, that's why I called the vet out.'

'Oh.' Livvy didn't quite know how to respond. Grudgingly she admitted that Giles did seem to be very fond of the horses. 'So . . . is there anything I can do to help?'

He looked mildly surprised. It was the first time she had ever spoken to him civilly. Usually she snapped his head off as soon as he opened his mouth so now he only spoke to her when it was strictly necessary. 'Thanks, but I don't think there is. I'm going to stay over here with her now till she's had the foal.'

'But that might mean spending the night here,' she pointed out.

'It wouldn't be the first time.'

Liberty, the horse in question, was one that her father had bred, and she had been one of his favourites. Livvy knew that had her dad been there he would have done exactly the same. 'Right, in that case I'll see to our horses and leave you to it.'

He nodded and she hurried away to see to Willow and Bramble.

When she entered the stables the following evening after work she peeped into Liberty's stall and was delighted to see a pure black baby suckling from his mother.

'He's a little beauty, isn't he?'

Livvy swung about to find Giles standing right behind her. He looked desperately tired but pleased as punch.

'She finally had him at three o'clock this morning with a little help from me,' he told her, coming to lean on the half door next to her. 'With his pedigree he'll be a real asset to the stables when he's older.'

Instantly her face set as she ground out, 'Oh, I might have known it would all come down to money.'

'We're running a business here,' he reminded her.

Two spots of colour flared in her cheeks and her eyes blazed. 'Quite! My *father's* business,' she said testily and stamped away, leaving him to shake his head. Women! He'd never understand them if he lived to be a hundred!

'So *now* what's wrong?' Sunday asked as Livvy stormed into the kitchen a short time later.

'It's that insufferable *pig*, Giles!' Livvy spat. 'I thought for a while last night that he actually had a heart when he stayed with Liberty to help her deliver her foal but all he thinks about is the money! As if he hasn't got enough owning Treetops *and* Dad's business.'

'It's hardly *his* fault if his grandfather chose to buy the house,' Sunday patiently pointed out. 'And if he hadn't bought it we would have had to sell it to someone else anyway, in case you've forgotten.' She was getting a little tired of the vendetta Livvy seemed to be waging against the Willerbys, but her words fell on deaf ears, for Livvy had already barged off to her room in a huff.

Oh, I'll just leave her to it, Sunday thought dejectedly. What with worrying about Kathy and Livvy's attitude towards their new neighbours she was just about at the end of her tether!

Chapter Eighteen

'Is anything wrong, love?' Sunday asked Kathy one evening late in August as she was just about to retire to bed. It had been a hot, humid day and everyone was drained. Everyone but Kathy that was, who seemed to be wandering about like a cat on hot bricks.

'No, I'm fine,' Kathy assured her as she paced up and down the small hallway, her hands on her back. 'I've just got this niggly backache. You go on up, I'll be following you soon when I've cooled down a bit.' Even now with the windows wide open there was not a stir of breeze and the house felt airless.

'All right, but call me if you need me.' Sunday made her way up to her room where she washed using the jug and bowl she had placed on the washstand ready. She slipped into her night-dress and after releasing her hair from its pins she brushed it thoroughly. But Kathy was on her mind so instead of climbing into bed she went back downstairs.

Kathy was still pacing, and a little worm of fear wriggled in Sunday's stomach. This couldn't be the start of the baby coming surely? There was still at least four weeks to go.

Kathy turned to say something to her but then stopped

abruptly as a small puddle of water appeared on the floor between her legs. The colour drained from her face as she stared down in shock. Part of her nursing training had been spent on the maternity ward in the hospital, so she knew only too well what this meant. Her waters had broken. Early or not, the baby was on its way. Suddenly she wished she didn't know what was coming and she was afraid.

Sunday meanwhile appeared to be perfectly calm, although her stomach was churning. 'Right, young lady,' she said cheerily. 'It looks like we're going to meet the new member of the family before too much longer so let's get you upstairs and into bed while I get everything ready.'

'But I haven't had any pains yet, only backache,' Kathy protested. 'Do I have to go up just yet?'

'I suppose not,' Sunday agreed. 'First babies are notorious for taking their time before putting in an appearance, so I'll make us a nice mug of cocoa and we'll see what happens next.'

Sunday filled a saucepan with warm milk and set it on the hob to heat, while Kathy sat in the fireside chair staring into the empty grate. She had truly believed that Ben would be back before the baby arrived but now she was forced to admit that he hadn't even taken the trouble to write to her and the hurt hit her like a blow. Up until now she had managed to convince herself that Ben had loved her, but doubts were creeping in and she had to face the prospect of bringing their child up alone. That is if she survived. Although she'd tried hard to push them away, thoughts of her mother had been preying on her mind more and more as the birth approached. Would she die too? What would happen to her baby then?

'Here you are, darling, get that inside you.' Sunday interrupted her thoughts as she pressed a mug of steaming cocoa into her hand.

Noticing the look of fear on her daughter's face, Sunday told Kathy gently, 'Don't be frightened. Giving birth is one of the most natural things in the world. You're going to be just fine. Now, drink that while I run up to the house and get John to phone the midwife for me. She needn't rush – you'll probably be hours yet. I'll just pop upstairs to get dressed first.'

As she was about to leave the kitchen, Livvy breezed in, with a sullen expression on her face.

'I've just spent the most *boring* night of my life listening to my date ramble on about his father's farm,' she grumbled, then seeing the look on Kathy's face she asked, 'What's wrong?'

'Nothing,' Sunday assured her. 'But Kathy's baby is on its way. I was just about to get dressed so I could go up to the house and ask John to get the midwife to come.'

Livvy's face paled to the colour of lint as her hand flew to her mouth. 'Oh crikey . . . the *baby* is coming . . . You stay here. I'll run up to the house.' And without another word she went sprinting off like a greyhound.

Sunday rolled her eyes at Kathy, sharing a grin. Livvy wasn't very good with things like this and would never have made a nurse.

'Right, I'm going to get dressed anyway,' she said, turning towards the stairs. 'I have an idea we may have a long night ahead of us.' Then she too was gone, leaving Kathy alone with her gloomy thoughts.

Livvy was back in no time with John close behind her and Kathy's pains started shortly after that, at which point Sunday insisted she should go upstairs.

'I'm terrified,' Sunday admitted to John when Livvy had gently led Kathy away. 'Kathy's mother died after giving birth to her. She was one of twins but the other baby, a little boy, died too.'

'Now we'll have no more of that silly talk,' he scolded gently. 'Kathy is going to be just fine. She's young and healthy and she'll come through this with flying colours, you'll see.'

Sunday was suddenly glad he was there. He had been so kind and understanding when she had told him that Kathy was going to have a baby and had shown no condemnation whatsoever.

'So, you just put that smile back on your face and get up those stairs and be strong for your girl,' he ordered. 'And meanwhile, I shall stay down here and make sure you have plenty of hot water. I'll send the midwife up when she comes, shall I?'

'You really don't have to stay, John. It could take hours yet,' Sunday objected but he wouldn't hear of leaving and so eventually she made her way up the steep stairs saying a silent prayer as she went.

When Nurse Bennett, the midwife, arrived she rolled up her sleeves and took control of the situation immediately. She was a stout, middle-aged woman with short, silver-grey hair and a stern expression, but those that knew her would vouch that she had a heart made of pure gold. Kathy had met her on a number of occasions when she had visited the new mothers at the hospital and knowing that she was in safe hands reassured her slightly.

'Hm,' Nurse Bennett said thoughtfully as she straightened after listening to the baby's heartbeat through her pinard.

Sunday's heart started to beat faster with panic as she saw the frown on the woman's face. 'Is there something wrong?'

'Not that I know of, dearie,' the woman answered calmly and turning her attention back to Kathy she told her, 'I'm going to examine you now and see how far on you are. Just lie as still as you can, there's a good girl.'

It proved to be easier said than done for Kathy, for the pains were coming thick and fast now but she grit her teeth and did the best she could, while Livvy escaped to wait downstairs with John.

'Ugh, I'm *never* going to have a baby,' she declared as she hurried into the kitchen. Normally she didn't even wish John good day if she could help it, but tonight she was too concerned about her sister to care about anything else.

'Oh, I'm sure you'll feel differently when you meet the right young man and settle down,' he told her, with a sparkle in his eye, but she was too busy pacing the room with her eyes fixed fearfully on the ceiling to even take in what he said.

The time ticked away, each minute feeling like an hour to those waiting and as the night progressed John and Livvy could hear Kathy's anguished cries getting louder.

'There must be something wrong. *Surely* it shouldn't take this long?' Livvy fretted. And then just before dawn, as the sky became a kaleidoscope of pinks, purples and oranges, a piercing scream rent the air and Livvy gripped the edge of the table as her eyes stretched wide. The scream was followed by a moment of uncanny silence followed by the indignant squawk of a newborn wail.

'Oh my goodness, I think she's had the baby.' Livvy was almost limp with relief as she and John strained to hear what was going on.

Upstairs Nurse Bennett handed a tiny little bloody bundle into Sunday's waiting arms.

'It's just as I thought,' the woman said as she bent to the new mother again. 'He's only a little scrap of a thing. Far too small for her to be the size she was. I reckon there's another one in here.'

And sure enough, ten minutes later another baby, slightly larger than the first born, was delivered. This time it was a girl and Sunday unashamedly cried tears of joy as she stared down into their little puckered faces.

'Well, they might be a little on the small side, but their lungs certainly seem to be functioning properly,' she laughed as the midwife checked them over.

'They'll do,' Nurse Bennett said with a satisfied smile and taking them from Sunday she placed them into their mother's waiting arms.

Kathy stared down at them in awe. They were tiny but beautiful and she could hardly believe that she had managed to produce something quite so perfect. The only thing that marred the birth for her was the fact that their father wasn't there to see them, and Kathy could only assume he didn't want to be. *But I won't think about that for now*, she told herself. *From now on I must concentrate on these two because they're surely the very best thing that has ever happened to me.*

Soon after, the babies were wrapped in towels and handed to Sunday, while the midwife saw to Kathy and with a smile on her face that stretched from ear to ear, she carried them downstairs for their first bath.

'It's a *boy*!' she announced joyously as she entered the room where John and Livvy were anxiously waiting for her. 'And a *girl*!'

'*Twins!*' Livvy clapped her hands in delight as she raced over to get her first glimpse of her baby niece and nephew. 'Oh, they look just like Kathy,' she declared as she stared at the downy dark hair on their tiny heads. And then she hurried off to fetch bowls of warm water and watched as Sunday tenderly bathed them one by one before dressing them in the tiny flannel nightgowns they had ready.

'They look just adorable, like little dolls,' Livvy giggled. It was already apparent that she was going to spoil them both shamelessly.

'I agree,' John said, and Sunday was sure his eyes were damp with emotion as he stared down at the babes. 'They're just perfect!'

Eventually when the midwife had washed Kathy and got her into a clean nightdress, Livvy retired to bed and the babies were taken back upstairs to their mother for their first feed as John and Sunday sat at the kitchen table, tired but happy.

'I've been thinking,' he said presently. 'It's going to be a very tight squeeze, all of you fitting into this little place. Kathy would be very welcome to move into the nursery up at Treetops if she wished to.'

Sunday was shocked at his kind offer although she already knew what Kathy's answer would be should he suggest it to her. Kathy would want to stay here with her.

'That's really kind of you,' she told him warmly. 'But I'm sure we'll manage very well here. Thank you, though.'

He shrugged. 'Just a thought. I quite like the idea of babies up at the house, and the way Giles is going I don't think I shall be having great-grandchildren anytime soon. But anything she needs, you just let me know. I don't want those babies to go without, or young Kathy for that matter, do you hear me?'

'Loud and clear,' Sunday answered, her eyes shining.

Cissie huffed into the room just then. 'They told me up at

the house Kathy were havin' the baby,' she gasped breathlessly, noting how close John and Sunday appeared.

'*Babies!*' Sunday corrected her happily. 'A boy and a girl, both doing well as is their mum.'

'Well, I'll be!' Cissie plonked down onto the nearest chair with a broad smile on her face. 'Ain't that just the best news ever? May the dear lord bless their little souls!'

Chapter Nineteen

Kathy named her babies Thomas, for her late father, and Daisy, after her father's sister, the aunt she had never known but who Sunday and Tom had told her so much about. In no time at all they had everyone who met them under their spell. They slept in their mother's room in two tiny cots Sunday had fetched from the nursery at Treetops and were such good babies that the people in the lodge hardly knew they were there. They only cried when they were hungry and when that happened everyone always rushed to try to be the first to pick them up.

John Willerby was as besotted as everyone else and the day after they were born, he had an enormous bouquet of roses delivered for Kathy. Friends popped in to get a peep at the new arrivals and Kathy got frustrated because Sunday insisted she wasn't to get up for at least a week.

'But I'm *bored* lying here,' she complained one morning as Sunday tidied the bed and tucked the covers about her.

'Make the best of it, once those two get a bit older you'll dream of being bored,' Sunday told her with a grin, and so reluctantly Kathy did as she was told, although within hours of the birth she had felt as fit as a fiddle.

The twins were five days old when there was a tap on the

front door and Sunday went to open it. She was surprised to see David Deacon standing on the doorstep clutching a colourful bunch of chrysanthemums and looking mildly embarrassed.

'I, er . . . heard that Kathy had had the baby – or should I say babies? Are they all well?'

'You'd better come in.' Sunday held the door wide and allowed him to step past her. 'And yes, they're all very well, thank you,' she said primly. She still had suspicions that David was the father and wasn't quite sure how she should greet him.

David shuffled from foot to foot uncomfortably before saying, 'I don't suppose there's much chance of me seeing Kathy is there?'

Sunday felt herself melting a little. She'd always liked David. In fact, she'd hoped at one time that he'd ask Kathy to marry him. She wondered suddenly if perhaps he *had* proposed, and Kathy had turned him down. It would be just like her stubborn daughter. And if that was the case, then she doubted Kathy would welcome the visit.

'I'm not sure that she'll want to see you,' she said in a slightly gentler voice. 'But if you don't mind waiting, I can pop up and ask her?'

'Oh yes . . . yes please.'

'Very well.' Sunday went upstairs to Kathy who was propped up on pillows breastfeeding Thomas. She had already fed Daisy, who was always the greedier of the two.

'You've got a visitor,' Sunday told her as Kathy leaned Thomas forward and began to pat his back to bring up his wind.

Kathy smiled. She welcomed visitors. They relieved the boredom at the moment. 'How lovely. Who is it?'

'It's David Deacon.' Sunday watched the smile slide from the girl's face and added hastily, 'But you don't have to see him if you don't wish to.'

Thomas gave a loud burp and Kathy handed him to her mother who lay the child back in his crib.

'I . . . I think I will see him,' Kathy said quietly. 'Will you pass me my hairbrush? I'd better try and make myself look respectable.'

Sunday did as she was asked before going back downstairs to David. 'She's in the first bedroom door facing you on the landing, go on up and I'll bring you both a tray of tea,' she told him and, without a word, he began to climb the stairs.

'Come in,' Kathy said, when he tapped at the door.

David took a deep breath and entered the room. Kathy was sitting up in bed eyeing him rather tentatively, but he thought he had never seen her look so lovely. Her dark hair shone and there seemed to be a glow about her. Since she had ended their relationship, he had tried to put her out of his mind and his heart. He had even stepped out with other girls, most of them nurses, but no one could take the place of Kathy in his affections.

'How are you?' he asked as he stood clutching the flowers, and then his eyes fell to the little cribs at the side of the bed and before he could stop himself, he found himself walking towards them and gazing down at the babies.

'Kathy . . . they're just . . . *beautiful.*'

She smiled and her whole face lit up. 'They are, aren't they? And they're *so* good. I can't wait to be up and about so I can take them for a walk.'

'Hm, well I should be careful if you do that. The weather's suddenly taken a change for the worse and it's raining cats and dogs out there. You wouldn't want them catching cold. It might be best to keep them in the warm until they're a bit bigger.'

138

He sounded for all the world like a protective father and just for a moment Kathy couldn't stop herself from thinking what might have been had it not been for Ben. But still she clung to the hope that Ben would come back, and while that hope remained, there could never be another man in her life.

Meanwhile, David was shocked at the emotions that were pulsing through him. He had expected to feel resentful towards the babies. After all, the way he saw it, they were the reason she had ended their relationship. He'd also had to put up with a lot of gossip after Kathy left the hospital and finished with him. Half of the staff were convinced that the babies were his, he was sure of it. And yet he felt a surge of something he couldn't describe as he gazed down at them. They looked so innocent that he just wanted to lift them into his arms so he could keep them safe. But he wouldn't, of course. He wondered again who their father might be but immediately put the thought from his mind – it was still far too painful to think of Kathy with another man. *And what a fool that man was*, he thought, *just look at what he was missing!*

'So . . . the birth went well?' Somehow, he managed to drag his eyes away from the twins but his voice came out as a croak and he realised he was sweating. This wasn't proving to be as easy as he had hoped it would be. 'Oh, er . . . and here . . . these are for you.' He pushed the flowers across the bed to her, scattering multi-coloured petals all over the bedspread, just as Sunday appeared balancing a tray of tea and a sponge cake she had baked that morning.

David was clumsily trying to gather the dropped petals together, but Sunday waved him to a chair and after placing the tray down she took the flowers from Kathy, telling him with a smile, 'Don't worry about those. I can see to them in a minute.'

She poured them both a cup of tea then swept away to put the flowers in water.

Once they were alone again, Kathy told him, 'In answer to your question, the birth went very well, thank you. Although I have to admit it was a shock when we discovered there were two of them. I can't believe neither the midwife nor the doctor picked up on it before.'

'Ah well, that would depend on how they were lying in the womb,' he answered as his doctor's training came to the fore. 'If one of the babies was lying behind the other two heartbeats wouldn't always be detected.'

'Hm.' She nodded in agreement and they slipped into silence as they sipped at their tea, both feeling slightly ill at ease.

'So . . . what will you do now?' David asked eventually and when she raised an eyebrow he hurried on, 'What I mean is, will you be coming back to work?' He desperately wanted to ask if there was any chance that she and the babies' father might get together again but decided to keep the conversation on safer ground.

Kathy sighed. 'I haven't really thought about it yet,' she admitted. 'I suppose when they're a little older I might like to return to nursing if I can get someone reliable to look after them. I know my mother would, of course, but she isn't getting any younger and I wouldn't like to impose on her.'

'I can understand that.' His eyes strayed back to the sleeping infants and for a second Kathy thought she saw a look of longing in them but then he shocked her when he said, 'In the meantime . . . I hope we can be friends again. I've hated us avoiding each other and if . . . Well, if you need any help, financially or otherwise, I want you to know I'm here. I'd hate to think that you or the babies would be going without anything.'

'Oh.' Kathy felt a lump form in her throat. He was so kind and she had missed him, so what harm could there be if they became friends again? Just friends of course. They could never be more when there was still a chance that Ben might come home.

'I'd like that,' she said softly. 'And thank you but we'll be very comfortable financially. Mum had more left over after selling Treetops and settling Ben's debts than she'd initially thought she would, and I always saved a bit of my wages so we should be fine.' *Oh Lord*, she thought. *I'm turning into a softie!* Since having the babies her emotions seemed to be all over the place, but then she supposed that was the old hormones kicking in.

'Right well, er . . . I ought to be thinking of going now. I'm on duty this evening and I don't want to overtire you. But would it be all right if I called again? I'd like to see how those two are coming along.' He rose, placing his cup and saucer back on the tray, and she nodded.

'I'd like that.'

He hovered uncertainly for a moment and she had the awful feeling that he was going to kiss her but instead he seemed to think better of it and turned to the door. 'Goodbye for now.'

'Goodbye, David . . . and thank you for the flowers.'

After he left, she lay staring thoughtfully into space, mildly surprised at how good it had felt to see him. How much easier things would have been if she could only have fallen in love with him.

Chapter Twenty

On Sunday 18 December shortly after Kathy's nineteenth birthday the twins were christened in the little church of St Peter's in Mancetter. At one point it looked unlikely that the baptism would go ahead for the country was lying beneath a thick carpet of snow but somehow they managed to get there. The service was beautiful, and the twins were as good as gold. And in their snow-white christening robes, lovingly stitched and embroidered by Sunday and Cissie over many long nights, the twins looked beautiful. Their little personalities were beginning to develop now. Thomas was the more solemn of the two; he rarely cried and was content to lie in his cot, whereas Daisy had a ready smile for everyone and loved to be picked up all the time, and they were adored equally by everyone around them.

George stood as the twins' godfather and Cissie and Livvy were their godmothers. John Willerby had insisted that the party that followed should be held at Treetops. At first Sunday had been against the idea but as he pointed out, there really wasn't enough room to hold it in the lodge so in the end, much to Livvy's disgust, she agreed.

It took them twice as long as it should to get back to the

house for the roads were treacherous and even impassable in parts but eventually everyone arrived safely to find John's maid Edith had fires roaring and a feast fit for a king laid out on the dining room table. Mrs Gay, the cook, had been busy baking for days and she had done them proud. There were whole hams, fresh from the oven, crispy joints of pork and beef and dishes full of vegetables, and roast and mashed potatoes as well as pies, cakes and all manner of delicious desserts.

Giles was one of the first to arrive home and stood in the hallway helping the guests off with their coats as they stamped the snow from their shoes, their faces glowing and their noses red with cold. A huge Christmas tree stood in one corner of the hallway and instantly there was a party atmosphere.

'May I help you off with your coat, madame?' Giles asked Livvy as she came through the door. There was a teasing twinkle in his eye, but she glowered at him.

It was the first time she had stepped inside Treetops since they had moved into the lodge and she had no intention of pretending to be pleased about being there.

'I can manage quite well, thank you!' she said icily, turning her back on him, and Sunday, who was right behind her, sighed.

'Can't you, at *least* for Kathy's sake, try to look as if you're enjoying yourself and be civil,' she hissed when Giles turned away to help someone else.

'*Huh!* What with that pompous *oaf* rubbing salt into the wound because he's in *our* house!' Livvy stamped off into the dining room and Sunday gave up. She was more than a little tired of Livvy's prolonged bitterness. She herself now visited Treetops to take tea with John regularly. Only the week before she had spent the afternoon helping him decorate the Christmas tree because, by his own admission, he was useless at such things, and she did have to admit it had been time well spent. It looked magnificent.

'My wife always saw to that sort of thing,' he had told her helplessly and she had taken pity on him. Most men were useless at that sort of thing – her Tom included. Thoughts of Tom sent a little shaft of pain piercing through her. It was so sad that he hadn't been here today to see his grandchildren christened. He would have been so proud, but then she pushed the sad thoughts firmly aside. She was going to have her hands full trying to stop Livvy causing a huge argument, and she didn't have time for these maudlin thoughts. So, plastering on a smile, she followed her daughter, determined to keep an eye on her.

It wasn't long before George, who had been looking increasingly uncomfortable in his suit and tie, left to go and check on the horses and despite the sullen look on Livvy's face the rest of the day passed pleasantly as the guests all billed and cooed over the stars of the day. Almost everyone Sunday cared about was there. The Locketts had braved the weather as well as Flora and Jamie and their two teenage daughters from the village, and Constance and her husband and baby, who'd been born a few months before the twins. A number of Kathy's friends, including David and some of the nurses she had worked with at the hospital, had also come along and Sunday noted with amusement the way they were eyeing Giles up. But then he was a very attractive young man. She just wished Livvy could see it but there seemed little chance of that happening now. Livvy had spent the day studiously avoiding Giles and at the earliest opportunity, she left.

Eventually David drove Kathy and the babies back to the lodge, insisting that she shouldn't walk down the drive in the snow that was still falling thick and fast, and soon the guests began to depart, eager to get back to their firesides before the afternoon darkened.

Both Cissie and Sunday stayed behind for a while after everyone had gone to help tidy up and as Sunday was carrying a tray of dirty pots into the kitchen, she passed Cissie in the hallway.

'David's been as good as gold to Kathy an' the twins, ain't he? I reckon he's got a real soft spot for them babies,' Cissie commented sadly. 'I allus thought those two would make a go of it.'

'I did too.' Sunday nodded then looked surprised when Cissie suddenly grinned and, changing the subject, said, 'You look like you've never left this place.'

Sunday frowned. 'What do you mean?'

'I should think it's as plain as the nose on yer face. John is smitten wi' you. Surely you've noticed?'

Sunday was shocked. 'Don't be so ridiculous. John and I are friends. We're far too old to be anything more!'

'Huh! You'd better tell him that then,' Cissie chuckled. 'Cos I reckon he sees you back here as the mistress again. An', may I add, you're never too old to fall in love!'

Sunday shook her head and hurried on to the kitchen, her mind whirling. *Surely Cissie must be wrong?* John had never behaved as anything other than a perfect gentleman towards her and she had certainly never considered him to be anything more than a friend, but Cissie's words got her wondering all the same and she was thoughtful as she handed the tray over to Edith.

Shortly after she and Cissie left too and, once outside, Cissie set off for her cottage, while Sunday walked the short distance to the lodge. On entering she found Kathy and David laughing at the babies who were lying on a rug in front of a roaring fire and she couldn't help but think what a pretty picture they made. They looked like the perfect little family. But she had come to accept now that Kathy had been telling the truth and David wasn't their father. Even so, it was more than obvious that he loved the babies – and Kathy too, if it came to that – and she had the feeling that even now he would have married her like a shot if she'd have him, which was all credit to him considering the babies weren't his. Most men would have wanted nothing more to do with any of them.

It's such a shame, she thought as she hung up her coat and slipped her feet out of the snow-caked boots, and once again she racked her brain as to who the twins' father could be. Whenever she asked Kathy, she just clammed up, so Sunday had stopped asking. Whoever he was he was certainly keeping his distance – if Kathy had even told him.

The following day John arrived mid-morning and with Cissie's words preying on her mind, for the first time Sunday felt awkward in his presence.

'I suddenly realised after you'd gone yesterday that I hadn't given the twins their christening present,' he told Kathy, while Sunday tripped away to put the kettle on.

Kathy looked puzzled. 'But you laid on the wonderful spread at your home, that's more than enough,' she protested.

'Nonsense.' John fished in his pocket and withdrew two envelopes, which he pressed into her hand. 'I'd like you to open them both an account at the bank and put this in for them to start their savings,' he told her and when she went to protest again, he held his hand up.

'Please! I'll be most offended if you don't take it.'

And so, Kathy had no choice but to gratefully accept.

It wasn't until after he had gone that she opened their gifts and when she did, she gasped. 'But there's fifty pounds in each of these,' she told her mother. 'That's *far* too generous.'

Sunday didn't quite know what to say so she merely shrugged. 'Well it will be a nice start to their savings, and he must have wanted to do it. I'm sure John would be upset if you were to tell him you can't accept it,' she pointed out. 'Just put it in the bank for them.'

Kathy nodded. She didn't have much choice, but she still secretly thought that it was a very extravagant and expensive gift.

Christmas arrived all too soon and though John had invited them all to spend Christmas Day at Treetops with himself and Giles, Sunday had decided that she, the girls and the babies would spend it quietly at the lodge instead because Livvy had flatly refused to go.

Cissie was there with her on Christmas Eve when John appeared laden down with presents, which he carried in and placed beneath the small Christmas tree in the living room.

'I was hoping to give these out tomorrow but, seeing as you've chosen to spend the day here, I thought I'd better drop them off,' he explained, looking slightly crestfallen.

Sunday's cheeks burned as she saw the amused twinkle in Cissie's eye and she thanked him graciously, passing him his gifts from her and the girls. When he had gone, she glared at Cissie. 'Why are you sitting there with that soppy grin on your face? It *is* usual to give gifts to friends at Christmas, isn't it?'

'Of *course* it is,' Cissie answered innocently, as she bit into one of Sunday's delicious mince pies.

With a sigh Sunday turned away. Cissie was her oldest friend and she loved her dearly, but she could be so annoying when she got a bee in her bonnet about something!

Chapter Twenty-One

March 1939

'I tell you, war is coming, and I reckon it will be sooner rather than later,' George solemnly informed Cissie and Sunday as they all sat together in the little kitchen of Cissie's cottage one windy morning in March. 'Neville Chamberlain has informed the House of Commons today that if any action threatened Polish independence and the Poles felt it vital to resist, Britain and France would go to their aid.'

Cissie paled. The newspapers had been full of doom and gloom for weeks and things seemed to be going from bad to worse with every day that passed. On 15 March, Hitler had made a triumphal entry into Prague and slept at Hradcany Castle. On the 23 March he had forced Lithuania to surrender Memel, under threat of air attack, and now he was demanding Danzig from Poland.

'They're sayin' that German troops are already movin' towards the Polish border so I can't see how we can avoid becoming involved now,' George ended glumly.

'But what could this mean for us?' Cissie asked fearfully. She could still remember the last war all too clearly.

George sighed. 'It's hard to say at present. We'll just have to wait and see what develops.'

Sunday and Cissie exchanged a concerned glance and fell silent, each of them lost in their memories.

On the 23 August, the signing of the Nazi–Soviet non-aggression pact shocked British leaders who reaffirmed their pledge with France to defend Poland, and by the end of the month another war seemed inevitable. The forces were mobil-ised in readiness, reserves were called up and children began to be evacuated from the major cities. On 1 September German aircraft and troops attacked Poland and just two days later everyone's worst fears were realised when Prime Minister Neville Chamberlain declared that England was now at war with Germany. The country fell silent as families huddled around their wireless sets to hear the grim news and almost immediately the air raid sirens began to wail across London, sending people scurrying to the shelters. Thankfully this time it was a false alarm, but it was a fearful indication of the destruction which might yet come.

'I almost feel glad that I never had a son,' Sunday confided. 'I'd be worried sick about him going off to fight if I had.'

'I know exactly what you mean,' Cissie agreed glumly, thinking of her own sons. 'I think John is afraid Giles may decide to sign up too but all we can do now is wait and see what happens over the next few weeks.'

Later that afternoon, John popped into the lodge to discuss the dreadful news. 'I think I'll offer to have a couple of evacuees here,' he told Sunday. 'I'm far too old to go and fight but at least if I do that I'll feel as if I'm doing my bit.'

'But will the children be safe here?' Sunday fretted, thinking of her own two adorable grandchildren. At two, they were mischievous, and running all over the place and sometimes she felt that she needed eyes in the back of her head. But even so she doted on them and was terrified what might happen to them. Thomas had now gone from being the smallest of the two to being the tallest, although Daisy was still the chatterbox and by the far the most bossy. Truthfully, she would have liked to take some evacuees herself, but the lodge was already over-crowded. 'We're only a stone's throw from Coventry and the car factories there are bound to be a target if they start bombing,' she pointed out.

John shook his head and spread his hands helplessly. 'I should think it would still be safer here than staying in one of the major cities.'

She nodded numbly as a horrible sense of foreboding swept through her.

Within days recruitment centres appeared in all the towns and cities across the country and young men were called up to join the forces.

'They were queuing up outside the recruitment office in Nuneaton,' John told Sunday sorrowfully one afternoon before admitting, 'I'm terrified that Giles will be called up at any moment. I find myself lying awake every night worrying about it.'

She could understand his fears. She could still remember how terrified she had been when Tom and Ben went away to fight in the first war, but as she pointed out, 'I imagine he'll want to feel he's contributing in some way, though. But what will happen to the horses when he goes? I'm not sure George could manage

151

everything in the stables on his own.' Unfortunately, young Billy, the groom John had first employed when he arrived at Treetops, had left soon after his arrival to return to his family so the onus of looking after the animals had fallen solely to George and Giles again.

'If it's anything like the last time the army will take the horses,' John said glumly. 'They'll just leave the very young and the very old probably. They'll probably take the gates and any metal they can get their hands on as well for making tanks and ammunition but we're just going to have to make the best of it.'

Dread ran through her veins like iced water as she again thought back to the last war. Their sons and daughters would not remember it, but she did, as if it was only yesterday. She could remember being in the town one day and watching the young men queuing to go to the front, she had known many of them and was painfully aware that the majority had never come home and now their bodies lay buried in foreign countries far away. Would it be the same this time? All they could do was wait and see.

When Livvy got home from work that evening she flung herself into a chair and pouted. '*Three* young men from our office alone went and joined up in their dinner hour today,' she told her mother. '*Three* of them just from one business, so how many more must be going? There would have been four, but Jeremy Garner got turned down for medical reasons. He has a heart murmur apparently and bad eyesight too. At this rate there'll be no men left here!'

Sunday and Kathy glanced at each other and shook their heads. It was all so worrying for everyone.

Kathy had just got the children up from a nap and she stood in the doorway with one on each hip. Her main concern was

152

for her children, but she hoped they would be safe as they lived in a village on the outskirts of the town. She settled the twins on the floor with a pile of wooden bricks then set about getting their tea. They were having boiled eggs and bread-and-butter soldiers this evening followed by jelly and cream – one of their favourites. They both had healthy appetites although Daisy was still the greediest, and they would eat most of what she put in front of them, which she was grateful for.

'Do you think there's any chance this Hitler chap might turn back and everything will fizzle out?' she asked hopefully, and Sunday snorted.

'Huh! This Hitler is some sort of power maniac. I think there's about as much chance of that happening as a snowflake in hell would have!'

Kathy bit her lip as she buttered the bread. It seemed they were just going to have get on with it as best they could.

Over the next couple of weeks training camps sprang up all across the country and the stations and trains were packed as the new recruits flocked to them, waved off by teary-eyed sweethearts and parents, who remembered the last war all too well. There were no celebrations to see them on their way this time, just the loved ones left behind on the deserted platforms, their faces etched with dread.

David called round one evening, as he often did, in time to help Kathy get the twins ready for bed. Normally he was laughing and playing with them but this evening, as they sat and watched them splashing in the bath, he seemed unnaturally quiet and thoughtful.

153

'Is everything all right?' Kathy asked eventually as she lifted Daisy first from the water and swaddled her in a big, warm towel. It wasn't like him to be so quiet.

'Yes . . . Well, it all depends what you mean by all right.' He stared at her solemnly. 'The thing is, I've been talking to Matron. You may be aware that the British Expeditionary Force has already crossed to France and taken up their position alongside the French army.'

'Yes, I was aware of that,' she replied, puzzled. 'It said in the newspapers that they'd arrived safely despite fears of them being attacked either by U-boats or the German army.'

'Hm, well, Matron informed me that at present a number of field hospitals are also being set up and the army are asking for doctors and nurses to volunteer to work in them. And so . . . the long and the short of it is, I went and signed up this afternoon. Myself and a number of nurses from the hospital will be taken to a port in the south of England then we'll be ferried across the Channel escorted by destroyers with all the medical equipment we'll need.'

The breath caught in Kathy's throat as she stared at him from frightened eyes.

'B-but you might be killed!'

He gave a tight little smile. 'I don't think we'll be anywhere near as at risk as the troops who'll be doing the fighting,' he assured her. 'But even if we are, it's a chance I'm prepared to take. I don't want to be considered a coward.'

'But you're *not*,' she said in a choky voice. 'And you're needed here! What about all the lives you save at the hospital?'

'I'm sure the older doctors will be more than capable of stepping in and filling the younger doctors' shoes while we're away.'

Kathy's heart was pounding with fear and emotions she

154

couldn't recognise. David was nothing more than a friend – that's all he had ever been, wasn't it? But she had come to depend on him and to care deeply for him. She hadn't realised just how much, and the thought of him going to war had her quite upset.

'And when will you be leaving?' she forced herself to ask as she began to rub Daisy dry.

'Within the next two weeks.'

Again, she felt as if all the air had been sucked from her lungs. It was so very soon, she would hardly have time to get used to the idea and he would be gone. A silence settled between them, as David lifted Thomas from the bath and began to dry him, while Kathy put Daisy's pyjamas on and brushed her hair. Normally this was such a happy time of the day but this evening even the twins seemed to sense that something was amiss, and they were strangely subdued. The adults sat them at the kitchen table when they were done and David carried the bath outside and emptied it, while Kathy gave the children some milk and a slice of bread and jam before carrying them up and tucking them into their cots.

David was sitting in the fireside chair when she came back down, and she made them both a cup of cocoa and joined him. Sunday had gone into the village to visit Flora and Jamie, as she often did, and Livvy had gone out with her friends, so now with the twins settled it was just the two of them.

'So, do you have any idea where they might be sending you?' she forced herself to ask. She wasn't sure that she really wanted to know.

He shook his head. 'None at all. It's all very hush hush for obvious reasons but . . . I'll write to you, if I may?'

'Of course you must write.' Suddenly the tears she had been

holding back spurted from her eyes and ran down her cheeks and with a sigh he was down on his knees in front of her holding her hands.

'I . . . I'll miss you,' she sniffed.

'I know,' he said gently as he stroked a lock of her glorious dark hair from her cheek. 'And I'll miss you too; more than you'll ever know.' His face was troubled as he wrestled with himself and then suddenly everything he had wanted to say for so long came spilling out of him. 'Oh, Kathy, you *must* know by now that I still love you? I've never stopped loving you—'

She opened her mouth to stop his flow of words, but he held his hand up to silence her. 'I know you don't feel the same. Your heart obviously still belongs to the twins' father, whoever he is, but I had to tell you how I felt before I went just in case I don't come back . . .'

'Don't *say* that,' she said in an anguished voice and threw her arms about his neck. 'I *do* love you, David, but not in the way you want me to. I love you as a dear friend, and I still can't bear the thought of you being hurt.'

At that moment Sunday appeared and seeing the tears on Kathy's cheeks and their arms about each other she asked with a hopeful smile, 'So what's going on here?'

As Kathy haltingly told her, Sunday's face became solemn. 'Then may God go with you,' she told David. 'And just be sure to keep in touch.'

'I will.' He rose slowly and headed for the door. 'I'll be round again on my next afternoon off, if I haven't been shipped out that is. But if I am, I'll be sure to let you know.'

Kathy could only nod; she felt far too upset to speak and she was even more upset when the door had closed on him and her mother rounded on her.

'Oh, Kathy, you little *fool*,' she snapped in an uncharacteristically sharp voice. 'Are you *really* going to let that poor chap go off to war without recognising how you feel about him and telling him?'

'What do you *mean*? David knows I love him as a dear friend!' Kathy snapped back.

Sunday shook her head and sighed. 'They do say as there's none so blind as those who don't want to see. Let's just hope you don't live to regret this!' And with that she stomped off to her room, leaving Kathy staring after her with a bemused expression on her face, and a feeling of dread in her heart.

Chapter Twenty-Two

David left for war ten days later after a tearful farewell from Kathy and soon the whole of Britain was in a state of uncertainty and anxiety. Hospitals were cleared of patients except for the gravely ill and mortuaries were stacked high with piles of cardboard coffins that the government feared would be needed for the first casualties. Everyone was urged to carry a label with their name and address on and identity cards and gas masks were issued. Suddenly blackout material was becoming hard to find and streetlamps remained unlit as everyone waited for the first raids that would surely come.

On a blustery morning in mid-October John visited Sunday to tell her that the two little evacuees he had agreed to house for the duration of the war would be arriving the following day.

'Really? Where are they coming from?' she enquired.

He grinned. 'The East End of London – two little cockney sparrows aged five and eight, so I assume I'm going to have my hands full! But Cook and Edith are looking forward to having children in the house. I'm not so sure Giles is that keen on the idea though.' His face became solemn then as he confided, 'Between you and me I'm still worried that he might go off and join up before he's called up. Oh, I know he'll have to go eventually but he's been very quiet for the last couple of days.'

'Oh dear.' His words once again brought back memories of when Tom and Ben had gone off to war. Ben . . . just the thought of his betrayal still cut like a knife, for no matter what he thought, she had loved him as her own. But that had clearly been what had festered in him for all these years. She had to admit that she hadn't taken it well when she'd discovered he was Tom's son, and he had obviously never forgiven her for that, despite the many years she'd cared for him before that. And when he'd returned from the war, he'd been so distant; it was as if he'd closed his heart to her. Then, once Kathy and Livvy had come along within months of each other, she'd always suspected he'd been jealous of them, although it hadn't been so much of a problem at the time as he'd had Maggie. But then he'd had the heartbreak of losing Maggie and his son, followed by the death of his father to contend with. Even so, she would never have believed him capable of stealing everything from her.

'I was wondering if you'd drive into Nuneaton with me to pick them up from the church hall tomorrow?' John asked her, bringing her thoughts sharply back to the present. 'To be honest, I'm not that brilliant with children. It's been a long time since our son was born and my wife did most of the caring back then. She always wanted at least four children, but Giles's father was our only one and when he was killed, I think it would have killed her too if she hadn't had Giles to take care of.'

'Of course I will.' Sunday pushed gloomy thoughts of Ben aside and smiled. 'I'm sure the children will be delightful, and Edith will probably do most of the looking after of them, if I know her. She's so good with the twins. It's such a shame that she never had children of her own.'

And so immediately after lunch the next day she and John drove to the church hall in town. It was total chaos inside. Bewildered children with their names written on brown cardboard labels hanging on string about their necks were sitting on chairs around the walls of the hall as the women who had escorted them from London tried to place them with the families who had volunteered to take them in. It appeared that most of the children had already been chosen or allocated.

'Name?' one of the harassed-looking women said shortly as John and Sunday entered the room.

'John Willerby.' John's eyes scanned the rows of children, wondering which two were the ones he had come for.

'Ah yes, here we are,' the woman answered as she quickly read down a list on the clipboard she was clutching. 'You're down to take two children. We thought you could take Bobby and Peggy Walker.' She led them across the room, weaving through a throng of people until they came to two children sitting silently and clutching each other's hands. It was so loud that the woman could barely make herself heard, but she smiled kindly at the children when they reached them.

'This is Mr Willerby who you'll be staying with, children,' she informed them and Sunday almost gasped with dismay. They were so small, more like a four- and a five-year-old, and they were painfully thin. Most of the children were carrying small cardboard suitcases but these two had a torn paper carrier bag with string handles that was clearly all they had brought between them. The little girl looked absolutely terrified, while the boy was glaring at John guardedly.

'I ain't going wiv him!' Bobby said instantly. 'He's an old geezer!'

'Bobby, how dare you be so rude!' the woman gasped but John merely laughed.

'You're quite right, Bobby,' he agreed. 'I *am* an old geezer, but I have a nice warm house and I promise I'll take very good care of you and your sister.'

Sunday held her breath as she watched for the child's reaction. Bobby was clearly the older of the two but although he might be small for his age, she noted he certainly wasn't afraid to say what he thought. She could see head lice running across the parting in his hair and her hands itched to scrub him clean.

'S'pose we'll 'ave to come wiv yer then,' he said resignedly, for all the world as if he were doing John a great favour. 'But just fer a little while!' And now the corners of Sunday's mouth twitched too.

'So, is she yer wife then?' Bobby stabbed a grubby finger towards her.

John shook his head. 'No, Bobby. Mrs Branning is just a very good friend of mine. She lives close to me so you'll no doubt be seeing a lot of her during your stay. But come along, I believe my cook has a nice hot meal waiting for you.'

John duly signed the necessary forms and once he had gently ushered the children from the hall and they approached his car, still clutching each other's hands, Bobby's mouth gaped open, making him look like a goldfish.

'Cor, is this *yours*?' he croaked incredulously. 'I ain't never 'ad a ride in a motor car before!' And when John nodded, he smiled for the first time since their introduction. 'Blimey, are yer rich or sommat?'

'Comfortable,' John assured him as he lifted Peggy into the back of the car and placed a rug across her skinny knees. He noticed that her stick-like legs were covered in bruises and wondered how she had got them.

Once they were on their way, Bobby couldn't stop smiling,

which John took as an encouraging sign, and when they drove down the drive leading to Treetops Bobby's eyes were on stalks as he asked, 'Which part o' this 'ouse is yours?'

'All of it,' John answered and just for a moment Bobby was rendered speechless. He could hardly believe the size of the house or the vast green expanse of lawn. And the fields, which held grazing sheep and cows, were the first he had ever seen, apart from dead ones hanging in the butcher's shop window. He had been brought up in the heart of the East End in a tiny terraced house with not a tree in sight and suddenly he felt as if he had entered another world, not that he would have admitted it.

Both Edith and Cook had been watching for them from the hall window and by the time John drew the car to a halt they were outside the front door on the steps, waiting to greet them with broad smiles on their faces.

'Welcome to Treetops, children,' Edith said as the two little ones clambered out of the car.

'I've got a lovely meal all ready for you,' Cook told them with a welcoming smile. 'Come on through to the kitchen.' She and Edith had thought that perhaps the new arrivals would feel more comfortable in there for now, rather than putting them in the formal dining room.

Soon the children were seated at the large, scrubbed oak table tucking into a roast-beef dinner as if they had never seen food before. In fact, Bobby was stuffing his mouth so full that he was making himself heave. It was almost as if he was fearful someone was going to snatch it away from him. It was the same when Cook served them jam roly-poly and custard and, as she and Edith stood at the sink, she shook her head sadly.

'Poor little souls,' she said. 'Just look at the state of 'em. I reckon we're goin' to have us hands full wi' this pair, or with the little lad, at least. The girl seems quieter. In fact, she seems to be jumpin' at her own shadow, the poor little mite.'

Edith nodded in agreement but wasn't fazed in the slightest. Never having had children she was more than ready to take them under her wing. She and her husband had dreamed of having a large family when they had first married but, sadly, he had been killed in an accident down the pit shortly after their first wedding anniversary. Soon after she had gone to work for John Willerby and his wife and that had been the end of her dreams of becoming a mother. Now she leaned towards Sunday and whispered, 'They both look like they could do with a good bath but what are we going to dress them in? The few things they've brought with them are little more than rags.'

Sunday smiled reassuringly. 'Don't worry. Up in the loft there should still be some trunks full of clothes that belonged to the children who lived here with me and Tom. That's if John hasn't thrown them out but I doubt he would have. There's bound to be something to fit them until John can get them some new things. Once they've finished eating, we'll go up and have a look, if you like, while John shows them round.'

She and Edith set off for the attics and half an hour later came back downstairs laden down with clothes that looked as if they might fit the new arrivals.

'Just look at this,' Edith said gleefully as she held up a little tartan kilt with a matching red jumper. 'Isn't it just the cutest thing you ever saw? I reckon little Peggy is going to look a treat in this. And there are some long trousers here for Bobby an' all. Poor little soul must be frozen in those old shorts he's got on.'

Cook winked at Sunday over Edith's shoulder. She had an

163

idea that Edith was going to love looking after the children and she had to admit that they had helped to lift the air of gloom that had settled over the house since the war was announced.

'Right, so all you have to do now is persuade the boyo into the bath,' she said with an amused twinkle in her eye. 'An' all I can say is, rather you than me!'

Chapter Twenty-Three

Going on Sunday's advice, Edith didn't even attempt to bath the children until it was close to their bedtime.

'If you do, you'll only highlight to them that you think they're dirty,' Sunday said wisely and Edith was happy to listen. After all, Sunday had had far more experience of caring for children than she had.

Sunday had kindly come back to help as bedtime approached, guessing that Edith might have trouble on her hands and in a very short time she was proved to be right.

'If you fink I'm gerrin' in there you've got anovver fink comin'!' Bobby announced after being led to the bathroom and eyeing the steamy suds. He had never been fully immersed in water as far as he could remember and had no intention of doing it now.

'But you'll feel so much better when you've had a bath,' Edith coaxed. 'And just look at these lovely warm pyjamas you can put on when you get out.'

Bobby stood his ground, planting his legs apart and crossing his skinny arms as he glared at her, so Sunday tried another approach.

'Well, that's a shame. We'll have to bath Peggy first then, so she'll get the first warm jam tarts straight out of the oven, oh, and her cup of cocoa too, of course.'

'*What?*' Bobby's ears pricked up as his mouth watered. 'Warm jam tarts?'

Sunday nodded. 'Yes, being as it's your first night here Cook thought she'd spoil you, but if you don't want any it doesn't matter.'

He seemed to weigh things up in his mind before saying reluctantly, 'All right then, I'll gerrin, but only if you two go outta the room while I get undressed!'

'Of course,' Sunday took Edith's elbow and led her out onto the landing and soon they heard a shout as Bobby stepped into the water.

'Bleedin' 'ell! This water is too hot! Are yer tryin' to scald me?'

The two women went back into him and the smiles died on their faces as they saw the bruises all across his small body.

'How did you get these?' Sunday asked gently as, much to Bobby's disgust, she began to scrub his lank, mousy-coloured hair with a bar of carbolic soap.

His lips set in a mutinous line and he remained obstinately silent. When his hair was thoroughly washed, Sunday took a fine-toothed nit comb from her pocket and began to rake it through as he protested loudly.

''Ere! I never said yer could do that! *Gerroff* me,' he shouted.

'The quieter you sit the sooner it will be done,' Sunday informed him firmly and to her surprise he became still, although he was cursing the whole time beneath his breath. 'There,' she said eventually, shocked to see how many nits she had dragged from his hair. 'Me and Edith will go out onto the landing now if you want to get dried. You can put those clean pyjamas on then.'

166

She and Edith walked sedately from the room and when he joined them, he was almost unrecognisable. He had looked dark before but now his skin glowed pink and instead of lying flat against his head his hair – which they had thought was dark – had turned fair and was already beginning to spring into little waves.

While Edith took Bobby downstairs for the treats he had been promised, Sunday went through the process again with Peggy, but thankfully she proved to be much more amenable and hardly moved throughout the whole procedure.

'Why, you look just like a little angel,' Edith declared when Sunday led her downstairs sometime later in the pretty nightgown they had found for her. Edith made to cuddle the child only for the little girl to cringe away from her and run to her brother.

'You keep yer 'ands off 'er,' Bobby warned as he hugged his little sister protectively and Edith looked so hurt that Sunday was afraid she might burst into tears. It was a situation she had come across many times during the years she had cared for children and she squeezed Edith's hand reassuringly.

'Just give them a little time,' she whispered. 'They have to learn to trust you.'

Edith blinked back tears. 'I hope they do,' she responded.

Soon after, Sunday glanced at the clock and sighed. 'I shall have to get back now,' she told Edith regretfully. 'Do you think you'll manage?'

'O' course I shall,' Edith told her. 'I've already sorted some story books out for when I tuck 'em in. Kids like a bedtime story, don't they? I've sorted out two bedrooms next door to each other as well, so they don't feel too isolated from each other.'

Sunday smiled her approval and after saying goodnight to the children she set off back to the lodge to tell Kathy and

Livvy all about the new arrivals. It had been nice to see children in Treetops again and she had an idea Edith was going to take to being a foster mum like a duck to water.

Back in Treetops, Edith's next problem came when she led the children up to bed. Their eyes grew round when she showed them into Peggy's room. Decorated in shades of soft green with a thick, warm carpet on the floor and a cosy fire burning in the grate, it was the prettiest room they had ever seen. The children seemed more than a little impressed with it but when she came to coax Bobby into taking a peep at his room, he planted his feet apart and glared at her.

'We sleep togevver!' he declared, placing his arm about his little sister's waist.

'But I have the room next door all ready for you,' Edith told him just as John entered the room.

'Do we have a problem?' he asked with a wink at Bobby who was looking very rebellious.

'Yeah, we do, mister,' he answered stubbornly. 'She wants us to sleep in different rooms but we allus sleep togevver!'

'Well, I don't suppose it would hurt just until you feel a bit more comfortable with things,' John agreed amiably with a smile at Edith. 'It's a nice big bed so there's plenty of room for the both of you. What do you think, Edith?'

'I suppose so,' she answered hesitantly and instantly the two children hopped into bed and pulled the blankets up to their chins, staring at the two adults warily. 'Would you like me to read you a story?' Edith asked, advancing on them with a book in her hand, but Bobby shook his head.

'We ain't babies, yer know . . . But yer could leave it 'ere fer us to look at the pictures, I s'pose.'

Edith gently placed the book on the bed and backed away, as did John.

'Right, children, we'll see you in the morning,' he said kindly at the door. 'Do you both like bacon and eggs? Our chickens lay delicious eggs. Oh, and I have to say Cook's porridge is very good as well, if you prefer that.'

Both children nodded vigorously, and the adults quietly left the room.

'Poor little mites,' Edith said softly once they were out on the landing. 'Peggy seems scared of everything, and I don't know what Bobby thinks we're going to do to her, but he hardly lets her out of his sight.'

'I think it would be safe to say they're both used to being knocked about, if the bruises all over them are anything to go by,' John answered solemnly. 'But give them a little time and patience and with fresh air and good food inside them they might come out of their shells.'

'I hope you're right,' she said as she left him to return to the kitchen.

Later, she peeped in the bedroom to check on them and smiled to see them curled up together, snoring gently in the big feather bed. They looked so innocent that it brought a lump to her throat as she gently closed the door and crept away.

The next morning, dressed in the clothes Sunday and Edith had sorted for them, the two children were almost unrecognisable and once more they tucked into their food as if they hadn't eaten for a month.

Giles, who had been busy working in the stables when they arrived, watched with amusement.

'So, who are you then?' Bobby asked in his own blunt way. 'Do yer work 'ere?'

'Well, yes I do, but I live here as well,' Giles told him good-naturedly. 'This is my grandfather's house, but I run the stables.'

'Do you 'ave any horses 'ere?' Bobby asked, spooning yet more porridge into his mouth. He was like a bottomless pit when it came to food.

'Yes, quite a number of them, although I don't know for how long now that we're at war,' Giles answered glumly.

'So, can I see 'em when we've finished eatin'? I like animals. We've gorra dog back at 'ome called Skippy!' Bobby's eyes were glowing with excitement. The only horses he'd ever seen before were the cart horses that delivered the milk. He had quite a nice little sideline going, following them about to pick up their mess before selling it to people to put on their roses, not that many people had roses where he lived.

'Of course you can see them,' Giles agreed and to his amusement Bobby began to eat even faster.

'They've eaten more than Mr Willerby an' Giles put together,' the cook chuckled once Giles had led them away. 'Not that I'm complainin', mind. It's nice to cook for someone with a hearty appetite.'

Edith nodded in agreement. She was going to visit the school in Church Road in the village later that morning to try and get the children enrolled there and she wondered how they would take to it. If she didn't miss her guess, the teachers would have their hands full with Bobby, but hopefully they'd settle in soon enough.

Chapter Twenty-Four

Over the next few days Bobby followed Giles about like a little shadow. Edith had managed to secure the children a place at the village school and they were due to start there the following week but until then Bobby adored being in the stables and despite his earlier misgivings about having children at Treetops, Giles seemed to have taken to them.

Edith was in her element too. Peggy slowly seemed to be coming out of her shell, but Bobby still wouldn't trust her with anyone other than Cook and Edith, so she now spent most of the time in the kitchen with them, while Bobby himself was off with Giles and the horses.

'So, do you help your mammy with the cooking?' Cook asked one morning as she and Peggy stood at the kitchen table. Cook was making a fruit pie and had given Peggy a little pastry to roll out.

Peggy frowned. 'Me ma don't cook,' she said matter-of-factly.

'Oh, so what do you eat then?'

Peggy shrugged her slight shoulders. Already a little colour was creeping into her cheeks, but she was still painfully thin. 'We just 'as bread an' drippin', or sometimes Ma gets us a pie on 'er way 'ome from work.'

'Oh yes and what sort of work does your ma do?'

Peggy frowned. 'I ain't sure. She goes out at night a lot an' comes 'ome late usually but I don't know what she does.'

'And what about your dad? What does he do?'

''E goes to the pub when ma comes 'ome wi' any money, but I don't fink 'e goes to work,' the child said innocently.

Sunday breezed into the kitchen then and the conversation came to an end.

She smiled at Peggy. 'Good morning, everyone. Did you have a good night's sleep, Peggy?'

'She had a bit of a bad dream and I had to go into her,' Edith answered for the child. 'But you were all right once I'd tucked you in, weren't you, pet?' she said to the child.

Peggy nodded solemnly and flushed. She had also wet the bed, but Edith didn't tell Sunday that. She didn't want to embarrass the child. She seemed perfectly at ease with Sunday, Edith and Cook now but they'd all noticed that she was still very nervous around men, even Giles and John, which made them wonder if perhaps it was her father who had inflicted the bruises she had arrived with. They were beginning to fade to pale yellows and mauves now and were nowhere near as noticeable as when she'd first come there.

'Can I come back to the lodge wi' you an' see the babies when yer go?' Peggy asked suddenly and Sunday nodded.

'Of course you can.'

Peggy was very taken with the twins and loved going to the lodge, although Sunday wondered if it was perhaps because there were no men there. The child was slowly opening up like a little flower to the sun but all of them realised that neither of the children could have had an easy time of it back in London from the very little they had said about their parents and their

172

home life. Only the day after they had arrived Edith had noticed that Bobby had seemed very nervous about filling in the stamped postcard each child arrived with informing their parents where they were staying.

'I bet yer ma and dad will be here to see you in no time,' Edith had said, and Bobby had scowled.

'Me dad won't come an' I doubt he'll let me ma come eivver,' he had said solemnly, which Edith had thought rather odd. Surely if their children were living in a strange place with strange people their parents would want to come and check everything out, but time would tell. On a few occasions she had tried to get him to speak of them but each time he had closed up like a clam, so she avoided asking anything now. As Sunday had pointed out, he would open up in his own good time and until then it was best that he was allowed to settle in with no pressure.

Giles and George came into the kitchen for their tea break, closely followed by Bobby, and instantly Peggy scampered to her brother's side and after ramming her thumb in her mouth, she eyed the men warily.

'I shall be going out for a couple of hours shortly,' Giles informed them, as he took a seat at the table and lifted the mug of freshly mashed tea.

'Can I come wiv' yer?' Bobby asked hopefully, but this time Giles shook his head.

'I'm afraid not but I shan't be too long and, while I'm gone, I'm sure George will find you something to do.'

'I certainly shall, you can help me with some diggin',' George assured him. He had been clearing some of the lawn in preparation for another vegetable patch as everyone had been instructed to do. After all, who knew when and if rationing would come into force again? They already had a very productive vegetable garden but as George had pointed out, 'What we can't eat some of the villagers will be glad of!'

Cook fetched some of her homemade biscuits to the table and everything else was forgotten as Bobby dived in, much to everyone's amusement.

Once Giles had left to get ready for his outing, and George and Bobby had gone back to work, Sunday went through to see John, who was in his study poring over some paperwork. As always, his face lit up at the sight of her.

'You must be sick of me dropping in.' She grinned. She had called in at least once a day since the children had arrived, to check that all was well.

He shook his head. 'Never!' His smile faded and standing up he went to close the door quietly behind her.

'Sunday . . . there's something I've been meaning to ask you for a very long time, and I suppose now is as good a time as any . . .'

She stared at him curiously. Whatever he was about to say was clearly something serious and she wanted to put him at ease. 'Ask away then, I don't bite,' she told him with an encouraging smile.

He gulped, making his Adam's apple bob up and down as he ran a finger around the inside of his collar as if it were suddenly too tight for him. 'The thing is . . . I, er . . . I've grown very fond of you since I moved here.'

'And I'm fond of you too,' she assured him.

'Ah! So, I was wondering . . . what I mean is . . . Oh damn! I'm making a right mess of this so I'm just going to come right out and say it. I love you, Sunday Branning. I think I have since the minute I clapped eyes on you, and I was wondering if you would do me the very great honour of becoming my wife?'

Sunday's eyes grew wide as her hand rose to cover her mouth

and for a moment, she was sure that she must have been hearing things . . . but no, one look at his face assured her that she hadn't. John was quite serious.

'I . . . I don't know what to say,' she faltered. 'Don't you think we're rather old to be contemplating marriage?'

'As I've recently discovered, you're never too old to fall in love,' he said, coming to gently take her hands in his. 'I must admit I never even thought about another woman after I lost my wife. Until I met you, that is. And what's wrong with wanting to spend our twilight years together? We get on well, don't we? And I'd love to see you back here in Treetops where you belong.'

'Oh, John, I'm flattered,' Sunday told him when she finally managed to find her voice again. 'And yes, we do get on . . . very well. But the thing is . . . I loved my husband dearly and . . .'

As her voice faltered, he held his hand up. 'Please, you don't have to give me an answer right now. But will you just agree to give it some thought? I know that wasn't the most romantic of proposals. I'm afraid I'm a bit rusty at this sort of thing, but I think we would do very well together.'

She nodded, still numb with shock. 'Very well, I will think about it. Just give me a little time.'

'As long as you need,' he assured her, bending forward to kiss her cheek.

Sunday made a hasty retreat, her mind in a whirl. John's proposal had taken her completely by surprise. Admittedly, Cissie had told her that she thought John had feelings for her, but she had never believed it for a minute, until now!

Cissie popped round to see her later that afternoon after finishing work at Treetops and seeing that Sunday was rather quiet and preoccupied, she asked, 'Are you all right?'

Sunday chewed on her lip as she wondered whether she should tell her or not, but she and Cissie had never had secrets from each other so haltingly she told her of John's proposal.

'Didn't I *tell* you he had feelings for you?' Cissie crowed delightedly. 'John is such a lovely man and just think, you'd be the mistress at Treetops again!'

In that moment Sunday made her decision. 'Yes, you're quite right I would,' she agreed. 'But the trouble is Tom wouldn't be the master there. I still love him, Cissie, and as much as I care for John as a dear friend, he could never take Tom's place – no one could. So, I'm afraid I'm going to have to tell him that the answer is no.'

Cissie sighed but she understood. She knew how much Sunday and Tom had meant to each other. *It's a shame, though*, she thought. She would have loved to see Sunday back in what she considered was her rightful place.

Chapter Twenty-Five

Giles returned from his outing late in the afternoon and he strode through the kitchen without acknowledging anyone, his expression stern.

The children were sitting at the kitchen table with a colouring book each and some crayons that Sunday had bought for them and Cook frowned as she popped a meat and potato pie into the oven.

'Looks like someone's upset him good an' proper,' she commented to Edith.

'Hm, he were a bit preoccupied, weren't he?' She went on peeling the potatoes for supper.

In the hallway Giles paused, then drawing himself up to his full height, he straightened his back and made for his grandfather's office. He was usually to be found in there at that time of day.

'Hello, lad,' John greeted him when he entered. 'Fancy a glass of port before dinner?'

Giles shook his head. 'No thanks, Grandpa. I have something to tell you.'

'Oh yes? And what would that be to make you look so

serious?' But already John had a good idea and he was praying that he was wrong.

'The reason I went into town today was to sign up,' Giles told him. 'I've put my name down to join the RAF. Tomorrow I have to go to London to do some exams and if I pass those and get accepted, I'll be leaving to start my training very soon after.'

'I see.' John carefully placed his glass down. His hand was shaking so much he was afraid he would spill his drink if he didn't. 'Then all I can do is wish you good luck. I'm not going to lie to you, you'll be sorely missed, and I shall worry every second that you're gone, but I'm very proud of you.'

'Thanks, Grandpa.' There were tears in their eyes as John strode over to hug him but then John stepped back from him and asked, 'What made you want to join the RAF?'

Giles shrugged. 'Well, you know I've always been fascinated with planes.'

'And where will you be doing your training?'

'Somewhere in Wiltshire, I believe. That's if I pass my exams, of course. It's a three-month course and then when I've passed the tests, I'll be sent to one of the airbases.'

'Then there's nothing to be said,' John said with a catch in his voice as he slapped his grandson on the shoulder. 'May God go with you, my boy!'

Later that evening as Giles settled the horses, Livvy strolled in and made for the stall where her horse was stabled.

'Evening,' Giles said shortly, and she glanced at him, surprised. Normally he went out of his way trying to engage her in conversation but this evening he had been as short with her as she normally was with him.

Giles continued to fork straw into one of the stalls and when he was done, he said abruptly, 'I shall be going to London tomorrow so I'd be grateful if you could give George a hand with the other horses as well as your own while I'm gone.'

'Why are you going to London?' She was curious despite the fact that she kept telling herself she didn't give a damn where he went.

'I'm hoping to join the RAF, as it happens, so I have to go and sit some exams and see if they'll accept me. If they do, I'll be leaving shortly after to begin my training.'

Livvy's eyes grew round as she stared at him incredulously. 'Then, er . . . good luck.' She could think of nothing else to say and he gave a wry grin.

'Don't you mean good riddance?'

She felt herself blush and was instantly on the defensive with him again. 'Of course I don't! I like to think I'm a little more adult than that. In actual fact I've been thinking of signing up myself.'

'*You!*' Now it was his turn to look shocked. 'Doing what?'

She sniffed and shrugged her shoulders. 'I haven't really given it a lot of thought yet but there's bound to be something I can do.'

As he stared at her standing there looking so dainty and delicate, he doubted it, and if truth be known he didn't like the thought of her being actively employed in the war at all, though he had no idea why he should feel that way – she'd been nothing but a pain to him since the day they had met.

'In that case good luck to you too,' he answered, and much

179

to her chagrin he turned and marched away without another word.

The following afternoon, Sunday went to see John and found him reading the newspaper. 'Have you *seen* this?' he asked. 'It says that Hitler has ordered the flogging of Jews and there are barbarous and systematic tortures being inflicted on them in both the Dachau and Buchenwald camps. Some of the poor devils have gone mad and others have pretended to try and escape so they will be shot rather than have to face the agony of living there! It's despicable! What sort of a monster is this Hitler, for God's sake!'

He took a deep breath and smiled apologetically. 'I'm sorry about that little outburst, my dear, but how could *anyone* read of such atrocities without becoming upset?'

'I quite understand. But now I'd like to speak to you about the proposal you put to me yesterday, if I may?' She'd had to force herself to come and get this over with because she knew if she put it off it would stand between them being friends.

Instantly his eyes were hopeful, and she looked away guiltily before she forced herself to go on.

'I'm most terribly flattered . . . but the thing is . . .'

Being the gentleman he was, John took it graciously. 'I understand,' he said softly when she had mumbled her way through her refusal and the reasons why. But it didn't make her feel any better, so she was feeling pensive as she went to the kitchen to see the children.

With every day that passed they seemed a little bit more settled and Peggy's eyes were slowly losing the haunted look they'd had when she first arrived, although Edith was concerned that the children still insisted on sleeping together. They were tucking into large dishes of rice pudding when Sunday entered and as soon as they had finished, they scampered off to find George in the stables, leaving Sunday to chat to Edith and Cook.

'I suppose you've heard about Giles goin' away? He's in London taking his exams today,' Cook said miserably.

Sunday nodded as she took a seat at the table and smiled as her eyes fell on the children's empty dishes. They were so clean they didn't look as if they'd been used. 'Livvy told me last night and strangely enough she seemed quite concerned about it, which is surprising seeing as those two are usually at each other's throats.'

Cook shook her head. 'I ain't at all happy about it either,' she confided. 'The thought of him flyin' across Germany droppin' bombs on the enemy scares me to death – not that there's anythin' I can do about it. What if the Germans drop one on him? I've known him since he was just a little boy, see? So, I'm bound to be worried about him.'

'I know what you mean.' Sunday's face was grave. 'Since David left for France a couple of weeks ago Kathy has been walking around with a face on her like a wet weekend. Surprising really, seeing as she insists she feels nothing but friendship for him.'

At that moment the children bounded back into the kitchen and Bobby was almost beside himself with excitement.

'Cor, George just told us Giles is going to be flyin' planes in the war,' he said admiringly. 'I reckon he's really brave, don't you?'

'Yes, he is,' Sunday answered. Thank goodness Bobby didn't seem to realise what danger Giles and all the rest of the RAF pilots would be putting themselves in.

Bobby's words suddenly reminded Edith of something, and hurrying over to the fireplace she fetched a postcard she had placed there. 'Look what came for you today.' She waved it at the children, 'It's a postcard from your mammy. Do you want me to read it to you?'

Bobby's face became solemn as he took it from her, saying, 'I can read it meself, fanks.'

Tongue in cheek he peered at the words and began.

Deer children, I ope yu are both settlin in to yur new place. Everyfin is all right ere so don't get worryin about me. I'll cum an see you when I can, love Ma xxx

Bobby blinked and just for second his slight shoulders sagged but then he forced a smile again. 'See, our ma's fine,' he told Peggy and she nodded. Still clutching the postcard, Bobby took Peggy's hand and as they wandered away again, Cook sighed.

'Poor little devils. It can't be easy fer 'em bein' so far away from home. But I wonder why their mam didn't mention their dad?'

'From what I can make of it their dad's a bit of a bad 'un,' Edith confided. 'Last night as I was tucking them in Peggy started to talk about him and Bobby came down on her like a ton o' bricks an' told her to shut her trap! Between you an' me I reckon he were the one who gave 'em all the bruises they had when they first arrived.'

'Hmm, an' from the bits I've picked up it sounds like their mam's a bit of a one an' all,' Cook commented. She glanced around quickly to make sure that the children weren't within earshot and went on, 'It sounds to me like their mam is on the game. You know . . . on the streets . . .'

'Surely not!' Sunday looked shocked but Cook was quite adamant. 'They dropped it out that she goes out after dark . . . to work. An' if she comes back an' she's got no money their dad wallops her. When she has, he takes it all off her and goes to the pub.'

'Poor thing.' Sunday looked distressed. 'Perhaps that's the only way she knows of making money, so who are we to judge her? If their father is a bully the poor soul probably doesn't have any choice.'

'That might be why the children were in such a state when they arrived,' Edith chipped in. 'If he's takin' all their money no wonder they didn't have anythin' decent to wear.'

'Well, at least they do now,' Sunday said kindly. A couple of days before Giles had driven Edith into town and she had come back loaded with new clothes for them, so with those and the ones from the attic the children were now very well rigged out. Sunday had a sneaking suspicion that Edith had bought some of the clothes with her own money and she could hardly believe the change in the woman. Since the children had arrived, she seemed to have blossomed and already it was clear that she adored them. Sunday just hoped that this wouldn't lead to heartache for her when the children had to return home, but for now she was content to see Edith so happy. They would face the separation when they had to.

Chapter Twenty-Six

'My, don't you both look just beautiful!' Edith said proudly as she surveyed the children dressed and ready for their first day at the village school, the following week.

Peggy's hair was tied into two neat plaits with red ribbons that matched the little kilt she was wearing, while Bobby was squirming in his smart shirt, tie and grey trousers.

'Why's we 'ave to go anyway?' he muttered, rubbing the toe of his highly polished shoe across the flagstones in the kitchen. He would much sooner have spent his time in the stables with Giles and the horses.

'To learn your lessons of course, young man,' Edith responded brightly as Cook looked on with an indulgent smile on her face.

'I can already read an' write,' he objected sulkily, but Edith didn't waver.

'So, you can but there's still a lot more to learn. Oh . . . and don't forget to wear your name tags an' take your gas masks.

Bobby frowned as she tied the name tag she had made for him about his neck and tucked it down underneath his shirt before doing the same to Peggy. She then lifted the two little boxes she had prepared for their lunch and after handing them one each she nodded at George who was waiting to take them to school in the horse and trap. That, at least, Bobby was pleased about; he loved the trap and Edith was sure he would have driven around in it all day had he been able to.

'Come on then,' George said amiably. 'Say ta-ra to Cook an' Edith. Yer don't want to be late on yer first day now, do yer?'

Edith quickly planted a kiss on each cheek, much to Bobby's disgust, then he reluctantly followed George from the kitchen, leaving Edith with tears in her eyes.

'Eeh, I hope they'll be all right,' she commented to the cook and the rosy-cheeked woman grinned.

'Now why ever wouldn't they be? They'll be meetin' some o' their mates from home there no doubt, an' anyway they'll be back afore yer know it.'

'I dare say you're right,' Edith said sadly as she moved to the window to get a last glimpse of them, then turning about she tried to concentrate on her chores and put the children from her mind.

'How did they go in?' she asked George the second he arrived back.

George lifted his cap to scratch his wiry head and grinned. 'Right as ninepence. Most o' the children that have been evacuated from London were there this mornin' from what I could see of it in the playground, so happen they'll meet up wi' some of their mates.'

Cissie who had just arrived nodded in agreement. 'O' course they will so stop frettin', Edith. They'll both be right as rain, you'll see.' She collected the lavender polish and went into the hallway to begin polishing the mahogany bannister rails as George went to stable the horse.

She glanced up as the post came through the door and picking it up, she noticed an official-looking envelope at the top of the

185

pile. Guessing instantly what it was, she took it through to the kitchen.

'This is fer you,' she told Giles with a catch in her voice. He had just popped in for a tea break and he slit the envelope and read what was inside as they all looked on.

'I've passed my exams and I've to report to a training centre in Wiltshire next Wednesday,' he told them.

The mood in the kitchen became solemn. None of them had had any doubt that he would pass the exams with flying colours. During the past few weeks, other than taking the children in, the war had not directly affected them but now it suddenly seemed very real.

Cook took a large white handkerchief from her apron pocket and noisily blew her nose just as Sunday came in.

'I popped over to see how the children went into school on their first . . .' Noticing the strained faces, she looked from one to the other of them before asking, 'Is something wrong?'

'Not at all.' It was Giles who broke the silence that had settled in the room. 'I've been accepted into the RAF and have just received the date to start my training. I shall be leaving early next Wednesday.'

'Oh . . . I see.' Like the others Sunday was deflated at the thought of what lay ahead of him, but she plastered a smile onto her face. 'Well at least you can make your plans now,' she said, managing to keep her voice cheerful. 'And I'm sure George will do a sterling job of looking after the horses till this is all over.'

'Huh! And I wonder how long that will be,' Cissie said pessimistically.

'I'm afraid that's a question none of us can answer,' Sunday sighed. 'But we won the last war and I'm sure with fine young men like Giles fighting for us we shall do the same this time.'

186

'Of course, we will,' Cook said. 'And in the meantime, till you leave I intend to cook you all your favourites.'

'That sounds good to me.' Giles quickly drank the rest of his tea and slid from his chair. 'But now if you'll excuse me, I'd best go and break the news to Grandad.'

The women stood silently, each of them thinking the same: 'Dear God, keep him safe!'

Later that afternoon, Edith went to collect the children from school, insisting that the walk would do them all good. She was amongst the first there, standing at the school railings waiting for the bell to ring.

Without even realising it there was a broad smile on her face. She had missed them terribly and the day had seemed endless, but the smile slipped away the second they walked out of the school and she clapped eyes on them. As usual Peggy was gripping tightly to her brother's hand and she looked much as she had that morning. But the same couldn't be said for Bobby for he looked as if he too had been in the war. His tie was skew-whiff, there was a hole in the knee of his brand-new trousers and he had the beginnings of a black eye forming.

A teacher was walking with them and, once they reached Edith, she drew her to one side to tell her, 'I'm afraid there was a small altercation in the playground this afternoon between Bobby and a child from the same area of London as him.'

Bobby scowled at her as he scuffed at the ground with the toe of his shoe.

'I see, an' has this boy been dealt with?' Edith asked indignantly.

'I have spoken to the family he is staying with,' the teacher assured her. 'And hopefully this will be an end to it. Isn't that so, Bobby?'

He sniffed. 'All depends on wevver or not he says bad fings about me ma again,' he shot back defensively.

The teacher shook her head and after a nod at Edith she strode away as Edith turned the children towards home. 'So, who's goin' to tell me what's gone on then?'

'Eddie Burrows called our ma a whore! What's a whore, Aunty Edith?' Peggy asked innocently as colour bled into Edith's cheeks.

'It's a . . . er . . .' For one of the very rare times in her life Edith was lost for words. 'Look, let's get home an' have a look at that eye, shall we? It looks nasty.'

'This is nowt to what Eddie looks like,' Bobby growled smugly. 'I made his nose bleed an' he squealed like a stuck pig. I bet he won't call me ma that again.'

Once more, Edith didn't know what to say, so taking Peggy's hand she marched them along in silence, her lips set in a grim line.

An hour later after milk and biscuits and having his eye tended to with a lump of raw liver, which Cook swore would take the swelling down, the children pottered off to find Giles, while Edith sat down in the kitchen to repair Bobby's trousers.

'I can't believe I'm having to patch them after the first time he's worn them,' she told Cook regretfully. 'An' he looked so smart when he set off fer school this mornin'.'

'Aye, well that's lads fer yer,' Cook replied. 'My two were just the same at that age; always into scraps, they were. But what was the fight about?'

'It seems that one of the evacuees that lived near Bobby called his ma a *whore*.'

'Really?' Cook's eyes stretched wide. 'An' from bits you've picked up from the children there could happen to be some truth in it, eh?'

Edith shrugged. 'There could be,' she admitted. 'And I have to say that I'm a bit disappointed she hasn't bothered writin' to 'em again. You'd think she'd want to know how they were gettin' on, wouldn't you?'

'If their dad is as bad as he sounds it could be that she's glad they're out o' the way somewhere safe.' Cook shook her head. 'Whatever the reason, I've caught Bobby lookin' for the postman every mornin', poor little tyke. I've noticed he rarely mentions his dad but to hear him you'd think his ma wore a halo.'

She got on with what she was doing then, preparing one of Giles's favourites – steak and ale pie. After all, she reasoned, he wouldn't be there for her to spoil for much longer and the thought made tears sting at the back of her eyes.

At that moment Livvy was just entering the stable where she found Giles talking to the children.

'Giles is goin' to go an' start his trainin' next Wednesday,' Bobby informed her excitedly. Giles was fast becoming his hero.

'Is he now?' Livvy suddenly felt as if someone had thumped her in the stomach, although her voice was level as she went on, 'I bet you wish you could go with him and learn to fly aeroplanes too, don't you, Bobby?'

'Not 'alf!' Bobby's eyes took on a dreamy look, until Peggy

189

grasped his hand and dragged him off towards the orchard, leaving the two young adults alone.

'So . . . you'll soon be off then?'

Giles nodded as Livvy tried to think of something appropriate to say. What could you say to someone who was prepared to risk his life for his king and country?

'I, er . . . hope the training goes well,' she muttered eventually.

'Thank you.' His deep-blue eyes were staring into hers and she felt her cheeks begin to burn before she quickly turned away.

'Right, I'd best get on then.' She almost tripped over her own feet in her haste to put some distance between them and all the while he watched her, with an amused little smile on his face, although he said not a single word.

'What's wrong with you?' Kathy enquired, when Livvy spilled into the kitchen shortly after with a sombre look on her face.

'Nothing!' Livvy bent to stroke Daisy's head and the little girl took her attention from the brightly coloured wooden bricks she was happily playing with to glance up and give her a toothy smile. 'Giles just told me he'll be leaving to start his training soon.'

'Oh, I see.'

'See what?' Livvy said defensively. 'It's no skin off my nose what he does, is it?' And with that she stormed away upstairs, leaving Kathy with a thoughtful expression on her face as she finished changing Thomas's trousers. He was almost potty-trained now but still had the odd accident.

When she had finished, he toddled off to sit beside his sister and she smiled sadly. She could quite understand Livvy's concerns about Giles going away. Could Livvy have known it she was worried about the welfare of two men: Ben and David. But at least she knew exactly what David was doing. She had no idea at all where was Ben was. She had still not heard so much as a word from him since the day he had left. Her only comfort was in knowing that it was the young men who were enlisting at present. Surely Ben would be too old now for active service? She looked at her children. They were her whole world and she had taken to being a mother like a duck to water. In fact, she couldn't imagine her life without the twins now and it hurt to know that Ben was missing so much. But all she could do was pray that eventually his conscience would get the better of him and he would come home. With a sigh she went to put the dirty nappy into the soak bucket. Somehow, they were all just going to have to get on with things as best they could.

Chapter Twenty-Seven

Liverpool Docks, late November 1939

As the noise from the street outside his bedroom window grew louder, Ben groaned and pulled the covers over his head in an attempt to shut it out. His head was throbbing, and his mouth felt like the bottom of a bird cage, as he tried to lose himself in sleep again. But it was no good. The noise was growing louder as the workers tramped towards the docks, so he dragged himself to the edge of the bed and peered at the thin curtains through narrowed eyes. For a moment he felt disorientated, but then gradually the night before began to come back to him, and he groaned again. He had no idea how many pints of beer he must have drunk – he'd lost count after ten – but he was certainly paying for it now. Glancing down, he saw that he was still fully dressed, and shame coursed through him. He'd done well to get back to his room, he supposed, considering the state he must have been in. He could remember going into the Dog and Duck and ordering a beer then getting into conversation with some chaps in army uniform. After that everything was blurry.

Suddenly something occurred to him and he reached down

to feel for his wallet, which had been in the back pocket of his trousers. It was still there but a quick examination when he opened it revealed that it was empty. There had been twenty pounds in there at the beginning of the night and now every penny was gone. Whether he had spent it, or it had been stolen he had no idea, but he knew that he couldn't go on like this. Thankfully the majority of the money he had swindled from his stepmother was safely locked away in the bank but even so he was aware that it wouldn't last long if he went on the way he was.

A sharp rap at the door had his hands rising to his head, which felt as if it was about to burst, as the rasping voice of his landlady sailed through the door. 'Mr Brannin'. Yer breakfast is ready. I ain't keepin' it warm so if yer want it yer to come down right now!'

He gulped. Just the thought of food made his stomach revolt. 'Thanks, Mrs Jennings. I'll give breakfast a miss this morning, if you don't mind.'

'Huh! Yer could have told me last night. All that good food goin' to waste.'

The woman's voice grew quieter as she thumped off down the stairs and Ben gave a wry smile. Good food indeed! Mrs Jennings's breakfasts consisted of a rasher of bacon swimming with grease, an overcooked sausage and an egg that was so hard he might easily have broken his knife on it. Still, he supposed for the rent he paid for his room he shouldn't really expect a lot more. Glancing about, he took in the gloomy surroundings. An old wardrobe stood against one wall with a chest of drawers that had seen better days standing beside it. There was an old washstand with a cracked jug and bowl standing on it and to the side of that a chair with a very wonky leg. That was it apart

193

from the bed, which again had seen better days. The mattress was so hard he sometimes felt as if he had slept on a door – when he did manage to sleep that was.

The streets beyond the warehouses that led to the docks were full of such lodging houses. Cheap and cheerful, his landlady had told him, but he hadn't managed to find anything cheerful about the place as yet. Most of them were inhabited by sailors who came and went on the ships that docked there. Dotted in amongst the lodging houses were a fair number of brothels and Ben had taken full advantage of them too. It was a far cry from the smart hotels he had stayed in when he first left Treetops. Strangely the novelty of staying in such places and being waited on hand and foot had soon worn off and Mrs Jennings's lodging house was quite good enough for him now. He had soon discovered that you could be just as lonely in a palace as you could in a slum.

He supposed to some it must appear that he had the world at his feet. He had money in the bank, and he was carefree and single and able to come and go whenever he pleased, so why, he wondered, was his new lifestyle giving him no joy? At the most unlikely times he would find himself thinking of Treetops and the life he had led there, and he would become maudlin. He missed his comfortable bedroom, the horses, and although he denied it to himself, even the people. And then there was the guilt. For most of the time he could convince himself that Sunday had deserved all she had got – she had never loved him as she did Kathy and Livvy. But then a little voice would whisper, 'But she *did*! You *know* she did.' And the only way he could quieten the voice was to drown himself in drink. Not forgetting Kathy! *Kathy*, the thought of her made him bow his head. She had told him she loved him, and he had taken full advantage of the fact just to get back at Sunday. He had always known how horrified

Sunday would be if ever she found out about their relationship, which she undoubtedly would have done by now. There was nothing he could have done that would hurt her more. Kathy had been just a young innocent girl with a crush on a much older man. He was old enough to be her father and they had been brought up in the same family. He had grown up with Kathy's mother, for God's sake! Sunday would look upon their affair as almost incestuous and he supposed he couldn't blame her.

His thoughts raced back across his life and he realised suddenly with a little shock that the only time he had been truly happy was when he was married to Maggie, the love of his life. His thoughts turned to his birth mother, who had abandoned him on the steps of the workhouse when he was a newborn. He'd never even met her. Did she not love him, then? Is that why she abandoned him? Then Sunday and Tom had adopted him and he could still see the look of shock on his father's face as he showed him the letter his mother had sent him. But his father had seemed happy to know he had a natural child. It was Sunday who had found it difficult to come to terms with it. His bitterness had begun then, even though his father and Sunday tried to make things up to him.

After he'd returned home from the war with his scars, there had been times when he had almost dared to let himself believe that Sunday truly loved him again. But then the girls had come along, and it felt as though they replaced him in her affections, and he was once again left out. After all, how could she ever love him as much as she did her own daughter? And as for Kathy, well, Kitty had always been everyone's favourite – even his for a time – so it stood to reason that Kitty's daughter would take that special place in Sunday's heart.

If it hadn't been for Maggie, he would have felt pushed aside.

But Maggie *had* loved him and married him, and for the first time in his life he had discovered what it was to feel truly happy. He had thought things couldn't get any better, but they had when she'd informed him that he was going to be a father. How he had looked forward to holding his child, his very own flesh and blood, in his arms, and to having his very own little family. But even that dream had been snatched away when both Maggie and his son had died in childbirth.

For years he had been haunted by the sight of his love lying pale and serene in her coffin with his tiny son nestled in her arms against her. Sometimes when he remembered, the pain was so intense that he was sure it would kill him. And then Kathy had declared her feelings for him, and he had seen a way to wreak revenge on everyone for the hurt he had suffered. But what was done was done now, there could be no going back to undo it, and he could only hope that Kathy would go on to meet a nice young man her own age.

Dragging himself from the edge of the bed he staggered across to the window and flipped aside the curtains, gasping with pain as the bright light attacked his eyes like daggers. Between the gaps in the warehouses he could see ships of all shapes and sizes bobbing in the murky water. He turned back and that was when he saw the official-looking document lying on the chest of drawers. As he lifted it and began to read his eyes stretched wide and his mouth fell open.

Will report for training in two weeks' time . . . His mouth fell open as suddenly everything began to come back to him. He had been with Bean, his rather disreputable friend, and after spending some time with the young army chaps, he suddenly recalled Bean getting all patriotic and suggesting they should sign up to do their bit for king and country.

A loud hammering on his door made his eyes swing towards it and when he opened it, Bean, looking somewhat dishevelled, burst into the room brandishing an identical letter to the one he was reading.

'Bleedin' 'ell, matie!' Bean, who was considerably younger than Ben, ran a hand distractedly through his thick, brown hair. 'What the 'ell 'ave we let 'usselves in for?'

Bean was a well-known figure about the docks. He made his living – a very comfortable one – wheeling and dealing with the goods that came in from abroad that just happened to fall into his possession. He would openly admit that he lived by his wits and had never done an honest day's work in his life. He was always the life and soul of any party but today his face was pasty, and Ben saw that his hands were shaking. 'Do yer reckon we can get outta this?' he asked, his voice cracking with fear. 'If we go back to the recruitment office an' tell the blokes there we were half-cut an' didn't know what we were doin' surely they'll tell us to rip these up?'

Ben's lips set in a grim line and suddenly he felt as sober as a judge as he recalled what it had been like in the First World War.

'No chance. It says here that because of my age I shall be a horse handler. What are you going to do?'

Bean swallowed. 'I'm army trainin'. That means I'll be sent to the front, don't it?'

Ben nodded. 'I should say so, but what made us do it?'

'Them young army chaps we were keepin' company with,' Bean said bitterly. 'They were eggin' us on an' sayin' as we were yeller bellies an' the next thing I remember we were at one o' the recruitment offices.'

Ben sighed. 'Well, we've done it good an' proper now. We've got no choice but to go.'

197

'You speak fer yourself. I ain't goin' to be shot down. I'm off. Me old mum will understand. There ain't many pickin's round 'ere anyway since the war started. Half the goods ain't comin' in anymore so I'll clear orf an' try me luck somewhere else till this bloody war is over.'

Ben shrugged. He wouldn't have expected any more of the lad, if truth be known. He was as shallow as a stream.

'An' what are *you* gonna do?'

Bean's voice brought Ben's thoughts back to the present. 'I shall be going,' he said quietly. This time there would be no one left behind to worry about him or write to him as there had been the last time. It was a sobering thought. Yes, he would go. Perhaps this was justice for what he had done. But first he intended to put his house in order . . . just in case he didn't come back.

Chapter Twenty-Eight

With his back to the station, Giles took a deep breath and took one last lingering look at his adopted hometown. It was market day and people were milling everywhere. He had always loved the market, especially the cattle market, and he would miss wandering about the stalls heaving with livestock. He had said his goodbyes to the family back at Treetops, insisting they didn't need to accompany him to the station, but now he was wishing he had allowed his grandfather to come with him. It was clear he wasn't the only one leaving to join the war. Young men were standing about surrounded by weeping mothers, sisters, wives and girlfriends, and turning about Giles kept his eyes trained straight ahead as he moved purposefully towards the platform, suddenly feeling very lonely. And then a figure caught his eye and his steps slowed before she turned and saw him.

'Livvy!' Giles couldn't keep the surprise from his voice as he came abreast of her.

She smiled to hide her embarrassment. Suddenly she wondered if this had been such a good idea after all. She didn't even know what had prompted her to come but she supposed that now she was here she may as well make the best of it.

'I, er . . . didn't get chance to say goodbye last night so being as I had to pop out on an errand from the office, I thought I'd call by to wish you all the best.'

'I see . . . thank you. It was good of you to think of me.' They faced each other, each looking decidedly uncomfortable and neither of them quite knowing what to say.

'So, will you be getting leave during your training?' It was Livvy who broke the silence.

He shrugged. 'I'm not sure, to be honest, but I shall certainly do my best to.' They were standing in the sunshine on the platform and he noticed the way it had turned her hair to liquid gold. And those eyes – they reminded him of the colour of the bluebells in the woods in the spring. It was funny, he'd never noticed how pretty she was before, he thought, but then they had always seemed to be at cross purposes so perhaps he just hadn't taken much notice.

A shrill whistle in the distance heralded the approach of the train and suddenly they were surrounded by people all clinging to each other and saying their tearful goodbyes.

'This is it then.' She looked at him levelly, at a loss for words again and he nodded as the train came into view further along the track.

'Yes . . . this is it.'

'You, er . . . just take good care of yourself and I'll look forward to seeing you when you come home on leave.'

Without thinking she took an involuntary step towards him and suddenly his arm was about her waist and his lips were on hers. Just for a moment she melted against him, responding to his touch, then self-consciously she took a step back, her cheeks aflame.

'Crikey, all this war stuff is making us all sentimental,' she said, suddenly her usual off-hand self again and he grinned, displaying a set of very white, straight teeth.

'Yes, that must be what it is.' The train had pulled into the station now and people were scrambling to get aboard. 'I . . . I'd better go.'

'Of course.' She inclined her head and watched as he climbed aboard.

Once on the train he leaned out of the window. 'Look after Grandad and the horses for me, and thanks for coming, Livvy.'

She nodded as the porter strode along the platform, blowing his whistle and slamming the doors. And then there was a loud whistle as the engine chugged back to life and slowly the train pulled away with Giles still leaning out of the window waving to her. She waved back till the train was lost to sight around a corner and then slowly her fingers rose to touch her lips where he had kissed her.

Don't be daft, it was just a spur-of-the-moment thing, it didn't mean anything, she told herself. And yet as she walked despondently away, her heart was thumping so loudly she feared people would hear it and there were tears in her eyes.

Three days after Giles had left for training, Livvy came home from work to find Peggy at the lodge playing with the twins. Bobby was now allowing her out of his sight for short periods, so long as his little sister was with people he knew, which Edith took to be a good sign. The twins were always getting into all sorts of trouble, much to Peggy's amusement. Their hair had grown and formed a halo of springy curls about their small heads and with their cheeky smiles and their deep-blue eyes everyone found them irresistible and spoiled them shamelessly.

'They love having Peggy to play with,' her mother remarked as she ushered her to the table for her evening meal, which she had been keeping warm for her. Kathy had slipped over to Cissie's cottage to pick up some sweet little nightshirts she had made for the twins. They were growing out of the ones they had again.

'Mm.' Livvy began to half-heartedly push the food about her plate and Sunday frowned.

'Livvy . . .' she began cautiously. 'You don't seem yourself. Is something troubling you?'

Livvy licked her lips and keeping her eyes on the plate she said quietly, 'There is actually. You see I've been thinking that I should be doing my bit towards this war.'

'In what way?' Sunday raised her eyebrow.

'I, er . . . I've been thinking of enlisting, as it happens.' Seeing the look of horror on her mother's face she rushed on. 'Lots of girls are doing it. I mean, it's not as if we'd be sent to the front like the men. They need people to work in the NAAFIs, as drivers or as radio operators, all sorts of things. What do you think?'

'I think it's a *ridiculous* idea,' Sunday answered sharply.

'But why? I mean I understand that the war hasn't really affected us in the countryside yet, but we need every hand if we're to win this war – men and women alike.'

Kathy had just come into the kitchen in time to hear what her sister said and after staring at them both for a moment she piped up, 'Well, I think that's an admirable idea. I'll tell you now if I didn't have the twins, I'd be signing up to work in one of the field hospitals.'

Sunday shot her a withering look, but Kathy stood her ground. 'Livvy is right, Mum,' she pointed out. 'Women are already doing the jobs that their men did before they signed up so why shouldn't Livvy be allowed to do her bit if she feels it's right? She's a grown woman and quite able to decide for herself what she wants to do.'

Livvy smiled at her gratefully as Sunday stood nervously wringing her hands. The children had become silent as they picked up on the tense atmosphere and eventually Sunday let out a long sigh. She knew when she was beaten and deep down she also knew that Livvy should be allowed to make her own decisions.

'Then in that case I suppose it's your choice. So, what will happen next?'

'I think I'll call into one of the enlisting offices in my dinner hour tomorrow to make a few enquiries.'

Her mother nodded. It seemed there was no more to be said.

Two days later Livvy enrolled in the WAAF. 'I shall be going to London to do six weeks' basic training,' she told Kathy and her mother when she got home later that day. 'Then if I pass, I'm going to put my name down to become a balloon operative.'

'But won't that involve being in dangerous places where barrage balloons need to be flown?' Sunday asked in a croaky voice.

Livvy smiled. 'I will have to do my training in London,' she admitted. 'But then I dare say we'll get shifted about the country.'

'And when will you have to leave?'

'I should get my papers within the week.' Livvy gave her

mother's hand an encouraging squeeze and John, who had popped in to bring some winter vegetables from the cottage garden, gave her a broad smile.

'I'm proud of you,' he told her. 'And I'm sure you'll look very smart in your WAAF uniform.'

Sunday blinked back tears and added her praise to his. 'I'm proud of you too, darling. But . . . I shall miss you dreadfully and worry about you every minute you're away.'

'I shall be fine,' Livvy said breezily, although were she to admit it she was a little nervous. Still, it was done now and there could be no going back.

Chapter Twenty-Nine

January 1940

'Have you seen this?' George asked, stabbing his finger at a page in the newspaper he was reading as he and Cissie sat in their cottage one evening in January. 'It says the River Thames has frozen over for the first time since 1818.'

'It don't surprise me,' Cissie replied from her seat by the fire where she was darning socks. 'I can't remember ever having such a bad winter. It's enough to freeze the hairs off a brass monkey out there an' there's no sign of it stoppin' yet. Still, at least the twins an' the children are enjoyin' the snow. It's a job to get young Bobby off that sledge you made for him.' Her face became solemn then as she remarked, 'I don't know why you even bother to read that paper anymore. It's full o' doom an' gloom. Another two million young men have been called up an' now we've got rationin'. We're fairly lucky 'ere but folks as live in the towns won't fare so well.' She eyed the toast he'd just spread with a generous helping of butter disapprovingly. 'An' you've got your entire week's ration on your toast. Two ounces a week is your lot. Unless you want to use marge. An' none of yer four teaspoons of sugar in yer tea

205

anymore neither. Twelve ounces! I use more than that when I bake one cake.'

George snorted; he had a sweet tooth and was already finding it difficult to adjust, but then he supposed they were still going to be a lot better off than most folks, plus they'd been through it all before – and not that long ago.

'Sunday had a letter off Livvy yesterday,' Cissie went on. 'Poor lass says the huts they're havin' to sleep in are freezin' but she's almost finished her trainin' now so hopefully wherever they transfer her will have a bit better accommodation.'

At that moment Livvy was sitting beneath her blanket in a hut with four other girls shivering like a jelly.

'It's so cold,' Nell Wiseman, one of the girls, complained. Nell was from Earlsdon in Coventry and was a sturdily built girl with straight, mousy hair and a spattering of freckles across her nose. Of the four other girls she had started training with, Nell was Livvy's closest friend. With Nell so tall and plump and Livvy so petite and delicate they looked an unlikely duo but nonetheless they had hit it off as soon as they'd met.

'I would have thought you'd be used to it by now,' Livvy responded.

Amanda in the next bed snorted. 'How is one *ever* expected to get used to living in such appalling conditions,' she complained as her straight, white teeth chattered like castanets. Unlike Nell, who came from a very working-class background, Amanda, who was the only child of wealthy parents, had been brought up in Bristol and had had the best education that money could buy.

Her father owned a string of restaurants – a fact she never tired of telling them. In the next bed was Susan, a farmer's daughter from Yorkshire. She was a sweet-natured girl with flame-red hair who was so homesick that she cried herself to sleep every night. And finally, in the very end bed nearest the draughty door, unfortunately for her, was Pauline. She hailed from London where she had been brought up in an orphanage. There had been six of them when they started but Pat had injured her ankle during the first week of physical training so that had been the end of her WAAF career.

Now Susan extricated her arm from the blanket and glanced at her wristwatch. 'The NAAFI should be open any time now for some cocoa and supper,' she commented as Livvy rose to throw some more wood onto the stove that stood in the middle of the room. It was a temperamental thing, often throwing out more smoke than heat.

'Ouch!' Livvy cried as she opened the door and it spat at her. 'I swear this ruddy thing waits for me to do that!' She hastily threw the log she was holding in and slammed the door shut, causing smoke to billow into the hut and make them all cough.

Amanda quickly took out her compact and applied lipstick and powder to her nose, then fluffing her hair up she asked, 'So who's coming then?'

As they had all discovered, Amanda hated being seen without her make-up, whereas the rest of them were usually bundled up in layers of clothing just intent on keeping as warm as they could with no thought to how they looked.

They all rose and when Nell opened the door a gust of snow blew in at them.

'Ugh! Bloody weather,' Susan grumbled as they stepped out

into the raging blizzard. 'Perhaps we should have put the kettle on the stove and made our own drinks tonight!'

'Ah, but some of those handsome RAF chaps could be in,' Amanda pointed out.

The RAF base was not far from theirs and when the pilots weren't flying they often used the NAAFI for a meal.

Susan and Livvy exchanged an amused glance, then, heads bent, they picked their way through the deepening snow and just for a moment Livvy thought of the warm, cosy little kitchen back at the lodge.

In the very kitchen that Livvy was thinking of, Sunday was just opening the door to John, who had popped in to check that all was well. Their relationship had undergone a subtle change since he had made the unexpected proposal. For a time, they had lost their easy relationship and she had felt slightly embarrassed when in his company and had stopped visiting Treetops as frequently as she had previously. But since the departure of Giles and Livvy they were becoming closer again, finding comfort in each other's company.

'How are you all?' he asked as Sunday quickly closed the door behind him and he stamped the snow from his boots. Already his coat was beginning to steam in the warm atmosphere, and she smiled as she ushered him to the fireside chair and hurried off to set the kettle on the range.

'We're fine. Kathy is upstairs getting the twins to sleep.' Without asking she spooned tea leaves into the pot from the caddy and lifted down two cups from the shelf. She knew exactly how John liked his tea. 'Any news from Giles?'

He shook his head as he held his hands out to the leaping flames. 'Not yet, but Cissie mentioned today that you'd had a letter from Livvy.'

'Yes, yesterday.' She lifted it down from behind the clock on the mantelshelf and handed it to him to read.

He smiled as his eyes scanned the page. 'It sounds like she's rather missing her home comforts.'

Sunday nodded as she poured the boiling water into the pot.

'Which brings me around to what I was going to suggest . . .'

Sunday raised a quizzical eyebrow. 'Oh yes, and what would that be then?'

He coughed to clear his throat before going on. 'Well, with the weather being so bad you and Kathy are a bit stuck in here with the twins and I was thinking that perhaps you'd all like to move back into the house. Purely on a no-strings basis, of course,' he added hastily when he saw her eyes widen. Then with a sigh he said, 'Look . . . I realise I was probably out of order when I proposed to you and you were most likely right – we probably are both a bit long in the tooth to be starting a new relationship – but that shouldn't mean we can't enjoy each other's company. I'm missing Giles and I know you're missing Livvy. And this place . . .' He spread his hands as he looked about the small room. 'As comfortable as you've made it it's hardly on the level of Treetops, is it? The twins would have more room to play and you'd be doing me a favour. You and Kathy could help Edith with Peggy and Bobby and I know they'd love to have the twins there.

'There's something else to think of as well. Anderson shelters are popping up everywhere. I was thinking that we could make the cellar suitable for a shelter just in case of a raid. You'd all be so much safer there. I think we've all been lulled into a false sense of security with us living out in the sticks. But what we have to remember is that all the car factories in Coventry are now making tanks or ammunition and they'll be a target. What if the Jerries decide to randomly drop bombs on us on the way there or back? Won't you at least consider it, if not for yourself for the children?'

Sunday paused in the act of pouring the tea and bit her lip as she thought about what he'd said. 'All right,' she agreed eventually. 'I will think on it, but I'm not making any promises, mind. I need to know what Kathy thinks of the idea too.'

'That's good enough,' he answered with a beaming smile and they went on to talk of other things.

But when Sunday relayed the conversation to her daughter the next morning, Kathy had very mixed feelings about the idea.

The thought of living back in her old home was tempting and because of his many kindnesses, she had long since lost any feelings of resentment she'd felt towards John. And she could see the sense in what he said; they would all be much safer there if the bombings were about to start. But still, like her mother, Kathy had her pride.

'It's very kind of him,' she said cautiously as she watched the twins pottering happily about. 'And John is right, we would all be safer there and the twins would have so much more room to play. But . . .' She paused. 'I suppose it would just feel strange being back there when it isn't really our home anymore. Not that I'm not grateful for the offer,' she added hastily.

'I know exactly what you mean,' Sunday agreed, much to Kathy's relief. 'I'll thank him but tell him we're happy here for now, shall I?'

Kathy nodded, hoping they were making the right decision.

As January came to a close, and much to her relief, Livvy's training had finally come to an end and the girls were waiting for the results of the test they had taken to see if they were to be accepted for the job of working the barrage balloons. There had been a lot more to it than Livvy had expected. No one would guess when they saw them flying like great grey elephants in the sky just how hard it was to get them airborne, nor how heavy and dangerous they could be for the people who operated them. Of the five of them only four would be accepted for the job and she hoped that she would be one of them.

Just then a female officer stepped into the hut, clipboard in hand, and they all instantly stood.

'Right.' The woman consulted her clipboard. 'Meadows.' Amanda instantly stepped forward with a smug smile on her face. 'Blake.' Susan was the next. 'Shaw and Wiseman.' Pauline and Nell took their place next to the others, casting a sympathetic glance at Livvy, who clearly had not been chosen as one of the balloon operatives. 'All go and report for duty,' she ordered them. 'And you, Branning, come with me.'

With a sinking heart Livvy managed a smile at her friends before following the officer from the hut with a glum look on her face. It would be just her luck to be chosen to work in the NAAFI, she thought miserably as they picked their way through the snow.

Once they had reached the office that was located at the end of the huts, the officer ushered her inside and Livvy stood before the desk, her back straight and her hands clasped behind her back, while the other woman took a seat.

'Branning, it's come to our attention that of the five of you hoping to become balloon operatives you were the quickest to pick the job up.'

Livvy was more confused than ever now. If that was the case, why had she not been chosen for the job?

'And so, what I have in mind for you is an even more important job,' the woman told her not unkindly. 'If you feel you're up to it, that is. It would of course involve a great deal more training but what we have in mind for you is a radio operator communicating with the pilots in the air.'

Livvy's eyes almost popped out of her head and a little gasp escaped her. She knew what an important job that was. Men's lives depended on the operators to guide them in and out of the airfields and also to keep track of them while they were airborne.

'So, what do you think? Would you like to do it?'

A broad smile spread across Livvy's face. 'Yes . . . ma'am, definitely.'

'Good, then go and pack your things. You'll be transported to an airfield in Lincolnshire this afternoon where your training will commence. And, Branning, don't let me down. It was me that put you forward for this. Good luck.'

'Thank you, ma'am. I promise I'll do my very best.'

Livvy was on such a high that she didn't even notice the snow leaking over the top of her boots as she raced back to the hut. She felt sad that she wouldn't get to say goodbye to her friends, though. She would probably be long gone by the time they came off duty. *Still*, she thought, *I can leave them a note telling them what's happened and asking them to keep in touch.*

Hastily she grabbed a pad and pen and scribbled a note, which she propped on Nell's bedside locker.

As soon as she was ready Livvy was transported to her new

headquarters. She couldn't help her heart beating a little faster with excitement. She knew how highly the operators were regarded, and now she had the chance to become one of them, she intended to take full advantage of the opportunity.

Chapter Thirty

May 1940

Ben sat shoulder to shoulder in the bowels of the ship with men and boys almost all of whom were many years younger than him. As the large craft ploughed through the icy seas towards their destination, Ben found, to his surprise, that he was looking forward to working with horses again; he had missed them. He knew, though, that what lay ahead wasn't going to be anything like being back in the stables at Treetops – in fact it wasn't going to be pleasant at all.

The day before he had visited a solicitor and left a letter for Sunday with strict instructions that it should be forwarded to her immediately should anything happen to him. It would be ironic, he thought, if the money he had taken so much trouble stealing from her should end up being returned.

Suddenly, the youth next to him, who had turned an alarming shade of green within minutes of leaving the port, leaned forward and deposited his breakfast all over the floor. *Poor little sod*, Ben thought as he eyed the lad, the thought of joining up had initially seemed like a big adventure but it appeared that already the reality of what he had done was coming home to him and he was openly crying. Ben awkwardly patted his shoulder, trying to ignore the stench of vomit. They were crammed in like cattle and there was no chance of cleaning the mess up. He glanced around the gloomy confines and shuddered as if someone had walked over his grave, and he wondered if this was a portent of what was to come.

David was in theatre in a field hospital in France battling to save a young man's life. He had been on duty for almost eighteen hours and his eyes were gritty from lack of sleep as he battled to stem the flow of blood from the stump of the leg he had just been forced to amputate.

The young man on the table looked to be no more than seventeen or eighteen years old at most and David's heart went out to him. Even so, he was one of the lucky ones. The two he had operated on before this boy had both died. One on the operating table and the other shortly after he had been taken back to the ward, which David looked on as his failure. Truthfully, no one could have saved them. The first had had half of his head blown away and the second had been so peppered with bullets that blood had spurted from his wounds like water from a colander. Eventually, David knew he had done all he could and as he turned from the table, rubbing his eyes wearily, the theatre sister pounced on him. 'It's time you took a rest now, Doctor. Dr Sayer will take over.'

David opened his mouth to protest but then promptly shut it again. When he was this tired it would be easy to make mistakes and his patient could pay for it.

'Very well, I'll try and catch a couple of hours sleep,' he

agreed as he snapped off his gloves. Already another wounded soldier was being wheeled into the theatre and David turned despondently and made his way to his sleeping quarters.

He was so weary that he didn't even bother to undress but simply dropped onto his bunk. He could hear the whistle and explosion of the guns in the distance as the men fought it out and again it hit him how pointless it was. There would be another influx of wounded this evening and another batch of telegrams going out to relatives informing them that they would never see their loved one again. He shut his eyes and tried to think of pleasanter things and instantly an image of Kathy and the twins flashed before his eyes. He could picture them all safe and cosy in the lodge with a lovely fire roaring up the chimney. The twins were growing like weeds and he imagined he would see a big change in them when he next got some leave. He just hoped they would remember him when he did see them again. His thoughts turned to Kathy then, but exhaustion quickly claimed him, and he slept with a smile hovering at the corners of his mouth.

In Wiltshire, Giles was facing his flight officer, back straight and arms at his side, looking straight ahead.

'You'll be pleased to know that you passed all your exams with flying colours,' the man told him. 'And so tomorrow, you'll be transferred to another airfield where you will start to fly Spitfires.'

'Sir.' Giles tried not to show how thrilled he was as he stood to attention and saluted.

Once outside he punched the air and gave a whoop of delight.

Spitfires, no less. His favourite plane. Then with a wide smile on his face he hurried away to find his friends to tell them the good news. Perhaps they'd get to have a celebration at the local pub that evening if they were all off duty. He'd have to write to his grandfather and tell him the good news too. He had an idea the old man would be quite proud of him. Whistling merrily and looking very handsome in his uniform he went on his way.

Chapter Thirty-One

November 1940

Cissie and Sunday sat together in the kitchen of the lodge listening to the wireless, which was reporting what was ever after to be known as the Coventry Blitz. It had apparently been the worst air raid of the war to date; hundreds were dead and the city lay in ruins.

'It don't bear thinkin' about.' Cissie shuddered as she thought of the devastation. Men were busily digging through the ruins of people's homes looking for bodies, and fires were raging everywhere. Even the fine old cathedral had taken a hit and people's spirits were low.

The month before the army had come to take all the horses apart from the elderly ones and Kathy and George had watched them go with tears in their eyes. Even before the horses had been taken, the beautiful gates that led into the drive of Treetops had been removed to be melted down and made into ammunition. Worse still, only months before, Nuneaton had been bombed by the Luftwaffe who had mistaken the town for Birmingham causing chaos and bringing home to them all the fact that they were now as vulnerable as the rest of the country.

All along the coast barbed wire had been strung along the beaches like lethal sparkling necklaces to try to prevent attacks from the sea and now everyone was fearful.

'It makes yer wonder where it's all goin' to end,' Cissie said fretfully and Sunday could only nod in agreement. She was now nearly seventy-one years old and sometimes recently she felt so tired that she wished she could just close her eyes and join her beloved Tom, but she knew that she wouldn't. Not until the war was over and Livvy was home safely. Only weeks before her daughter had managed to get a forty-eight-hour pass and had made a fleeting visit, much to her mother's delight.

Sunday had been shocked when she first saw her, for in the time Livvy had been away she seemed to have grown from a girl into a level-headed young woman. She held a very responsible job, and although Livvy enjoyed the challenge, Sunday knew it could be very hard sometimes. She'd told Sunday about a time when she suddenly lost contact with a pilot who was out on a mission only to learn hours later that he hadn't made it home. Even so, Livvy tried to concentrate on the ones who did make it safely back and made sure that despite a number of flirtations she never got serious with any of the young pilots. It would have been just too heartbreaking to become attached to one who might be shot down.

Kathy came into the kitchen then, to find her mother and Cissie hanging over the wireless, and sighed. She was struggling with frustration. Daisy and Thomas were a mischievous pair who kept her on her toes every minute of the day. She was looking forward to them starting school the following year when she would be able to return to part-time nursing. Admittedly both her mother and Cissie had offered to watch them for her if she wished to go back sooner but Kathy didn't feel right about placing such a responsibility on their shoulders, particularly as they were both in their seventies now.

On top of that, they were all feeling the strain of the war. Rationing was tight, even new clothes were difficult to come by now and they had had to resort to trying new recipes as the food rationing got tighter still. Only the day before Cissie had baked a carrot cake that Thomas had declared was 'disgusting', which had won him a clip around the ear, despite their amusement.

'Well yer either eat it or go wi'out,' Cissie had told him sternly. 'We none of us get enough sugar to go wastin' it on cakes now an' the prime minister keeps tellin' us, we're to make do an' mend.'

Thomas had gone off in a huff, although Daisy had eaten his and then asked for another slice. But then Daisy was like a bottomless pit and would eat anything if it was halfway edible.

All their thoughts were gloomy, until Cissie suddenly said, 'I'm a bit concerned about young Bobby. He's taken to seekin' out the newspapers when Mr John has read 'em an' he's frettin' somethin' terrible about the bombin's in London. He's worried about his mam an' I'm feared he'll take it into his head to try an' go an' check she's all right.'

'But he's far too young to try and go all that distance alone,' Kathy said worriedly as she watched Daisy's rear end disappear into the Morrison shelter that took up one wall in the kitchen. It was a great cumbersome thing, but John had insisted they should have it just in case there was an unexpected air raid and they didn't have time to get down the drive to the cellar at Treetops. Both Kathy and Sunday hated it, but the twins had made it into a little den, which Kathy supposed was something, although how they were all supposed to squash into it should the need ever arise, she had no idea.

'You'll just have to keep a close eye on him and see that he doesn't disappear,' Kathy told Cissie, and the older woman snorted with derision.

'Oh, an' just *how* am I supposed to do that, may I ask? I ain't got eyes in the back o' me head an' he does have to go to school. Still, Edith is keepin' as close an eye as she can, bless her. She surely loves them little 'uns as if they were her own.'

They all nodded in agreement. Edith adored both Peggy and Bobby and thanks to her loving care they were now almost unrecognisable from the poor little waifs they had been when they first arrived.

Kathy filled the kettle at the sink, and she had just placed it on the hob to boil when there was a rap on the front door.

'I'll go,' she volunteered and seconds later the women in the kitchen heard her scream with delight. 'David . . . whatever are you doing here? Why didn't you let us know you were coming? Oh, hark at me rattling on, come on in out of the cold.' She took his arm, which seemed much thinner than she remembered, and hauled him over the step, then laughing she prodded him towards the kitchen, saying, 'Look who's here. Isn't this a lovely surprise?' Turning back to David she told him bossily, 'Give me your coat and hat and get yourself over by the fire to get warm. I was just making some tea. How long are you here for?'

He slowly removed his coat and after greeting Cissie and Sunday he answered, 'I've been sent home for two weeks leave. I'm actually on my way to stay with my parents in Yorkshire but thought I'd pop in and see you on the way. It seems ages since I've seen Daisy and Thomas.'

Suddenly two little heads appeared out of the Morrison shelter and when they saw who it was Daisy screeched with happiness and charged across to him, while Thomas hung back shyly with his thumb jammed into his mouth

'Crikey, you two have certainly grown.' David chuckled as he tousled Daisy's hair and held his other hand out to her brother.

'Have you got anything for us, Uncle David?' Daisy asked hopefully, remembering how he had never come without a treat for them and he laughed.

'As it happens, I have.' He fumbled in his jacket pocket and produced two sugar candy canes, causing the twins' eyes to grow round with anticipation.

'Thank you,' they chorused greedily. 'Can we eat them now, Mummy?'

Kathy gave them an indulgent smile. 'I suppose so, just so long as you promise to eat your dinner,' she warned. Then turning her attention back to their guest, she said, 'You may be on your way home to Yorkshire but surely you could spare us just one night of your company at least? You could sleep in Livvy's room. Is that all right, Mum?'

'Absolutely, you can stay for as long as you like,' Sunday told him warmly, noting the way Kathy's cheeks were glowing. Could it be that the old saying was true? Absence makes the heart grow fonder.

'In that case I'd be delighted to,' David answered gratefully. 'To be honest I am a bit tired. All the train stations leading into Coventry are closed because the lines have been bombed and it was a bit of a mission to get here. I've been travelling since early yesterday morning. I'm sure I could sleep the clock round!'

'That's settled then. Now how about I get you something to eat?' Kathy prattled on, feeling quite ridiculous. Her heart was thumping so loudly she was afraid they would hear it and it was all she could do to stop herself from throwing her arms about him. It had been almost a year since they had last seen each other, and she could hardly believe how he had changed in that time. He had lost so much weight that his clothes hung off him and his face looked haggard, but then she supposed that was to be expected with the terrible sights he had probably seen and the gruelling hours he had to work.

He had written to her every single week and although he had always tried to keep his letters light-hearted, she had glimpsed the heartache behind them. David was a very conscientious doctor and she could only imagine how terrible it must be for him to be presented time and time again with patients that he had no chance of saving.

In no time at all she had made him big doorstop cheese sandwiches, just to keep him going until dinner time, she explained, and after he had eaten them and drunk three cups of tea a tiny bit of colour began to creep back into his cheeks, although he still looked as if he was about to drop with exhaustion.

'Right, it's up to bed for you, young man,' Kathy told him bossily as the twins giggled. 'We'll wake you up for your evening meal.'

'Are you quite sure you don't mind?' David asked. The last thing he wanted was to be any trouble, but Kathy was determined.

'Of course we don't mind. I don't want you falling asleep where you sit. Come on, I'll show you which is Livvy's room. The bed is all made up although it is quite cold up there. I'm afraid we can't manage fires in the bedrooms now that coal is harder to get. But never mind, once you're in bed I'll bring you a hot-water bottle up and you'll be snug as a bug in a rug.'

David gave everyone a weak smile and followed Kathy up the stairs as meekly as a lamb.

'There,' she said, opening the bedroom door with a flourish before hurrying across the room to close the curtains. 'Hop in and get warm. You look worn out and you've come such a long way.'

'I've come from hell,' he said quietly, and his eyes were haunted as he thought of all the terrible things he had witnessed.

'I've no doubt you have but try not to think about it for now and get some sleep. Things won't look quite so bad when you've had a good rest.' Kathy reached out to stroke his arm and was surprised as a little shock rippled through her fingers. She still couldn't believe how thrilled she was to see him, and it struck her then, like a blow between the eyes, just how much she had missed him. She turned quickly and hurried away, her emotions all over the place. *What's wrong with me?* she asked herself. *I love Ben. I've always loved Ben and he's the father of my children so why am I so pleased to see David?* And yet, she was aware that it was becoming harder to picture Ben's face now. With a shake of her head she went back downstairs to make David a hot-water bottle.

It was very dark when David woke and for a moment he was disorientated as his eyes adjusted to the gloom in the unfamiliar surroundings. But then, remembering where he was, he stretched luxuriously and narrowing his eyes he peered at the wristwatch on his wrist, shocked to see it was after seven o'clock at night.

224

Hurriedly, he rose and got dressed. What must Kathy and her mother think of him? he fretted. He'd turned up out of the blue and then promptly slept the day away. However, he needn't have worried. When he walked into the cosy kitchen-cum-sitting room the twins ran to him and Kathy gave him a dazzling smile.

'Ah, here you are. We've kept your dinner warm for you on a pan of water on the stove. We didn't want it to dry up in the oven.'

'I'm so sorry, you should have woken me,' he mumbled apologetically as she ushered him to the table.

'You looked so comfortable I didn't have the heart to.'

He noticed that the twins were in their pyjamas, washed and ready for bed and once she had fetched his meal they began to protest as she tried to get them upstairs.

'No, Mammy, we want to stay with Uncle David,' they protested loudly.

David grinned at her. 'Can't you just let them have another half an hour? They can tell me all they've been up to since I last saw them.'

'We got lots to tell you,' Daisy told him importantly as she scrambled up onto the chair next to him. 'They came an' took all the horses away 'cept two an' Mammy an' Uncle George cried!'

'Yes, they did,' Thomas agreed with a solemn nod of his head.

'Well, let's just hope they bring them all back safe and sound one day,' David replied, although he knew there was very little chance of that happening. Although horses weren't being used in battle nearly as much as they had been in the last war, they still worked desperately hard, pulling heavy equipment across difficult terrain. Many of them ended up dying of exhaustion. But how did you explain that to four-year-olds?

'Mum's gone over to Cissie's for an hour,' Kathy told him when she could manage to get a word in edgeways. 'So, when these two are in bed we can have a good catch-up.' Thankfully after a good sleep she noted that he looked slightly better although he was still terribly pale and there were dark circles beneath his eyes.

'I'll look forward to that.'

Again her heart did a little flip and deeply embarrassed she turned to wash the few pots that were soaking in the sink.

Chapter Thirty-Two

Livvy settled into her seat in the station next to the airfield and put her headphones on before looking at the list in front of her on her desk. There would be four Spitfires and three Hurricanes on stand by that evening and it was up to her to try to keep track of the pilots. Her friend, Monica, had told her that three new pilots had joined the team that afternoon but as Livvy had slept the day away she hadn't yet met them. Now she flicked down the list of names and as her eyes rested on one particular one her heart missed a beat – *Giles Willerby!* Could it really be the same Giles Willerby of Treetops? Livvy couldn't believe it.

Giles was here and tonight he would fly one of the Spitfires. She gulped as she tried to compose herself but then the alarm sounded and the familiar announcement of '*Pilots to your planes*' rang through the loudspeakers, indicating that enemy aircraft had been spotted heading towards England, and suddenly the whole place was hustle and bustle.

Through the window of the viewing tower Livvy watched the pilots racing across the runway towards their crafts, although she could have no idea which one was Giles. They scrambled aboard still fastening their helmets and goggles, then one by one their noses turned and pointed down the runway and they were off, gathering speed before they rose gracefully into the sky in perfect formation to chase down the enemy bombers that were threatening their country.

'Come in Tango Delta,' Livvy shouted into her mouth-piece and instantly the voice of the pilot in the first plane answered.

'Receiving loud and clear, approaching one hundred feet.'

One by one she made contact with the five planes, although because of the crackling on the receiver she had no idea which one was Giles, but soon they were swallowed up by the night sky and all she could do was listen with concern in case any of them reported they were in trouble. From the direction the bombers were taking it appeared that they were heading yet again for London and Livvy's heart was in her mouth as she wondered how many poor, unsuspecting victims would lose their lives that night. It was a clear, moonlit night with stars twinkling high in the heavens, making the towns and cities easy targets for the deadly planes, and Livvy began to silently pray.

In London, Susan and her friends would be hoisting Nellie, as they had christened the barrage balloon they flew, high into the sky and the ack-ack guns would be peppering the sky, but as they all knew to their cost, these were only partially successful deterrents against the deadly German bombers.

'I say, have you seen the new pilots?' Monica asked the next morning as she brushed her hair in the mirror above the sink in the washrooms before twisting it into a neat bun. 'A couple of them are very dishy indeed.'

'Are they?' Livvy finished brushing her teeth, which were chattering with cold. Unfortunately, the washrooms were very primitive indeed.

'Hm, I'm hoping we'll get another glimpse of them at breakfast,' Monica chuntered on as she straightened her tie in the mirror. 'Although it's unlikely, I suppose. They didn't get back to the airfield till the early hours of the morning, did they, so they'll probably still be sleeping. It was a very successful night, wasn't it? All of our boys came back in one piece and they shot one of the Jerries' planes down and it went into the River Thames in flames. Good riddance to bad rubbish, that's what I say. I just wish we could shoot the lot of the murdering bastards!'

Livvy raised an eyebrow. 'I dare say the Germans aren't all bad,' she pointed out as she began to brush her own hair, but her heart was hammering painfully. She'd had very little sleep the night before.

Monica snorted disdainfully. 'Everything that comes out of Germany is rotten,' she insisted. 'But get a move on. You know what the chaps are like. All the decent bacon and sausages will be gone if you don't hurry up.'

The canteen was teeming with people when they arrived and as they approached the counter Livvy quickly scanned the room and was surprised to feel slightly disappointed when there was no sign of Giles.

'Yes,' she heard one of the pilots in the queue ahead of her say. 'The swines targeted the East End last night. God knows how many lives must have been lost. The way those bloody Dorniers were dropping the bombs those below wouldn't have stood a chance.'

Livvy sighed and suddenly she didn't feel quite so hungry as she wondered where it was all going to end.

Back at Treetops Bobby was sitting as close to the radio as he could get and as he listened to the report of the devastation that had been wreaked in his place of birth the night before, tears sprang to his eyes. Would his mam be all right?

Edith, who had tried to persuade him not to listen, suddenly reached across and firmly switched the wireless off.

'Whaddya do that for?' he shouted indignantly as colour crept up his neck.

Seeing how angry her big brother was, Peggy stuck her thumb in her mouth and began to suck it noisily. She hated it when Bobby was upset.

'Because it's not doing you any good at all to listen to that,' Edith explained patiently. 'Don't forget there are Anderson shelters in almost every back garden in London now so there's every chance your parents would have been in one of them and they will be just fine.'

'But you can't be sure o' that can you?' Bobby said with his hands curled into fists.

Edith sighed. 'No, I can't, luvvy. But worrying about it won't make things any different, will it? If anything had happened to them someone would get word to us, so no news is good news. Now come on an' finish your breakfast. You'll be late for school at this rate.'

She was somewhat surprised when Bobby seemed to suddenly calm down and do as he was told and shortly after, clutching their lunch boxes and wrapped up warmly, she waved them off down the drive.

As the village school gates came into view Bobby stopped and turned to Peggy. 'I want you to go on from 'ere on your own. OK?'

Peggy frowned. 'But *why*, Bobby? Why ain't you comin' in? Miss Kitely'll be angry.'

'Just tell 'er I've 'ad to 'ave a day off cos I ain't very well.' Then seeing her confusion, he suddenly and quite uncharacteristically leaned forward and gave her a peck on the cheek. 'Look, if you must know I'm goin' back 'ome to check on Ma, all right?'

'But 'ow will you get there?' Peggy was frightened now.

'Don't you get worryin' about that. Just be a good girl an' do as I ask you, eh? I'll be back afore you know it. An' don't tell Edith where I've gone neivver, all right?'

Peggy swiped a tear from her cheek with her mittened hand as Bobby turned and marched away into the snow, then she walked on and through the gates leading to the school.

After a time, Bobby stopped to stuff the food in his lunch box into his pockets then after discarding the box and his gas mask, which Edith insisted they should carry at all times, he resolutely moved on towards the railway station. It seemed to be a long, long walk, particularly in such bad weather conditions, but his steps never faltered and at last the station came into view. Once inside, he dropped to his knees and crawled past the ticket office so as not to be seen, only standing again when he reached the platform. It was quite deserted. The people who were waiting for the next train to Euston were all huddled around the fire in the waiting room. Bobby slunk into a corner and at last he heard the roar and hiss of a train as it approached the station.

When it came to a halt he watched as a guard went systematically along the rows of carriages opening doors to let folk off and on. Then, waiting until the man was at the very far end of the platform, he made a dash for the luggage carriage at the back of the train and slid inside to hide amongst the suitcases.

The journey seemed never-ending. The atrocious weather frequently slowed the train and even stopped it completely a few times as snow was cleared from the tracks. Bobby's hands and feet were so cold that he had lost all feeling in them, although he was aware that he must have dozed off when the sound of the brakes made him start awake.

There were no windows in the luggage carriage, so he was unsure if they had reached their destination, until the engine became silent and the sounds of doors slamming reached him. Then suddenly the door was flung open and as a surprised porter caught sight of him, he shouted, ''Ere, nipper, wharra you doin' in 'ere?'

Bobby was shocked to discover that it was already completely dark outside and the gloomy light that penetrated the luggage van made him blink but the next second, he was up on his feet, regardless of his frozen toes and he sprinted past the guard like a whippet and hared off across the platform. He didn't pause for breath until he emerged into Euston Square where he came to an abrupt halt as he stared about, horrified. It seemed that the whole city lay in ruins. Once-fine buildings were now nothing more than smouldering ruins and gas pipes and water pipes jutted out of the ground like so many writhing snakes, as weary soldiers and civilians dug amongst the wreckage looking for survivors.

Bobby took a deep, shuddering breath then set off to find what had become of his parents and his home.

Chapter Thirty-Three

Peggy slunk into the kitchen late that afternoon with a guilty look on her face and as Edith, who was preparing some hot, buttered scones made with dried eggs and carrot, turned to her, the smile died on her face.

'Where's Bobby?' She was staring over Peggy's shoulder and for some reason her stomach had started to churn.

''E . . .'e's gone to London to make sure our ma is all right,' Peggy told her in a small voice with her eyes downcast.

'*He's what!?*' Edith suddenly felt sick. Bobby was just a little boy. He had no money. How would he get there? Would he be safe? '*When* did he go?' She was holding Peggy's shoulders now and the little girl's eyes filled with tears as she looked up.

''E went afore school this mornin',' she admitted as Edith sat down abruptly, her face bleached of colour.

That was hours ago, Edith thought despairingly. *He could be anywhere by now.* Then standing up abruptly she raced from the kitchen to inform John. He would know what to do.

'I don't really see that there is much we can do,' John said worriedly when she had breathlessly informed him of what had happened. 'I'm going to report him missing to the police and then I'm afraid all we can do is wait. It would be like looking for a needle in a haystack to try and find him in the city. I'll go and ring them right now.' He got up to go to the study, leaving Edith wringing her hands in distress.

'Do you *really* have to go today?' Kathy asked glumly the next morning as David helped her to wash up the breakfast pots.

After tucking the twins into bed, the evening before they had sat up until the early hours chatting in front of the fire and now suddenly she couldn't bear the thought of him leaving again.

'Well . . . my parents don't know I'm coming so I suppose I *could* stay a little longer if you're sure I wouldn't be imposing,' he answered uncertainly.

'*Imposing!*' Kathy laughed. 'Why you'd be doing me a favour. The twins seem to behave so much better for you than they do for me and I know they'd love to have you for a little longer.'

'In that case I'd love to . . . providing you clear it with your mother first,' he hastened to add.

'Clear what with me?' Sunday had just come down and she smiled at him.

'I was asking David if he couldn't stay for a while longer, but he seems to be worried that it would be a problem for you,' Kathy explained.

'Not at all,' Sunday responded. 'We'd love to have you. Stay as long as you like.'

The twins' ears had pricked up and now they whooped delightedly. 'You can take me out on our sledge,' Thomas suggested hopefully. 'Mammy says we can't cos it's too cold so perhaps just the boys could go?' Which earned him a slap on the arm from his sister.

234

The next minute they were rolling about the floor and, reaching down, Kathy caught them both gently by the scruff of their necks and hauled them to their feet. 'See what I mean?' she laughed. 'I think they lack a father's discipline.' And then realising what she had said she blushed to the roots of her hair as Sunday looked on with an amused twinkle in her eye. Could it be that her daughter was finally discovering this young man's worth? She sincerely hoped so for there was nothing she longed for more than to see both of her girls happily settled before she died.

An hour later hoots of laughter sounded from the grounds of Treetops as David patiently hauled the children about the garden on the sledge and helped them to build a snowman. They embarked on a snowball fight then and for just a short, sweet time, David's terrible memories of the war were pushed to the back of his mind.

'Looks like someone's enjoying themselves,' John commented as he called in to see Sunday at the lodge later that morning.

They stood together at the kitchen window, watching the grown-ups and children playing – even Kathy had joined them now – and Sunday nodded.

'Yes, and it's so lovely to see Kathy smiling. I think she's missed David more than she realised.'

He stared at her from the corner of his eye. He knew how much Sunday loved her daughters. 'Well, don't forget if it's meant to be it will happen,' he warned softly. 'You know how stubborn Kathy can be and if she thinks you're trying to match-make she might clear him off again.'

Instead of being insulted Sunday laughed. 'I know. And don't worry, I'm quite happy to take a back seat. But have you heard anything from Giles?'

He shook his head. 'Not since last week when he was being

transferred to an airfield in Lincolnshire somewhere. Look well if it's the same one that Livvy's stationed at. They'll be at each other's throats again in no time.'

'Actually, I don't think they would.' Sunday poured hot milk onto his coffee. 'Again, with those two I have a sneaky feeling they like each other more than they're letting on.'

'Really?' He held his hands out to the fire. 'That would be a bit of a turn-up for the books wouldn't it? What I mean is, when anything happens to me, Treetops will go to Giles and if he and Livvy got together she'd end up back where she's always felt she belonged.'

'Ah well, what will be will be,' Sunday said quietly as she carried his drink to the table. 'But now come and have this while it's hot. And take those boots off. There's snow melting all over my clean floor.'

With a guilty grin he did as he was told.

'And now you can tell me what else is wrong,' Sunday said bossily when he was seated and staring into his cup with a worried expression on his face. She knew him well enough by now to know that something was on his mind.

'It's young Bobby. He set off for London yesterday to check on his family and we've no idea where he is. I've reported him missing to the police, of course, but all we can do now is wait and pray that he turns up safely.'

Sunday frowned. They had all grown to be very fond of John's little evacuees, especially Edith, and Sunday could only imagine how upset she must be.

'Try not to worry; he'll turn up. He's a tough little chap,' she said reassuringly as she gently squeezed John's hand and they both lapsed into silence as they thought of the missing child and prayed that he was safe.

At the RAF airfield in Lincolnshire, Livvy was heading for the canteen. She had just done a ten-hour shift straight through the night and was so tired she was sure she could have fallen asleep on a clothesline. It had not been a good night. Two of their pilots had not come back. One of the pilots who had returned safely had chokily told them that he had witnessed one plane take a direct hit and go up in a ball of flames, so there was little hope the pilot had survived. The other plane had been hit in the wing and the pilot had managed to bail out as the plane spiralled to earth. Now all they could do was hope he had made it safely to the ground and managed to escape, or at worst been taken prisoner. So, all in all, Livvy was not feeling or looking her best as she entered the steamy canteen that smelled strongly of boiled cabbage and mince. There was no need to guess what they would be having for lunch today.

She was standing at the counter with a tray in her hand when someone tapped her lightly on the shoulder and, turning quickly, she found herself staring up into Giles's handsome face. He was dressed in his flying gear and due to go out on a raid in less than an hour.

'Small world, eh?' he said teasingly. 'Fancy seeing you here.'

She wondered whether she should tell him that she'd known he was there but then quickly decided against it. He would only wonder why she hadn't sought him out.

'Hello, Giles, how are you?'

'Oh, you know, fine at the minute though that could change in the blink of an eye in this job, as you're well aware. Still, we have to look on the bright side, don't we? How are you? I hear you're very highly regarded here.'

'That's nice and I'm fine thanks.' It was hard to be rude to him when he was smiling at her like that.

Once she'd been served, he carried her tray to a table for her and without waiting to be asked he sat down to join her with his mug of tea.

'So, you're off out this afternoon then?' she asked rather unnecessarily as she pushed the soggy cabbage about her plate with her fork. It really did look very unappetising.

'Yes, Berlin today. I'm flying one of the Hurricanes for a change.'

Livvy knew that Hurricanes were heavier and not quite as nippy as the Spitfires, which meant that should they become involved in a dogfight, Giles could be at a much higher risk.

'Then I wish you a safe, successful journey,' she muttered.

He shrugged. 'It should be all right. It will be dark by the time we get there and hopefully we can be in and out without the Luftwaffe even knowing.'

They stared at each other for a moment, each aware of the risk the pilots took every time they took off. Then hoping to lighten the atmosphere he asked, 'Heard anything from home lately? Dad told me the army took the horses some time ago and I was gutted. They only left the two old nags, apparently, which is hardly surprising. They're not really fit for much but the knacker's yard.'

'Ah well, at least the little ones have still got them to ride round on,' Livvy answered sympathetically. Giles might be an arrogant so-and-so, but she was well aware of how much he had loved the horses.

'Treetops seems an awful long way away now, doesn't it?' he said wistfully, and she could only nod in agreement.

After a pause, he asked, 'When is your next day off?

Surprised at the change of subject she blinked. 'Saturday as it happens. Why do you ask?'

'You've been here longer than me and I thought you might show me something of the place. Where is the nearest civilisation to here anyway?'

'Lincoln.' She grinned. 'Me and some of the girls usually get a lift in one of the jeeps and find a pub where we can have a sing-song. Most of the theatres are closed so there isn't a lot else to do. You're quite welcome to join us, if you like.'

He smiled but then glancing at the wall clock he hurriedly drained his mug and stood up. 'Right, I'd best be off. Hopefully I'll see you sometime tomorrow.'

She nodded and as he turned to leave, she suddenly said, 'Giles . . .'

He turned and cocked an eyebrow, 'Yes?'

'Just . . . take care.'

He gave her a cheeky wink and then he was gone, leaving her feeling strangely uneasy and deflated. It would be many long hours until he returned from his mission and suddenly she wasn't sleepy at all.

'Ooh,' Monica teased when Livvy strode into their hut shortly after. 'Didn't take you long to latch on to one of the dishy new pilots, did it? I had my eye on that one myself, as it happens.'

'Actually, I already knew Giles,' Livvy said tiredly. 'I'll tell you all about it sometime.' But not now, she thought. She was far too wound up thinking of him preparing for take-off and praying that he would come back safely, although why she should care quite so much, she had no idea.

Chapter Thirty-Four

Bobby woke with a start and peeped out into the road from the shop doorway where he had slept. He was so cold that his teeth were chattering and the air, which was heavy with smoke from the hundreds of fires that were still raging, was making him cough.

It had been too dark for him to try to find his way home the night before and so he had huddled in the first shop doorway he came to and curled into a ball to try and keep warm. The food that Edith had lovingly packed for him the morning before was long gone and now as well as being cold, his stomach was grumbling with hunger. Just for a moment he wondered if he had been right to come back but he knew that he would never have settled until he knew that his ma was safe, so the best thing to do now was go and check on her and then head back to the Midlands.

The trouble was the streets all looked so different now and he wasn't even sure he was heading in the right direction. Nothing looked as he remembered. Whole streets had been flattened and there were piles of bricks and rubbish that had once been people's homes everywhere he looked. The sight struck fear into his heart. What if his own home was now just a pile of bricks? What if his ma had been buried underneath? Suddenly he didn't feel quite so hungry anymore and, swallowing back the tears that had sprung to his eyes at the thought of his mother lying crushed beneath their home, he squared his shoulders and set off through the choking smoke that hung over the entire city in a thick black cloud, and when he glanced down, he saw that his clothes were already covered in a fine dusting of soot.

Fire engines were still desperately trying to put out fires, while haggard-faced men continued to work tirelessly amongst the flattened buildings to find survivors. Bobby had to climb over perilous piles of rubble to get through the streets. After what felt like hours, he at last spotted some familiar buildings and soon after he turned into the street where he had lived only to come to an abrupt halt. One side of the street was intact, apart from the fact that most of the windows had been blown out and tiles had fallen from the rooftops. But his own home was nothing more than a smoking ruin.

With his heart in his mouth Bobby silently stared ahead. Part of him didn't want to move forward, he was afraid of what he might discover, but it was as if his legs were moving of their own volition until he was standing in front of the ruins of what had been the only home he had ever known before he had arrived at Treetops. He stood there with tears burning behind his eyes as he tried to take in what he was seeing. And then suddenly he heard a familiar voice.

'Is that you, young Bobby?'

He turned to see Mrs Cotton, a neighbour from across the road, staring at him from her front door. She was wearing a huge flowered wrap-around pinny and had a scarf tied turban-like about her head. She was nice was Mrs Cotton. Many a time she had bathed a black eye for Bobby or Peggy after one of their father's drunken episodes, and many a time she had taken them in and given them a meal when their ma didn't have so much as a crust of bread in the house.

'Y-yes it's me, Mrs Cotton,' Bobby answered in a shaky voice. 'But where's me ma and dad? . . . An' Skippy?'

At that moment a little tan-coloured mongrel flew from between the woman's legs and launched himself at Bobby with his tail wagging furiously and part of his question was answered at least.

'Skippy were in the street when the 'ouse got bombed,' Mrs Cotton told him. 'Your dad must 'ave turfed 'im out an' it were a good job an' all. I took 'im in an' I've been feedin' 'im. But why don't you come in' an' all, lad? I bet you could do wi' a nice hot sup o' tea an' a bite o' sommat to eat, per'aps?'

'But me ma an' da? . . . Where are they?'

'Come away in now. The road is no place to talk.' She put her plump arm about his shoulders and, without a word, led him into the house.

He immediately noticed that Mr Cotton had boarded up the broken windows and a fire was burning in the grate.

'We're 'aving to cook on the fire at the moment,' Mrs Cotton told him as she pushed the kettle onto the coals. 'All the gas pipes were blown up. Still, we're better off than mo—' She stopped abruptly. She could feel the boy's eyes burning into her back and was dreading what she was going to have to tell him, poor little mite. The way she saw it he'd had a raw deal of it one way or another. Although she noted that he'd put weight on and was looking a lot healthier than when he'd been evacuated. Not surprising, she supposed, since that father of his had always spent every last penny he could get his hands on an ale.

'M-Mrs Cotton . . . me ma?' His voice came out as a squeak but again she didn't tell him anything, instead she hurried off to fetch a loaf of grey-looking bread from the pantry and began to scrape it with margarine. It was hard to get good white flour now, as it was most things. People were having to make do with what they could get their hands on and every day she thanked God that her own children had been evacuated to the country, despite missing them every minute.

She added a dollop of jam to the bread and pushed it in front of him, while she pottered off to make the tea but suddenly he had lost his appetite as he sat and stared dumbly at it.

''Ow 'ave you got back 'ere anyway?' she asked presently as she prepared two cracked mismatched cups. The explosions in the street had knocked most of her treasured china off the shelves and all she had left now was what she had managed to salvage.

He simply stared back at her from frightened eyes. After the extreme cold outside the heat in the room had made his face glow and his hands and feet were tingling painfully as the feeling returned to them, but he was oblivious to the discomfort and she realised that she would have to tell him the worst now. There was no point in putting it off any longer. She just wished that her Bert were here with her to help her, but he was out digging for survivors with the rest of the ARP wardens.

'The thing is, son . . .' She gulped and licked her lips. 'Both your ma and your dad were in the house when the bomb dropped . . . I'm so sorry but they didn't stand a chance. They were pulled out o' the wreckage two nights ago.'

Bobby sat as if he had been turned to stone. His ma and dad gone, dead . . . just like that!

'Wh-where are they now?' he asked eventually as he rapidly blinked back scalding tears.

The kindly woman reached across to touch his hand, wishing she were a million miles away. 'They'll 'ave taken 'em to a morgue an' then they'll probably be buried in one o' the mass graves.'

He nodded and rose from the table as she stared at him in distress. 'But where are you goin'?'

'Back to Peggy,' he stated. 'The family we're stayin' wi' will be worried about me. I'll take Skippy wi' me, fanks for lookin' after 'im.'

'But, luvvie, 'ow will you get 'ome?' She was deeply concerned now. He was far too young to be wandering about all on his own. 'Just stay 'ere wi' me an' my Bert'll get in touch wi' 'em for you then they can come an' fetch you. It ain't safe for you to be 'ere on your own. We could 'ave another raid any time.'

The words had barely left her lips when the sound of the air raid siren filled the room and she groaned. 'Dear God, not again. Come on, Bobby. We'll go out the back into the shelter.'

He shook his head as he backed towards the door. 'No, it's all right. Me an' Skippy will be fine.' And then before she could stop him, he was gone, racing off down the road, slipping and stumbling across the scattered debris with Skippy close on his heels and there was not a thing she could do about it.

'Bobby . . . Bobby, stop *please*!'

Her voice followed him, but he ploughed on as the tears he had held back spurted from his eyes and all the time the sky overhead grew darker with enemy planes intent on dropping their deadly cargo. The furious sound of ack-ack guns suddenly added to the noise and somewhere in the distance he heard a loud explosion. Seconds later a great black cloud rose into the sky telling him that some other unfortunate blighters had copped it. Still he ran. Occasionally someone would shout to him to get to a shelter, but Bobby ignored them. He had no idea what direction he was running in, he only knew that somehow he must leave the terrible news Mrs Cotton had told him far behind. But no matter how far he ran, he knew deep down that there was no getting away from it. And then there was the sound of another explosion, closer this time and the ground beneath his feet seemed to tremble.

'Come on, Skippy.' Bobby dived into the nearest shop doorway and huddled back as far as he could go with his arms about the dog. The poor thing was shaking with terror as he looked up at him from velvet-brown eyes and Bobby affection-ately kissed his head.

'It's all right, boy,' he soothed, although he was trembling himself. Skippy stared at him trustingly. He wasn't the prettiest of dogs, if truth be told: his legs were short and squat and he had one ear that pointed to the sky, while the other hung flat against his head. His tail was bushy like a fox's and his body looked out of proportion with the rest of him, but all the same Bobby loved him unconditionally and had missed him while he had been away.

'It's just you an' me now,' he muttered, wiping tears and snot from the end of his nose with the back of his sleeve. 'Ma's gone an' she can't come back.' Strangely enough he felt no sorrow at the loss of his father. He had been a bully and Bobby was relieved that he would never have the chance to take his belt to him again . . . but his ma . . . Oh, his ma. He had loved her unreservedly and he knew that things would never be the same without her.

What would happen to him and Peggy now? he wondered. Would they be shoved into some orphanage until they were old enough to look after themselves? It was a fearful thought and he shuddered, as yet another bomb dropped dangerously close to where he was hiding. This time he could hear the sound of houses collapsing around him and breaking glass and now the air was so full of soot and smoke he could hardly breathe or see more than a few feet ahead. In the distance he could hear the sound of fire engines, for what good they could do, and men shouting, and now venturing from the doorway he urged the dog out behind him. A little further down the street, or the remains of it, he found a length of rope, which he tied round Skippy's neck.

'Come on,' he urged above the wail of the dropping bombs. The ack-ack guns didn't seem to be having much success. 'We 'ave to find us somewhere safer to 'ide.'

Bricks were scattered all across the road and within minutes he had slipped so many times his hands and knees were skinned but still he kept doggedly on, praying that the train station hadn't been hit. If the trains were still running at least then there was a chance that he could slip onto one and get himself and Skippy away from the city. As he ran, he briefly thought that this must be the hell his Sunday school teacher had told him about. Fire and deafening noise all around him.

Soon he was surprised to see Petticoat Lane to the left of him, or rather what was left of it. There were no stalls or stall-holders shouting their wares today. Like the rest of the city it had been bombed and as he stared at the smouldering ruins it was hard to remember it as it had been, but at least now he could get his bearings again.

'Come on,' he urged the dog, who was beginning to flag a little. 'The train station is this way.' Suddenly he had an over-powering urge to see Edith. Admittedly he had been wary of her when he had first arrived at Treetops, but her patience and kindness had won him over and now he wanted nothing more than to just fall into her arms and sob his heart out.

Soon the station appeared in the distance and Bobby allowed himself to lean against a wall for a moment to ease the stitch in his side. He bent to stroke the dog reassuringly and as he straightened, he became aware of a deafening whistling sound. Glancing up he saw a bomb hurtling down straight towards him and seconds later it crashed into the road only yards away from him. As he felt the bricks in the wall behind him begin to collapse, he just had time to throw himself down over Skippy and he thought briefly, *I hope our Peggy'll be aw'ight*, and then, as the wall began to cave in on top of him, there was only darkness and he knew no more.

Chapter Thirty-Five

'*No . . . nooooo . . . Dad, don't!*'

'Shush now, pet.'

Peggy started awake from a terrible nightmare as Edith clicked her bedroom light on and hurried towards her to gather her into her arms.

The child was wet through with sweat and was in a tangle of damp sheets. 'It's all right now. You were just having a nasty dream but it's all over now.'

Edith rocked her to and fro and very slowly the child's cries subsided into hiccupping sobs that tore at her heart. 'That's better. Now, what was so bad to make you dream like that?' she asked softly. It wasn't the first time Peggy had had nightmares, but she had been worse since Bobby had gone.

For a moment Peggy remained silent and Edith thought she would clam up as she usually did when this happened. The child seemed to be considering whether to say anything or not but then haltingly she told her, 'It . . . it were me dad . . . He did bad things to me an' he 'urt me.'

'With his belt you mean?' Edith questioned softly but Peggy shook her head.

'No . . . 'e did bad things to me down 'ere.'

Edith's heart sank as the child pointed to her most private parts and inside she was crying, *No, no! Surely no father would do that to such a young child?* Yet deep down she knew that they would, she had always suspected it and now Peggy was finally telling her rather than leaving her to surmise it. Fighting to hide the wave of sickness that had risen in her, Edith held on tight to the child and managed to keep her voice light.

'That was very bad of him, pet,' she said with a slight wobble in her tone. 'Why ever didn't you tell your mother?'

'Dad said the devil would come an' get me in the dark if I told anyone,' the child said with a hitch in her voice. 'An' he only done it when Bobby an' Ma were out. I think Bobby knew, though, an' that's why he started to sleep in my bed back at 'ome so's he could try an' keep me safe.'

'Oh, my *poor* darling,' Edith muttered and now she could stop the tears from falling no longer and they rained down her face as she thought what the poor child must have gone through.

'I . . . it were my fault,' Peggy said. 'Dad said I made him do it . . . Will the devil come nows I've told you?'

'No, he will *not*! There is no such thing,' Edith retorted as her anger rose. 'And it *wasn't* your fault, pet. What your dad did was very wrong. Things like this should never happen to little girls . . . *ever*!'

At that moment John appeared in the open doorway in his dressing gown and, wiping the sleep from his eyes, he asked, 'Is everything all right in here?'

Peggy instantly shrank into Edith's side as she stared at him fearfully and now at last Edith understood why the child was so nervous around men.

'Everything is fine,' she told him. 'We've just had a little accident, that's all, so you go and put the kettle on and when we've changed the bed and got Peggy into clean pyjamas I'll come down to the kitchen and join you for a drink.'

She knew there would be no point in going back to bed; she'd hardly slept a wink since Bobby had disappeared and she had come to a decision. She was tired of waiting for the police to bring news of him and had decided that the very next day she would go to London to look for him herself. But for now, she concentrated on making Peggy comfortable and once the bed was changed and the child was tucked in again, she planted a gentle kiss on her forehead. 'There now,' she said softly. 'You snuggle down and get some sleep. And don't get worrying. I promise you that I'm going to see to it that your dad never hurts you again.'

Peggy nodded trustingly as Edith passed her the teddy bear she had bought for her and seconds later the little girl's eyelids were closing. Satisfied that she could do no more for now, Edith crept from the room.

John was waiting for her in the kitchen with a pot of tea on the table ready when she got downstairs and he asked, 'So what's all the fuss about then? Is she worrying about Bobby?'

Slumping onto a chair Edith passed a hand across her weary eyes and slowly told him what Peggy had said. By the time she had finished there were tears in John's eyes and he looked devastated.

'It makes me ashamed of my sex,' he muttered. 'I can't believe that a father could do that to his own child!'

'Oh, but some do, I assure you,' Edith said regretfully. She herself had been beaten as a child, which was why she had left home and married at the earliest opportunity. Not that she had ever admitted it to a living soul, not even her own late husband.

The shame had gone too deep, but it meant that now she knew exactly what Peggy had been through.

'So, what do you think we should do about it?' he asked as anger replaced the shock.

'We could report it, I suppose, but the problem is it would be Peggy's word against his,' Edith said flatly. 'And nine times out of ten the police don't have time for things like this, particularly when there's a war on.'

'Well, one thing is for sure, she won't be going back to that brute!' John stated.

Edith gave him a sad smile. 'I really hope not. But right now, I'm worried about Bobby. I was thinking of going to London to try to find him myself tomorrow. We know the address where he lived so there's a fair chance someone will have seen him, if he managed to get there. I can't just sit around waiting for the police to bring word of him, it's driving me mad.'

Seeing the strain on her face he patted her hand affectionately. She was a good woman, was Edith. 'I think you've rather taken to these children, haven't you?'

'I love them like me own,' she admitted. 'And I don't mind telling you I've been dreading them going home, especially now we know what's been going on with little Peggy.'

'Somehow, we'll sort it,' he promised, for he too was more than a little fond of the young waifs they had taken in. 'And you don't need to go to London; I will. I don't want to have to be worrying about you too. Plus, Peggy needs you here. The trouble is I just heard on the radio that all the lines into Euston are closed at the minute because of the bombing so I'm afraid we're going to have to be patient until they're up and running again.'

Frustrated, Edith nodded as she poured the tea and then

they sat in silence, each trying to take in what poor little Peggy had confided. It was just too horrible to imagine what the child must have gone through. It also explained why Bobby was so protective of her. But now they were both determined that somehow they would ensure it never happened again.

Early the next morning, Sunday decided to give David and Kathy some time alone with the twins and called in to Treetops, where she found Edith bleary-eyed and tearful. George had taken Peggy to school as Edith felt that routine would be better for her than staying at home, and when Edith told her what Peggy had said the night before Sunday was just as horrified as she had been.

'Poor little mite,' she said. 'The man should be put up against a wall and shot. Even animals will protect their own. But never you fear; her dad will get his comeuppance.' Little could she know that he already had.

It was mid-morning when the phone rang, and Edith instantly flew into a panic as John hurried from his study to answer it.

Edith hovered, watching his expression closely and by the look on his face, she was sure it was news about Bobby and her heart began to thud painfully.

'Yes, yes of course,' he said eventually. 'I shall be there as soon as I possibly can. Good day and thank you.'

Slowly he replaced the receiver and turned to Edith and Sunday, his expression grave.

'That was the police in London,' he said solemnly. 'It appears that Bobby and Peggy's parents were killed when their house was bombed some nights ago.'

'Eeh!' Edith placed a hand against her wildly thumping heart. 'Oh, those poor children! Although I can't say as I'm sorry to hear that bastard of a dad of theirs has copped it. For an awful moment there I thought you were going to say the call was about Bobby.'

He stared back at her and for a moment the words he was about to say froze on his tongue. But then, realising that he must tell her the dreadful news he licked his lips and said quietly, 'I'm afraid it was, Edith. The police managed to speak to one of the children's neighbours, a Mrs Cotton, who was most helpful by all accounts, and she informed them that Bobby had been there. She felt obliged to tell him what had happened to his parents and when she did, he was so distraught that he ran off with his little dog, Skippy.'

'So where is he now then?'

John looked away from the hope in her eyes. 'Soon after he left, London suffered yet more bombing and last night rescuers retrieved the body of a boy matching Bobby's description with a small dog beside him near Euston Station. They have the body in a hospital morgue, and they have asked if I will go and identify it.'

'But it might not have been him,' Edith gasped, clutching at straws as Sunday placed a comforting arm about her.

John sighed. 'It appears he was wearing the name tag you always insisted the children should wear about his neck and the name on it was Bobby Walker . . . I'm so sorry, Edith, but it sounds like it was Bobby they found.'

'No!' Great, fat tears welled in Edith's eyes and she sagged against Sunday as her legs turned to jelly. John helped her into the kitchen, while Sunday ran to fetch the smelling salts, which they wafted beneath the distraught woman's nose. Slowly she began to get a grip of herself, although the tears continued to fall.

'I think I knew deep down that he wasn't going to come home,' she said brokenly. 'I just had this horrible feeling in here.' She thumped her chest close to her heart. 'But what will happen now if it is Bobby?'

'I shall go and bring him home and he'll have a decent burial,' John promised with a catch in his voice.

As something else occurred to Edith she broke out in a cold sweat. 'And what about Peggy? If their parents are dead, she's an orphan now. What will become of her? Will they push her into some horrible orphanage?'

'Let's cross each bridge as we come to it,' John urged, and they all fell silent with grief as they thought of the mischievous little boy who had come to mean so much to them.

Chapter Thirty-Six

Two days later John left for London. Edith had wanted to go with him but knowing how distressing what he had to do would be he had persuaded her to stay at home to look after Peggy, who was broken-hearted at the death of the big brother she had idolised.

'What'll 'appen to me now?' she had asked piteously when John and Edith had broken the news to her as gently as they could.

'Nothing for now,' Edith had assured her. 'You're quite safe here with us for the time being.' But already she knew what she was planning to do, and she just prayed that her employer would go along with the idea. But first they must know without doubt that the child who had been killed was indeed their Bobby.

At the lodge, David and Kathy were getting along famously. He had already stayed far longer than he had intended but somehow, now that he was there, it was very hard to leave. He was the closest thing to a father figure the twins had ever had and they clearly adored him.

'I really should be thinking of setting off for Yorkshire tomorrow,' he told them all as they sat enjoying their lunch after yet another morning of playing out in the snow on their sledges with him.

He saw the way Kathy's eyes suddenly narrowed and his heart did a little skip. He had loved her ever since the day he had first set eyes on her. Even the fact that she had become pregnant by another man had not been able to dim that love and now he wondered if finally she might be feeling something more than friendship for him. He could only pray that she might, and meantime he intended to enjoy every moment spent with her and the children.

'No,' Daisy said petulantly, flinging her chubby arms about his neck and planting a sticky kiss on his cheek. 'Me an' Thomas loves you an' we wants you to stay here with us!'

'Oh, all right then, perhaps I could manage just another couple of days,' David answered. He was easily persuaded and heartened to see that Kathy looked happy with the idea. 'So, what do you want to do this afternoon?'

'We could go skatin' on the duck pond, it's frozen over,' Thomas suggested hopefully, and David chuckled and agreed.

In Lincolnshire, it was Livvy's day off and she had agreed to take Giles into Lincoln that evening – if they could get a lift there, that was. Thankfully they found a jeep that was already taking some of the others into the city and they crammed inside it.

'Blimey, this must be what it feels like to be in a tin of sardines,' Giles laughed as yet another pilot piled in beside him, squashing him yet further along the seat

Livvy was very aware of the warmth of his body through their uniforms as they sat pressed together and she felt herself blushing. *Daft oaf*, she scolded herself. *He's not coming because of you, he just has nothing better to do.* And yet suddenly she was painfully aware of how handsome he looked in his smart uniform.

There was much laughter and chatting as the jeep bounded along the rough country lanes and more than once Livvy would have ended up on the floor had it not been for Giles placing a steadying arm across her. But then at last they were there, and the jeep stopped to let them out as the driver promised to pick them all up later that evening. Most of the people shot off, leaving Livvy and Giles to trail behind.

'So where do you suggest?' he asked. 'Don't forget this place is new to me.'

'We usually wind up in the Lion and Snake in the High Street,' she answered. 'There's often a bit of a sing-song and a knees-up going on in there. The High Street's quite close to the cathedral.'

'Then the Lion and Snake it is.' He grinned and gallantly crooked his arm with a theatrical little bow and after a moment's hesitation she slid her hand through it, and they walked on. It was quite dark as all the streetlamps were out and the windows of the houses they passed were covered in blackout curtains, but thankfully Livvy knew her way about quite well by then and soon the sound of people having a good time in the pub reached them.

'So, what will it be then?' Giles asked as they pushed their way to the bar. There were a lot of RAF personnel in there and they called greetings.

'I'll have a gin and tonic please. And while you get those I'll go and see if I can find us a table. But I'll get the next round in, mind.'

He shook his head and grinned as she pushed her way back through the crowd, noting the way her hair shone gold in the dim lights. He had thought her pretty when they had both been at Treetops but since then she had grown into a very beautiful young woman. She didn't seem quite so cutting either, which was something to be grateful for. Perhaps she was finally forgiving him for living in her former home?

Minutes later he shuffled back, balancing their drinks precariously.

'That hits the spot,' he said approvingly as he lit a cigarette and took a long swig of his beer. 'I was ready for that, but now tell me, have you had any leave lately?'

'Not for some time but I'm due a forty-eight-hour pass next month. What about you?'

'Same here.' His face became serious. 'We've lost four of our pilots over the last month and, until some more join us, there's not much chance of getting any time off at all. Still, remember me to my grandad and everyone there when you go.'

'Of course.' They started to chat and before they knew it people were standing to leave.

'It can't be that time already, surely,' Livvy remarked as she glanced around. 'It feels like we only just got here.'

'Ah well, you know what they say – "time flies when you're having fun".'

She opened her mouth to pass some icy remark but then seeing the mischief twinkling in his eyes she promptly closed it again. Much as she hated to admit it, he had been very good company, although she would never have told him so.

They trailed through the streets of Lincoln with the rest of the crowd to the pick-up point and as they made their way across the treacherously slippery pavements it seemed the most natural thing in the world to hook her arm through his again.

'I've enjoyed tonight,' he told her as they jolted their way back to the camp in the jeep. 'Perhaps we could do it again on our next night off?'

'Perhaps.' She answered in an off-hand manner, but in actual fact she had enjoyed herself just as much as he had, not that she would ever admit it, not even to herself.

For the next few days they saw little of each other except to say hello occasionally in the canteen. But Livvy was aware that he was flying most days and she found that it bothered her. And then one evening as she was coming off duty, she found him waiting for her with a grave look on his face.

'Hello, is anything wrong?' Just one glance at his face told her that something was amiss.

'There is actually,' he answered, taking her elbow and drawing her into the shadows. 'I've had a letter from grandad today and . . . Well, I don't quite know how to tell you this, but young Bobby ran away from Treetops when he heard about all the bombings in London on the radio. He went to check on his family, I dare say, only to find when he got there that they had died in an air raid. But that's not the worst of it, unfortunately. Poor Bobby was killed too. They think he was probably trying to get back, but he got caught in a raid with his little dog just near the station. It seems they were both killed instantly when a wall collapsed on them.'

'Oh *no!*' Tears sprang to Livvy's eyes as her hand rose to cover her mouth. 'The poor little scrap.'

Giles nodded. 'Apparently Grandad arranged to have his body taken back to Treetops and he's going to be buried in

259

Mancetter churchyard in two days' time. He says in the letter that he felt it was the least he could do for little Bobby.'

Livvy gulped as she tried to take it all in. Bobby had been just a little boy and to die like that . . . all alone. She shuddered, then making a decision she told him, 'I'm going to go and see my officer and see if she'll grant me some compassionate leave. If I can go tomorrow, I'll be there for the funeral. I have a feeling everyone will need some support. They were all so fond of the children, especially Edith.'

He nodded in agreement as a picture of Bobby playing with the horses back in the stables at Treetops flashed in front of his eyes. 'Do you know what, I reckon I might try to do the same,' he said. 'It's not a good time when we're so many pilots down, admittedly, but it's worth a shot. I'll go and see my flight officer too and, if I do get leave granted, we could perhaps travel home together? Meet me back in the canteen in an hour so we can find out how we got on.'

An hour later, as arranged, they met in the canteen. By that time Giles had not been to bed for over eighteen hours and his eyes were gritty and sore from lack of sleep. He had only come back from a mission three hours before to find the letter waiting for him and after that sleep had been impossible.

'I don't know how I wangled it, but I managed to get a forty-eight-hour pass, it will mean I have to set off back here straight after the funeral but at least I'll be there to show my respects and offer some support. What about you?' Giles asked Livvy.

'Same here,' she said with relief. She could only imagine how upset her mother and the women back at home must be. And, although she wished it weren't under these circumstances, she had to admit she was looking forward to going home and seeing her family. 'I've arranged a jeep to run me to the station at eight in the morning. The train leaves at nine so you can come with me, if you like. But now why don't you go and try to get some rest. You look awful!'

'Thanks.' He grinned wryly. 'You sure know how to make a chap feel good about himself.'

Despite the awful news she found herself smiling. Rather than finding him arrogant anymore she was fast discovering that he actually had a very dry sense of humour.

'Don't suppose I could tempt you to come and bunk down with me?' he teased.

She scowled at him and put her nose in the air. 'Don't push your luck otherwise you might find yourself walking back to Nuneaton.' And with that she turned on her heel and marched away with her back ramrod straight, leaving him to stand there with a wide grin on his face. She was a feisty little thing, there was no doubt about it. And good-looking into the bargain.

Chapter Thirty-Seven

After what had happened, David decided to write to his parents and promise that he would try to get to see them, as soon as possible. Thankfully, they had had no idea that he had been on leave so he knew that they wouldn't be too disappointed. It would mean that he could spend the rest of the time he had left with Kathy and attend the funeral. Everyone was upset, even the twins, although luckily they weren't quite old enough to understand the finality of death.

'But if Bobby has gone to heaven why can't he come back sometimes to visit us?' Thomas queried with tears trembling on his thick lashes. Sometimes Kathy thought he looked so much like Ben she was amazed no one else had picked up on it.

'Because once they are in heaven God likes them to stay there safely with him,' Kathy tried to explain inadequately.

Thomas snorted in disgust. 'Then I think that's very selfish of God,' he exploded.

Daisy meanwhile had been listening with a worried expression on her face. 'You told us that Patch our dog had gone to heaven,' she told her mother accusingly. 'But I saw George dig a hole and plant him in the garden like a flower. How can he be in heaven if he's in the garden? And he never grew back neither,' she ended accusingly.

Kathy was at a loss as to how better to explain but thankfully David saved the day when he asked, 'Who wants to come for a walk to the shop in the village for some gobstoppers?'

'I do!' The twins chorused and Kathy flashed him a grateful smile.

Bobby's body had been brought home and he was now lying in the day room at Treetops in a heartbreakingly tiny coffin until the funeral, which would take place the next day. Kathy was dreading it, as they all were. The telegram boys bearing tragic news were now a common sight in the town as they cycled about telling families that their loved ones had been killed in action, and yet the death of an innocent child seemed infinitely worse. At least the young men who had gone away to fight had had some sort of a life, whereas Bobby's had barely begun.

Sighing, Kathy hurried away to get their warm clothes and as she glanced through the window she gasped with delight when she saw Livvy and Giles walking towards the lodge in their uniforms.

Heedless of the bitingly cold weather she raced outside and grabbed Libby in a fierce hug. 'Oh, Liv, it's *so* good to see you,' she said as fresh tears started down her cheeks. She felt as if all she had done was cry ever since the terrible news about Bobby had reached them. 'This will cheer Mum up no end. She's up at the house at the minute. Edith is in such a state we don't like to leave her alone at present. But come on in out of the cold.'

Giles touched his peaked cap as he strode on, while Livvy allowed herself to be dragged unceremoniously into the lodge.

'Aunt Livvy.' The twins raced towards her with cries of delight.

'Hello, my lovelies,' Livvy laughed. Then glancing up over their heads she was surprised to see David. 'Hello, David. Now calm down and let me catch my breath, won't you. And my goodness – how you've grown! I hardly recognised you.'

'Bobby's gone to be an angel in the sky with God,' Thomas told her solemnly as he plugged his thumb into his mouth and Daisy nodded in agreement.

'Come on, children. The shop will be sold out of gobstoppers at this rate,' David told them hastily, hoping to lighten the mood. 'Let's get on and then you can see your Aunt Livvy when we get back.'

Muffled up in their warm clothes, the children went off happily enough, and Kathy went to put the kettle on.

'Little monkeys,' she said ruefully. 'I don't think there's anything they wouldn't do for gobstoppers.'

'That's kids for you,' Livvy agreed as she peeled her gloves off and looked around. It felt strange, but lovely to be back after being away so long. 'But what's David doing here?'

Kathy flushed prettily. 'He just called in to see us last week on his way home to Yorkshire and somehow the twins persuaded him to stay.'

'Did they now?' Livvy grinned and raised an eyebrow. 'And how do you feel about that?'

Kathy tried to shrug nonchalantly. 'Well, we've always got on and been friends, haven't we?'

'Hm, I'd say from the way he was looking at you just now he thinks of you as a lot more than a friend.'

'What about you marching up the road with Giles, then?' Kathy retorted defensively. 'I'd say you two looked more than a little chummy too.'

The two sisters glanced at each other and grinned.

'Touché!' Livvy said and then listened intently as Kathy told her about all that had been happening.

'But what will happen to little Peggy now?' Livvy asked with concern.

Kathy sighed. 'John had a phone call from the welfare department in London that deals with war orphans and they're going to come and see him once the funeral is over.'

'Surely they won't put her into an orphanage?' Livvy was horrified at the thought.

'Between you and me, I think they'd have a fight on their hands with Edith if they tried to,' Kathy confided. 'She's intimated that she wants to officially adopt her, but I have no idea if that would be allowed.'

They went on to speak of what they had both been up to as they waited for their mother to arrive, which she undoubtedly would as soon as Giles told her that Livvy was home.

Overnight the snow turned to rain and they woke the next day to find the sky dark and heavy. It was now also treacherously slippery underfoot but when Livvy suggested to her mother over breakfast that it might be better if she stayed at home to avoid any nasty falls, Sunday almost snapped her head off.

'I'm not quite decrepit yet, young lady!'

'I wasn't suggesting that you were,' Livvy assured her hurriedly. 'But funerals are never nice things and I thought you might prefer to stay in the warm.'

'Then you thought wrong.' Sunday began to plaster marmalade onto her toast as Livvy raised her eyebrow at Kathy across the table. She had certainly made a mess of that! However, by the time the meal was over Sunday was back to her usual good-natured self, and after glancing at the clock she told them, 'You'd best get the children up to Treetops to Cissie, girls. The funeral is in two hours' time and we have to get ready and get there yet.'

Unlike Sunday, Cissie was not keen to risk a fall on the icy paths, so she had volunteered to stay behind to take care of the twins and Peggy while the rest of them attended the service, as they had all agreed that the children were too young to see such things. And so, just over an hour later, with Cissie entertaining the children in the vast, warm kitchen at Treetops, Sunday, Kathy and Livvy waited on the doorstep for the hearse that would transport Bobby's body to the church to arrive.

It was a solemn procession that wended its way to Mancetter Church following little Bobby on his final journey. John had insisted that the child should have the finest mahogany coffin that money could buy but, because Bobby was so small, it had had to be especially made and it was heartbreaking to see it and remember the child who lay inside whose young life had been cut short so abruptly. Edith was inconsolable and wept all the way through the service, but then so did most everybody else.

Eventually Bobby was laid to rest beneath the shelter of a yew tree in the churchyard. The last rites were read by a solemn-faced vicar and the sad procession made its way back to Treetops.

Cissie, in the meantime, had kept the children occupied as best she could but it had been no easy task. Although they had explained to Peggy that Bobby had died, she would not accept it and every single day she asked when he would be coming home. Bobby had been her hero, the one person in her who had always defended her and stood up for her. Many a time he

266

had taken the beating their father had intended for her, or given her his food when there wasn't enough for the two of them, saying he wasn't hungry, and now without him she was bereft.

'Time is a great healer,' Sunday told Edith as she sobbed on her shoulder. 'And one day you'll be able to remember the joy Bobby brought you in the short time you had him, and smile.'

At that moment Edith very much doubted it. Already now she was fretting about what might happen to Peggy. One thing she was sure of, should the authorities try to take her away from them, she would fight them like a tiger.

Chapter Thirty-Eight

Ben dragged himself back to his hut, his eyes burning from lack of sleep, and the terrible sights he had witnessed that day.

Admittedly, unlike the last war when he had fought on the front line with the rest of the men, this time he was not in the thick of the fighting. His job was to keep the horses fit so they could pull the carts that moved the heavy guns and equipment wherever they were needed. Soldiers also used the horses when they patrolled the tricky desert terrain around them. But sometimes, when he needed to take the terrified horses into an area where there was heavy fighting, the sight of so many fallen soldiers, and the smell of cordite, blood and death, on top of the deafening explosions and the rattle of gunfire, brought back the dreadful memories of those nightmare years during the last war. He couldn't seem to get away from it, even in sleep. On the rare occasions when he did manage to nap, his dreams were full of images of the beautiful animals he was tending dropping like stones, their nostrils flaring with panic as they frothed at the mouth with fear. Even though this time the horses weren't often in the line of fire, the screams of those long-dead horses he had watched mown down on the battlefields of France echoed through his nightmares and brought him starting awake in a tangle of sweat-drenched sheets.

His biggest dread was that he might be confronted with one of the horses he had reared at Treetops, as he was sure they would have been requisitioned by now, but thankfully as yet that hadn't happened, which was one blessing at least.

Only that evening he and an officer had almost come to blows when the man had mounted a young stallion that Ben was trying to keep quiet after the poor animal had nearly gone mad with terror when he had been taken into the battle zone. The animal had reared up when the officer had leapt onto his back and brought his whip crashing down on the terrified animal's rump. Ben had snatched it from his hand and snapped it in two across his knee.

'That won't do any good,' Ben had roared at him. 'The poor beast is scared. You need to take a different horse tonight.'

The officer had been red in the face as he tried to bring the horse under control. 'How *dare* you!' His eyes had glittered with rage. 'I could have you court-marshalled for that, you ignorant oaf! And as for this damn animal, if it's not going to do its job then I'll put a bullet in its head.'

Ben's young assistant, a spotty-faced youth with thick glasses who had been unable to join up for the fighting because of poor eyesight, had raced across to calm the situation down, which was just as well because Ben had been ready to drag the arrogant officer from his saddle and beat him to a pulp.

'I'll see to this, Corporal Branning.' He had pushed Ben towards the tent where the horses were kept as he grabbed at the reins and talked soothingly to the horse, and Ben had walked away with murder in his heart. As it happened, he wouldn't have to confront that particular officer again. Both he and the horse had been shot by a sniper as they patrolled through a ruined town on the edge of the desert and although Ben grieved for the poor horse, he felt nothing for the officer.

When Ben arrived back at the hut that was home to him and a number of other men he stared around despondently. It was almost as cold inside as it was out and the hard beds and thin blankets offered little comfort or protection against the biting cold, despite the smoky old stove that stood in the centre of it. His stomach was empty and growling with hunger, but Ben couldn't be bothered to go to the mess to see what meals were available.

It hit him then, like a blow between the eyes, that he had no home to go to now. Nobody would care if he should die tomorrow and, deep down, he knew it was all his own fault. He had tried not to think of what he had done to Sunday and the family but tonight for some reason it was playing on his mind. Where were they now? he wondered. They would have been forced to sell Treetops, of that he had no doubt, so where would they be living? Was Sunday even still alive? She would be an elderly lady now. And what would his father think of what he had done to her if he were still alive? He shuddered to think, for Sunday and Tom had adored each other. She had never been the same since his father's death, but it was too late to right the wrong he had done her.

The money he had stolen was tucked safely away in a bank doing no one any good, especially him. It had never brought him any joy, if truth be told, and certainly hadn't protected him from the war. And Kathy! As he thought of her tears came to his eyes. He had taken advantage of her, thinking that when it became known it would hurt Sunday, but what about Kathy? He could only hope that Kathy had put him from her mind and moved on with her life. As guilt stabbed at him, he lowered his head into his hands and sobbed like a baby.

On the morning of David's departure, the mood in the lodge was dark.

'Please don't go,' Daisy sobbed as she clung to his leg with tears streaming down her chubby cheeks. 'We loves you, Uncle David.'

'And I love you too,' he told her, his own voice husky as he stroked her silky curls.

Thomas added his own pleas to his sister's. 'We'll be *ever* so good if only you'll stay,' he pleaded.

'You're always good. But I have to go back to the hospital now.'

'Will you come back soon?'

'I can't promise how soon,' David told them honestly. 'But just as soon as the war is over this will be the first place I'll head for,' he promised, silently praying that he would be alive to keep it.

'An' when you come back will you be our daddy?' Daisy implored innocently.

Kathy's eyes stretched wide as David looked at her over the twins' heads and suddenly she realised how much he had come to mean to her. She had dreamed of Ben returning for so long, but now it hit her that he had never really cared for her, let alone loved her. She had offered herself to him on a plate but now she could see what had happened for what it was. To him it had been no more than a fling: she was there, she had made herself available to him and he had taken advantage of the fact.

She wasn't even sure now that she'd ever loved him, not truly – it was more like idolisation, a silly teenage crush, nothing at all like what she now realised she felt for David.

Conscious that David was still staring at her avidly she gave him a wobbly smile as he finally answered, 'If your mummy would allow it there is nothing I would like better than to be your daddy.'

Then somehow, she was in his arms and his lips were on hers and she felt her heart swell with love for him.

'I think that's an excellent idea,' she said gruffly when they finally drew apart. Sunday was watching with a broad smile on her face, and suddenly feeling self-conscious, Kathy gently pushed him away, saying, 'But now you'd better be off. You don't want to miss your train.'

'Come on, children, let's go and wait outside while David and Mummy say their goodbyes,' Sunday urged, shepherding the twins ahead of her.

'Did you mean it, Kathy, or did you say that just for the sake of the children?' David looked as if all his birthdays and Christmases had come at once as he took her in his arms again and she laid her head against his shoulder.

'I mean it.' She stared up at him with tears glistening on her long lashes. 'I think I've loved you for a long time but didn't admit it to myself.'

Her words, so long awaited, were like music to his ears. 'Well now you have and from now on I want you to write to me at least once a month. I want to know everything you and the twins have been up to. Do you promise?'

She nodded but there was no more time for at that moment they heard George stop outside in the pony and trap to give him a lift to the station. Petrol was heavily rationed and hard to come by and David had told George that he could walk, but George wouldn't hear of it.

'The exercise will do the horse good,' he had insisted.

David looked deep into Kathy's glorious eyes for one last time, committing every feature of her face to memory. 'I love you more than you'll ever know,' he said throatily, then lifting his kitbag he slung it across his shoulder and strode away before he broke down. At the door he paused just once to tell her, 'And when I get home after this bloody war is over, we'll be married as soon as possible. All right?'

She nodded numbly and wept as the door closed softly behind him. She had been such a fool. *But I'll make it up to him*, she promised herself. And then she prayed with all her being that he would come home safely. It would be just too cruel if he didn't.

'Well it certainly took you long enough to realise what a lovely chap David is,' Sunday remarked when they had tucked the children into bed later that evening. 'But at least you saw sense in the end.'

Kathy grinned. She hadn't felt so happy for a long time. 'We're going to be married as soon as the war is over,' she informed her mother and Sunday's face lit up.

'I'm delighted to hear it. At least that's one of you I won't have to worry about. Now I just have to make Livvy see the light.'

Kathy cocked her eyebrow as she carried the children's dirty clothes to the wash basket. 'What do you mean?'

'I should think it's obvious.' Sunday grinned as she poured

some milk into a saucepan for their cocoa. 'She and Giles are mad about each other, it's as clear as the noses on their faces, but the stupid pair are too stubborn to admit their feelings for each other.'

Kathy frowned. She had never really thought about it before but now, as she pictured them together, she supposed that her mother could be right.

'Ah well, what will be will be,' she said, and Sunday nodded in agreement.

'You're quite right. I just hope they make it soon.'

Chapter Thirty-Nine

May 1941

'Kathy, *wake up*! The sirens are wailing,' Sunday urged as she hurried into her daughter's room and urgently shook her arm. 'We need to get the children downstairs into the shelter.'

'Wh-what?' Kathy mumbled groggily as she knuckled sleep from her eyes, and then hearing the sirens she was instantly awake. Scrambling out of bed she rushed into the twins' room and as she lifted Daisy, who didn't even stir, Sunday crossed to Thomas's bed and lifted him. They made their way downstairs in darkness with the children clutched tightly in their arms and struggling towards the shelter in the kitchen they knelt down and gently laid them on the blankets that they always kept there. This was not the first raid that Nuneaton had suffered, and they had got into a routine now.

'There, they didn't even wake up.' Kathy gave a big yawn. 'Let's hope it doesn't go on for too long so we can get them back to bed.' Crossing to the fire she stirred it into life with a poker and then threw on some of the wood that she had collected from the copse. Even coal was getting harder to buy now but as they were surrounded by trees, thankfully they always had enough fuel to keep the house warm and cosy.

'Fancy a brew?' Kathy asked as she lit the oil lamp. Scarcely had the words left her mouth when they heard the drone of enemy planes overhead.

Sunday shuddered. 'I bet they're heading for Birmingham again,' she muttered tiredly. 'God help the poor souls.'

Kathy nodded and she had only just filled the kettle when the sound of an explosion sounded in the distance. 'Dear God, it sounds like our town is getting it again,' she muttered. 'Let's hope it doesn't go on for too long.'

Dousing the light, she crossed to the window and twitched the blackout curtains aside to peer up into the sky. 'My God, they're dropping incendiary bombs,' she gasped, horrified. 'And with the moon so bright tonight and the fires from the incendiaries everything beneath will be an easy target.'

Sunday joined her and her heart leapt into her mouth as she watched the deadly planes releasing their bombs. It looked like the majority of the town was being hit and she could only pray that being a little way out of it they would be safe.

They were still there when an urgent banging came on the back door and when Sunday hurried to answer it, still in her dressing gown with her long grey hair hanging in a plait across her shoulder, she found John standing there with George behind him.

'We've come to take you all up to the house,' he told her in a voice that brooked no argument. 'It's not safe for you all to be here.'

'But the children are safe and asleep in the Morrison shelter,' Sunday pointed out.

He shook his head. 'That's as may be but where will you

and Kathy shelter if they drop any bombs before they get to the town? There isn't enough room in that for all four of you, so come along and stop arguing. I won't take no for an answer. I have a horrible feeling this is going to be the worst raid yet.'

Seeing that he meant business, she allowed him and George to push past her to get the children.

'I'll just get dressed and then I'll follow you,' she told him, but he shook his head.

'Just throw a coat and some shoes on. There's no time for messing about. I have the cellar all ready for us.'

Sunday and Kathy did as they were told and soon they were hurrying along the drive, which was thankfully shrouded on either side by trees that were now in leaf. The sounds of the planes overhead and the explosions were so loud outside that they couldn't hear themselves speak so they just concentrated on getting the children to safety as soon as possible.

Once inside Treetops John urged them towards the cellar door and as they descended the stairs, she saw Edith there with Peggy fast asleep on her lap. Cissie was there too and Sunday was pleasantly surprised at how cosy they had made it. An oil lamp and candles were burning, illuminating the long row of wine racks and John had taken down a table and some chairs and a primus stove, on which stood a kettle that was just coming to the boil. He had also brought some old wing chairs down from the loft for the adults to sit comfortably in and there were padded benches arranged along one wall for the children to lie on.

'There, they'll be as snug as bugs in rugs on there,' Cissie declared once the children were comfortably settled and covered in blankets. 'Now, who's fer a nice cup o' tea?'

She set out some cups then produced a cake tin full of scones she had made earlier that day.

'There's carrots instead o' fruit inside 'em,' she apologised. 'An' I'm afraid I never thought to bring any jam. But at least they'll fill a hole till breakfast.'

'The good lord knows what we'll find out there tomorrow,' John said sombrely, once they had settled back in the chairs and were tucking in to the scones, and they all nodded in agreement, their thoughts and prayers with the people in the town.

It was a very long night, and just as George had forecast it was the worst raid they had had to date, and it seemed to go on forever. It was almost dawn when the all-clear finally sounded and by that time it didn't seem worth waking the children to go to their beds.

'Let them have their sleep down here,' Cissie whispered as the adults all climbed the stairs and went outside. They were horrified at the sight that met their eyes for a huge black cloud of smoke hung over the town in the distance.

'We'd better get dressed and drive into town to see if there's anything we can do,' John said to George soberly. 'They might need volunteers to dig for survivors if any houses have been hit.'

'But ain't you two a bit long in the tooth to be doin' things like that?' Cissie asked bluntly. 'Why don't yer leave it to the young 'uns?'

'Most of the young men are away fighting,' John pointed out. 'And judging by that cloud I have a feeling the town will need all the help it can get. What say you, George?'

'I'm up for it,' George said heartily. 'We ain't quite past it yet. You wait there an' I'll go an' get the car. I should be savin' petrol really, but this is an emergency.'

Ten minutes later the men set off to see what could be done to help leaving the women to see to the children.

The extent of the damage became apparent when they reached the bottom of Tuttle Hill and turned into Manor Court Road. Whole houses lay in ruins, some still ablaze as firefighters battled to douse the flames. In other places women and children were digging amongst the ruins with their bare hands as they desperately searched for survivors.

The bodies that had been recovered had been laid out at the sides of the road and covered with sheets provided by people whose houses still stood, and a tiny little girl clutching tight to a teddy bear was sitting on a kerb, her hair thick with brick dust as tears streamed down her dirty cheeks, leaving white trails through the grime.

'Poor little bugger,' a firefighter who saw John looking towards her said. 'Luckily she was asleep in a Morrison shelter when we found her but her mam, dad an' brother all copped it. The neighbours have sent for her grandparents so hopefully they'll take her in.'

Grim-faced, John nodded before asking, 'What can we do to help?'

Training his hose higher onto the fire he was trying to bring under control the fireman told him, 'Just dig if you're able. But be careful – if you smell gas step away. This whole place is a ticking time bomb with so many damaged gas pipes about.'

As the morning progressed more bad news filtered through to them. The majority of the town had been hit and already over a hundred dead had been found. Chilvers Coton Church and the surrounding churchyard had taken a hit too and they heard that there were headstones and the bones of disturbed bodies all over the place.

John shuddered at the thought. It seemed that the Luftwaffe had no respect for the British people whatsoever, be they alive or dead. Even the injured had had to be turned away from the hospital because that had been hit too.

Women from the WVS appeared bearing flasks of tea and sandwiches as the morning wore on and George and John stopped to take a well-deserved break. They had both seen sights during the day that would stay with them forever: an old couple still in their bed, which had fallen through the ceiling, their arms clasped tight about each other. Dead cats and dogs – someone's beloved pets. Children with wide, staring eyes, their mouths open as they had screamed for their parents. The two men felt as though they had been caught in the grip of a nightmare. And then shortly after lunchtime the army appeared and an officer approached John and George to tell them kindly, 'Why don't you two go home and get some rest now? My lads will take over. But thank you for all you've done. The people hereabouts have told me you've both worked like slaves all day.'

Both men were now almost dropping with fatigue and they nodded numbly. Their clothes and shoes were ruined, every muscle in their bodies was screaming a protest and yet had they been asked they would both have said they would not have done things any differently. The one bright spot in the whole day had been when they had managed to pull a screaming baby from the ruins. How the little tot had managed to survive beneath all the bricks and debris they had no idea, but it had made all their hard work worthwhile.

'What do you reckon, George? Shall we call it a day?'

George nodded. 'Aye, I reckon so. An' when I get home, I'm gonna sleep the clock round. That's if there ain't another raid tonight o' course.'

The following day they discovered that over ten thousand homes had been damaged, three hundred and eighty had been completely destroyed, and a hundred and thirty people had lost their lives. Most of the munition factories had been flattened as well as the church and part of the hospital. It had been the worst raid that the market town had suffered so far during the war and one that those who had survived it would never forget.

Chapter Forty

Throughout May the war seemed to escalate, and London was bombed relentlessly, but then the British people knew sweet revenge when the German's newest and fastest battleship, the *Bismarck* – the pride of their fleet – was chased by over a hundred British vessels and sunk in the Atlantic.

'Serves the buggers right!' George said heartily as they all sat in the kitchen at Treetops listening to the radio report. At John's insistence Sunday, Kathy and her family had not returned to the lodge since the night of the raid, except to collect their clothes, and although it had felt strange to be back in Treetops at first, sometimes now Sunday found it hard to believe that they had ever been away. John had even ensured that both Sunday and Kathy were back in their old bedrooms and all in all the arrangement was working well.

The twins loved living there and now that she had them to play with Peggy was slowly coming out of her shell again after the loss of her brother.

That was why it was such a shock when Sunday opened the door one bright May morning to find two very official-looking people standing there, a man and a woman.

The man was smartly dressed in a trilby hat and overcoat while the woman was small and straight-faced.

'We've come to see Mr John Willerby,' the woman informed Sunday imperiously. 'Are you the maid?'

'No, I am *not* the maid,' Sunday answered indignantly. 'But if you'd care to come in, I'll see if I can find him for you.'

She showed them into the drawing room, which was scattered with toys the children had been playing with earlier, before hurrying off to track John down. As she had expected, he was ensconced in his study and after tapping at the door she went in. 'There are two people here to see you, John, and I have a feeling they might be something to do with Peggy.'

His face clouded. 'Oh dear!' But then with a nod he rose and followed her back across the hallway.

'Good morning, I am John Willerby. How may I help you?' he asked as he entered the room and held out his hand.

'Actually, I believe it is we who may be able to help you,' the small, bird-like woman answered with an oily smile. John instantly took a dislike to her.

'I am Miss Tyler from the welfare department in the East End of London and Mr Parsons here is the housemaster at an orphanage we use to place children who have been bereaved of their parents. I believe you have Peggy Walker staying here with you?'

John nodded. 'We do and she's doing remarkably well, all things considered, which I told you on the phone the last time we spoke.'

'Good, good,' she said with a false smile as she seated herself and folded her hands neatly in her lap. 'It has been very good of you to allow her to come here as an evacuee. But of course we must be responsible for her now that she has no family to return to when the war is over.'

'Why?' John said brusquely. 'The child is quite welcome to stay here.'

'Ah, but you must understand that it isn't as simple as that,' Miss Tyler twittered. 'We have a responsibility to the child.'

'Like you had when she lived at home and her father interfered with her?' John spat and the little woman paled as her gloved hand rose to her mouth.

He leaned towards her then to tell her in no uncertain terms, 'Peggy is happier here than she ever was in London. She's safer too because we live in a village so have less chance of being bombed. It's taken her a while to get over the deaths of her brother and family and now *you* turn up out of the blue and tell me that you know what's best for her? I don't think so! You've never even met her!'

'Really, Mr Willerby, there is no need to take this attitude,' Miss Tyler stuttered. 'We are only here in the best interests of the child.'

'In that case leave her where she is,' he retorted. 'My house-keeper is a fine, upstanding woman who is longing to adopt the girl. I would myself but I realise that I'm a little old to be taking on a child of her age.'

'I . . . I see.' Miss Tyler had well and truly had the wind taken out of her sails. 'Well, I would of course have to assess this woman to see if she was suitable.'

'Of course,' John conceded and then turning to the gentleman he said shortly, 'And you, sir. Your establishment must be full of orphans at the moment? Would a generous donation help towards some of their keep?'

'Well, er . . . yes, it certainly would,' the man babbled, his greedy eyes lighting up. 'Of course,' he added hastily as Miss Tyler glared at him. 'All donations go towards making a better life for our poor unfortunate orphans.'

Hm, and I bet some of them end up in your back pocket, John thought wryly.

However, his voice was calm as he asked Miss Tyler, 'Would you like to meet Edith? She has been with me for many years and should she be allowed to adopt Peggy they will have a home here where Peggy is settled for as long as they like.'

'Yes, very well,' Miss Tyler answered doubtfully. 'But you must understand the decision would not be up to me alone. I would have to take her details back to the department and there would have to be meetings to consider if it would be a suitable place for the child.'

'Of course, I understand that,' John agreed. 'And once you have spoken to Edith you are welcome to speak to Peggy also. Surely what she wants should be taken into account as well? The child has suffered quite enough heartbreak and upheaval without her having to enter an institution where she knows no one. You are also quite welcome to see her bedroom, speak to the school she attends and inspect my home, if you so wish? So now, shall I send Edith in to you?'

The woman inclined her head and without another word John left the room.

Edith entered the room shortly after as if she was going into a boxing ring. She was prepared to do whatever was necessary to keep Peggy, as the two officials soon discovered. Just before the interview ended John appeared again with a sizeable cheque made out to the orphanage and Mr Parsons's eyes lit up like light bulbs at the size of it.

'Why, Mr Willerby . . . this is *more* than generous,' he

announced, pocketing the cheque quickly as if he were afraid the other man might change his mind. 'And I have to say, I think Edith would make a wonderful mother, don't you agree, Miss Tyler?' he said ingratiatingly.

Once again, she glared at him as she rose from her seat. 'It just remains for me to see Peggy now. Is she here?'

'She's in the kitchen, as it happens,' Edith told her. 'I'll fetch her in to you.'

Minutes later the little girl appeared, looking from one to the other of the strangers fearfully.

'I's ain't goin' wiv you if you've come to try an' take me away,' she announced with a quiver in her voice. 'I loves Edith an' livin' at Treetops an' all me friends is 'ere now.'

'I see.' Miss Tyler noted the way the child clung to Edith's skirts. 'Well, before I can tell you what is going to happen, I have to contact your school to get their opinion of how you are doing and then it will be down to my superiors,' she told her as if she were talking to an adult. 'But now, before we catch the train back to London, perhaps you would like to show me your bedroom?'

Peggy led her from the room skipping up the stairs ahead of the visitors, and in truth they couldn't find fault with what they saw. With John's permission, Edith had painted the room in a pretty shade of pink and dolls and books were scattered all around it. Thick, velvet curtains lined with blackout material hung at the windows and a handmade patchwork quilt that had taken Edith many hours to lovingly make covered the bed.

'I dare say this is quite satisfactory,' Miss Tyler sniffed. Even she could not criticise it. 'So, we will take our leave of you now and you will hear from us in due course with our decision.

Good day to you.' And with that she waltzed away with her nose in the air as if there was a bad smell beneath it.

'Old witch,' Edith muttered as she cuddled Peggy protectively. 'Don't you get worrying about her, sweetheart. I'm not going to let anybody take you away from me. But come on now, let's go out into the sunshine for a while, shall we, and get some colour back into your cheeks?'

She smiled to herself as they made their way downstairs. Had it been anyone else she would have asked George to give them a lift back to the train station in the trap as it was a very long walk, but let them make their own way there. In fact, she heartily hoped they got blisters and got lost on the way.

Chapter Forty-One

'So, how were they?' Sunday stared at her daughter's tear-stained face.

Kathy sniffed. It was clear that she had been crying although she would never have admitted it. 'They walked in with their new teacher as right as rain and never even looked back.' She grinned. 'I don't know if that made it better or worse, to be honest. I can't believe that they've started school. They looked so little lining up with the other children in the playground. Of course, it would have been awful if they'd clung to me crying. But then it hurt that they went off without a tear as well.'

Sunday chuckled. She knew exactly how Kathy was feeling – she had felt exactly the same the day Kathy had started school.

'I'm sure they'll be absolutely fine,' she assured her. 'And Peggy will love having them there even if they are in different classes. She'll look out for them, never you fear. But what will you do with your time now? Knowing you, you won't want to be sitting about all day waiting for them to come home.'

'You're quite right,' Kathy agreed. 'So, I was wondering, if George were willing to pick them up after school each day, do you think you could manage them for a couple of hours if I went back to work? I know the hospital is screaming out for doctors and nurses and I'd like to feel that I'm doing my bit.'

'Of course I could manage,' Sunday assured her. She had been half expecting this. Kathy was an amazing mother, but now that the children were off her hands during the daytime, she'd guessed that she'd want to make herself useful again, and she'd always enjoyed working.

'In that case I'll go into town today and have a word with Matron.' Anything would be better than sitting moping about the children, she'd decided, and so she hurried away upstairs to get ready before making her way to the hospital.

Once there, she made her way straight to the matron's office, relieved to see that, despite the bomb damage, little had changed there.

'Kathy, why how lovely it is to see you,' Matron said with genuine pleasure as Kathy entered her room. 'You're looking very well. I hope those lovely children are too? But how can I help you?'

'Actually, I was hoping that it was me that might be able to help you,' Kathy told her as she returned her smile. 'You see, the twins started school today, so I was thinking of coming back to work, if you'll have me, of course. I could only do part-time as I'd need to get the children to school before I started each day, and I might be a little rusty now admittedly but . . .'

Matron held up her hand to silence her before she could go any further. 'My dear young woman, nursing is a little like riding a bike, you never forget how it's done, so rusty or not I'd be grateful of any hours you could do. I should warn you though – we have some very bad cases here that have filtered through from the military hospitals,' she warned. 'Do you think you could handle it?'

'Of course – I'm a nurse,' Kathy told her confidently.

After a little discussion it was agreed that Kathy would start back the following Monday and though she was delighted, Kathy found she was in a strange mood as she returned to Treetops after doing a little shopping for Cook. It felt funny to be going back to work and she would miss the children dreadfully, but it was also nice to think that she would have a measure of independence again and she found she was looking forward to it.

'So, all decided, is it?' Cissie asked when Kathy strolled into the kitchen shortly after lunchtime with her basket of shopping.

'Yes, all sorted. I'm starting back next week.' Kathy's eyes were drawn to a letter on the mantelpiece and her heart lifted as she recognised David's handwriting.

'Postie brought it about an hour or so ago,' Cissie told her as Kathy eagerly lifted it down.

'Right, I'll just go and read what he has to say then I'll be back to help you and Cook prepare the dinner,' Kathy promised as she scooted out of the kitchen and headed for the privacy of her room.

Once there, she tore the envelope open eagerly and settled on the bed to begin to read.

My Dear Kathy,

As always, I can't begin to tell you how much I am missing you, Daisy and Thomas. I pray that you are all safe and well. It's as hot as hell here, no pleasure at all, I'm afraid when I'm in the operating theatres all day . . .

The next few lines were heavily censored, and Kathy sighed with frustration as she read on.

Have the twins started school yet? I know sometimes the letters take a long time to reach you so I am surmising that they will have by now. At school! It's hard to take in, they're growing so quickly.

The next part of the letter had been deleted too but continued further down the page.

I can hardly wait for this war to be over now. It seems to be going on forever, but when at last it is over, we will be together for always and I cannot wait. It seems so long since I've seen you, but you are the first person I think of every morning when I wake and the last one I think of before I sleep – not that I get much of that. We are losing so many young men daily. It breaks my heart that although myself and the other doctors do our best some are beyond help. It's the noise that is the worst, the constant sound of gunfire and . . .

Kathy sighed with frustration as she saw that the censor had been at work yet again. And then finally he ended:

Stay strong, my love, this war cannot go on forever. Take good care of yourself and the children. Thinking of coming home to you is all that is keeping me going now,
   With all my love
   David xxxx

As Kathy placed the letter back in the envelope there were tears in her eyes. David sounded tired, she thought worriedly, but then she supposed he would be. From previous letters he had written she knew that sometimes he had to stand in the operating theatre for up to eighteen hours a day and the terrible injuries he saw would be enough to get anyone down.

She shuddered to think of it and prayed David would stay strong enough to cope with all he had to deal with. In some ways she wished that she could have joined him, but then she would never be able to bring herself to leave the children so, for now, she would have to settle for doing what she could in the local hospital.

The children were in a happy mood when Kathy picked them up from school later that day.

'We's had great fun,' Daisy told her animatedly. 'An' I's done you a picture. It's in my bag an' I'll give it you when we get home.'

'And what about you?' Kathy questioned Thomas, who was looking nowhere near as smart as he had when she'd left him at school that morning.

He beamed up at her as he picked his nose. Normally she would have told him off but just for today she decided she would let him get away with it. 'Me an' the other lads played football in the playground at break time.' It was quite a novelty for Thomas to have boys his own age to play with and he intended to make the most of it.

'Don't worry, I kept my eye on 'em for you,' Peggy informed her solemnly and Kathy gave her a grateful smile.

'That was very kind of you, Peggy,' she told her, and the child's chest swelled with importance. As yet there had been nothing more from the welfare department but as Kathy had told Edith, 'No news is good news!' and now all they could do was keep their fingers crossed that Peggy would be allowed to stay. Somewhere along the line she had become very much a part of the family and they all adored her.

When they reached Treetops, Edith and Cissie were waiting for them with glasses of milk and little rock buns straight from the oven.

Sunday, who was sitting by the empty fireplace, watched them tuck in with a smile on her face, and said nostalgically to Kathy, 'I don't know, it doesn't seem more than a minute since it was your first day at school. Make the most of every moment, darling, because before you know it, they'll be grown and flown the nest.'

Kathy sighed as she thought of her mother's words. As yet their true father had never even seen them and she doubted now that he ever would, so he would never know what he was missing. It was doubtful he even knew of their existence but suddenly it didn't matter anymore. Had he intended to ever come back he surely would have long ago. She could accept the fact now because she realised that if only David could come through the war unscathed the twins would have the chance of growing up in a real family unit. Thoughts of David brought a smile to her face and she wished she had realised what a truly wonderful man he was years ago. Now all she could do was wait and pray that he would stay safe because she couldn't picture her future without him.

Chapter Forty-Two

On the following Monday morning, after first dropping the children off at school, Kathy caught a bus into town and reported for duty at the hospital. It felt strange being back in her nurse's uniform, but she was looking forward to working again.

Matron met her, delighted to have her back, and led her into her office where she warned her, 'You will be working on the men's ward today, Nurse Branning, but I should warn you there are some very bad cases in there. Truthfully, all we can do for some of them is offer them palliative care, poor souls. Others you will find have been horrifically injured. The military hospitals on the coast are full to bursting with new patients arriving daily so every bed we have is full. The patients are then transferred to whichever hospital has room for them. Every one of the nurses and doctors we have left without exception is exhausted, which is why I am so delighted to welcome you back, even if it is on shorter hours. But now, if you would like to report to the ward sister, I'm sure she will be happy to go through the patients' charts with you.'

Kathy nodded and after hanging her cloak in the small nurses' staff room she went straight to the ward where the sister was waiting for her.

She too greeted Kathy effusively before going through each patient's notes with her.

'The young man in the second bed on the left isn't expected to last the day,' she told her regretfully. 'He suffered major burns to most of his body, so we are keeping him heavily sedated, so he won't be in too much pain. There is nothing else we can do for him.'

Kathy glanced towards the young man but all she could see was a head swathed in bandages above the sheets, although thankfully he appeared to be sleeping and showed no signs of distress.

'In the next bed is Mr Jakes. He has had both his legs and one arm amputated after standing on a land mine.' The sister shook her head. 'I have every reason to believe that he will pull through but the problem there is he doesn't want to. He considers himself less of a man now and won't even allow his wife to come and see him.'

She then briefly went through the rest of the names on the list and although Kathy had expected things to be bad, nothing could have prepared her for some of the injuries she was hearing about, and to think that David had to deal with this, and worse, on a daily basis! Even so she was determined to do her best for each and every one of them and soon she was back in her stride and it was as if she had never been away.

After a very short lunch break, Kathy returned to the ward to find the young man with burns had taken a turn for the worse and began to cry for his mother.

'Unfortunately, his mother is having to come from London,' the sister told Kathy. 'We sent a telegram very early this morning to tell her how serious his condition is, and we got one back within an hour saying that she would get here as soon as possible.

But with the way the trains are running there's no way of knowing if she will get here in time.'

'How awful,' Kathy answered 'Sister, would you mind if I sat with him to offer what little comfort I can? I would hate to think of anyone leaving this earth with no one holding their hand.'

'How kind, of course.'

Kathy hurried over and pulled a chair up to the side of his bed and started to speak to him soothingly.

'Your mum is on the way,' she told him gently. 'And I don't mind betting she's so proud of you. Where were you stationed before you became injured?'

'Africa,' he said throatily. 'It were 'ot as 'ell out there but nowhere near as 'ot as these bloody burns.' All that was visible were his lips and eyes, which stared up at her, full of pain and suffering. Every other inch of him was swathed in bandages making him look like an Egyptian mummy.

'And do you have a girlfriend, Jimmy?' she asked after checking his name on his chart.

His head moved just a fraction. 'Yes, 'er name is Carol an' she's a right little sweet'eart. She's in the WRENs so she can't get to see me but I 'ad a letter off 'er while I were in the hospital in Portsmouth.'

As Kathy stared at the bandages, she wondered what he had looked like before the war. She could see by the notes on the end of his bed that he was just twenty-one years old but even as she was trying to picture him, he winced and tried to raise his arm.

'I'm going to get you some more painkillers,' she told him and after she had administered an injection he thankfully drifted off into a drug-induced sleep. Fortunately, his mother appeared at the door an hour later and after pulling the curtains about Jimmy's bed to give them some privacy Kathy hurried away to see what could be done for the rest of the patients.

By the time she finished her shift at five o'clock she was worn out and downhearted.

'How did your first day go?' Sunday asked when she entered the kitchen some time later and Kathy promptly burst into tears.

'Oh, Mum, those poor men! I know we read about what they suffer in the newspaper and hear it on the radio, but nothing can prepare you for actually seeing it. And they're all so brave.' She went on to tell her mother about Jimmy. He had died within an hour of his mother arriving, almost as if he had been waiting for her, and Kathy had cried unashamedly. It was such a waste of a young life, but Jimmy was only the tip of the iceberg. Thousands of young men just like him were dying daily and still there was no end to the war in sight. Still, she consoled herself, at least she was doing her bit to help now, and she still had her adorable twins to come home to. No one could stay sad around them for long.

'Corporal Branning, get up this instant. What's wrong with you!' The officer standing at the end of Ben's bed was rattling the iron footboard irritably, but Ben was almost oblivious to his presence as he lay there shaking. He was soaked with sweat and the officer soon realised that something was seriously amiss.

'Get over to the hospital and ask one of the doctors to come over and take a look at him as soon as possible,' he barked to the young corporal standing beside him. 'And in the meantime, you'll have to deal with the horses. He's clearly in no fit state to.'

'But, sir . . .' The young man looked concerned. 'I ain't got the foggiest idea how to handle horses.'

'Then learn!'

'Yes, sir!' The young man saluted and turning about he fled out of the hut.

Fifteen minutes later he was back with David in tow, but the officer had long gone about his duties.

'It's this chap here,' he told David. 'His name is Ben Branning.'

David started. *Ben Branning* did you say?' His mind was working overtime. Wasn't Kathy's half-brother called Ben? The one that had run off after stealing all Sunday's money?

Pulling himself together he leaned over Ben and asked, 'Are you feeling ill, old chap?' But he didn't really need to ask. He could see at a glance what the problem was. This chap had shell shock, or battle fatigue as they were now calling it. He was shaking convulsively, and his eyes were wide and staring so the only thing he could do was recommend that he be shipped home until – or *if* – he recovered.

'Name?'

Somehow Ben managed to answer him. 'B-Branning . . . Ben Branning.'

'And where are you from, Branning?'

'The Midlands . . . Treetops.'

David swallowed hard. Yes, it was him all right. He'd recognise him anywhere. The thief. The one that had ensured his wife-to-be had been turned out of her home. He had never been fond of Ben, even before he had stolen from Sunday. He could remember when he had first started to visit Kathy at Treetops how unwelcome Ben had always made him feel. But he mustn't allow personal feelings to affect his duty so he told the young corporal behind him, 'Go and tell the sister I shall be admitting him then arranging that he be shipped home, unfit for duty.' At least he wasn't lying there. From the looks of him he wouldn't even be able to look after himself, let alone the horses. In this state he was neither use nor ornament.

Twenty minutes later Ben was lying in a hospital bed in a ward reserved for the men who were suffering from the same condition as him. Unfortunately, it could be some time before he was returned home for the physically maimed and injured had priority over the men suffering with mental breakdowns.

David visited him over the next couple of days as often as he could and although Ben was still far from well, with rest he did seem to recover slightly, to the point that he could answer questions and speak.

'Don't you remember me?' David asked one day and Ben stared at him curiously. 'We've met before.'

'When?'

'I'm a friend of Kathy Branning's.' David hesitated. 'In fact, she's my fiancée.'

Ben's eyes stretched wide. *'You're* engaged to Kathy?'

'I most certainly am,' David told him proudly. 'And as soon as this damn war is over, we're going to be married and I'm going to adopt her twins.'

'Kathy has twins!' Ben gasped.

'She does, and they're the most delightful, mischievous children you could ever wish to meet,' David said fondly.

'And how old are they?' Ben forced himself to ask.

'Hmm . . .' David had to think. 'They were four on the twenty-eighth of last month, I believe. They've just started school, as it happens. They agreed to take them a little early so that Kathy could get back to nursing.'

Ben closed his eyes and groaned deep in his throat. The

children couldn't be this doctor's if he was speaking of adopting them and to his knowledge Kathy hadn't had a boyfriend, apart from himself before he left so . . . *No!* His head wagged from side to side in denial. Surely Kathy couldn't have been pregnant when he left? But then as he groggily tried to work out the dates everything fitted together. The children *must* be his, but why hadn't she told him that she was with child?

Because you never gave her a chance to, you just used her, a little voice in his head said accusingly and burying his face in his pillow he began to shake again as it hit home what a total mess he had made of his life.

Chapter Forty-Three

Three weeks later, as Kathy read the letter that had just arrived from David, she began to tremble, and her hand flew to her mouth as panic set in.

> *Benjamin Branning, Sunday's stepson, has just been shipped back to England suffering with battle fatigue. He was admitted to the hospital and when I saw him, I realised who he was.*

If David had found Ben, would they have spoken about her? Would David have mentioned the twins? She had never told a living soul, not even her mother, who the father of the twins was, but if David had told Ben about them would Ben put two and two together and realise they were his? She had spent the first years of the children's lives longing for him to come back and meet them and yet now she fervently prayed that he would stay away.

Taking a deep breath, she tried to calm down. Of course Ben would never dare to show his face here again. He would be too afraid of reprisals, surely? For all he knew Sunday could have reported him to the police and they could still be searching for him even now. She looked at the date on David's letter. It had been posted over two weeks ago so Ben would likely be back in Britain now, in some hospital somewhere, she supposed. But what if he did come back? a nagging little voice asked.

'Mummy . . . I'm clean now,' Daisy's voice floated to her from along the landing and bundling the letter back into the envelope she shoved it into her pocket and hurried to the bathroom.

'Come on, sleepy head.' Kathy smiled as Daisy clambered out of the bath and her mother dried her with a large, fluffy towel. 'Thomas is waiting for your story and then it's off to the land of nod for you two. It's school tomorrow.'

Once Daisy was clad in a clean nightdress Kathy gave her a cuddle then bundled her along the landing and into the bedroom she shared with Thomas, who was already yawning.

Lifting the story book, Kathy began to read to them but before she had got to the end of the third page, they were both snoring softly so, laying the book down, Kathy smiled and tiptoed quietly from the room.

On the way downstairs she wondered if she should mention what David had told her to her mother, but then decided against it. It would only worry and upset her and that was the last thing Kathy wanted. Sunday was no spring chicken and Kathy didn't want to alarm her. For now, at least, she would keep the news as her secret and wait to see if anything developed from it.

It was a blustery, wet day at the airfield, and Livvy was having a cup of tea in the mess with Giles and the rest of the air crew that would be flying that day. 'I wonder if the flights will be cancelled. The weather forecast is appalling, gusty strong winds and rain,' Livvy remarked.

Giles shrugged. 'I doubt it; we're targeting an arms factory and a big airfield in Berlin today so it's going to be an important raid from what our flight officer told us.'

Livvy bit her lip as she glanced out of the window anxiously. It was mid-October now and already the weather had turned, and the leaves were beginning to flutter from the trees. She could see the trees bending in the strong wind and shuddered to think of the pilots who would soon have to fly the large Lancasters that had recently been delivered to their site. The planes were enormous and heavy, and she knew that controlling them in such bad weather conditions made flying them all the more difficult.

Not that Giles seemed concerned. Over the last few weeks they had gone out together on a number of occasions when their time off coincided and although she hated to admit it to herself, she had grown fond of him to the point that each time he was out on a mission she would watch anxiously for his return.

Already the pilots were kitted out in their flying suits and Livvy, who would be one of the operators guiding them out of the base, was due at work in ten minutes' time. 'Take care then and have a safe journey.'

He grinned at her. 'You bet. I'll see you when I get back, if you're not already tucked up in bed by then, that is. I can't see us being back until very late tonight at the earliest.'

She nodded and headed out to the station where soon she was seated with her headphones on. From the control tower she could see the pilots walking across the runway and climbing into their planes and then she saw the great beasts shudder into life and watched as one by one they turned to point their noses down the runway.

'Oscar Tango, get into position and prepare to take off,' she told Giles over the radio when it was his turn. She knew exactly which plane he and his crew were in.

'Oscar Tango to control, receiving loud and clear.'

She saw the plane begin to taxi down the runway before lifting to join the others. Soon the perfect formation of aircraft was nothing more than a dot in the sky.

'Stay safe!' she whispered to herself.

'What was that you said, Livvy?' the operator on the next table asked as she took off her headphones and Livvy flushed.

'Oh sorry, Sylvia, I was just muttering to myself.'

Flustered and unable to shake off the deep feeling of foreboding that had settled on her, Livvy turned her attention back to the job in hand. Another crew should be returning from their mission any time now and the operators were holding their breath as they waited to see if they had all made it back.

By the time the planes reached Berlin a heavy fog had settled, which made flying as well as finding the right targets very difficult.

'Do you think we should turn back?' Giles's flight engineer asked worriedly as he peered out of the cockpit. 'I'm always afraid we might end up dropping the bombs on houses in this weather, be they German or not, innocent women and kids don't deserve to die in air raids.'

'Mission control would have instructed us if they wanted us to abort the mission, and anyway we're almost there now so we may as well go and drop our loads then hightail it back home. I don't know about you but I'm dying for a cuppa.'

The planes were all still flying in exact formation but suddenly Messerschmitts appeared from the mist and instantly the Spitfires that were flying behind the heavy Lancasters flew into action, guns blazing.

'Christ, I reckon Drew in the next plane has just taken a hit,' Giles's navigator exclaimed as he peered out of the window. The plane was dropping behind and losing height and suddenly it dipped forward and started to nosedive towards the ground with one of its wings on fire.

'I hope the chaps had time to eject,' Giles said through gritted teeth as he steered sharply to the left to avoid a German plane. The next ten minutes were a nightmare, during which Giles saw another of their planes take a hit, as well as three of the German ones. At least the Spitfire pilots were doing a good job and according to the radio contact they were now above their target.

'Fire!' Giles screamed at his bomb aimer and seconds later the undercarriage of the plane slid open and the bombs went whistling towards the earth below. The explosion they caused as they landed was so loud the crew could hear it even at their altitude.

'Job done,' Giles stated grimly as he turned the nose of the plane. 'Now let's get the hell out of here.'

Suddenly there was a loud crack and as Giles looked to the side, he was appalled to see his navigator lying back in his seat with blood pouring from a gaping wound in his chest. The wind was whistling through the broken window, which made it almost impossible to keep the plane on course and then he noticed his left-side wing smoking before bursting into flames.

This is it, Giles thought as he pressed the eject button and offered up a prayer, and then he was hurtling towards the ground, and strangely, the last face he thought of before he crashed into a field, and darkness claimed him, was Livvy's.

Chapter Forty-Four

'Why don't you go and get some rest?' the radio officer told Livvy in the early hours of the next morning, but she shook her head. She had stayed on long after her shift had finished to see the planes return and now most of them were back. There were only four missing and the pilots who had already landed had told them that at least three had taken a hit. That meant there was still a possibility of one coming back, but would it be Giles's plane? She had lost radio contact with him and some of the other planes when they were somewhere over Berlin early that evening and now she couldn't rest until she knew he was safe.

Suddenly there was a low droning noise over the tower and the last Lancaster dropped into view before bumping along the runway to eventually come to a shuddering halt. Without thinking, Livvy flung the headphones aside and was out of her seat and racing out of the door and across the runway, only to come to an abrupt stop when a weary pilot, closely followed by his crew, climbed down from the cockpit.

It was Giles's good friend, Will, and at the sight of her he hung his head.

'*Giles?*'

He looked at her and shook his head at the question in her eyes. 'Sorry, Livvy. He was flying right next to me when his plane took a hit.'

'But didn't he try to get out?' There was panic in her voice now.

He nodded wearily. 'Oh, he ejected all right, but I couldn't see if his parachute opened or not. It was too foggy. I'm so sorry. He was a good chap was Giles.'

'Yes . . . yes, he was,' she said brokenly as she turned and blindly made her way back to her hut. 'He was a very, very good bloke.' She only wished now that she had taken the time to tell him so.

Cissie was cleaning the hall windows when something on the drive caught her eye and glancing up her heart sank as she saw the telegram boy furiously cycling towards her, his legs going like pistons.

'Oh, dear God,' she muttered as she looked towards the study door. John was in there with Sunday enjoying a cup of tea; should she fetch him? Deciding to answer the door herself she took a deep breath and flung it open.

'Telegram for Mr John Willerby,' the boy said and Cissie nodded, her heart in her mouth.

'I'll see that he gets it, son . . . thank you.'

The boy handed it over and flew off down the drive like the wind as Cissie stared numbly down at the brown envelope. Eventually she squared her shoulders, took a deep, shuddering breath and went to tap on the door.

'Cissie, how many times have I told you, you don't have to

knock,' John scolded gently, but then as he saw the envelope in her hand the colour drained from his face.

'I'm afraid it's for you.' Cissie held it out to him and for a moment it was as if he was frozen to the spot, but then he reached out and once he had taken it, he stared at it numbly.

'Would you like me to open it for you?' Sunday asked in a small voice and he nodded as he handed it over.

Shaking, she slit the envelope with her thumb and after hastily scanning the contents she looked at him, her eyes brimming with tears. 'It . . . it says that Giles is missing in action, presumed dead . . . I'm *so* sorry, John.'

John nodded as his hand rose to his heart and then to their horror he dropped to the floor like a stone.

'Cissie, run into the hall and call the doctor,' Sunday said urgently as she fell to her knees beside John's prone figure.

Cissie raced away and minutes later she was back with George close behind her.

'Let's get him through to the drawing room and onto the settee,' George said, taking control of the situation. The women were obviously in such a tizz that they barely knew if they were coming or going.

With George holding John beneath his arms and Sunday and Cissie taking a leg each they somehow managed to carry John to the sofa and then Edith dashed away to fetch blankets and a pillow.

'He's still breathing,' George told them. 'I reckon the shock might have caused him to have a heart attack, but we'll know soon enough when the doctor comes.'

It was twenty minutes before the doctor arrived, by which time John was semi-conscious again although he seemed disorientated and was unable to speak. They had all noticed that one side of his mouth had dropped, and George shared his concerns with his wife.

'I reckon the poor devil has had a stroke; I don't think it's a heart attack,' he whispered and Cissie nodded in agreement as they and Edith looked towards where Sunday was holding John's hand and talking soothingly to him.

They all left the room as the doctor arrived and when he came out, having completed his examination, his face was solemn. 'I'm afraid it is a stroke,' he confirmed. 'Poor chap. It's no wonder after the shock he's just had but now would you like me to have him admitted to the hospital? If I can find a bed for him, that is. I'm afraid the hospital is bursting at the seams at present.'

'There'll be no need for that. We can nurse him just as well here if you tell us what to do,' Sunday said. Since coming back to the manor, they had all become like a family and she knew that John would want to stay in his own home. When Cissie and Edith nodded in agreement the doctor heaved a sigh of relief.

'All you can do for now is let him rest and make sure you get plenty of fluids into him,' he advised. 'We won't know how severe the stroke is for a few days but peace and rest for now is the best advice I can offer. Can you manage to get him to his bed?'

'No problem,' George assured him. 'Soon as Kathy gets home, we'll get him upstairs between us. She's a nurse so it'll be a godsend having her to hand.'

'Good, then I'll bid you good day and I'll be back sometime tomorrow to see how he is, but should you need me before don't hesitate to call the surgery.'

It was only later that evening when John was safely tucked

up in his own bed that they all had the chance to speak about Giles.

'Missing in action don't necessarily mean that he's dead,' Cissie said optimistically as a great fat tear rolled down her cheek. 'He could have been captured by the Germans and taken prisoner.'

'I'm not sure if that would be better or worse, but that's about the best we can hope for right now,' Sunday agreed, although after reading in the newspapers about some of the atrocities the prisoners of war were having to endure in the camps, the very thought of Giles being incarcerated in such a place made her blood run cold.

That night, she, Cissie and George took it in turns to sit beside John in case he should need anything, but although he appeared to be wide awake now, he simply lay staring unseeingly up at the ceiling with tears sliding from his eyes and soaking into the pillows.

'Poor bugger,' George said feelingly as they sat down to a breakfast that none of them really wanted the next morning. 'I know all our brood have flown the nest now and are scattered far and wide, but I'd be heartbroken if anythin' were to happen to any of 'em. An' Giles was all John had, his only grandson. It's no wonder he's taken it so hard.'

They all nodded in agreement as they sat thinking of the handsome young man they might never see again. Edith, especially, was unnaturally quiet, for besides having the terrible of news of Giles and what had happened to John to contend with, she also had another concern now. God forbid if anything should happen to John, she might no longer have a stable home to offer to Peggy and she was terrified this might affect her chances of adopting the child. But all they could do was pray

311

that John would recover; although deep down they knew that even if he did, he would never get over this terrible loss.

'Look sharp, Livvy,' the young WAAF who occupied the bed next to Livvy warned. 'The officer will be here any minute for kit inspection and we all know what a tartar she is.'

Livvy finished polishing the shiny brass buttons on her jacket and slipped it on, then checking that everything was neat and tidy in her locker and the bed was made just so, she went to stand to attention at the end of her bed.

The officer appeared minutes later and after she had finished her inspection, she paused in front of Livvy. 'Come to my office in ten minutes, Branning.'

'Yes, ma'am.' Livvy saluted smartly and once the officer had gone the girls breathed a sigh of relief.

'Phew,' Gilly Morris said as she tugged at her tie. 'I'm glad that's over, but I wonder why she wants to see you, Livvy?'

Livvy shrugged. She had lived in a fog of despair since Giles had been lost and didn't really care.

'Can you think of anything you might have done wrong?' Gilly persisted and Livvy shook her head.

'Not off hand, though I dare say I haven't been concentrating quite as much as I should have since . . .' Her voice trailed away, and the others glanced at each other meaningfully. They were all aware of her connection to Giles and had seen how his failure to return to base had affected her.

'Well, I shouldn't worry,' one of the other WAAFs piped up encouragingly. 'Everyone knows that you're one of the best radio operatives there is here.'

Livvy managed a little smile before setting off to find out what the officer wanted her for.

Soon she was standing to attention in front of the woman's desk.

'Stand easy, Branning.'

Livvy relaxed a little, keeping her eyes trained somewhere over the officer's head as she listened to what the woman had to say and ten minutes later, she left the office in a daze.

'So, what did she want?' the others asked when she came back into the hut.

'Actually, she was lovely,' Livvy told them. 'She offered her condolences about Giles and said that seeing there was a connection between us she felt I should have some leave to come to terms with what's happened. She said that what had happened was bound to affect my concentration and that could be dangerous for the pilots.'

Gilly whistled through her teeth. 'You jammy thing, you! How long did she give you and when can you go?'

'She gave me four weeks starting immediately.' Even as she spoke, Livvy was dragging her kitbag from behind the locker and ramming anything she might need into it. When she'd finished, she smiled sadly at her friends.

'That's it then. I'll go and see if there's a train heading home now. I might even be lucky enough to get a lift into town. Bye for now, girls.' And then with a heavy heart she set off, half dreading what she might find at home. Obviously, everyone would be grieving for Giles so she didn't envisage it being the happiest of breaks but somehow she would just have to make the best of it.

Chapter Forty-Five

Ben had been at the hospital in Portsmouth since being shipped home a couple of weeks before and with each day that passed, he was feeling slightly better. Admittedly the smallest thing could turn him into a gibbering wreck again – only the day before the tea lady had dropped a cup, which smashed on the floor and instantly Ben was shaking uncontrollably as his ears rang with explosions and the frantic screaming of the terrified horses.

Even so, as the doctor examined him, he was pleased with his progress. Ben was actually one of the least traumatised of the patients they cared for. Some of the poor souls would never be sane again and were destined to end their tortured lives in an asylum.

'So . . .' the doctor stared at Ben thoughtfully. 'Do you feel up to facing the outside world again yet, Branning? You're nowhere near well enough to go back to your unit, but I'm thinking that some time in your home might be beneficial to you. Would that be possible?'

Ben's mind went into overdrive. Home, the doctor had said, but where was home? He could no longer class Treetops as such. It would have been sold by now and he didn't even know where his stepmother would be living – not that he would have expected her to welcome him with open arms even if he had. But common sense told him that she, Kathy and Livvy would never have gone far. Nuneaton was their hometown, so it was likely that they still lived there somewhere . . . with his children.

Since the young doctor had told him of the children's existence, Ben had found himself thinking of them constantly. He hadn't dared to ask where they lived but suddenly his mind was made up and he nodded.

'Yes, I would like to finish my recuperation at home,' he told the doctor.

'In that case you can give the sister the address of your GP at home and we will write to him. He will then tell you when he considers you fit enough to return to your regiment. You may go as soon as you like, Branning, if you feel up to making your own way there? And good luck, old chap.'

Ben assured the doctor that he was capable of returning alone and after shaking his hand the doctor left the room, leaving Ben to put his possessions, which were pitifully few, into a bag that the ward sister provided.

Two hours later he was on a train headed for Nuneaton and as he stared from the window, he wondered what he would find there.

It was early in November and Sunday was counting the days because Livvy only had two weeks of her leave left. Since the day she had arrived so unexpectedly she had been such a great help to them all that Sunday wondered how they would have managed without her. The minute she had breezed in she had taken over the lion's share of caring for John, who thankfully was improving with every day that passed. Though the doctor had warned him that he should take the stroke as a warning.

'You're not as young as you used to be,' the doctor had said solemnly. 'This time you've every chance of making a nearly full recovery but next time you might not be so lucky, so slow down.'

Now John was able to sit in the chair at the side of his bed for short periods and he had regained the use of his speech, albeit slightly slurred. His right side was slightly weakened too, although the doctor had assured him that with light exercise this should return to normal eventually, so all in all he had come off quite lightly.

John had been a little afraid of doing the exercises the doctor had recommended, for he was worried they might bring on another stroke, but Livvy had been strict with him and ensured that he did them every single day. Edith and Mrs Gay had been cooking him good nourishing food to help build up his strength again and Livvy bullied him into eating every mouthful that was put in front of him, and her endeavours were paying off.

'We'll miss her when she goes back,' Cissie sighed as she and Sunday sat in the kitchen one morning with a pot of tea in front of them. 'She's certainly took a great weight off our shoulders, bless her. And I don't mind telling you that I'm finding it harder to do as much as I used to these days.'

'She's always been a hard-working girl,' Sunday said proudly as Livvy appeared bearing John's empty tray.

'I don't know what you've said to perk John up, but he seems to be improving by the hour,' Cissie told her.

'That's because he has hope.' Livvy placed the tray down and helped herself to a cup of tea from the pot. 'I've told him that

I don't believe Giles is dead. Oh, I did at first admittedly, but now I feel in here that he's still alive somewhere.' As her hand rested on her heart, her mother frowned.

'And since when did *you* care so much about Giles? If I remember rightly you two were always at each other's throats before you both joined up.'

'We were, or at least I was always at his,' Livvy admitted with a guilty flush. 'But then when we found we were both based at the same station we got to know each other better and the long and the short of it is . . .' she hesitated before plunging on. 'I love him. It's as simple as that but I didn't realise it until it was too late to tell him.'

Sunday was so shocked that she spurted the mouthful of tea she had been in the process of swallowing all across the table. 'Well, that's a turn-up for the books,' she spluttered as she hastily dabbed at the spillage with a tea towel. 'And I just pray that you're right and he is alive somewhere even if he is in one of those dreadful prisoner-of-war camps.'

'They're not *all* dreadful,' Livvy pointed out. 'Look at the one they've opened up in the grounds of Arbury Hall for the German prisoners of war. The Germans there are actually rebuilding Chilvers Coton Church and the local people seem to have quite taken to them. Not all Germans are bad.'

'Hm, you could be right.' Just then Sunday glanced towards the window and for a second she could have sworn she saw someone disappear round the edge of the stable block. She frowned. It couldn't be George or Kathy. George had gone into town, Kathy was at the hospital and the children were playing at a friend's house, so who could it be? She wandered outside on the pretext of needing some fresh air and cautiously began to look around, but her search revealed no one so eventually

317

she returned to the kitchen thinking she had either imagined it or it had been a trick of the light.

That evening, long after their elders had gone to bed, Kathy and Livvy sat chatting in the kitchen.

'So, we'll be having a wedding when the war is over, and David comes home then?' Livvy said teasingly.

'The sooner the better,' Kathy agreed. 'I can't believe I didn't realise I had feelings for him long before, but I was just so busy bringing the twins up. But what about you and Giles?'

Livvy sighed and shrugged. 'I shall have a lot of making up to do to him when he does come home,' she admitted. 'Just like you with David I couldn't see what was right beneath my nose.'

'But what will you do if he *doesn't* come home?' Kathy asked tentatively.

'He *will*,' Livvy answered with conviction. She had to believe it otherwise there was no reason for living.

'Have either of you girls moved some straw in the stables?' George asked the next morning when they had all gathered in the kitchen for a break.

Livvy and Kathy shook their heads. It was a Sunday and a rare day off for Kathy.

'That's strange.' George removed his cap and scratched his head. 'Now we've only got the two old nags I keep 'em at one end o' the stable block an' I keep the rest o' the stalls cleaned out but today it looked almost as if someone had made a bed o' straw in the end stall.'

'A lot of people from Coventry and the surrounding towns

that have been bombed are making their way further out into the country for safety,' Sunday pointed out. 'Perhaps it was someone who was looking for shelter for the night?'

'It could've been,' George admitted, and he dismissed the incident from his mind as they went on to talk of other things.

The following evening following a long shift at the hospital, Kathy was striding up the drive, keen to get out of the dark and the driving wind, when suddenly a dark figure loomed out of the trees ahead of her and her heart leapt into her throat.

'Who's there?' she asked loudly as she narrowed her eyes and peered into the gloom, her heart racing.

'It's me.'

It was a voice she had never expected to hear again and as the figure advanced on her she gasped.

'Ben . . . What the hell are you doing here? I heard you were in Egypt.'

'Now that's hardly the way to greet your long-lost love, is it? And yes, I was in Egypt. I suppose that fancy doctor chap of yours told you, but I was sent home to recover because I was ill. I'm due to rejoin my regiment soon, as it happens, but I couldn't go without coming to see you and my children first, could I?'

'*Your long-lost love!*' Kathy scoffed, her voice scathing. 'I can assure you it's been a very long time since I thought of you as *that*. And yet do you know? I don't blame you for what happened between us. Looking back, I have to admit that it was me that did all the chasing. I'd hero-worshipped you since I was a little girl and I suppose I saw you through rose-tinted glasses. But then you stole every single penny that my mother possessed. Money that it had taken her and your father a whole lifetime to accumulate and you left me with my belly full.'

'Well, I couldn't have taken everything if she had enough left to stay in this place and I didn't know you were pregnant when I left, did I?' Ben said defensively.

'My mother had to sell Treetops,' Kathy spat. 'We moved into the lodge down by the gates but now she stays back in Treetops with the new owner where it's safer for the children until the war is over. Not that *you* give a damn what becomes of them,' she said harshly.

Ben stared down at the ground as he muttered. 'I've seen them. I watched them when they came out of the lodge. The girl looks like you and the boy looks like . . .'

'*You!*' Kathy snarled. 'Yes, he does but thank goodness he's nothing like you in nature. I don't even know why you've bothered to come here. We've done without you all this time so why show this sudden fatherly interest now? I suggest you get away while you can because after what you did to me and my mother one word in the police's ear could see you locked up for a very long time and it would be no more than you deserve.'

'What . . .? You mean the police aren't looking for me already?' he asked, bewildered.

Kathy shook her head. 'No, they're not. My mother refused to report what you'd done even though for a time it looked as if we might not even have enough left after the sale of Treetops to keep a roof, *any roof*, over our heads. And do you know why she didn't report you? . . . Because despite what you'd done she *still* loved you. You're still family to her. Treetops had been her home for all her married life and was her last connection to her mother. It almost destroyed her to lose it because she loved every single brick of it, but even so she wouldn't risk you being arrested. So now tell me what you're doing here and then go.'

320

Bitterly ashamed, Ben bowed his head. 'I . . . I suppose I wanted to see my children,' he muttered.

'*Your* children!' Kathy barked. 'But they're not *your* children. Anyone can make a child, but it takes a *real* man to raise one. They've *never* been yours; you abandoned the right to call them yours before they were even born and you're just a stranger to them. David has been far more of a father to them than you could ever be, so now I suggest you leave. Any feelings I had for you died a long, long time ago and I pray that I never have to see your face again. If I do, I should warn you I shall have no hesitation in reporting what you did to the police. My mother loved you as her own and yet you took everything that was precious away from her. You're *despicable!*'

As she stared at him, she felt only contempt and yet she knew that once upon a time she would have laid down her life for him. But that seemed like a lifetime ago and now all she saw standing before her was a very old man. *How could I ever have thought that I loved him or even found him attractive?* she asked herself.

Ben stared at the beautiful face in front of him. Kathy had been just a naïve little girl when he left but she had turned into a beautiful young woman. And the children. Oh, how he wanted to get to know the children. Hidden amongst the bushes he had watched them, and his heart had lifted at the sight of them. But Kathy was right. He deserved everything she had said to him. It was too late to ask for her forgiveness, he had treated her shamefully and she had the handsome young doctor to care for now. But it wasn't too late to make things right with the children. They were *his* children after all. He stared at the lovely face before him for one last time, then, turning, he slipped away and was soon swallowed up by the darkness.

Chapter Forty-Six

Livvy's leave seemed to have passed in the blink of an eye, but now it was nearly over, and much as she loved her job, she was wishing she didn't have to go back – her mother needed her at home. But there was nothing she could do about it apart from pray the war would soon be over. Thankfully John seemed to be much better. Admittedly he would have to take his time from now on and heed the warnings the doctor had given him, but he continued to improve each day. And then one day as Livvy came down the stairs with an armful of dirty washing, she glimpsed the telegram boy cycling down the drive and she gasped.

Dropping the washing in an untidy pile she raced to the door just as the boy reached it and took the telegram from him without a word. *Please God don't let it be bad news about David*, she silently prayed. That on top of the news about Giles would be just too much for all of them to bear. Thankfully, though, she saw that the telegram was again addressed to John so she could only assume that it must be something to do with Giles. Pounding back up the stairs she burst into John's room and waving the envelope told him breathlessly, 'This just came for you. It must be something concerning Giles. Shall I open it for you?'

John was sitting in a chair at the side of the bed and he nodded solemnly. If this was to tell him that they had recovered Giles's body, he knew that he would lose the will to live. He held his breath as Livvy opened the envelope and began to read. Then suddenly she was dancing about the room laughing wildly before racing back to him and grasping him in a bear hug with tears streaming down her cheeks.

'Giles is *alive!*' she squeaked joyfully. 'Do you hear me? *He's alive!* They've located him in a prisoner-of-war camp, which won't be any picnic for him admittedly, but Giles will be coming home when the war is over.'

Now John was unashamedly crying too and when Cissie, Edith and Sunday, who had heard the commotion, came dashing into the room they found John and Livvy with their arms wrapped about each other.

Livvy threw the telegram to her mother who also whooped with delight after she had read it. She knew this news would do John far more good than any medicine the doctor could prescribe and soon she and Cissie were crying tears of joy too. The news was more than any of them, apart from Livvy, had dared to hope for and the air of gloom that had settled on the house began to lift.

'It says that in due course the RAF will inform us what camp he is in and we'll be able to write to him and send him parcels,' Livvy said excitedly.

Suddenly John looked ten years younger and for the rest of that day they all walked about with broad smiles on their faces.

Now, even having to return to her unit didn't seem quite so daunting to Livvy and she set off with a spring in her step, assuring them all that she would get back just as soon as she had some more leave due.

On the same day that Livvy returned to her unit, Ben stood gazing through the railings at the children in the school playground. It was now mid-November and the children were muffled up in hats, scarves, gloves and warm coats, with only their small faces showing. But he still would have recognised his two anywhere. It was funny, really. If he was honest, he had never yearned to have children, nor even given it a thought before he met Maggie; and then his tiny son had been cruelly snatched away from him. He had thought his chances of becoming a father had died with him and now here were Daisy and Thomas. It was like being offered a second chance and he was desperate to get to know them, to tell them that he was their father. It was a bitterly cold day and the biting wind whipped around his face as he stood there, his hands thrust deep into his coat pockets. The day before he had visited the doctor who had told him that he should be well enough to return to his regiment within the next couple of weeks. But Ben had no wish to return now. He wanted to spend time with Daisy and Thomas. But how he was going to do that he had no idea. Kathy had made it more than clear that she no longer had any feelings for him, and she never wanted to see him again, and now the clock was ticking.

At that moment a teacher appeared and rang a bell and the children formed straggly lines and were promptly marched back into school leaving Ben feeling bereft. He turned despondently and began the long trek back into town where he had rented a room in a rather seedy bed and breakfast in one of the back streets close to the town centre. He had been coming to the school fence for the last few days, watching his children avidly at break times like a starving man might eye a feast, but now he was getting desperate. Somehow, he must come up with a plan for them to be together – they were his own flesh and blood, after all.

'George been spoiling you, has he?' Cissie asked the next afternoon when Peggy, Thomas and Daisy arrived home from school, each clutching a bag of aniseed balls. It was usually George who collected them, apart from the rare days when Kathy wasn't working.

'No, it weren't me,' George said defensively as he hung his coat on a nail in the back of the door. 'I know Cook don't like 'em to have sweets afore their dinner.'

'So where did you get them then?' Cissie queried as Peggy skipped off to find Edith. Daisy and Thomas shrugged.

'From the nice man who stands outside the school fence,' Daisy told her innocently.

Cissie scowled. '*What* nice man? And did he give any of the other kids sweets?'

'No,' Thomas said, his cheek bulging with the treats. 'He just likes us.'

'Hm, well just mind what I said about talking to strangers,' Cissie warned as she placed a glass of milk each on the table for them. 'And make sure as Cook doesn't see you eatin' 'em afore your meals an' all, else she'll have your guts for garters.'

The children giggled as they greedily slurped their milk and, for now, the incident was forgotten.

The next day, George drove the car into town to do the shopping. Because petrol was now so hard to come by, he hardly used it anymore, but the two old nags were being shod, and the car needed a little run now and then to keep the engine in good condition. Unfortunately, on the way home he had a puncture in one of the tyres and he'd had to abandon the car and walk to the nearest garage to get it repaired, which meant that by the time it was fixed he was running late for picking the children up from school.

'The shoppin's in the car,' he told Cissie breathlessly when he finally arrived home. 'I'll have to leave you to unload it yourself else I'll be late for pickin' the children up. I had a puncture on the way home an' it's put me a bit behind.' And with that he was off like a shot from a gun.

At that moment, Ben was standing in the trees over the road from the school entrance watching the children come out. His heart was thumping. Normally by this time George was here waiting for them but so far today there had been no sign of him. Could this be his chance? At that moment Daisy and Thomas appeared in the school doorway, their little satchels and gas masks slung over their shoulders, and when they reached the gate they paused to glance up and down the lane for George who had told them they must wait there for him should he ever be late. There were just the two of them today as Edith had kept Peggy at home because of a bad cough. Deciding that it was now or never, Ben stepped from the shelter of the trees and hurried across to them. He had been wrestling with his conscience ever since he had spoken to Kathy, but now he had convinced himself that he deserved a chance to get to know them.

'Hello, you two.'

Looking up they found themselves staring at the kindly

stranger who had been treating them to sweeties and they smiled at him.

'I'm Ben, a friend of your mummy's,' he told them jovially. 'George can't fetch you today, so she asked me to pick you up. But first I'm going to take you both on a little adventure.'

The smiles slid from the children's face as they stared doubtfully at each other. If what he was saying was true, why hadn't Mummy told them about him? She had always told them they must never go off with a stranger, but then he wasn't *really* a stranger, was he? They had seen him quite a number of times over the last few days and he'd always treated them kindly. Furthermore, if Mummy had told him to pick them up from school, she would be angry if they didn't do as he asked, wouldn't she?

'All right.' It was Daisy who made the decision. 'But what sort of adventure are you taking us on?'

'You'll see. It's a surprise,' Ben told them, as he took their hands and led them away in the opposite direction to which he knew George would come. 'First of all, we're going to have a ride on a bus into town. And then I'm going to take you on a train ride.'

Thomas still looked a little doubtful, but Daisy's eyes were shining. 'A train ride! Cor, I *love* trains,' she exclaimed. 'David takes me trainspottin' sometimes when he comes home on leave.' And almost before they knew it, they were on a bus heading into town.

As the end of her shift approached, Matron came up to Kathy, who was dressing a wound in one of the wards.

'Nurse Branning, would you come with me, please? Nurse Wilson can finish doing that, I need to speak to you and it's rather urgent.'

Kathy wiped her hands on the towel she had laid ready and followed Matron into the small hospital foyer where she found her mother and George waiting anxiously for her.

Her mother looked pale and George was nervously twisting his cap in his hands as they looked towards her and Kathy suddenly felt sick.

'Has something happened to one of the children?' It was her first thought and now her heart was hammering so loudly that she was sure they must be able to hear it.

'No . . . Yes . . . Well, actually we're not quite sure,' George stammered. 'Y'see, I was a few minutes late fetchin' 'em from school today cos of a puncture I got in the car. It were only a few minutes late, mind, but when I got there they were gone. There weren't a sign of 'em.'

'What do you mean . . . they were *gone*?' Kathy said accusingly. 'Gone *where*?'

'We don't know,' George admitted guiltily. 'The teachers didn't see 'em leave an' I walked up an' down the lane fer ages but I didn't get so much as a sniff of 'em.'

'Perhaps they got invited to one of their friends' for tea?' Kathy suggested, clutching at straws.

George shook his head. 'I've already called round the houses of every one o' their friends I could think of, but they weren't at any o' them.'

Kathy began to anxiously chew on her knuckles as she glanced towards the window. It was already very dark, and a thick hoar frost was beginning to form on the grass.

'Then we must go straight to the police,' she said urgently.

Suddenly a thought occurred to her and she gasped fearfully. *Ben!* Could it be that he had taken them off somewhere? As yet she hadn't mentioned his visit to her mother for fear of upsetting her but now she knew that she must risk it.

'Mum . . . I'm afraid there's something I haven't told you,' she began in a small voice and by the time she had finished her tale Sunday was as pale as lint.

'But surely you don't think Ben might have taken them, do you?' she asked and when Kathy nodded, she frowned.

'But why ever would he do that?'

It was time for the terrible secret that Kathy had kept for all those years to be told. 'Because . . .' she began falteringly. 'Ben is their father . . .'

Chapter Forty-Seven

'It seems that a man and two children matching your descriptions boarded a train for London late this afternoon,' a police officer informed Kathy later that night. The police had been scouring the town for them ever since Kathy had reported them missing.

'*London!*' Kathy was shocked. 'But it's so dangerous there! And it's so big. What are our chances of finding them if he's taken them there?'

The officer sighed. 'To be completely honest with you, not a lot,' he admitted. 'Unfortunately, by the time we thought to check the train station they would have already arrived in London and what with all the bombings and the state that place is in . . .' He shrugged his shoulders. 'It's going to be a bit like looking for a needle in a haystack. But don't worry,' he went on hastily, seeing Kathy's deep distress. 'We've already spoken to the police there and given them the children's descriptions. They'll be keeping a lookout for them, so don't give up hope.'

Tears spilled down Kathy's cheeks. *Why* hadn't she guessed that Ben might be capable of doing something like this? And why hadn't she told her mother about his visit? But it was too late for regrets now. Somehow, she had to find them. They would be so frightened in such a big city without her once they realised that Ben wasn't going to bring them back. Another thought occurred to her then and the tears fell faster. David had told her Ben was suffering from shell shock, so why hadn't she realised that he wouldn't be thinking straight? He probably wasn't even capable of looking after himself properly, let alone the children, so what would become of them? And all the bombings that were taking place there – look at what had happened to poor Bobby when he returned to London. What if her babies were killed? She wouldn't be able to bear it.

'*Please*, tell the police to keep looking,' she sobbed, and the policeman nodded and after replacing his helmet left quietly by the back door.

'Oh, darling, *why* did you never tell me that Ben was their father?' Sunday asked.

'I . . . I suppose I was too ashamed to; I thought you'd be shocked,' Kathy answered with a catch in her voice. 'Even though he was my stepbrother I thought I loved him, and I thought he loved me too. It took a long while for me to realise that he never had. I was just some part of his plan to hurt us all before he cleared off. Then I suppose my pride was hurt and I convinced myself that I could bring the children up without him . . .'

'And a very good job you've made of it,' her mother told her as Cissie nodded in agreement. George, however, was silent as he sat in the chair by the fire, his head bowed, blaming himself. If only he'd been on time to pick the little ones up none of this would ever have happened.

As if she could read his mind Sunday suddenly told him, 'George, why don't you try to get some rest? You've been out searching with the police since late afternoon and you look exhausted. And, George, please don't get thinking any of this is your fault. What happened to you could have happened to any one of us.'

Kathy raised her streaming eyes to nod her agreement. 'She's right, George. I couldn't have gone back to work if it weren't for you agreeing to meet the children from school each day for me, and any one of us could have been delayed getting there, so please don't blame yourself. Ben was clearly just biding his time to grab them. In fact, I wouldn't mind betting he's the "nice man" they spoke of that has been hanging around the school giving them sweets and getting them to trust him. If only I'd put two and two together, I could have put a stop to it, so if anyone's to blame it's me.'

'No, it isn't,' Sunday told her sharply. 'It isn't anyone's fault but Ben's. He's always had a chip on his shoulder the size of a house brick. He seems to think he's the only one who's ever lost someone he loves – I can't make excuses for him anymore, so let's hear no more of who's to blame. There's absolutely nothing more we can do tonight, and it's been a very long day, so I suggest we all try to get some sleep so that we're fresh for tomorrow.'

Cissie and George took their leave to return to their little cottage and Edith and Cook retired too, leaving Sunday and Kathy sitting by the fire.

'I can't believe you've kept this secret from me all this time,' Sunday said brokenly. 'Didn't you trust me enough to tell me?'

'It wasn't that; I just thought because Ben and I had been brought up in this house together that you'd disapprove.'

'Well, if I'm honest I suppose I would have found it hard to come to terms with – he is so much older than you that it would never have occurred to me that you'd ever look at him that way,' Sunday admitted. 'But then you aren't blood related, so you were doing nothing wrong. Come along, I think we should go up now too. Tomorrow is another day and who knows what it might bring.'

Arm in arm they climbed the stairs although neither of them managed to sleep a wink for worrying about the missing children.

'I don't *like* it here,' Thomas stated emphatically the next morning when he woke in the poky little room that was the only place Ben had managed to find for them to stay the night before. There were two single beds in it. Ben had slept in one and Thomas and Daisy had slept end to end in the other. 'The sheets smell funny,' he went on with a wobble in his voice. 'And I want to go home to my mummy!' He promptly burst into tears.

'Shush, we will just so soon as we've finished havin' our adventure,' Daisy soothed as she placed her arm about his shoulder, though in truth she hadn't been having the best of times up to now either. *Still*, she thought optimistically, *today is bound to get better.* There were so many wonderful things to see and places to visit in London that their teacher had shown them in books; perhaps they would get to see some of them in real life today? For now, though, her main concern was hunger; her tummy was rumbling ominously, and she was desperate to use the toilet as well. Ben had woken her up a couple of times during the night when he had called out in his sleep but thankfully Thomas had slept through it, which was just as well, Daisy thought, cos her brother wasn't as brave as she was.

Ben's eyes suddenly snapped open and he sat bolt upright in bed, his eyes staring, causing the children to huddle together but then catching sight of the two frightened little faces he forced himself to relax.

'Good morning, you two. Sleep well, did you?' There was no answer, so he went on. 'How's about we have a bit of a wash and go down an' see what the landlady has for our breakfast, eh?'

It was only when they had washed as best they could with the cold water in the jug that Ben realised he had no clothes or even a hairbrush for them and that could prove to be a problem with no clothing coupons.

'We'll just finger-comb your hair for now,' he told Daisy, as he awkwardly tried to tie the springy curls into a ribbon at the nape of her neck.

'We haven't got our toothbrushes neither,' Daisy told him accusingly. 'And Mummy says we should clean our teeth every morning and every night before we go to bed.'

'And quite right Mummy is,' Ben said cheerfully. 'But don't worry. We'll go and buy you both new ones right after breakfast.'

As they descended the stairs of the small house the landlady – a small, grubby-faced woman with a hooked nose and untidy grey hair who put Daisy in mind of the witch in one of her story books – appeared from a door in the hallway.

'Ah, good morning,' Ben greeted her cheerfully for the sake of the children. 'I hope we're not too late for breakfast?'

'Breakfast? Where d'yer think you are, the Ritz?' the old woman snorted derisively. 'Yer won't get no breakfast 'ere on the money you paid for the room, sonny!'

Daisy had shrunk into Thomas's side and now even Thomas looked wary.

'Will yer be wantin' the room again tonight? If yer will I wants the money up front. Rooms is 'ard to come by round 'ere an' yer were lucky to find it!'

'Er . . . thank you but no,' Ben told her hastily, and he ushered the children out into the street.

'Are we goin' home now?' Daisy asked tearfully, raising her frightened face to Ben's.

'Well, we'll see. There's so much to do first,' he told her, taking a firm grip on her hand.

As they walked through the ruined streets both children became more and more distressed. This London was nothing like the one they had looked at in Miss Price's picture books at school. This London was dirty, dismal and cold with ruins of what had once been houses everywhere they looked.

'It's not all like this,' Ben tried to reassure them. 'So, we'll go and have a good breakfast in a café somewhere and then we'll find somewhere nice to go.' Although secretly he wondered if there was anywhere nice left in London. The Luftwaffe had done a very good job of destroying the place since he had last been there. At last they found a small café in a back street and Ben urged them inside out of the cold.

'I'll have three teas and three lots of eggs on toast,' he told the woman behind the counter who had a cigarette dangling from her lips and a newspaper spread out in front of her.

'Only got powdered eggs,' she told him abruptly.

'Oh, I see . . . then perhaps three bacon and sausage with toast?' Ben was trying desperately to keep his patience. The woman clearly didn't care if she served them or not, but the children were hungry.

'No bacon, only sausages!'

'Then that will do nicely, thank you.'

335

He slapped the money down on the counter and returned to the children whose eyes were fixed on him.

The tea when it finally came was lukewarm and unsweetened and the sausages were so hard that Ben was certain he could have soled his shoes with them, but they were all hungry, so they ate them anyway.

'Now,' he said when they had eaten. 'Where would you like to go?'

'Home,' the children chorused, and Ben wished he hadn't asked them. But then he supposed it was early days. Once they got to know him, they would come to love him, wouldn't they?

'We'll go and get some fresh air,' he told them and miserably the children followed him outside.

The further they went into the city the worse the damage they witnessed but at last they came to a bridge spanning the River Thames, which had so far escaped the bombing.

'Ugh! It's all dirty and sludgy!' Thomas said in disgust as they stared down at the murky brown water.

'I need a wee!' Daisy piped up and Ben sighed.

He hadn't realised how hard it was to care for children. In fact, as the time wore on, he realised he hadn't really thought about the consequences of taking the children at all. There was no way Kathy would have just let them disappear without raising a hue and cry and even now every policeman in London could be out looking for him. And he still had no idea how he was going to clothe them considering he had no clothing coupons. He also needed to find them somewhere a little more salubrious than the place they had stayed in the previous night, before it got dark. The days were short now and it was so cold that there was no pleasure whatsoever in wandering the streets. They trudged on, knocking on doors, hoping to find decent lodgings. Because he guessed the police would be looking for him, Ben didn't dare risk staying at a hotel, even though he could well have afforded it. But hotels would probably be the first places the police would look and so Ben was limited in his options. But it was pointless, thousands of people had lost their homes and every place he tried turned him away, until eventually he had no option but to return to the house they had stayed in the night before.

'Huh! I thought yer'd be back,' the old woman scoffed when she answered his knock at the door. 'Want the room again, do yer?'

Ben forced himself to smile pleasantly. 'Yes, please.'

'Then give us the money.' She sniffed. 'I don't want yer clearin' orf in the mornin' wi'out payin'. An' what's up wi' the little 'un?' She nodded towards Daisy who was crying with the cold.

'Oh, she's just tired,' Ben said hurriedly as he pushed the children onto the cracked and faded lino in the hallway. He handed the money over and shooed the children ahead of him up the stairs.

'An' don't forget to pull them blackout blinds afore yer turn the light on,' the landlady's voice followed him, and he gritted his teeth. She really was the most unreasonable little woman he had ever had the misfortune to meet!

The bedroom felt only slightly warmer than outside and Daisy was crying again now.

'Look, can I trust you to watch your sister for a little while?' Ben asked Thomas. 'I saw a fish and chip shop just down the road. I'll run and get us all some, that'll make you both feel better, won't it? And then we can snuggle down in our beds and get warm.'

Thomas nodded hesitantly and Ben slipped away leaving the children alone.

'I want to go home,' Daisy whined tearfully.

'So do I,' Thomas admitted, bitterly regretting ever agreeing to go with Ben in the first place. They huddled together, listening to every little sound that reached them from the road outside.

Soon Ben returned bearing three small parcels wrapped in newspaper. 'Here we are.' He placed a parcel each on their laps. 'Lovely, piping-hot fish, chips and mushy peas.'

The children ate every scrap and did feel a little better with their stomachs full. They then got undressed down to their underwear and scrambled into bed and despite feeling so home-sick they were fast asleep in no time, their arms tightly wrapped about each other.

Tomorrow I shall tell them who I really am, Ben promised himself as he stared down at their little faces. *They're bound to love me and want to be with me when they know that I'm their real dad.* On that comforting thought he too climbed into bed and slept.

Chapter Forty-Eight

Early in December, the residents of Treetops sat in the kitchen listening to the radio, their faces grave as they heard that Japan was now at war with the United States and Britain. Several hours earlier 360 Japanese warplanes had made a huge surprise attack on the US Pacific fleet in its home base at Pearl Harbor in Hawaii.

'The Yanks will become involved now,' George said solemnly. 'An' it might not be a bad thing. We need all the help we can get at the minute.'

Sunday nodded in agreement as she glanced towards Kathy, who was standing at the window staring off down the drive, just as she had every single day since the children had gone missing. The police were still doing their best to find them but up to now their search had been fruitless and it was as if the children had disappeared off the face of the earth as the endless days stretched on.

Sunday doubted if Kathy had even heard about the attack on Pearl Harbor. She listened keenly for news of London, terrified that it was being bombed again, but if it was about anything else, she turned away. All she could think about were the children, which was understandable. She had not been to the hospital once since they had gone missing, but Matron had been very understanding about it and had even taken the trouble to visit Kathy at home when she'd found out what had happened.

'Just take as much time off as you need,' she had told her kindly, even though the hospital was dreadfully short-staffed. 'And don't give up hope.'

Hope was all Kathy had to cling to now and every minute she prayed her babies would come home, but as time wore on – each day seeming like a lifetime – the possibility of her ever seeing them again seemed to be more remote.

She had lost weight and her eyes were haunted but there was nothing anyone could do to help her; nothing anyone could say to make her feel better. All they could do was pray that the nightmare might soon be over, and the children would be back where they belonged again.

In London Ben was also feeling the strain. He and the children had spent the last few nights in a shelter in the underground station close to where they were still staying in the grubby little bed and breakfast. He had managed to find the children some ill-fitting clothes on a second-hand stall in the local market, but the children constantly cried to go home now, even Daisy who at first had tried to be brave for Thomas. The stress of caring for them and knowing that they didn't trust or like him was beginning to tell on Ben and the nightmares had returned with a vengeance. The children would lie in their bed watching with terrified eyes as he thrashed about and called out in his sleep. Often now a whole day could go by without them even saying so much as a single word to him. One night, Daisy came up with the solution to their problem.

'Soon as he goes out next time we're going to run away,' she whispered to her brother.

'B-but where will we run to? We don't know our way home,' Thomas whimpered.

Daisy frowned, then came up with an idea. 'We'll find a policeman an' tell him that he took us away from our mum. Granma always told us to do that if we got lost.'

Ben had sat them down and told them that he was their father some time ago but neither of the children believed him. Their mum had told them that David was going to be their dad, so this man must be lying.

Now Thomas nodded. 'All right, but we'll have to be careful,' he whispered back. 'If we run away an' he finds us he'll be angry.'

They huddled together in the darkened room waiting for daylight when they could hopefully put their plan into action. Apart from being taken to the shelter when the air raid sirens sounded, they had barely been out of the room for the last two weeks for it was far too cold now to be walking the streets. Ben would go off from time to time and bring back food for them then get annoyed when they refused to eat it.

'You'll be ill if you don't eat,' he had snapped the day before when he had returned to the room with hot pies, which they showed no interest in.

Sometimes Ben would shout at them with frustration, at other times he would get upset and tell them how much he loved them, but the children didn't believe that any more than they believed he was their father. Everyone at Treetops loved them and they never shouted at the them, or made them stay in cold, smelly rooms for days on end. And then there was his constant pacing. Up and down, up and down the room he would go, muttering to himself as if the children weren't even there, until they would cling together shaking with fear, cold and hunger.

Their chance soon came when later the following morning Ben put his coat on and told them, 'I'm going to go and get us some breakfast. I shan't be long.'

He smiled at them and left, closing the door softly behind him and they listened carefully as his footsteps clattered away down the bare wooden staircase.

'Right, Thomas, grab your coat,' Daisy told him, her heart hammering. 'He won't be gone for long so's we have to be quick.'

Thomas hurriedly did as he was told, fumbling with the buttons on his coat and side by side they approached the door. They sighed with relief to find it unlocked then inched it open. Satisfied there was no one in sight Daisy took her brother's hand. 'Come on but be quiet. We don't want the witch stopping us from getting out.'

Step by step the children tiptoed down the staircase and at last they found themselves in the damp-smelling hallway. Thankfully there was no sign of the landlady, so they approached the front door. It creaked alarmingly when Thomas managed to open it but at last they were standing on the pavement outside in a thick smog.

'W-which way shall we go?' Daisy asked falteringly. She could barely see more than a few feet ahead of her and suddenly she was frightened. What would Ben do to them if he found them trying to run away from him?

Thomas glanced up and down the street. They could hear the ship's hooters in the docks, which were not very far away, and making a decision he took her hand and told her, 'Let's go this way.' He led her away from the noise and at the end of the road they came to a slightly busier one.

Thomas swallowed as he looked up and down at the passing traffic. Suddenly he had taken charge for a change. 'Look for a policeman,' he instructed her as, keeping close to the wall, they moved on. Suddenly the all-too-familiar sound of an air raid siren pierced the air and Daisy froze, her eyes stretched wide with fear. Suddenly people were running past them, as if they were invisible. They flattened themselves against a wall.

'What shall we do now?' Daisy asked fearfully as she clung to Thomas's hand like a limpet. At that moment a middle-aged lady wielding a large wicker shopping basket stopped abruptly right in front of them

'My dears, whatever are you doing out here all alone?' Her voice was kindly, and Daisy started to cry as she and Thomas stared numbly up at her.

'Look, come with me, we need to get you into a shelter.' She ushered them in front of her and at the end of a street she shooed them into an open doorway and down some steps. They found themselves in a large cellar that had clearly been adapted into a shelter and she told them reassuringly, 'You'll be safe here now until the raid is over and then you must go home.'

Daisy and Thomas slid onto a long bench that was fast filling with people and soon after there was a loud droning overhead and the sound of the ack-ack guns began to sound.

Shortly after they heard loud whistling noises followed by earth-shaking explosions as yet more bombs were dropped on the already dreadfully damaged city and the children could only sit there and pray that it would be over soon. As the day wore on there seemed to be no let-up and eventually someone lit some oil lamps, casting ghostly shadows over the faces of those that were sheltering there. A baby was crying, and small children were becoming fractious as their mothers tried to entertain them but at last the all-clear sounded and slowly the people rose and began to leave, afraid of what they would find above ground. Taking his sister's hand Thomas encouraged, 'Come on, we can't stay here on us own.'

It was then that the kindly lady who had taken them there stopped in front of them again to ask, 'Will you be all right getting home by yourselves? Have you far to go?'

For a while, the children stared numbly up at her and then starting to cry again, Daisy blurted out, 'We don't know our way home. It's a long way away. Ben took us away from our mummy.'

Bending to her level, the lady took a large white handkerchief from her pocket and mopped at Daisy's tear-stained face before saying, 'Right, I think we need to find someone to help you. Just stay there for a while, I'll be back very soon, I promise.'

True to her word she was back moments later with an ARP warden who smiled at them encouragingly.

'Right then, children,' he said cheerily. 'This 'ere lady says you need some 'elp. Why don't you tell me all about what's been goin' on, eh?'

And so, between them the children haltingly told them all about Ben taking them from school and making them stay with him and when they were done, he asked, 'An' where is this Ben now?'

Daisy shook her head. 'We don't know. We stayed in a smelly little room an' when he went out this morning to get us some food we run away. We want to go home to our mum!'

'Of course you do.' The man patted her head. 'Let's get you

down to the police station, eh? The policeman can let your mum know where you are then and you'll be home in no time, you just see if you ain't, me beauties.'

And so, they trustingly allowed him to take their hands and lead them out into the bomb-damaged streets, praying that he was telling the truth and their nightmare might soon be over.

Chapter Forty-Nine

'Here we are then,' Ben said cheerfully as he entered the small rented room holding a bag of food. 'I've got us a few . . .' His voice trailed away as he stared at the children's empty bed and his heart sank.

'*Thomas . . . Daisy . . .*' he called, as if speaking their names might make them miraculously appear, but only silence greeted him and he sank heavily onto the side of the bed as the bag fell from his hands, scattering the contents all over the floor. They had gone. His attempts at being a father to them had failed dismally. He should have realised how unhappy they were. When the air raid siren started to wail, he just sat on, not much caring if he lived or died. He had made a complete mess of his life and he had nothing left to live for. Curling himself into a ball on the crumpled sheets he started to shake. It would be pointless trying to find them, they could be anywhere by now, but if they should be killed in the raid it would be all his fault for taking them away from the safety of their home. As the enormity of what he had done struck home he began to cry great gulping sobs that threatened to choke him.

Kathy was standing at her usual position at the window peering down the drive into the gathering gloom of the afternoon. Leaning towards Cissie, Sunday whispered, 'I don't think her nerves can take much more of this. If the children aren't found soon, I swear she'll crack!'

'No, she won't. Kathy is made o' sterner stuff than that,' Cissie assured her, patting her hand. The strain was showing on Sunday too now, and she was beginning to look her age.

Behind them, Kathy gave a gasp. 'Th-there's someone coming down the drive,' she said with a catch in her voice. 'I-I think it's a policeman!' And suddenly she was racing towards the green baize door that led into the hallway, the others following behind at a more sedate pace.

The policeman arrived at the front door at the same moment she did, and she ushered him inside and quickly closed the door behind him. It was the same man who had been keeping them informed of the search and he respectfully took off his helmet and beamed from ear to ear.

'I've got good news,' he told the group gathered around him, not wishing to keep them in suspense for a moment longer than he had to; he had seen how they had suffered during the time the children had been missing. 'The children have been found. They're safe and well in a police station in London.'

The shock of his words made Kathy sway and had it not been for George taking a firm grip of her elbow she might have collapsed.

'A-are you quite sure it's them?'

He nodded. 'Sure, as I can be. An ARP warden took them to the police station after a raid and they told the sergeant their names and what town they lived in. Seeing as the London police already had all their details it didn't take much for 'em to put two an' two together. So, it looks like all's well that ends well.'

'But what were they doing out on their own?' Kathy asked.

'They ran away from the chap that took 'em by all accounts,' the policeman told them and now Kathy was sobbing with relief, although she knew she wouldn't settle properly until she had them back in her arms.

'So, what will happen now? Must I go and fetch them?'

'No need, they're already on their way,' he assured her. 'The police contacted the welfare department and they've sent a lady to bring 'em home. They're on the train even as we speak so they should arrive later this evening.'

'I'll go and get the car out. We can go and wait at the station for them,' George said, and Kathy nodded her agreement, and without thinking, she threw her arms about the policeman's neck and gave him a loud smacking kiss on the cheek, causing him to blush a dull, beetroot red. She rushed away then to get her coat and soon she and George were on their way to the station.

'We might have a long wait ahead of us,' George pointed out as he steered the car past the five-sailed windmill in Tuttle Hill, but Kathy laughed for the first time in weeks.

'I don't care if we have to wait all night,' she said. 'They're coming home! Oh, George, I can hardly allow myself to believe it! There have been times when I thought I might never see them again and if that had been the case, I don't think I would have been able to bear it.'

'Well, you won't have to now, will you?' His face was wreathed in smiles. 'An' young Peggy will be made up an' all. She's been mopin' about somethin' terrible since her mates have been gone, bless her. She were hoppin' from foot to foot wi' excitement when I told 'er just now we was goin' to fetch 'em!'

The next two hours were spent restlessly pacing up and down in the waiting room on the station platform but at last the distant sound of the train approaching was heard and both Kathy and George dashed outside to meet it. It was quite late by this time and few people alighted from the train but then, suddenly, the twins appeared and when they caught sight of their mother they shrieked with joy and flew towards her, their feet barely touching the ground.

'*Mummy, Mummy!*'

They were all laughing and crying at the same time as Kathy clutched her children to her as if she would never let them go again. 'I missed you *so* much,' she said through her tears as she rained kisses onto their grubby cheeks. 'Are you both all right?'

'We are now,' Thomas said solemnly. 'But we didn't like living with Ben. He said he was our daddy but that's not true, is it, Mummy? He's not our daddy, is he?'

'Er . . . we'll talk about it later,' Kathy hedged. 'For now, I just want to get you safely home.' Turning to the woman who had brought them back she gave her a grateful smile. 'Thank you so much. Have you somewhere to stay for the night? I doubt the trains will be running back to London again at this hour. Why don't you come with us and you can catch the first train back in the morning?'

The woman, who was portly with soft, brown hair and a kindly face, smiled her thanks. 'Thank you, if you're quite sure I wouldn't be imposing I'd love to take you up on your offer. To be honest I was so keen to get them home to you I didn't give a lot of thought as to how was I going to get back.'

Moments later they were all bundled into the car, Kathy in the back with her arms about the twins, and Miss Blake, as the woman had introduced herself, in the front with George.

The twins were drooping with exhaustion by then. They didn't look as if they had had a bath or their hair washed since they had gone missing but for tonight all Kathy wanted to do was see them safely tucked up in their own little beds with full bellies. They looked as if they had lost a little weight to her. There would be time for baths and more explanations the next day.

They received a rapturous greeting when they arrived back at Treetops, even little Peggy had been allowed to stay up to see them and everyone cried tears of joy at their safe return.

Cook had prepared a large pan of nourishing chicken soup and despite being tired the twins tucked into it ravenously.

'They're beautiful children,' Miss Blake commented later as Sunday led her to the cosy room Edith had made ready for her.

'Yes, they are,' Sunday agreed. 'But then they're my grandchildren so I may be a little biased. It's been a very difficult time for all of us.'

'I can imagine.' Miss Blake nodded sympathetically.

Sunday opened the door of the bedroom and turned to clasp Miss Blake's hand. 'Thank you from the bottom of all our hearts,' she said, tears in her eyes.

Miss Blake smiled gently. 'I'm just happy to have been able to help.'

Sunday squeezed the woman's hand then turned and walked away. For the first night in weeks she knew that she would sleep like the dead.

Despite the late hour, in London, Ben was striding towards the deserted docks. Once his mind had cleared, he had spent the afternoon writing letters that he had then delivered to the bank where his money was deposited and to his solicitors.

When he arrived at the docks, he stood for a time watching the many different-shaped boats bobbing up and down on the water. As he stood there, he felt the first flakes of snow begin to fall and he realised with a little jolt that it would soon be Christmas. Suddenly he was remembering the snowy Christmases past at Treetops. He could see himself and the family opening their presents beneath the tree and sledging in Hartshill Hayes with his father. He could almost taste the delicious Christmas dinners they used to have and hear the carol singers that would come to the door of Treetops for hot punch and mince pies. Then he pictured his beloved Maggie waddling about, so happy and excited as she awaited the birth of their child. It all seemed so long ago now, and those happy times could never come again. And it was all his own fault.

For too long he had wallowed in self-pity. Too late he realised that it hadn't been his birth mother's fault that she had abandoned him. And Sunday had always loved him, deep down, he knew that. She'd cared for him from when he was a little child, how could he ever have doubted her love? Even when she had first learned that he was her husband's illegitimate son, she had never been unkind. Instead, she had done her best to make him feel that he belonged. If he thought about it now, it was the war that had changed everything. Coming home scarred and with those terrible nightmares . . . And then Kitty had died, and though he loved Maggie by then, Kitty had been his first, childhood love and he had grieved for her.

He shook his head. Maybe everything would have been all right, if only his Maggie had lived. Maybe he wouldn't have let bitterness cloud his mind. He had loved Sunday fiercely when he was a child, after all. Why had he not allowed her back into his heart? He had never realised what he had until it was gone and now there was no one to care what became of him. Tears burned his eyes as a great wave of loneliness washed over him. He was quite alone now; he had no one. But no, as he stared across the floating jetsam Maggie's lovely face appeared through the snowflakes; she was smiling and holding her arms out to him.

'*Come on, darling, there's no need to suffer anymore,*' Ben heard her say softly, and he felt a measure of peace settle in his tortured mind for the first time in many years. Behind him he could hear the clanging of fire engine bells as they raced from place to place struggling to put out the fires caused by the latest wave of bombings. The air was heavy with smoke, but it didn't matter anymore, Maggie was waiting for him.

'I'm coming, Maggie.' Ben held out his arms and stepped forward and as he dropped into the water and slipped beneath the floating debris, he was heedless of the cold as it closed over him. For the first time in years he was at peace and he smiled.

Chapter Fifty

Sunday stared at the large envelope that Cissie handed to her curiously.

The postman had just delivered it and it looked official. 'I wonder what this is?' she said, sitting down at the kitchen table to open it.

Her face blanched and her mouth fell open, as she pulled the contents out. 'It's from a solicitor in London,' she told Cissie. 'It's concerning Ben. He went to see him some days ago and he's . . .' She swallowed and forced herself to go on. 'He's given all my money back; almost every penny he stole. All I have to do is transfer it from this bank account back into my own.'

Cissie's eyes were on stalks. 'He's *what*?' she said incredulously, hardly able to believe her ears.

'It's true . . . Look for yourself.' Sunday handed her the letter.

'But why would he do that now?' Cissie shook her head. 'After all the bad things he's done!'

Sunday withdrew another letter, handwritten this time, and in Ben's handwriting.

Her hand shook as she opened it and began to read.

Dear Mum,

I dare say this letter will come as something of a surprise to you after all the bad things I have done, but now I feel that I must at least try to put some of them right starting with the money I stole from you. You will find it all here, all you have to do is instruct the solicitor to pay it back into your account. If it is any comfort to you, you can be sure that it never brought me any joy. I can only say that for some long time I have not been in my right mind. I see that now. I thought I had got over what I had been through in the Great War but realise that I never did and losing Maggie, the baby and Dad just tipped me over the edge. Suddenly I began to see everything as being your fault. I convinced myself that you loved Kathy and Livvy more than me, which is why I took advantage of Kathy when she said she had feelings for me. I thought it would hurt you. But when I discovered from Kathy's fiancé that I had left her expecting a child I was mortified and suddenly had a need to see them.

Taking them away from you all was unforgivable. I thought they would grow to love me – that they would become my family too, but they never did. They cried for you and Kathy the whole time I had them. But please believe me when I say that I never wished to cause them any harm and I pray that they have been safely returned to where they belong. They are a credit to Kathy, who has done a wonderful job of bringing them up, I can't begin to imagine how hard it was for her, particularly alone.

There is not much left to say. By the time you get this letter I will probably be dead. I will have been classed as AWOL by my regiment by now, I have no family left, and so there is nothing for me to live for anymore. I am not asking for your sympathy. You were the best of mothers to me and didn't deserve any of the terrible things I did to you. All I ask, if you can possibly manage it, is that you will think fondly of me from time to time.

Affectionately, Your stepson,

Ben xxxxx

Tears slid down Sunday's cheeks as she withdrew the final letter from the large envelope. Once again it was from the solicitor informing her that a body had been fished from the docks matching Ben's description. Ben's name was also engraved on the dog tag he had been wearing about his neck so there was little doubt that it was him and the solicitor was asking what she wished to do with his body. Even if they had been estranged for some time she was after all Ben's next of kin.

'Would you ask George to ring the solicitor and ask him to arrange to have Ben's body brought home?' she asked Cissie. 'He will be buried in the churchyard next to his father. It's what Tom would have wanted.'

'*What . . .?* After all he's done?' Cissie said incredulously.

'Yes,' Sunday said. 'Ben hadn't been mentally stable since he came home from the war and I think losing Maggie and the baby and then his father was just too much for him to handle. We have to try to put all the bad things he did behind us now, otherwise we'll never know any peace either.'

Cissie shook her head. 'Well, if you're sure, but goodness knows what Kathy will have to say about this! I have a feeling she ain't goin' to be so ready to forgive him as you are. Poor lass will hardly let them kids out of her sight since she got them back.'

'You leave Kathy to me.' She gave Cissie a watery smile as Cissie went off to find George.

Cissie was proved right and when Kathy got home from the hospital that afternoon, she was incensed to hear the news. She now always finished work in time to collect the children from school herself and seemed terrified of letting them out of her sight. The large Christmas tree John had ordered had been delivered that day and Kathy had promised the children that they could dress it that evening but now she was so angry she wasn't sure she'd be able to concentrate.

'So, he's dead then?' She sat down heavily as she let the news sink in but all she could feel was relief. At least now she wouldn't have to live in fear of him kidnapping the children again. But to bring him back here and even have him buried next to Tom!

'Can't you just have him buried somewhere else?' she asked bluntly.

'I'm afraid not.' Much as she loved her daughter, Sunday was prepared to stand her ground on this. 'I know he put us all through hell, but I spoke to his doctor this afternoon and he confirmed that Ben was very mentally unstable. Apparently, he had told Ben a short while ago that he should soon be fit to rejoin his regiment but now he regrets it, as clearly Ben was still very unwell. He would never have done what he did had he not been so ill. Surely you can see that? I know he hurt you more than any of us; it was unforgivable the way he took advantage of a young girl who trusted him, but he also gave you two beautiful children, for which we should be grateful.'

It was clear to Kathy that her mother would not budge on

this, and though she despised Ben for all he'd done to them, she knew from her mother's set face there was no point trying to change her mind. But her anger was bubbling within her and she turned and marched out of the room. At the door she paused and looked back at her mother. 'You do what you have to, Mum. But I will *not* be going to that man's funeral, and I never want to hear his name again.' Then she ran out of the room, slamming the door behind her. There was no way she would ever be able to forgive the man who had caused her so much heartache, no matter how ill her mother said he had been.

Ben's body was brought back to his hometown the following week and taken to an undertaker where he would lie in the chapel of rest, until the funeral took place two days later.

'I shan't be going,' Kathy said emphatically when she heard of the arrangements.

Sunday sighed. 'And I cannot force you to,' she admitted sadly. 'But whatever he did he was the father of your children and once he knew of their existence, in his own strange way I think he wanted to be part of their lives. Still, you must do what your heart tells you, Kathy. It's going to be a very small affair with only a few people attending and because of the circumstances there will be no wake afterwards. All I can say is, if I can find it in my heart to forgive him then perhaps you should?'

That evening as Kathy was tucking the children into bed, Thomas surprised her when he asked suddenly, 'That man, Ben, Mummy . . . the one that took us away. He told us he was our daddy, but you told us that our first daddy was dead.'

Kathy swallowed, trying hard to keep calm. Thankfully the twins appeared to be unscathed by the whole episode and within a couple of days of returning home they had not mentioned Ben at all. But now it was apparent that he was still very much on their minds.

'I never actually said that your daddy was *dead*,' she began haltingly, knowing that now was the time for honesty. The children had a right to know the truth. 'I said that he couldn't be with us because he had had to go away.'

'But we thought that meant he had died,' Thomas answered innocently.

Kathy sighed. 'Ben *was* your daddy,' she told them, as they stared at her with wide eyes. 'But he went away long before you and Daisy were born, and he didn't even know about you till he came back.'

'But *why* did he go away?' Thomas persisted and Kathy licked her lips.

'Because he didn't love me,' she forced herself to say and now Thomas frowned.

'But *we* love you . . . and he told me and Daisy that he loved *us*! He could be very kind sometimes when he wasn't being strange.'

She nodded. 'And I believe he did love you. He wasn't a bad man, not really. But the thing is . . . your daddy wasn't well, up here.' She tapped her head. 'He was in another war a long time ago and he saw lots of nasty things that made him poorly.'

'Is that why he said strange things and had nightmares?'

She nodded. 'Yes, I'm sure it is. So, you see he wished you and Daisy no harm when he took you away. And I'm sure he would never have hurt you. But he is in heaven now.'

'So, he *has* died now?'

A nod from Kathy confirmed his question and he stared off into space for a time before asking, 'How did he die?'

Kathy's breath caught in her throat as she thought of the best way to answer. She didn't want the children to know that Ben had taken his own life. It might prey on their minds and make them think that they had somehow been the cause of it.

'Unfortunately, he fell into the water and drowned when he was down at the docks,' she answered eventually.

'Oh, so it wasn't our fault for running away from him then?'

'Not at all.'

'And he can't come back from heaven and take us away again?'

'No, he can't.'

Thomas snuggled down into his bed and once again Kathy was shocked at how accepting children could be.

'Then perhaps we should forgive him for taking us away if he was poorly,' he said quietly as he stifled a yawn and Kathy felt a sharp pain in her heart. If such young children could forgive him so readily perhaps she should try to do the same.

'Goodnight, my darlings, sleep tight, hope the bedbugs don't bite.' She kissed them both soundly and left the room, closing the door softly behind her and once out on the landing she sagged against the wall as tears burned at the back of her eyes. She could only hope that she had handled the children's questions sensitively. They certainly seemed to have accepted things and now they had a wonderful future to look forward to with David when the damned war was finally over.

On the day of the funeral Kathy woke to an eerie grey light and after glancing out of the window she saw that a carpet of snow lay thick on the ground.

It had been agreed that Edith should remain at Treetops with the children, while Sunday, Kathy, Cissie and George attended the service. It had also been agreed that the coffin should be taken directly to the church as Kathy was concerned that it might be too confusing and upsetting for the children if it were to come to Treetops. As her daughter would now be attending the funeral, Sunday had been only too happy to agree to this. So, when it was time, they set off, the car's headlights making the snowflakes sparkle like diamonds in the eerie light.

As they drove down the drive, in her mind's eye, Sunday could see Ben as a little boy having a snowball fight with his father on the lawn. She could hear his laughter and her heart was heavy to think that his life had ended as it had.

Much to Sunday's regret, other than themselves there was no one else to mourn Ben at the church. After Maggie's death he had been rather reclusive, venturing into town only when it was absolutely necessary, and he'd cheated so many local trades-people out of their money when he'd fled that they all kept away.

The service was short and before they knew it, they were following the coffin to Ben's final resting place, the beautiful wreath of red roses and holly Sunday had insisted he should have standing out in stark contrast against the dark mahogany of the coffin and the snowy scene.

'Ashes to ashes, dust to dust.' The vicar's voice droned on as he performed the last part of the service and when it was finally over Sunday's eyes travelled to Tom's grave, so very close to his son's. She just hoped that wherever they were they were together again. She turned away and leaning heavily on George's arm they picked their way amongst the headstones to the lych-gate and the waiting car. Just once she turned to see the grave diggers begin the task of throwing the frozen earth into the grave but then she looked ahead again. It was done and hopefully Ben would be at peace now.

Chapter Fifty-One

'So, you're a very wealthy woman again,' John teased a couple of days later when Ben's solicitor rang from London to tell her that her money was now safely back in her account. The family were trying to get back to some sort of normality and were now looking forward to Christmas.

'I suppose I am,' Sunday agreed as she busily unpicked one of Peggy's old cardigans, which she would then remake into woollen socks for the troops. She paused for a moment and looked out onto the lawn where the children were making a snowman. 'Not that I need it at my age. Still, it will be nice to think that I can leave Kathy and Livvy an inheritance. When this war is over, they might decide to use some of it to buy themselves a house each.'

John scowled at her. 'When this war is over, you'll still be here so they'll have to wait a while,' he told her

She grinned. 'None of us can go on forever,' she pointed out. 'And I am getting on, you know.'

They were sitting in the drawing room where Kathy and the children had adorned a Christmas tree with pretty glass baubles and tinsel, and with the fire glowing in the hearth it was warm and cosy.

The phone ringing in the hall interrupted their conversation and as Sunday rose to answer it, John said, 'Stay where you are, Edith will answer it.'

He was right for at that moment they heard the sound of footsteps and someone lifting the receiver, so Sunday sank back into her seat. However, she had barely had time to lift the cardigan again when the door burst open and Edith erupted into the room in a most unladylike manner, her cheeks glowing and her eyes shining like stars.

'That was Miss Tyler. You know . . . the little woman who came from the East End welfare department with the chap from the orphanage about Peggy! And you'll never guess . . . they've decided to let me adopt her! Oh, I'm *so* happy, I can hardly believe it. They're going to start the proceedings straight after Christmas and because everything is so straightforward and there's no one to contest it, it should all be done and dusted in a couple of months!'

'Oh, Edith.' Sunday's eyes welled with tears. She seemed to have done nothing but cry recently but this time they were happy tears. 'I'm so thrilled for you . . . and for Peggy, of course. I'm sure she couldn't have chosen a better mum than you.'

'Hear hear!' John piped up. 'That's wonderful news. Just what we needed to put us back on track for a happy Christmas, eh? But now run and tell the others. I'm sure they'll be as delighted for you as we all are. Oh, and don't forget to tell Peggy as well.'

Edith scooted away hardly able to contain her excitement as Sunday and John smiled at each other.

'Oh, it's so nice to hear happy news for a change, isn't it? If only Giles, Livvy and David could be home for Christmas it would be perfect, but I fear there's not much chance of that happening!'

'Let's just count our blessings,' John said wisely. 'They're not likely to be with us admittedly but at least for now we know they are all alive and hopefully safe, so I'll settle for that for the time being.'

Sunday was reminded of Christmases past when she woke early on Christmas morning to hear the children pounding excitedly along the landing. Smiling she got out of bed and pulled her dressing gown on, then slipping her feet into her slippers she followed the children downstairs to the drawing room where their presents were spread about the tree.

Edith was there with Peggy, hovering over her like a mother hen, while Kathy was trying her best to stop Thomas and Daisy from grabbing at the nearest gaily wrapped packages. Cissie and George had gone to spend a few days with their youngest daughter and grandchildren in Yorkshire, promising to be back to see the New Year in at Treetops and Sunday was missing them already, even though they had only left the day before.

'Right now, this one is for you, Peggy,' Kathy said as she read the names on the gifts. 'And here's one each for you, Thomas and Daisy.'

The children tore the packages open and whooped with delight. For Peggy there was a very pretty baby doll with a ceramic face and long hair and eyes that opened and shut, while Thomas and Daisy found themselves the proud new owners of a wooden train and a pretty little china tea set.

'Looking at that pile of presents you could be some time.' Sunday grinned at the two women. 'So, while you help them open them, I'm going to seek refuge in the kitchen with John and Cook and get a cup of tea.'

She had just entered the hallway when the front door suddenly opened letting in a gust of snow, and Sunday gasped with joy.

'*Livvy!* Oh, my love, what are you doing here? This is the best surprise I could have had!'

Livvy giggled as she stamped the snow from her boots and took off her overcoat. 'I didn't know I was coming myself until last night,' she admitted as she hurried over to give her mother a hug. 'My boss gave me a forty-eight-hour pass, but I wasn't sure if the trains would be running, then luckily, I found out that one of the RAF chaps at our base was going to spend Christmas with his parents in Leicester, so he gave me a lift.'

Kathy was overjoyed. After all they had gone through during the past year this was the best Christmas present she could have wished for and she intended to make the most of every second of it.

'Come along.' Grabbing Livvy's arm she hauled her towards the kitchen. 'Let's go and surprise everyone. They'll be so thrilled to see you.'

After all the presents were exchanged and they had eaten a hearty breakfast, Livvy and Kathy set to helping Cook peel the Brussels sprouts and carrots they were having for dinner and the atmosphere was light.

'Any news from Giles?' Kathy asked as they sat at the kitchen table with the pile of vegetable peelings growing between them.

'Not as yet.' Livvy's pretty face clouded. She had sent numerous letters and two parcels to the prison camp but had heard nothing in return, which worried her dreadfully. They were all aware of some of the wicked camps the Germans had set up. However, when she had expressed her concerns about Giles, the officers at her base had assured her that not hearing from him was nothing to worry about. The prisoners were not always supplied with pens or paper they had told her, so Livvy had decided that she would include some in the next parcel she sent.

'And how is David?' Livvy asked to try and take her mind off Giles.

Now it was Kathy's turn to look sad. 'Oh, I hear from him regularly, although at least half of every letter is heavily censored,' she said bitterly. 'I know he gets terribly frustrated at the number of patients he's unable to save. Still, this war can't go on forever, can it?' she said optimistically.

'Let's hope not,' Sunday said with a heartfelt sigh.

At that moment, David was actually enjoying a temporary lull in the fighting as a truce had been called for Christmas Day. There were still the injured in the hospital to tend to, however, and as usual he was doing his rounds of the wards. The nurses had done what they could to make the wards look festive and more than one of the patients had a tiny bit of mistletoe hidden so that they could try and pinch a kiss from the young nurses.

When he had finished his rounds, David headed to the canteen for a well-earned cup of tea, trying hard to muster up some Christmas cheer. But he found it difficult after tending to so many injured men. Each and every one of them was someone's son, brother or sweetheart and he had no doubt it was the same for the other side. He couldn't imagine the German soldiers wanted to be out here in the desert any more than they did. With a sigh his thoughts turned to Kathy and he wondered what she and the children would be doing on this special day. God willing this time next year they would all be together again but only time would tell.

At Treetops the Christmas morning service at the church had to be abandoned because of the weather conditions but the atmosphere in the house was happy as the children laughed and played with their toys. Somehow despite the rationing Cook had managed to produce a Christmas dinner fit for a king. A local farmer had provided them with a plump goose, which was served with Cook's homemade stuffing and fluffy mashed potatoes. There was also a selection of vegetables, crispy roast potatoes and thick, creamy gravy followed by a delicious Christmas pudding, which Cook had had soaking in brandy for weeks, and lovely sticky yellow custard. The children tucked in as if they'd never been fed and Peggy squealed with delight when she found the shiny silver sixpence in the pudding.

'That's lucky,' Edith told her affectionately. 'Close your eyes and make a wish.'

The child closed her eyes and for a moment they all felt sad as they saw her lip tremble. She was clearly thinking of Bobby and they could all guess what she was wishing for, but unfortunately, if they were right, this was one wish that would never come true. Bobby, like thousands and thousands of others, had lost his life because of the war and none of them could ever come back.

However, the sombre mood that had settled across the table

didn't last for long because at that moment John glanced towards the window and saw the local farmer's truck ploughing through the snow in the drive.

'Ah.' He grinned. 'Now I have to go and see Mr Wilcox in the kitchen for a moment and then when you've finished eating, I want you all to come through and I shall hopefully have another present for you children.'

The mood lifted instantly as the children stared at him excitedly.

'What is it?' Thomas asked eagerly as John headed to the door, but John merely laughed.

'You'll know soon enough. Now finish your food.' And with that he was gone, leaving the children in an agony of anticipation.

'I bet he's got Farmer Wilcox to make us a new sledge,' Daisy piped up excitedly, but Thomas shook his head.

'It won't be that. We've already got one each with the new one that George made us.'

Sunday smiled indulgently. 'Well, why don't you just do as John suggested and finish your pudding then we can all go through and find out, can't we?'

Within minutes the rest of the food in their dishes had disappeared like magic, just in time to see the farmer's truck trundling off down the drive again.

'Please may we leave the table?' Thomas asked, already clambering down, and the adults nodded and followed behind as the children raced along the hallway.

They entered the kitchen to find John sitting at a chair with a large cardboard box at his feet.

'So, who wants to have a guess at what's in here then?' he teased as the children all stared at it curiously, but the words had barely left his mouth when the box suddenly moved and each of the children started.

Laughing, John bent down and opened the lid and instantly a tiny bundle of fur, its tail wagging furiously, spilled out onto the floor.

'It's a *puppy!*' Thomas cried ecstatically as he dropped to his knees and began to fondle the silky ears with a rapturous expression on his little face.

'A Golden Labrador puppy to be precise,' John laughed. 'I picked him out of the litter for you about four weeks ago, but you must all share him and take care of him. We grown-ups have enough to do.'

All three children were down on their knees now, giggling uncontrollably as the puppy jumped up and tried to lick every part of them he could reach.

'Oh, Uncle John, thank you,' they chorused. 'But what's his name?'

John shook his head and they all noticed then that Peggy sat back on her heels. They guessed that she would be thinking of her Skippy, the dog that had died with Bobby.

'Why don't we see if Peggy has any good suggestions?' John suggested kindly and Peggy smiled shyly.

'I think we should call him Skippy.'

Thomas and Daisy thought about it for a moment as they eyed their new pet, then nodded in agreement. 'I think that's a great name for him seeing as he can't keep still,' Thomas giggled.

'I just hope as he don't go piddlin' all over my clean floor,' Cook grumbled.

'Oh, don't worry, we'll take him out all the time and train him not to,' Thomas promised.

'I suppose that's all right then,' Cook sniffed, but in actual fact she was as taken with the new arrival as the children were and in time she'd be spoiling him with treats and scraps as he kept her company in the kitchen.

That night, long after everyone else had retired to bed, Kathy and Livvy sat in the kitchen enjoying a glass of sherry and a mince pie in front of the fire. Outside the snow was still falling but inside it was warm and cosy and Kathy sighed with contentment as she held her bare toes out towards the glowing fire. 'So, I wonder what next year will bring?' she mused.

Livvy shrugged and her eyes became sad as she thought of Giles locked away in a prisoner-of-war camp. After everything she'd heard, she just prayed Giles was strong enough to survive it.

'So, when did the sudden change of heart towards Giles take place?' Kathy asked as if she could read her sister's mind. 'I always thought you couldn't *stand* the poor chap.'

Livvy squirmed with embarrassment. 'I didn't think I could either,' she admitted guiltily. 'But I suppose when we were both stationed at the same place and we started to go out a bit together he just sort of grew on me. He doesn't know how I feel though, unless he got the letters I wrote,' she sighed. 'I told him in the letters because I wanted him to know I'd be here waiting for him when he came home, but the chances are he won't feel the same about me anyway.'

Kathy shook her head as she sipped at her sherry. 'Oh, I don't think you need worry on that score. Between you and me, I think he had a soft spot for you right from when he and John moved in here. If I recall rightly it was always you that was off with him.'

'Don't remind me,' Livvy answered guiltily. 'But I shall make it up to him if he comes home . . . *when* he comes home, that is! But what about you and David? You had rather a turnaround with him as well, if I'm not very much mistaken.'

'Yes, I did.' Kathy looked sheepish. 'I suppose it took the twins to make me realise what a lovely man he was and how stupid I was to spend my life thinking that I'd ever meant anything to Ben. For years I prayed every day that he would come back, and then when he did and took the children away it turned into a nightmare. Still, I don't like to think about that now. Things turned out all right in the end, thank goodness.'

'You must really hate Ben for what he did.'

Kathy stared into the fire for a moment before slowly shaking her head. 'I did at first,' she admitted. 'But then I slowly came to realise that he was very unwell and not really responsible for everything he did, and I was able to forgive him. And now Mum has her money back as well.'

'Hm, but she doesn't own Treetops anymore, does she?' Livvy said regretfully.

Kathy shrugged. 'Maybe not but she still lives here and who knows what the future might hold? They do say everything happens for a reason, don't they?'

The two sisters lapsed into a companionable silence, enjoying the peace and quiet after such a busy day, and making the most of each other's company. All too soon, Livvy would be returning to her base and who knew when they might be together again?

Chapter Fifty-Two

March 1945

By 1945, the tides of war had truly turned in the Allies' favour and everyone was feeling more optimistic that the end of the war might be in sight.

Livvy had still not heard from Giles and when John told her that he had been informed that his grandson had been transferred to the Belsen Camp in 1944 her spirits had sunk. Belsen had been set up as a camp for Jewish prisoners so they had no idea why Giles should have been sent there. They'd heard many horror stories of the atrocious conditions the prisoners were forced to live in and now their hopes of seeing him alive again were slim. It was reported that the camp was severely overcrowded, and the prisoners were living on starvation rations in appalling sanitary conditions that led to outbreaks of typhus, tuberculosis, typhoid fever and dysentery. When John rang Livvy at her base to tell her the news she openly wept.

'Stay strong, darling,' her mother urged her on the phone. 'Giles is a young man and he'll come through this.'

Livvy wasn't so sure, but she never gave up hope completely.

Kathy was also worried about David. The year before he had been brought back to England on a hospital ship, suffering from a severe case of dysentery, and when she had visited him at a hospital in Portsmouth, she had barely recognised him. He was so thin that he was almost skeletal, and he looked years older than his age.

'Hey, you're supposed to be out there looking after everyone else,' she had teased him as she plastered a bright smile on her face.

He had shrugged. 'I suppose I'm just a bit run down . . . but don't worry. As soon as I'm well enough I shall be out there again.'

As it happened, seeing Kathy was the best medicine he could have had and within a month he was shipped back to the field hospital. She had not seen him since but now every day she lived in hope that the war would soon be over, and they could finally begin their life together.

The years had also taken their toll on both Sunday and John who still lived compatibly side by side at Treetops.

Sunday had slowed down considerably, and though she still spent much of her free time unravelling any old woollies she could get her hands on and reknitting the wool back into socks for the troops, she rarely ventured into town anymore.

'I'm afraid our age is finally catching up with us. And not just us. Poor Cissie's knees are playing up and George is needing the children to help more and more with mucking out the stables,' she told John regretfully one evening as they sat enjoying a cup of cocoa before retiring to their rooms and he could only nod in agreement.

One evening, as they all sat in the kitchen eating their dinner, Sunday suggested, 'Let's have a party!'

'A *party*?' Kathy had just arrived home from the hospital and she looked astounded. 'What sort of a party?'

Sunday smiled. 'I've just got an urge to see as many people from Treetops' past as we can. I still keep in touch with quite a few of them.' She paused to look at John and asked, 'Would you mind?' Sometimes it was hard for her to remember that Treetops belonged to him now.

'Not in the least,' he assured her. 'But you have to remember that many of the young men you and Tom cared for will still be away fighting in the war. Perhaps you should wait a while?'

Sunday shook her head. 'No, it's not wise at our age to put off till tomorrow what can be done today. We might not be here.'

'*Mum*, what an awful thing to say,' Kathy scolded, but Sunday just shrugged and would not be put off from her plan.

'Let's do it,' she said enthusiastically, and her eyes grew misty as she thought back to other parties at Treetops she had enjoyed when her mother and Tom had been alive. 'When Lady Lavinia, your grandmother, owned Treetops, it saw some wonderful parties and balls,' she told Kathy dreamily. 'There would be an orchestra and the women looked like brightly coloured butter-flies as they glided round in their beautiful gowns. They were all the colours of the rainbow but not one of them ever managed to outshine your grandmother. She was truly beautiful, inside and out.'

'Yes, I remember,' Kathy agreed with a smile. She had very fond memories of her grandmother. 'But then you were very beautiful too, still are, in fact.'

Sunday chuckled. 'I'm an old woman,' she said with accept-ance. 'I don't feel old inside but when I look in the mirror, I wonder who the old woman is staring back at me. And sometimes

374

now I just yearn to go and join your father. It seems so long since I saw him, and I get so tired. But don't worry. I have no intentions of going anywhere until this damn war is over and I see you and Livvy settled. I promised your father I would look after you both and I will.'

'Don't talk like that. You're not going to leave us for a very long time,' Kathy said. 'And just where are we supposed to get all the food for this party?' she asked, ever sensible. The entire country was heartily sick of the enforced food rationing now.

'Don't you get worrying about that. If your mother wants a party, then a party she shall have.' John grinned and tapped the side of his nose. 'I have a few friends who might be able to get certain things on the black market. Not that I approve of it, of course, but sometimes needs must.'

'Oh yes, and who is going to prepare it all?' Mrs Gay, the old cook, had retired and gone to live with her daughter close to Brighton the year before and now Cissie and Edith did the cooking between them. The children had all missed her terribly when she first left, probably because of all the treats she used to cook for them.

'I'm sure me an' Edith can manage that so long as you don't want nothin' too fancy,' Cissie piped up. 'But why don't we plan it for when the weather is a bit better? It's early in March already so why don't we aim to have the party in May? People can spill out into the gardens then like they used to. In fact, I reckon George said only the other day that he'd come across the lanterns we used to hang in the trees in the back o' the barn somewhere. We could use 'em again providin' the mice ain't been at 'em.'

'I suppose that does make sense,' Sunday admitted. 'And it

will give us all something to look forward to.' She broke off then to pass Skippy a piece of meat beneath the table as they continued to make plans for the party. Sunday looked around the table with satisfaction; she'd been right to suggest it, the thought of the party had already lifted their spirits, and now she couldn't wait for the warm weather to arrive.

As March gave way to April it really appeared that the end of the war was in sight, and then on the thirtieth word reached them that Adolf Hitler had killed himself rather than admit defeat, and the people of Britain cheered. He had shot himself and died with his lover, Eva Braun, whom he had married the day before, but no one had a shred of sympathy for him. He had been an evil man and was responsible for hundreds of thousands of deaths so no one would mourn him.

Shocked soldiers were liberating the concentration camps and the full horror of what had taken place there was being revealed. But for many of the people who had been held there, rescue had come too late. In Belsen alone British soldiers had found 40,000 prisoners, many of them beyond help, suffering from starvation and many terrible diseases. Lying beside the survivors were piles of naked, rotting corpses with the little children who were still strong enough to stand playing beside them. It was a horrific testament to the cruelty and callousness of the SS guards. Almost all of the living were grossly emaciated, stick-like figures, their skin pulled so tight to their skulls that they were hardly recognisable as human beings and their rescuers openly wept at the sight of them.

They were shipped to makeshift hospitals but despite the

doctors' and nurses' best efforts, hundreds of the ex-prisoners were still dying every day.

'Livvy and John are beside themselves with worry,' Sunday confided to Cissie. 'They still don't know if Giles has survived.'

'He'll survive,' Cissie said confidently. 'He has to cos I think it would kill his grandad if he didn't.'

'I know what you mean,' Sunday agreed. John was hovering about the phone like a ghost, praying for it to ring with good news of his grandson, but so many people had been incarcerated in Belsen it was taking some time to get all the names of the survivors. Livvy was phoning daily for an update but all they could do was wait and pray for good news.

David meanwhile had been transferred to a field hospital in France after D Day the year before. Now the doctors and nurses didn't have as many casualties each day and were concentrating on the patients they already had. In his most recent letter to Kathy he had written:

Word has it that it's almost over and everyone here is optimistic. And then when I come home, I shall have a surprise for you, my darling, and God willing we shall never be parted again.

The letter lifted Kathy's spirits considerably and now everyone waited for news of the end of the war with anticipation.

And then at last, on 8 May came the announcement they had all been waiting for. Vast crowds had gathered in the streets around Whitehall and Buckingham Palace for the Prime Minister's announcement at 3 p.m. when he told them, 'The German war is at an end, hostilities will cease at midnight.'

Suddenly sirens and hooters were sounded all over the

country. Bonfires were lit and pubs and churches were filled to bursting. Flags and brightly coloured bunting in red, white and blue appeared everywhere, and in London, Winston Churchill's car was swamped by a jubilant crowd as he made his way to the House of Commons. Later he made an impromptu speech from a balcony above Whitehall. *'This is your victory!'* he told the cheering mass. *'God bless you all!'*

Beside him, Labour's Ernest Bevin led the crowds in singing, 'For He's a Jolly Good Fellow!'

Soon after, King George and Queen Elizabeth appeared on the palace balcony with Princess Elizabeth and Princess Margaret to wave to a rapturous crowd and, that evening, for the first time since war had been announced, Buckingham Palace, Big Ben and the Houses of Parliament were floodlit, while searchlights illuminated the sky. Britain was in a party mood and in London the streets were full of people dancing and singing, and there were chains of people doing the hokey-cokey, or singing 'Knee's Up Mother Brown' as they trailed behind anyone who possessed a musical instrument. Then at midnight when Big Ben sounded the hour of the official cease-fire a great roar went up, the tugs on the River Thames sounded their sirens, fireworks exploded, and bells pealed all across the land.

Everyone at Treetops had waited up to hear the excitement on the radio and their eyes were damp as they hugged each with sheer relief.

'Now please God our loved ones will come home, and we can all try to get our lives back to some sort of normality,' Sunday said as she dabbed at her wet eyes.

'I'll second that,' John said archly as he filled crystal glasses from a bottle of his very finest champagne, which he had saved for just such an occasion. 'And here's a toast to all the poor souls who will not be returning home who laid down their lives for our king and country. May God bless their souls.'

As they chinked glasses there was not a dry eye amongst them, for although they were elated at the victory, they were also painfully aware of the cost.

Chapter Fifty-Three

Although the war for Britain was over, the war in Japan still raged on but that didn't stop the people of Britain celebrating their victory.

'The people in the village are planning a street party,' Kathy told her mother and Cissie when she arrived home from the hospital late one afternoon in May, shortly after the joyous news had been announced. 'Why don't we bring our party forward and have it on the same day? We could have it here during the afternoon so that all the children could come too?' she suggested as Skippy leapt up at her, giving his usual rapturous welcome.

'What a good idea,' Cissie said approvingly. 'I'll get George to nip into town and get some flags and bunting . . . if you're happy with the idea, Sunday?'

Sunday nodded. 'I most certainly am. We can invite all the villagers as well as the people I was going to invite, and they can all bring a contribution to the food if they wish. Perhaps a bowl of jelly or some cakes for the children? If the weather is fine, we can have the tables out on the lawn and the children can run about to their hearts' content. If it's raining, we've still got plenty of room to accommodate everyone inside. We could

380

perhaps pin the invite up on the noticeboard in the church hall at the Holy Trinity. What do you think?'

'It would certainly save a lot of time having to go round the village inviting everyone individually,' Kathy agreed.

And so that evening they wrote the invite out and George took it along to the church hall and put it in pride of place on the noticeboard the next morning.

From then on Edith and Cissie spent every hour in the kitchen baking bread and cakes. John meanwhile was true to his word and delighted them when he presented them with six large tins of corned beef, a huge round cheese and enough dried, mixed fruit to make at least a dozen large cakes.

'I won't ask where they come from seein' as they have American labels on 'em.' Cissie winked as she whisked the things safely away into the pantry.

John gave a guilty grin. Sometimes it paid to have friends in high places.

The day of the party finally dawned, and everyone was suddenly rushing about preparing the tables. Bunting was hung in the trees and the children helped to carry the food out and place it on the long trestle tables. Neighbours had been dropping in all morning with their contributions and soon the trestles were groaning beneath the weight.

There were three types of sandwiches – corned beef, cheese and jam made with the fruit that Cissie had picked from the blackberry bushes the year before. There were dishes full of brightly coloured wobbly jellies and a variety of cakes. Sausage rolls fresh from the oven and huge bowls full of various pickles.

One of the villagers had brought in a big tray of scones, another two quivering dishes of blancmange, and as the children greedily eyed all the treats their stomachs rumbled with anticipation.

On the end of each table were big jugs full of homemade lemonade for the little ones. John had provided two large barrels of beer for the men and a selection of wines and spirits for the women, so all in all it looked set to be a very good party indeed.

'Eeh, we couldn't have asked fer a better day,' Cissie said contentedly as she eyed the feast they had laid out. 'It's as if him upstairs is smilin' down on us.'

George glanced up at the cloudless blue sky and nodded agreement. 'Aye, well happen after all the heartbreak this country has seen over the last few years, we deserve a bit o' sunshine now.' He hurried off then to help John and some of the village men who had volunteered to help carry the piano out onto the terrace. Finally, there was no more to be done and the women went to get ready for the first guests to arrive.

Sunday looked very regal in the outfit she had chosen to wear. It was a navy-blue calf-length skirt with a fitted jacket, which showed off her still-slim figure. Around her neck she wore the treasured string of pearls that had been a twenty-first birthday present from her mother, and on her finger the diamond engagement ring that Tom had bought her so many years ago sparkled as it reflected the light. There were also tiny diamond studs in her ears and her still-thick silver hair was dressed in a simple chignon at the back of her head.

As John commented admiringly to Cissie, 'She looks like a queen. No one would ever believe she was almost seventy-five years old, would they?'

'No, they wouldn't,' Cissie agreed with an envious little sigh.

Sunday had always been a looker. 'She can still turn heads when she's a mind to. But if you think she's pretty now you should 'ave seen 'er when she were young!'

'Well, if you don't mind me saying you're looking very fetching yourself today,' John said gallantly and Cissie giggled.

'Get away wi' you. Flattery will get you everywhere.' And then she hurried off to help with all the last-minute details with a happy flush on her cheeks.

By mid-afternoon the garden and the house were teeming with people. The wine and beer were flowing like water and everyone was having a fine old time. The children's laughter floated on the air as they raced about the lawns and Sunday was transported back in time. There were so many of the children she and Tom had cared for there, all grown up with families of their own now. There was Flora and Jamie, Janet, her late beloved Kitty's friend, and so many more that it took her all her time to catch a moment with each of them. And then there were all the people that had come from the surrounding villages, Witherley, Fenny Drayton, Mancetter and Hartshill. Some people had even come from Nuneaton town.

As evening descended George lit the lanterns that he and Cissie had hung from the trees and John sat down to plonk out some well-known tunes on the piano on the terrace, and suddenly everyone was up dancing, feeling happy and full after the lovely meal they had eaten.

They sang along to some of Gracie Fields's much-loved songs: 'Wish Me Luck as You Wave Me Goodbye', 'Sally', and Vera Lynn's 'White Cliffs of Dover'. But as the tempo increased, soon they were boogying to the 'Lambeth Walk' and even Sunday and Cissie were persuaded to get up and join in the fun for a time, till Cissie declared breathlessly, 'Phew, I don't know about you but I reckon I'm getting' too old fer this lark, I'm afraid. I think I'll sit this one out an' leave it to the young 'uns.'

'And I'll sit it out with you.' Sunday smiled as they claimed two seats and sat back to watch the merriment. They both became quiet then as they thought of the loved ones that could not be with them. Tom, David and Giles.

At one point, Sunday glanced towards Kathy who was trying to get a great lump of jelly out of Daisy's hair and when she saw the wistful expression on her daughter's face, she knew that she was thinking of David too. Livvy, meanwhile, was dancing with Thomas who was red in the face and giggling.

As the evening wore on people began to drift away but not before they had assured Sunday that it had been one of the best parties they had ever attended. The men had drunk the barrels dry and Sunday noted with amusement that they swayed slightly as their wives ushered them down the drive.

Cissie, Kathy and Edith were beginning to clear the tables now but at that moment Sunday noticed someone striding up the drive and her heart did a little skip . . . It was getting dark now and she was sure her eyes must be playing tricks on her but no . . . As the figure loomed closer, she knew she wasn't mistaken, and a sob caught in her throat just at the moment that Kathy glanced around and saw the figure too.

The pots she was holding suddenly crashed to the table as a look of pure joy spread across her face and then she was off like the wind haring towards him.

'*David!* Oh, David, I hardly dare blink in case I'm imagining this, and you disappear.'

Catching her in his arms he swung her off her feet and twirled her about as if she weighed no more than a feather.

'You can blink as much as you like because I'm here to stay,' he told her with a catch in his voice and then they were in each other's arms oblivious to everyone and everything around them, as they kissed as if they might never come up for air. When at last they did, she stared up at him starry-eyed. 'But how did you manage this? And why didn't you let me know you were coming?'

'I didn't know myself till a couple of days ago and I wanted to surprise you. But now, stand still . . . I have a surprise for you.'

He fished in his jacket pocket, pulled out a document and handed it to her. She studied it closely before whooping with delight and throwing her arms about his neck again.

'Can I take it that's a yes then?'

'Yes, yes and *yes*,' Kathy cried, and grabbing his hand she said excitedly, 'Come on, we must go and tell Mum and find the children, they're about here somewhere and they're going to be so thrilled to see you.'

'David.' Sunday greeted him warmly as he approached. 'I'd say you're about the perfect end to a perfect day. Are you home for good now?'

'I most certainly am.' Then looking slightly nervous he told Kathy, 'You'd better show your mother what I've just given you and I hope she'll approve.'

As Sunday read through the small document that Kathy passed to her, her smile grew broader. 'Why, it's a special marriage licence. Does this mean . . .?'

David let out a sigh of relief. 'It means that in three days' time, with your permission, I am going to make this very beautiful daughter of yours my wife.' He knew that most mothers dreamed of seeing their daughters float down the aisle in a swathe of satin and lace and sadly there would be no time to organise all that fuss now, but even so his future mother-in-law seemed happy with the idea.

'If Kathy is happy then so am I,' she assured him.

'In that case we'll go and see the vicar at St Peter's in Mancetter first thing in the morning and organise it.' David guessed that this was where Kathy would want to be married because her father was buried there. He was just sad that Tom wasn't there to give her away. And so, before the party was even properly finished, they were organising another one and as Sunday saw the radiant glow on her daughter's cheeks, she couldn't have been happier about it. The twins spotted David just then and they leapt all over him, smothering him with kisses as Skippy bounded about with his tail wagging furiously.

'You won't go away again, will you?' Thomas asked solemnly when they finally drew apart and David smiled as he ruffled the child's thick, dark hair.

'No, I won't be going anywhere. In fact, in a few days' time I'm going to be your new daddy. How do you feel about that?'

The smiles on their faces gave him their answer and Sunday slipped discreetly away to give the new little family some time to themselves. It truly had been the most wonderful day. All they had to wait for now was news of Giles, and should it be good news then everything would be just perfect.

The next morning the happy couple borrowed John's car and used up some of his precious petrol to drive to Mancetter to set the date for the wedding and when they came back the glow on their faces told its own story. 'In three days' time you'll be Mrs David Deacon,' David told Kathy happily. Suddenly the smile slid from his face as something occurred to him. 'Crikey! In all the excitement I hadn't given a thought as to where we're going to live!'

'I think I can help you there,' Sunday told them. 'You're more than welcome to live in the lodge. We all lived quite happily there and only moved here because it was safer for the children when the bombing was going on. It might need a good clean and an airing though. It's been empty for some time now. Of course, now that I have the money back that Ben stole, I'd be quite happy to buy you a house if you'd sooner live somewhere else?' Sunday offered.

Kathy and David glanced at each other and shook their heads.

'Actually, I intend to carry on working at the hospital, for now at least,' Kathy explained. 'And David will be going back there too so it would be wonderful if we stayed here because we'd still have all of you to keep your eyes on the children. They love living here anyway and I think it would be a wrench for them if we were to take them away.'

'In that case, me and Cissie will go down to the lodge and start getting it ready for you this morning,' Sunday promised. 'And then this afternoon, young lady, you and I are going shopping. I've saved all my clothing coupons so there are bound to be enough to get you something nice to wear for the wedding. I'll get George to drive us into town and if we can't find anything suitable there, we'll go into Coventry tomorrow.'

Kathy agreed meekly. She knew better than to argue with her mother when she had made her mind up about something.

As it happened, they found exactly what they were looking for in a small dress shop in the marketplace. It was a two-piece costume in cream with a straight skirt and a smart little jacket that made Kathy's waist look tiny. They even found a small hat with a little veil to match it and although it took every coupon Sunday had and a few more of Cissie's it was so perfect that it was worth every one.

'You look beautiful,' Sunday said with a lump in her throat when Kathy came out of the changing room. Now once again they would have to start preparing the small party that John had insisted they should have at Treetops following the wedding.

When they returned home, they were greeted with yet more good news. Livvy had phoned to say that her commanding officer had granted her leave to attend the wedding.

'Now there will only be one family member missing,' John said wistfully, for he had thought of them all as family for a long time now. They all felt for him. They knew that he was thinking of Giles.

Chapter Fifty-Four

As the ship that was taking him home crested a large wave before crashing back down again, Giles leaned over the side of the bed and heaved into the bucket one of the nurses had placed there. Most of the men in the beds dotted around them were doing the same and the nurses were hurrying from one to another doing their best to make the patients as comfortable as they could. They had been at sea for two days when they hit the storm but bad as it was Giles still had enough about him to know that this was nowhere near as awful as the prison camp had been.

He and the men he was journeying with had spent two weeks in a makeshift hospital before being taken aboard the ship. Sadly, many of his comrades had not even made it this far and two more had passed away since they had set sail. But at least now they were being treated with kindness instead of cruelty and there was food always available had they been able to eat it. Unfortunately, the starvation rations they had become used to had ensured that their stomachs had shrunk alarmingly so they could eat no more than one or two mouthfuls at a time.

'Still,' the kindly doctor who had first tended them had said cheerily, 'a little and often, eh, lads? We'll get you well again, never you fear.'

Many of the men were also suffering from horrific bed sores, some so big that they could have put their hands in them. This was due to the cramped and dirty conditions they had been living in and the fact that they had been sleeping on a concrete floor with no bedding of any kind. Sometimes Giles was surprised that any of them had survived. Each day the SS guards had entered their hut and thrown them a stale, grey loaf that would have to feed at least thirty of them for the day. They would then walk amongst them, lifting the bodies of those who had died during the night and throwing them onto the growing pile at one end of the room. Even now if Giles closed his eyes, he could smell the terrible stench that had come from them and once again his stomach would revolt and throw up any food he had managed to swallow.

But the weakness was the worst. The complete feeling of fatigue that meant he wasn't even able to sit let alone stand unaided. There had been no exercise allowed for the prisoners in Belsen and after weeks and months of lying on a cold, hard floor their muscles had wasted away to almost nothing. Again, the doctor had assured Giles that he would regain his strength in time but sometimes Giles had his doubts.

When he had first been incarcerated in Belsen he had received parcels from home but by the time they reached him they had been torn apart and any food or items of value had been removed. Even so it was the letters that had kept him going. Especially the ones from Livvy. In them, she had told him that she had feelings for him, but would she still want him now? he wondered. He was only half the man he had been before he had bailed out of his aeroplane on that fateful night over Berlin and he wondered if she would even recognise him anymore.

Head lice had been rampant in the camp and so they had all hacked off as much of their hair as they could with anything they could find. It was better than being driven mad scratching but now as he weakly managed to raise his hand to his scalp he frowned. His hair, or what was left of it, stood up in little untidy tufts and he knew that he must look a terrible mess if any of his comrades were anything to go by.

His thoughts were interrupted when one of the nurses, a kind young woman who had told him her name was Sally, asked, 'Is there anything I can do for you?'

He managed a weak smile. 'Yes, you could stop the ship from rolling.'

'If only I could,' she answered with a grin, clinging to the side of the bed as the ship dipped again. 'But never fear, the captain just told us that we should be out of the storm very soon and before you know it, you'll be back on home ground.'

He nodded and finally gave up trying to overcome the tiredness that had hit him again and within seconds he was fast asleep.

'Oh, my darling girl! You look *just* beautiful,' Sunday told Kathy on the morning of her wedding. 'I don't think I have ever seen a more beautiful bride. Your other mum would be so proud if she could see you.' She often thought of her Kitty, for as this lovely girl had grown, she had become the double of her.

'Now, Mum, don't start crying or you'll start me off,' Kathy warned as she pulled the little veil on her hat down over her eyes. 'Pass me that posy, would you? And then I think we're all ready to go.'

George had run the groom and the rest of them to the church some time ago and had now come back for Kathy, her mother and John, who would give the bride away. He had become quite emotional when Kathy had asked if he would consider doing it and had assured her that it would be a very great honour.

Sunday lifted the tiny posy of white roses and baby's breath and handed it to the bride then, after exchanging a kiss, side by side they set off down the stairs.

John too looked quite teary-eyed at his first glimpse of Kathy and told her sincerely, 'You look absolutely stunning, my dear. Now . . . are we ready to do this?'

'Oh *yes*,' Kathy breathed. She could hardly wait to be David's wife and so they all clambered into the car for the short journey to the church.

John looked as proud as punch as he walked down the aisle with Kathy on his arm. Peggy and Daisy walked behind them with broad smiles on their faces in their pretty bridesmaids' dresses with little crowns of flowers on their heads to match the tiny posies they were carrying, while Thomas stood proudly at David's side with Kathy's wedding ring resting on a small cushion, his tongue in his cheek as he concentrated hard on not dropping it.

Kathy and David had eyes only for each other as they solemnly took their vows, and almost before they knew it, they were pronounced husband and wife and David lifted her from her feet and gave her a smacking kiss on the lips, while the sun shining through the stained-glass windows painted them all the colours of the rainbow. Once outside they were showered in rice and rose petals and the air was full of laughter, then Kathy tossed her posy high into the air and it plummeted down and landed smack in Livvy's hands.

'There you go, little sis,' Kathy teased. 'It's your turn next.'

Could she have known it the words tore at Livvy's heart, for if she couldn't have Giles, she had decided she would never marry anyone, but she somehow managed to keep her smile in place and the moment passed.

Soon they were back at Treetops and once more a party was in full swing.

Edith and Cissie, who hadn't wanted to miss the wedding, had laid out a buffet of cold meats and pies before they left, and everyone tucked in.

'I wish you'd let me pay for you both to have a few days away somewhere as a honeymoon,' Sunday said regretfully, but both David and Kathy shook their heads.

'Thanks, Mum, but we're quite happy to spend a few days at the lodge with the children,' Kathy promised her, then dropping her voice she confided happily, 'The twins are calling David Daddy already. I'm just *so* lucky!'

'Well, you deserve to be,' Sunday told her warmly. 'And I have a feeling you're going to be very happy indeed together.'

'I hope so.' Kathy's adoring eyes met those of her new husband, and she hurried over to give him yet another kiss.

It was growing dark when the newlyweds set off down the drive with the twins skipping ahead of them, as Cissie and Sunday watched from the doorstep with broad smiles on their faces.

'What a wonderful month it's been,' Cissie said contentedly. 'First the war finally ends, then the party an' now the wedding. It couldn't get much better than this, could it?'

'It could if we could only have word that Giles is safe,' Sunday pointed out and Cissie frowned.

'You're right, of course. But who knows what tomorrow may bring, eh? Let's just hope as our good luck holds out.' And arm in arm the two old friends went back into the house.

Later that night, as Sunday and John sat enjoying a little quiet time before retiring, a thought suddenly occurred to Sunday, and glancing towards him she frowned.

'I've only just realised that I could now afford to buy my own place rather than put on you any longer,' she said quietly.

'You are not, as you put it, putting on me,' John snorted as he helped himself to a small brandy and poured one for her. 'If you must know I'm glad of your company. It will be hard enough to get used to not having Kathy and the twins about without you deserting me as well. We get along fine, don't we?'

'Oh yes, yes, of course we do,' Sunday assured him quickly. The last thing she wanted to do was hurt his feelings. But on the other hand, she didn't want him to think that she was taking advantage of his good nature either.

Sensing her unease, he sat forward in his seat and confided, 'To be honest, having you and the family here has been a life-saver for me, especially since Giles went missing. I think I would have gone mad had I been on my own, so in actual fact you'll be doing me a huge favour if you'll only stay. One day, God willing, this house will pass to Giles and it occurred to me the other day that should Giles and Livvy get together, she'll be the mistress here. We'd be sort of keeping the place in the family between us and I like that idea. Our grandchildren would grow up here and Giles and Livvy will be able to tell them stories about what an odd old couple we were.'

Sunday chuckled, feeling vastly relieved. She had no wish to move house at her age. In fact, the thought of leaving Treetops filled her with dread and now that she knew John didn't feel she was imposing on him her mind was at rest. She also liked the thought of her grandchildren growing up there and tried to picture them. But that was still just a pipe dream. First, they must wait to find out if Giles had survived and if he had they would have to stand back and let nature take its course.

Chapter Fifty-Five

The following morning yet another telegram was delivered and this time they all eyed it with dread. Would it tell them that Giles had not survived his incarceration in Belsen? Or would it be good news?

'Oh, give it to me, I'll read it,' Sunday said nervously when John stood staring at it as if it might bite him.

Taking the envelope from his limp hand she hastily opened it and then she started to cry. 'He . . . he's *alive*,' she said croakily. 'And even as we speak, he's on his way to a hospital in Plymouth. It says they'll send us an address where we can contact him in due course.'

John paled to the colour of lint and George rushed across to help him into a chair.

'Cissie, make some tea and put plenty of sugar in it, he's in shock,' Sunday said urgently.

John's breathing was shallow, and he was clutching his chest. 'And, George, would you go and ring the doctor please?' Sunday said as she knelt beside him chafing his hands and when he appeared to be a little calmer, she helped him into the drawing room and onto the sofa.

'I . . . I can't believe it,' he gasped as tears slid unashamedly down his cheeks. 'I prayed that he'd come home but I'd almost given up hope.'

'Well, your prayers have been answered,' she said softly. 'And now you have to calm down or you'll be ill and then you'll be no good to him at all when he comes home, will you?'

He gave her a crooked smile and her heart sank as she saw the way one side of his lip had dropped. It was becoming increasingly clear that he had suffered another stroke.

The doctor confirmed it when he arrived shortly afterwards. 'All you can do is get him up to bed and keep him quiet,' he told them solemnly. Sunday nodded and as soon as the doctor had left with promises to come back the next day, she and George helped John up the stairs to his room.

As the day wore on John appeared to be calmer and they all hoped that he would come through the latest attack.

'Poor chap has been living on his nerves,' Edith said as they all sat together in the kitchen later that day. 'But he's a tough old bird, and he'll come through it, you'll see.'

They could only hope that she was right.

Two days later another telegram arrived informing them which hospital Giles was in and John became agitated again. 'I should go and see him,' he fretted, but Sunday shook her head. 'You're not well enough,' she pointed out sensibly. 'But I know someone who will go. We rang Livvy on the day we found out he was coming back, and she already has a forty-eight-hour pass on standby. I've no doubt that now we know where he is, she'll be on a train to visit him like a shot.'

John was frustrated but could see the sense in what she said, so Sunday rang Livvy's base.

'Oh, I still have to keep pinching myself to make myself believe that he's alive,' Livvy said ecstatically after her mother had told her the good news. 'I shall be on the train to see him this very afternoon. I've already cleared it with my boss. I should get into Plymouth this evening then I'll find somewhere to stay, and I can be at the hospital first thing in the morning. And, Mum, be sure to tell John I'll ring him just as soon as I come out of there to let him know how he is.'

'All right, darling,' Sunday said, and then hastily as an afterthought. 'And oh, it might be best if you don't tell Giles just yet that his grandfather is ill. He might not be in a very good state himself after all he's been through and we don't want to worry him and make him worse.'

'Of course,' Livvy agreed before hastily hanging up, eager to start her journey. It would be a trek from her base and would involve a number of train changes but thankfully they were running smoothly again now and even if they hadn't been, Sunday knew that her daughter would have travelled twice the distance if necessary.

As the train sped across country, Livvy found herself sitting amongst many men who were being demobbed. They were easily recognisable as they were all wearing the standard demob suits that the army issued. Double-breasted, three-piece in either dark blue or grey. Almost all of them were returning home to their families and the atmosphere on the train was light.

'Are you off home an' all, love?' One of the men in the carriage asked Livvy cheerily.

She grinned and shook her head as she stared down at her uniform. 'Not yet. My unit should be dispersed within the next couple of months and I can't tell you how nice it will be to wear my own clothes again. I'm actually going to visit my . . . er . . . a friend who is in a military hospital in Plymouth. He was in Belsen.'

The man's smile faded as he glanced towards the man sitting next to him. 'Well, in that case don't get expectin' too much, love,' he said solemnly. 'Them places were hell holes so he might not be in very fine fettle at the moment. Still, at least he survived it so I wish him all the best.'

'Thank you.' Livvy stared out of the window thinking on his words. She was half longing to see Giles but was also half dreading what state he might be in. *But*, she told herself, *he's alive and that's the main thing*. Whatever condition he was in she was sure he would recover once he was back at Treetops. Everyone would make sure of that.

It was early evening by the time she alighted at Plymouth and it took her some time to find somewhere to stay. She finally found a small room in a little bed and breakfast place just outside the city that was only a short bus ride from the hospital where Giles was being cared for. The room left a lot to be desired but seeing as she was only going to be staying there for one night, Livvy wasn't concerned. She would have slept under a hedge if it meant being close to Giles, and despite the fact that she was exhausted after the journey she hardly slept a wink for excitement. She was up with the lark the next morning and after eating a fatty fried breakfast and getting directions from the slovenly landlady, she left.

The bus stopped outside the gateway of what had once been a rather stately manor. The enormous gates, which had once marked the entrance to the drive, were long gone, no doubt melted down to make ammunition for the war, but the drive was tree-lined and pleasant and reminded her a little of the drive at Treetops. As Livvy walked along she noted that the sweeping lawns on either side were well kept and when the house came into view, she paused to admire it. It was a huge place with many enormous windows sparkling in the early morning sunshine, and ivy and Virginia creeper climbing up the walls. On either side of the two stout oak doors in the centre of the house were flower-beds that were a profusion of colour.

Now she was so close, Livvy's heart began to hammer painfully and her mouth went dry. Giles was somewhere beyond those doors and very soon she would see him. It was the day she had prayed for and yet suddenly she felt apprehensive. What if he didn't want to see her? She had treated him appallingly when they had both lived at Treetops. But then she had let him know that her feelings towards him had changed – if he had even got the letters, that was. Taking a deep breath, she decided in for a penny in for a pound. She had come too far to turn back now. So, after mounting the three carved marble steps, she rang the bell at the side of the doors. It was answered almost immediately by a young nurse wearing a crisp, white apron.

'I've come to see Flight Officer Willerby,' she informed the nurse and the young woman smiled and nodded, ushering her into an enormous foyer with a black-and-white-tiled floor and a sweeping staircase on one side leading up to the first floor. A desk stood against the opposite wall and the nurse hurried over to it and after checking a register that lay open on the desk she nodded.

'Ah yes, here we are. He has a room on the first floor, would you like to follow me?'

Livvy's mouth went dry as they climbed the stairs. At the top of them was a large room in which a number of patients were sitting, some in wheelchairs and others in the wing chairs that were dotted about. Two of them were playing a game of chess, another two a game of cards, but the majority of them just sat staring into space as nurses hovered between them.

'That's one of the day rooms,' the young nurse told her as she saw Livvy looking in. 'There's another on the ground floor for the more able-bodied patients who are able to get about a little more easily.'

Livvy nodded as she followed her along a very long landing that still had an element of grandeur about it. Livvy could almost imagine women in beautiful ball gowns drifting along it in times gone by. But then her thoughts were brought back abruptly to the present when the young nurse stopped in front of one of the many doors that led off it.

'He's in here,' she informed Livvy, her face solemn now. 'But don't expect too much. He only arrived a short while ago and I'm afraid he is still very weak and very traumatised.' Seeing the distress on Livvy's face she added hastily, 'He will get better, of course. He's severely malnourished but if we can get some good food inside him, he'll start to improve in no time. Now, would you like me to tell him you're here?'

Livvy shook her head as she stood straight and smoothed her skirt. 'No . . . no thank you. I'd rather surprise him.'

'As you wish. I'll leave you to it then but do shout if there's anything you need. The tea trolley should be round shortly.' She tripped away and Livvy took a deep breath and tapped on the door before cautiously opening it and stepping into the room. This was it and she was painfully aware that her whole future could hinge on these next few minutes.

Her eyes quickly scanned the room and for a moment it was hard to believe she was in a hospital. A large rosewood wardrobe with a matching chest of drawers stood against one wall and heavy velvet curtains in a deep-rose colour hung at the window, which overlooked the sprawling lawns where she could now see patients being pushed about in wheelchairs. There was a small desk and chair in front of the window and on the other side of the room was the only evidence that this was indeed a hospital – a hospital bed. But surely that couldn't be Giles lying in it? His once thick, dark hair was now completely grey and stood up in untidy tufts across his head and he was so thin that even after staring she couldn't be at all sure that it really was him. He was truly unrecognisable from the handsome young man she remembered. She approached the bed cautiously, trying hard to stem the tears that were trembling on her lashes.

'Giles,' she said softly and suddenly his eyes blinked open and she knew that it *was* him! No one had eyes as blue as his.

But her pleasure was short-lived for almost instantly he turned his head away and growled, 'Go away, Livvy . . . *please*!'

Chapter Fifty-Six

'After the trek I've had to get here I most certainly will not!' Livvy answered indignantly and, pulling up a chair, she plonked herself down on it.

For over ten minutes she sat there, obstinately mute until, still with his face turned away from her, he asked resignedly, 'So just what do you *want*, Livvy?'

'I want to see *you*, of course,' she snapped. 'And a right old hike I've had to get here, let me tell you, so I've no intention of leaving until you speak to me.'

'But I don't *want* you to see me like this. I don't want *anybody* to see me,' he muttered. 'I'm just a shadow of the man I used to be.'

The tears she was holding back were choking her, but she kept them in check as she said angrily, 'Don't be so full of self-pity. It doesn't suit you. Why, you're damned lucky compared to most of the poor blighters in here! Some of them have no arms or legs, others are blind or horrifically burned, whereas you will make a full recovery given time.'

Silence hung heavy between them but eventually he slowly turned his head to look at her and the haunted look in his eyes almost broke her heart.

'You always were an *obstreperous* little devil,' he said with the ghost of a smile and suddenly she saw that somewhere in that bag of bones was still the man she loved.

'Did you get the letters I wrote to you while you were in the prison camp?' she asked with her chin in the air.

He nodded, his eyes on hers.

'So, you know then that I love you and *still* you try to send me away?'

'But I'm not the same man who used to show you off around Lincoln. Look at me . . . I'm a wreck.'

'*Huh!*' She sniffed disdainfully. 'More of a mess than a wreck,' she said frankly. 'Your hair is a bloody disaster, but I suppose that will grow back in time, and now I'm getting used to it I quite like that grey colour, it makes you look distinguished. And all right, you're not much more than a bag of bones at the minute but I've no doubt Edith, Cissie and Mum will fatten you back up in no time when you get home.'

Suddenly for the first time in a very long time he started to laugh, and tears began to roll down his cheeks.

'Livvy, you don't change at all,' he told her with a shake of his head. 'It would be a very brave man indeed who took you on.'

She tossed her head. 'You're quite right, so are *you* brave enough?'

'I dare say I shall have to be. I'm too scared of you to say no,' he answered with a twinkle in his eye and suddenly she was leaning over the bed and kissing every inch of his face.

'Right, in that case you'd better hurry up and get yourself out of here so that we can be married,' she told him bossily. 'I shall be out of the WAAFs in a short time and I don't like to be kept waiting when I've made my mind up about something.'

'Yes, boss,' he answered as he held her awkwardly and suddenly he had a future to look forward to again.

'How is John?' Livvy asked when she rang home that night.

'The stroke was nowhere near as bad as last time, thank goodness,' her mother told her, sounding relieved. 'But what about Giles?'

Livvy smiled. She was standing in a telephone box not far from the hospital having spent the whole day with him. She had decided to stay another night in the grotty little B & B so that she could see him again briefly before she set off back to the base the next morning. 'He's very malnourished and weak. In fact, he looks like a skeleton with skin stretched across its bones,' she admitted. 'And his hair has gone completely grey, what's left of it. But I'm sure once we get him home, he'll soon be on the mend again. And, Mum . . . I ought to warn you, as soon as we're both home we shall be getting married.'

'Oh, darling! That's *wonderful* news,' Sunday cried delightedly. 'I'm sure when I tell John this will perk him up no end! Am I allowed to?'

'Of course you are,' Livvy chuckled. 'You can tell the whole world if you like!' And then noticing someone was waiting to use the phone, she said hurriedly, 'I have to go, there's a queue for the phone here but I'll call you when I get back to the base. Bye, Mum, I love you.'

Sunday smiled as she placed the phone back in its cradle. It seemed that both of her daughters were going to be settled before very much longer and she couldn't have been happier about it.

'How is he?' John asked anxiously when she went into his room a short time later.

'Hm . . . let's put it this way.' Sunday smiled as she straightened the covers on his bed. 'You have to hurry up and get well because Livvy has just informed me we have another wedding to organise as soon as they're both home.'

John beamed like a Cheshire cat. '*Really?* Well I'll be, isn't that great news?'

'It is indeed but after the last wedding and organising the party I need some help with this one so just think on what I said.'

Three weeks later Livvy was home for good.

'It feels strange wearing my own clothes again,' she told her mother as Skippy danced around her feet.

'Yes, I'm sure it does but I think we ought to start thinking about what you're going to wear for the wedding now,' Sunday answered. She hadn't given up hope of seeing at least one of her daughters all in white, but that idea went out the window when Livvy snorted.

'I'd be happy to wear a paper bag so long as I could marry Giles. And don't go planning on a big posh wedding, Mum,' she warned. 'Because Giles won't be up to it. It's going to take some time before he's completely well again, so we just want to keep it plain and simple with no fuss.'

'But you will at least get married in church?'

Seeing the hopeful look on her mother's face, Livvy sighed. 'All right, if that's what you really want, I'll ask Giles how he feels about it. But then we'll just come back here. We don't want any great huge reception.'

It had already been agreed that Giles and Livvy would live at Treetops for the time being once they were married and then they would decide if they wanted to move elsewhere when he was fully recovered. Livvy had been to see him the week before and had been thrilled at how much better he looked already. Admittedly he was still painfully thin, but he had lost the skeletal look and with his hair growing and a little colour seeping back into his cheeks he was beginning to look like the man she had fallen in love with.

The following week she went to see him again but when she suggested a church wedding his face fell and he looked panicked.

'Look, I hate to let your mum down, pet. But I don't think I can face it. Can't we just slip away and get married quietly on our own? I'm sure the oldies would forgive us eventually under the circumstances.'

'Let me see what we can do,' Livvy said and without another word she slipped away to have a word with the matron.

That evening she rang home to tell her mother that she would be staying in Plymouth for at least another week. Giles would hopefully be strong enough to be discharged by then and if that was the case, she would travel home with him on the train and there'd be an ambulance ready to pick them up from the station.

'All right, darling, but just make sure you have somewhere nice to stay,' Sunday told her. 'And give him all our love. We're all so looking forward to seeing him again.'

The news that Giles would soon be returning home worked better than a tonic on John. Thankfully because the last stroke had not been as severe as the first one, he was now pottering about, although everyone was making sure that he didn't overdo things.

'I wish you women wouldn't keep fussing over me,' he groaned in frustration, but they simply smiled and took no notice. Already people was chipping in with ideas for Giles and Livvy's wedding and although Livvy had stated they only wanted a very quiet, simple do it looked in danger of spiralling into a much bigger affair.

Kathy, David and the twins were now happily settled into the lodge and if their bright eyes and smiling faces were anything to go by married life was suiting them very well. Immediately after they had married, David had applied to legally adopt the twins and, because there was no opposition from their birth father, they had been assured that permission should be granted very soon. There was absolutely nothing to stand in his way and already the twins were happily addressing him as 'Daddy', so all in all Sunday felt that had worked out very well.

A little over a week later, an ambulance drew up outside Treetops and as Livvy helped Giles down from the back of it they found a welcoming committee standing on the doorstep.

There was Sunday and John, Cissie, George, Edith and Peggy. Kathy had also taken a day off from the hospital and David was beside her with the twins on either side of him and Skippy leaping about in his usual madcap manner.

'Welcome home,' they chorused joyfully as he stood at the bottom of the steps leaning heavily on a stick with Livvy supporting him. He was still very weak, but the doctors were certain that with love and care he would eventually make a full recovery.

Giles felt tears sting at the back of his eyes. There had been times when he was locked away in the camp that he had truly thought he would never see their beloved faces again but here they all were.

'Come along in,' Cissie said bossily. 'You look tired and you're all skin an' bone. I can see I 'ave some serious fattening up to do wi' you, young man.'

They headed to the kitchen where the kettle was singing on the hob and the delicious smell of roast chicken filled the air. For at least half an hour one or another of them chatted non-stop as they caught up on everything, but it was Sunday who eventually said, 'And now we have another wedding to plan, how *wonderful*.'

Giles and Livvy exchanged a guilty glance and the room became silent as everyone stopped talking and looked quizzically towards them.

'Have I said something wrong?' Sunday asked with a frown. 'I wasn't trying to rush you if that's what you're thinking, only I—'

'Mum, it isn't that,' Livvy interrupted as she took Giles's hand. 'It's just that . . . Well, I'm not sure how you're going to take this, so I'll just come out and tell you . . . Giles and I were married three days ago in the hospital chapel in Plymouth. I'm *so* sorry to spring it on you like this, we both are, but Giles still has a long way to go before he's fully well again and we just couldn't face a big fuss.'

Sunday looked astounded and for the first time she noticed the thin, gold band on Livvy's left hand glinting in the sun that shone through the window.

'B-but how did you manage that?'

Livvy gave another guilty grin. 'We had a long chat to the matron there – she's such a dear soul – and we told her how we felt and, bless her, she organised everything from the licence to the service. She even stood as one of our witnesses. But you didn't miss a lot, really! It was a very, very quiet affair, I promise you . . . Do you all forgive us?'

She held her breath as she glanced at each of them in turn. For a moment there was a stunned silence, but then they surged forward to shake Giles's hand and kiss Livvy.

'Of *course* we forgive you,' her mother told her with tears in her eyes. 'If you're happy then we're happy. You're both home safe and sound and that's all that matters. Congratulations. I know you're both going to be very happy, my darling. And, John, you wouldn't happen to have another bottle of champagne, would you? We might have missed the wedding but there's nothing to stop us drinking a toast to the happy couple, is there?'

'Indeed, there isn't,' he agreed. 'I shall go down into the cellar this very minute, just carry on chatting without me. I'm not as quick on my pins as I used to be.' He pottered away with a wide smile on his face. It wasn't the sort of wedding he'd always envisaged for his only grandson, admittedly, but he couldn't have been happier with his choice of bride and that was all that mattered.

Much later that evening when the newlyweds had retired to bed, Sunday and John sat in the kitchen enjoying a last hot drink together when suddenly, to Sunday's surprise, he reached across the table and tenderly took her hand.

'Now don't get going all soppy on me again just because we've got the newlyweds home,' she warned with a little grin. Since the night John had made the marriage proposal to her so long ago, he had behaved like the perfect gentleman. But she needn't have worried.

'I wasn't about to,' he assured her with a grin. 'But what I *do* want to do is let you know that you and your family – or *our* family I should say now, shouldn't I? – have come to mean a very great deal to me. I'm thrilled with the way things have turned out for all our children and I want to thank you most sincerely for all you've done for me.'

'I think it's more a case of what *you* have done for me,' Sunday told him. 'But why are you getting all sentimental on me?' That strange sense of foreboding that sometimes came over her had crept up on her again and it was unsettling.

'I just wanted you to know that I think of you as my dearest friend. And now we shall change the subject, my dear.'

Soon after, they both retired to bed but for some reason Sunday's mind was working overtime and she tossed and turned all night.

She rose at dawn the following morning and for no reason that Sunday could explain she went to tap on John's door.

'John . . . John are you awake?' There was no answer, so she tapped again, slightly louder this time.

She paused before inching the door open and peeping into the room. John was lying in bed with a peaceful smile on his face and she knew before she reached him that he was dead. He had said his goodbyes to her in his own inimitable way the night before. Leaning over him she bent to kiss his cold forehead as a tear slid down her cheek.

'Goodbye, dear friend. And thank you,' she whispered and then turning she quietly tiptoed from the room.

Chapter Fifty-Seven

July 1946

'Do you *really* have to go into town today, darling?'

Kathy glanced at her mother in the mirror as she brushed her hair. She had only popped in to Treetops to check on Sunday on her way into town.

'Yes, I do,' she said. 'And I wish you'd stop fussing over me, Mum. I'm pregnant, not ill.'

'Well, I don't think anyone could doubt that looking at you,' her mother quipped. In actual fact Kathy was positively glowing with health. 'But you are very close to your time and I don't like you going out alone.'

'Oh, Mum, do stop fussing.' Kathy grinned. 'If I felt anything happening in town, I wouldn't have to go far to the hospital now, would I? And I have a few last-minute things that I need to pick up before this little one – or should I say *not* so little one – makes an appearance. Honestly it can't happen soon enough for me now. I feel like a beached whale and I've forgotten what my feet look like! But don't get worrying, I shall be back in plenty of time to meet the children from school. I think Giles is taking the twins and Peggy swimming this evening. Meantime you just take your time and put your feet up.'

'I'm perfectly all right, thank you,' Sunday said.

'Oh yes, so why did the doctor call round to see you again on Friday?'

'I just asked him to call to prescribe me a tonic,' her mother said a little too quickly and Kathy frowned.

'You would tell me if something were wrong, wouldn't you?' she persisted, and Sunday scowled.

'Oh, get away with you if you're going. Didn't I say I was fine? Or at least as fine as a woman of seventy-six can hope to be. You'd hardly expect me to be leaping about like a spring chicken now, would you?'

Kathy grinned and, snatching up her bag, she headed for the door, stopping on her way to plant a kiss on her mother's cheek and tell her, 'I love you, Mum.'

'I love you too, now shoo!' Sunday watched Kathy waddle off down the drive where she would wait in the lane for the next bus into town. Very soon now Sunday would have two new grandchildren, for Livvy was also expecting her first baby in September and she and Giles could hardly wait.

It had been a terrible shock for Giles when his grandfather had died the very day he returned, and it had put back his recovery quite some time. She shook her head, not wanting to dwell on those sad memories. It had been a shock to all of them, coming after so many happy events. She sighed. But that was how life worked, as she knew all too well. Still, gradually, with Livvy's loving care, Giles had recovered and now he was building their stud business back up with horses from tried and trusted breeders.

Sunday stared across the lawns through the open window.

She felt every year of her age now and often she wished she could just go to sleep and not wake up. She had felt that way ever since John had died. It was only after he had gone that she'd realised how much she had come to care for him. Not in the way she had cared for her Tom, admittedly, but they had been very close all the same. And now there were times when she felt almost redundant. Both of the girls had their own lives to lead and she dreaded becoming a burden to them. And Livvy and Edith had Treetops running like clockwork with the help of a woman from the village who came in three times a week to do the laundry and help with the cleaning.

Cissie and George had eventually retired shortly after last Christmas, but they were still living in the cottage close by, and every afternoon Cissie would come and the two of them would sit with a cup of tea and their feet up talking about times past.

'We're a right old pair o' biddies now, ain't we?' Cissie had chuckled only the day before and Sunday could only agree with her.

'You're right, if we were horses, we'd be put out to grass.'

Sunday smiled slightly at the memory. She loved the quiet times she spent with Cissie – she was her oldest friend after all – but today, once again, the bad feeling was on her and rising slowly from her chair she leaned towards the window and peered down the drive for a sign of Kathy, but she had long gone from view, so Sunday headed for the kitchen to see if there was a cup of tea going and to keep herself occupied.

Cissie was already there enjoying a tea break with Edith when she entered the room and she asked instantly, 'What's up wi' your face then? Yer look like you've lost a bob an' found a sixpence!'

'Oh, it's just me being silly really, I suppose.' Sunday plonked herself down beside her old friend. 'I was just the same when Kathy was having the twins but now that she's getting close to her time I'm fretting again. I keep thinking about what happened to her poor mother when she gave birth to our Kathy.'

'That was a long time ago,' Cissie pointed out. 'And Kathy is the picture o' health so get this cup o' tea inside yer an' stop bein' so daft.'

Sunday smiled but the bad feeling remained.

On a whim, Kathy decided to get off the bus at the end of Manor Court Road and walk to the hospital to see if David was about. She wanted to talk to him about her mother because she was sure there was something Sunday wasn't telling her, and she was worried. She knew it would be no good asking the doctor why he had been visiting her more frequently of late, patient confidentiality would mean he wasn't allowed to say anything, even though he had known Kathy all her life, but there was *something* wrong, she just knew it!

It was a beautiful day with the sun riding high in a cloudless blue sky, but Kathy was so lost in thought she hardly noticed it until suddenly she heard a woman scream and, glancing up, she saw a car careering along the road towards her. The driver appeared to be slumped across the steering wheel, but she had no time to register anything else because as it drew closer it mounted the pavement and suddenly she had the sensation of flying as it hit her full on. Seconds later she hit the ground with a resounding thud and a pain tore through her stomach as her hand dropped to protectively cover her unborn child. And then thankfully a welcoming darkness claimed her, and she knew no more.

'Get the theatre ready immediately. We have a heavily pregnant woman coming in who has been hit by a car. It seems the driver of the car had a heart attack and lost control.'

David had been coming out of his office when he heard the ambulance screech to a halt outside and heard the nurse's voice.

Two ambulance men were lifting a prone figure on a stretcher from the back of the ambulance and as they dashed inside with it, David felt his heart turn over. It was Kathy . . . *his Kathy!*

Matron had run from her office and taking stock of the situation immediately, she ordered David, 'Go back into your office, Dr Deacon. Dr Greaves will handle this.'

Dr Greaves, the other surgeon who worked at the hospital, was there that day, thankfully. Matron knew it would be far too hard for David to have to operate on his own wife.

'I think the baby is on the way,' a grim-faced ambulance man informed her as they hurried past.

'Very well, get her into that side ward so we can see the extent of the injuries.'

David was still standing as if he had been turned to stone and everything seemed to be happening in slow motion.

'Nurse, get Dr Deacon a cup of hot, sweet tea,' Matron ordered as she swept past at Kathy's side. And still David stood there as if he had been rooted to the spot. Suddenly he seemed to come to his senses and sprang forward to follow them only to be stopped by a restraining hand on his arm.

'Come on, David.' He glanced up to see one of the ward sisters looking at him sympathetically. 'Let them assess her before you go in.'

He allowed himself to be led away, still in a state of deep shock and minutes later there was a steaming cup in front of him.

'Get that down you. It will make you feel better,' the kindly sister urged but he shook his head numbly.

This wasn't how he and Kathy had planned the birth of their baby to be at all and he felt completely useless. The minutes dragged by, each one feeling like an hour. After what seemed an eternity, Matron reappeared in the doorway.

'Kathy is in theatre,' she told him gravely. 'Dr Greaves is going to deliver the baby then see what we can do for Kathy, but I should warn you it appears that she has serious injuries. I'm *so* sorry.'

He sat on until the door opened again.

'You have a very beautiful little son,' Matron informed him.

His head snapped up. 'And Kathy . . .?'

Gravely she shook her head and as his heart began to thump painfully, he saw that there were tears in her eyes. 'I'm so sorry, there was nothing that could be done for her.'

As David's whole world collapsed around him, he lowered his head and wept.

'I can't believe it,' Sunday muttered brokenly to Cissie later that evening. 'We lived all through the war and then we lose my girl to a car accident! Didn't I tell you this morning that I had a bad feeling? It's like losing my Kitty all over again.'

Cissie squeezed her arm gently. 'It's tragic what's happened, but we have to stay strong for David and the new baby now, love. And the twins. They're going to need us all to stay strong for them. It's what Kathy would have wanted. We've lived through enough heartache in our time, we'll come through this, you'll see.'

And yet as she stared at her beloved friend, she wasn't so sure. This latest tragedy seemed to have broken Sunday completely and Cissie was concerned for her. She was also worried about how the news had affected Livvy. She was close to the birth of her own baby now and heartbroken at the loss of the girl who had been brought up as her sister.

The funeral took place two weeks later on just the sort of day Kathy would have loved – bright and sunny – which made it all the harder. She was laid to rest not far from Tom and Ben, with all the people she loved gathered around, and the next day the baby was allowed home from hospital. David named him Edward and, having taken indefinite leave from work, insisted on caring for all the children himself. His parents had travelled from Yorkshire to help and they fell in love with their new grandchildren immediately. And so, it was no surprise when David visited Sunday one bright, sunny morning to tell her, 'I, er . . . I've made a decision and I need to speak to you about it.'

Sunday stared at him from dull eyes.

'The thing is . . . I've spoken to my parents and they've asked me to go back to Yorkshire so that the children and I can live with them. Mum will take care of them when I go back to work.

I hope you can understand, there are just too many memories here for me and we'll have a fresh start there.'

Sunday sighed; she had half expected this. The twins' adoption had been finalised some months ago and so Daisy and Thomas were now legally his.

'Don't worry, I shall bring all the children to see you as often as I can,' David rushed on, feeling guilty. Poor Sunday had lost her daughter and now she was about to lose her grandchildren too. But surprisingly she nodded.

'It might be for the best. We old codgers are past caring for them properly now and, as you say, they'll have a fresh new start there.' And then suddenly they were in each other's arms crying for the beautiful young woman they had both loved so much.

Two weeks later, on the day before they were due to leave, David took the children to place flowers on their mother's grave.

'I miss Mummy,' Daisy said tearfully.

'I know you do, sweetheart, we all do,' David said gravely as he cuddled baby Edward close to his chest. 'But she'll always be with us in our hearts and we still have each other.'

They stood for a few moments letting the peace of the place wash over them as they listened to the birds in the trees, then slowly they all made their way back to the car.

The following day, Sunday waved them all off from the steps of Treetops with a smile on her face, and it was only once they'd gone that she gave way to the tears she'd been holding back.

'I'm so *tired* of life, Cissie,' she sniffed. 'I'm worrying about how Livvy's birth will go now.'

'Don't be so silly,' Cissie scolded. 'Livvy is blossoming, or she was until this happened. She'll be absolutely fine. What happened to Kathy was just a tragic accident.'

Thankfully Cissie was proved to be right when Livvy gave birth to a fine, healthy little girl in September, who they named Eva Katherine. She was a delightful baby, only crying when she was hungry, and she went a very long way to lightening the mood at Treetops. Giles and Livvy were besotted with her and now at last Sunday felt that things might improve.

Eva was a week old when Edith took a cup of tea up for Sunday one morning and she told her, 'I think I'll have a day in bed, if you don't mind, dear? I'm feeling rather tired. I think everything that's happened the last few months is catching up with me.' Edith nodded but she was concerned. 'It just isn't like her to want to stay in bed,' she confided to Cissie. 'Do you think we should ring the doctor to come out and take a look at her?'

'Yes. In fact, I'll do it meself right now.' Cissie marched away to make the call. She had never really cared for the telephone and avoided using it whenever possible, but today she would make an exception.

Chapter Fifty-Eight

'Aw *please*, lass, just try a mouthful,' Cissie implored as she held the rich chicken soup to Sunday's lips, but she merely gave her a weary smile and turned her head towards the window.

'I don't want anything,' she said quietly. 'I'm waiting for Tom. He'll be coming for me soon and I must be ready.'

Sunday had now spent almost three weeks in bed getting weaker by the day and the doctor had told a very concerned Livvy and Cissie that there was nothing more to be done.

'She has had an irregular heartbeat for some time,' he confided – there seemed no point in hiding it from them any longer. 'But it's as if she's given up now and wants to die. I think losing Kathy so tragically was the last straw. All you can do is keep her comfortable.'

Livvy began to cry and Cissie put her arms about her shoulder as Edith saw the doctor out.

'There must be *something* we can do,' Livvy sobbed, feeling totally helpless.

Cissie shook her head. 'I'm afraid she's just worn out,' she said softly. 'You must remember she had a very hard life until she came to live at Treetops, and even then she worked harder than anyone I know. She's been a mother to dozens of children as well as her own.'

'I know,' Livvy sniffed. 'But she still has so much to live for. We are all grieving for Kathy, but we have Eva now, and little Edward, surely that should give Mum the will to live?'

'Ah, but she knows that Eva has a mummy and daddy who love her more than life itself, and Edward has David,' Cissie pointed out. 'And your mum is old and tired now. She still misses your father so much, so let's just do what the doctor said and see how it goes, eh? It could be that she'll rally round.' But knowing Sunday as she did, deep down Cissie doubted it.

For the last few days she and Livvy had taken it in turns to stay with Sunday throughout the night. It was Cissie's turn next and, as darkness fell, she took her place at Sunday's bedside and lifted her knitting – she was making a little matinée coat for Eva. For some reason, though, Sunday seemed unnaturally restless and talkative that night so Cissie put the knitting aside and pulled her chair closer to the bed.

'We've had a long and good life, haven't we, Cissie?'

'Aye, we have. It ain't always been an easy one but we got by,' Cissie agreed with a nod of her head. They talked of their past then, going right back to the awful time they had spent in the Union Workhouse in their childhood. They spoke of the joy when Sunday had been finally reunited with her mother, Lady Lavinia, and of the night they had found their Kathy's mother on the doorstep of Treetops. It all seemed so very long ago now and so much had happened in between.

Slowly the evening shadows filled the room. It was early October and there was a nip in the air at night now and the first leaves were beginning to flutter from the trees. At one point,

Livvy came in with baby Eva and Giles to say goodnight and Sunday kissed her beautiful new granddaughter affectionately.

'May she grow in beauty and grace,' Sunday whispered as they turned to leave the room.

'Don't talk like that, Mum, you sound as if you're never going to see her again,' Livvy scolded gently and after planting another kiss on her mother's wrinkled cheek they quietly left the room.

'I reckon it's time to draw the curtains an' put the light on now,' Cissie said, feeling vaguely uneasy as she made to rise from her chair, but Sunday shook her head.

'No, leave it as it is. I want to see the stars.'

Cissie sat back down. Outside the window was a black velvet sky with millions of stars twinkling, and taking Cissie's hand Sunday whispered, 'I never had a sister, Cissie, but if I had, I would have wanted her to be exactly like you. You have been my rock through all these long years and all the trials and tribulations, and I want you to know that I love you dearly.'

'I love you an' all, yer daft old thing,' Cissie said chokily as she sat close, holding Sunday's hand.

They settled into a companionable silence and shortly after that Sunday smiled and seemed to focus her attention on the shadows at the end of the bed. Cissie felt the hairs on the back of her neck stand on end as she followed Sunday's gaze, and just for a moment, she could have sworn she saw a shape there. She blinked and it was gone, and turning back to Sunday she saw that she was holding her hand out with a beautiful smile on her face that wiped away the years like magic.

'Tom . . . I *knew* you'd come,' she sighed and at the same instant Cissie felt the gentle pressure on her fingers slacken as Sunday's eyes closed for the very last time.

'Sunday . . . wake up . . . can yer hear me?' Tears were

streaming down Cissie's plump cheeks as she gently shook her beloved friend's shoulders, and yet already she knew that she had finally gone to a better place to be with the man she loved.

Bending, she placed a gentle kiss on her friend's cheek before stumbling blindly over to the window and there she stopped abruptly as she stared down at the garden below.

Lanterns were strung in the trees and somewhere an orchestra was playing as a young Sunday in her beautiful ivory wedding gown glided across the lawn in the arms of Tom, her handsome bridegroom, in the moonlight. They were laughing and happy as they looked adoringly at each other and slowly Cissie smiled through her tears. Sunday's passing would mark the end of an era and Cissie would always be grateful for being a part of her life.

'That's it, me lovelies,' she whispered. 'You have yer last dance an' may yer both rest in eternal peace.'

Acknowledgements

As always, I'd like to say a huge thank you to my amazing team at Bonnier for all their help and support during the writing of my Days of the Week collection. I can't believe it's ended!

Also special thanks to a very special lady, my wonderful agent Sheila Crowley, and to my copyeditor Gillian Holmes, who always helps to put the final polish on the finished book with me.

Thanks to all my lovely readers who take the time to get in touch with their feedback. It always makes my day when I hear from you.

And last but never least, my wonderful husband and family and my fur babies. I am so lucky to have you all!

Welcome to the world of
Rosie Goodwin!

Keep reading for more from Rosie Goodwin, to discover a recipe that features in this novel and to find out more about what Rosie Goodwin is doing next . . .

We'd also like to introduce you to MEMORY LANE, our special community for the very best of saga writing from authors you know and love, and new ones we simply can't wait for you to meet. Read on and join our club!

www.MemoryLane.club

Dear friends,

I hope you are all having a lovely summer after the awful wet winter we had! And now for those of you who haven't read the hardback, it's time for the paperback of *Time to Say Goodbye* to hit the shelves. I hope you'll enjoy it!

In this one I wanted to bring you all up to date with Sunday, who you will remember was the main character in the first of the series, *Mothering Sunday*. In *Time to Say Goodbye*, we meet Kathy, who is the daughter of Kitty, who died giving birth to her in *The Little Angel*. Kathy is all grown up now and in this one we will follow her and Sunday's trials through World War II.

I can't believe that this is the last of the series, and I have to admit I've shed tears throughout this book. I have been able to bring back many of the characters that you will remember from the previous stories. There's Ben, Flora and Jamie, Verity and Edgar, Cissie and George – to name but a few – as well as lots of new characters that I hope you will come to love as much as I did.

This has been such a lovely series to write and I've really enjoyed all of your feedback, but I suppose all good things must come to an end.

However, as sad as it is to say goodbye to them all, I can tell you that once I'd dried my eyes, in no time at all I'd begun another series, which I hope you will all enjoy just as much! The first book of this new collection, *The Winter Promise,* will be out for Christmas this year. It will be The Precious Stones collection, in which each of our main characters will be named after a gemstone. In the first one you will meet Opal, whose brother is sent to Australia on a convict ship, leaving the poor girl to cope all on her own.

The second one is about an orphan girl called Pearl. I've now completed that one too and am working on Ruby, the third of the series and am loving it! Each of the characters becomes so real to me that I laugh and cry with them and, as always, I'm enjoying the research! It's amazing that nowadays we can go anywhere in the world on our computer without even moving out of our chair!

In March I was delighted when my last book, *A Precious Gift*, was shortlisted for the RNA romantic sage of the year award and I had a wonderful evening in London with my lovely editor, Sarah and her assistant, Katie, at the awards ceremony – apart from getting locked in the toilet for fifteen minutes, that is! The lock on the door broke and a maintenance man had to come and break the frame to rescue me! Ha ha, it could only happen to me but it didn't spoil the evening.

Do join the Memory Lane Club on Facebook if you haven't already done so. There are some wonderful competitions on there and lovely prizes to be won, and you'll also be kept up to date with what's happening with all the Memory Lane authors.

It is strange now to think that while writing *Time to Say Goodbye*, me and my family had been spending as much time as we could at the coast with our dogs and loving it. I know many of you will have had your holiday plans postponed or cancelled and my heart goes out to you – I miss our lodge at the seaside and, of course, my family. At the time of writing this letter, this terrible Coronavirus has worked its way around the world and has us all on lockdown – it's very frightening. I hope that by the time you're reading this, we're back outside and reunited with our loved ones. I know it has been a difficult time for everyone and I am sending my best wishes to every single one of you. I've received some lovely messages from people reading my books during self-isolation and I am so pleased if I've managed to bring any comfort or distraction to my readers – I know I certainly turned to books, and almost ran out!

I hope you all manage to enjoy the summer, and I look forward to hearing from you as always.

Take care and much love,
Rosie xxx

Cissie's Roast Chicken

This delightful chicken dish inspired by Cissie is sure to bring warmth and an incredible aroma into your home.

You will need:

1 whole chicken	1 lemon, cut in half
1 chopped onion	Few sprigs of thyme
2 chopped carrots	30g butter

Method:

1. Preheat your oven to 170°C/190°C fan/gas mark 5
2. Put the chopped onion and carrots around the base of the roasting tin.
3. Season the cavity of the chicken with salt and pepper, then place both lemon halves and the thyme inside the chicken.
4. Place the chicken on top of the carrots and onions and rub all over with butter, then season with salt and pepper.
5. Put the roasting tin in the oven and cook for 1 hour and 20 minutes. To check if the chicken is cooked, the outside should be golden brown and the juices should run clear.
6. Remove from the oven and rest the chicken for 15 minutes.
7. Serve with roasted potatoes and other vegetables, and enjoy!

Read on for a sneak peak of Rosie Goodwin's next novel, *The Winter Promise*, the first in her new Precious Stones series.

Prologue

Fenny Drayton, December 1867

'*Please*, Opal . . . can we stop now? Me feet are hurtin' an' me tummy aches.'

'Not yet, sweetheart, we have to find somewhere to stay first, before it gets properly dark.'

Opal Sharp stared down at Susie, her six-year-old sister, and gave her an encouraging smile, as she shifted the weight of her two-year-old brother, Jack, on her hip. He was fast asleep, although how he managed it she had no idea. She had wrapped him tightly in her shawl, then tied it about her waist, but despite the bitter cold she could feel the burning heat of him against her chest and she was gravely concerned. He obviously had the fever that had taken their father just days before, and she was all too aware that he shouldn't be out in the bad weather – but she had had no choice in the matter.

The cottage they had lived in was tied to the farm that her father had worked for, and once he had died the farmer had turned up on the same day as the funeral, telling her that they must all be out by late afternoon. Left with no alternative, Opal had instructed Charlie to load whatever he could of their possessions onto the hand cart, and now they were in search of somewhere to shelter from the storm. The snow was coming down thick and fast, getting deeper underfoot by the minute and behind her she could hear fifteen-year-old Charlie grunting softly with exertion as he yanked at the handles of the small wooden cart. Thankfully a kindly neighbour had offered to take in the rest of their possessions until they found somewhere to stay.

'I'd have you all 'ere in a sigh,' she had told them sympathetically, 'but I daren't upset Farmer Gold or else my Stan might be out of a job an' all.'

'We – have – to – find – somewhere – soon,' Charlie gasped. 'I don't know how much further I can pull this thing.'

'We'll find somewhere, you'll see,' Opal answered, with a confidence she was far from feeling.

They had already tramped for miles, first down the old Roman Road, then through the village of Hartshill. They had then slid and slithered their way down Bucks Hill and now they were on the ground known to the locals as Rapper's Hole. It was nothing more than a wasteland of fields with an odd scattering of huts and dilapidated cottages scattered here and there, but Opal could think of nowhere else they could go. Even a run-down cottage would be some shelter from the cold, if they could only find one.

They trudged on, getting more dispirited by the minute. At last, a building suddenly loomed up out of the snow ahead of them and, dropping the handles of the cart, Charlie rushed towards it. It was what appeared to be a very old derelict cottage.

'It's empty,' he shouted excitedly. 'Perhaps we could rest here for the night, Opal?'

As she approached, she saw that there was a large hole in

the roof on one side of the building. It was surrounded by a picket fence from which an old gate hung on a single hinge. The tiny leaded windows – or what remained of them – were black and bleak looking and it looked barely habitable, but then she supposed Charlie was right – any port in a storm would be welcome at that moment.

As Susie raced ahead, Opal followed as fast as she could. On entering, she found herself in what she presumed must once have been a small kitchen cum sitting room, although it was hard to see in the all-enveloping gloom. The roof in this room seemed to be intact, so, quickly deciding, she told Charlie, 'Go and grab the cart. We'll light some candles and we'll try to get a fire going.'

He was gone before the words had left her mouth and, minutes later, she heard him grunting as he yanked the cart down the small overgrown path. Placing Jack in Susie's arms, she soon located the candles and matches. Once she had managed to light one, they looked around. Luckily there were odd bits of broken furniture lying about, so at least they would have some dry wood for the fire. A small inglenook fireplace was set into one wall and, after scraping out the dead ashes onto the hearth with his hands, Charlie immediately began to break the wood into pieces and set them into the fire basket.

Soon after he had it alight and, now with the candle burning and the faint glow from the fire, they could better see the room. A grimy deep stone sink stood against one wall and low beams framed the ceiling – but at least this room was fairly dry. The floor was littered with dirt and from the terrible smell that hung in the air, Opal suspected animals had found refuge there.

She couldn't believe how quickly their lives had changed, that they were now having to sleep here, but she couldn't think about that now. Pushing her worries aside, she rooted about in the cart and pulled out the blankets she had packed then shook the snow from them. Little Susie was struggling to keep her eyes open, and Opal immediately laid some of the blankets on the floor in front of the fire, instructing Charlie, 'Take the kettle and fill it with snow. I'll make us a brew of tea and at least it will warm us.'

While Charlie was doing that, Opal quickly settled Susie and Jack on the blankets and blocked up the broken panes in the window with rags or anything that came to hand. Soon after that, the kettle was placed on the fire and it gradually got a little warmer. Opal rooted in the cart for the half a loaf she had bought with them and tore chunks off it.

Susie took hers and hungrily began to gnaw on it, but Jack turned his head away as beads of sweat stood out like jewels on his forehead in the glow from the fire.

'He really needs to see a doctor,' Charlie said worriedly and Opal snorted.

'I don't even know how we're going to *eat* tomorrow, let alone pay for a doctor's visit!' she snapped and was instantly repentant. 'Sorry, Charlie, I'm just tired,' she explained guiltily.

'It's all right.' He awkwardly patted her arm and fell silent, as she poured the now boiling water into the old brown teapot and set it on the hearth to mash. She found the mismatched cups and poured them their tea and, minutes later, Susie was snoring softly.

Opal almost envied her. She was only a child and had no idea what a terrible position they were in. It was hard to believe now that only a few short months before they had been a close-knit happy family. True, her mother had suffered from ill health for some time, which was why Opal had given up her job in the little village shop – she was needed to help at home. But even then they had been comfortable with the wages that her father and Charlie earned on the farm. But then their hearts had all broken when their mother had died giving birth to their new baby sister, who was stillborn. And just nine weeks later their world collapsed when their father was suddenly struck down with the fever, and soon followed their ma. Now here they were, with no home, no parents, no money and no prospects.

'What are we goin' to do, Opal?' Charlie's face was fearful. Although he was only a year younger than his sister, he usually depended on her to make the decisions.

'Whatever we have to do to survive,' she answered. She dreaded what might be ahead.

'I think we may well have to put the little two into the work-house,' he said tentatively. 'At least there Jack will get the medical attention he needs and they'll both be fed.'

Opal was so horrified that she almost dropped her cup, and slopped hot tea over her leg. 'Ouch! . . . *Over my dead body!*'

'Well, have you got a *better* idea?' Tears stung at the back of Charlie's eyes as he pictured the cold grim façade of the Union Workhouse up on the Bullring – but he pushed back his mop of thick, curly brown hair and blinked them away. Just the mention of the place could strike terror into the hardest of hearts, but what choice did they have? At least if he knew the little ones were being looked after, he and Opal could find work and somewhere to live, and hopefully they could get them back out of the place before too long.

'It would only be until we could find somewhere decent to live and have enough money coming in to feed them,' he said gently.

'I know – but I can't bear to think of them in that place, or

of us separated. We're the only family they've got now – we need to stick together.' Opal hung her head as she stared at her two younger siblings. With their thick black hair and their tawny brown eyes, they looked like two little peas in a pod. They all did, if it came to that; they all took after their late mother in looks. She could hear her father even now, laughing and teasing that it wasn't fair that not one of his children had taken after him.

As the painful memories of happier times rushed back, Opal rose and went to stuff an old sack beneath the door to try and stop the wicked draught that was whistling beneath it.

'Let's try an' get some sleep, eh?' Charlie suggested, seeing that Opal was almost at the end of her tether. 'Jack might be a lot better in the morning and things will look brighter. An' at least we have somewhere dry to sleep.'

She managed to raise a weak smile, but as she curled up beneath the thin blanket she wasn't so sure, and when she finally fell into an exhausted sleep, there were tears on her cheeks.

Chapter One

Early the next morning, Opal woke to an eerie grey silence, and as she stared towards the window, all she could see was the snow piled high on the ledge. The fire was almost out and it was bitterly cold again, so she hastily broke up what was left of an old chair and threw it onto the fire.

Charlie stretched and yawned and, pulling himself onto his elbow, asked, 'What time is it?'

Opal shrugged. 'I don't know. We took the mantel clock to the pawnbrokers last week, if you remember?' She could have added, 'along with everything else decent we owned' but thought better of it.

'Ah, yes.' He sighed. Then, pushing his blanket aside, he rose and lifted the kettle. 'I'll go and get some more snow. At least we can have a hot drink.' They had no sugar or milk, but they'd grown used to drinking their tea without over the last weeks. After slipping his boots on, he attempted to open the door and was almost knocked over by the drift that had piled up against it during the night, as it spilled into the room.

'Cor blimey,' he breathed. 'Would yer just look at that!'

As far as his eye could see was nothing but a vast white

wilderness and it was eerily silent. He suddenly felt as if they might be the only people left in the world. Even the birds were not singing and the snow was still coming down like a thick white blanket. Hastily he stooped and filled the kettle, then, kicking what he could of the snow back out of the door, he quickly closed it again.

Susie also stirred at that moment and, when she looked towards the window, she clapped her hands with delight. 'Ooh, look at the snow,' she chirped. 'Will I be able to go out on me sledge, Opal?'

Opal smiled indulgently as she smoothed the fall of black curls from the little girl's face. Suddenly she felt old, for not so long ago she would have been excited to see the snow, too. Now she could only see the problems it would bring.

'Your sledge is back at Mrs Kitely's, love,' she explained and Susie pouted.

But then she began to cough. Opal quickly felt her forehead. It was hot and her heart sank. It looked as if Susie was about to come down with the fever, too.

Charlie also looked concerned as he saw the unnatural flush in his little sister's cheeks, but he said nothing as he wedged the kettle into the heart of the fire.

'Right now, let's see what we've got for breakfast,' Opal said in a falsely bright voice, as she rummaged in the small food bag in the cart. 'Ah, we have some oats here – look, that should fill us up.' They had no milk so she would have to boil them in water and they would be fairly tasteless – but she supposed it was better than nothing.

'I'm not hungry.' As Susie burrowed down beneath her blanket again, Charlie and Opal exchanged a worried glance.

Opal boiled the remainder of the oats and somehow, she and

Charlie washed them down with tea, but Susie refused it and Opal decided it was best to let Jack sleep.

'We're going to have to get some food in,' Opal muttered, glancing worriedly at the blizzard beyond the window. 'Though goodness knows how we're going to get through this lot. The nearest store is in Stockingford from here.'

'I know where it is,' Charlie assured her. 'And don't worry, I'll get through. But do we have any money left for food? And where are we going to stay tonight?'

'It looks like we'll have to stay here,' Opal replied. 'I can give the room a clean and at least it's dry. And yes, I do have a little money left from the money we got at the pawnbrokers, but not much.'

As she rummaged in the pocket of her dress and withdrew a few pennies, Charlie sighed. 'We're not going to get much with that.'

'We'll just get basics, some flour, a twist of tea and a pat of butter. I can bake some bread then. There's a small oven in the side of the inglenook look, though I dread to think what state it will be in. But never mind, I can soon scrub it out while you're gone. I'll have a look round the other rooms as well and see if there's anything we can use to make ourselves a little more comfortable. It looks like we're going to be stuck here at least until the snow goes now.'

Charlie pulled his boots on and wrapped up as warmly as he could. Then, with a nod at his sister, he set off. The two smaller children were snoring softly, so now that it was light Opal decided to see what state the rest of the rooms were in.

A door was set into the wall at the side of the fireplace and, on opening it, she found herself in what had clearly once been a bedroom. It was so cold in there that it almost took her breath away, so she quickly stepped inside, shutting the door behind her to keep what warmth she could in the kitchen. She clutched her shawl more tightly about her. There was a yawning hole in the roof and a pile of snow was heaped in the centre of the room. Against one wall was an old iron framed bed with what remained of a straw mattress on it and against another wall was a chest of drawers with one drawer missing.

Well there's no way we can use this room until the roof had been repaired, she thought despondently, kicking at what appeared to be the remains of a wooden chair. At least the wood could be used to keep the fire burning though. She quickly stooped to gather it up and carried it back to the kitchen, before cautiously starting up a staircase that was little more than a ladder and led to the upper storey.

She found herself in a small room which was surprisingly dry, with yet another old bed against one wall. The roof sloped in here, and she could only stand up in the centre of the room, but even so she could see that without too much work it could become usable.

She went back down the stairs as quietly as she could so as not to wake the children and headed for the last door to the other side of the fireplace. Once inside she found herself in what had clearly once been used as a small sitting room. An old sideboard that was thick with dirt and grime stood beneath the window but a quick glance around showed that all the rest of the furniture was broken and probably beyond repair, apart from a solid looking oak table that took pride of place in the centre of the room.

With a sigh, she made her way back into the kitchen and began to remove some of the cleaning things she had loaded into the cart, deciding that she could clean the kitchen up at least. Next, she refilled the kettle with snow again and, after heating it on the fire, she filled a bucket and attacked the floor with a broom, making dust fly everywhere. She was pleased to find that although filthy there were old quarry tiles on the floor. Many of the cottages thereabouts only had earth floors and after scrubbing them they began to look quite nice. She attacked the windows once that was done and now that all the rubbish was piled at the side of the inglenook ready to be burned the room began to look much better and her spirits began to lift a little.

Charlie looked about in amazement when he returned almost two hours later, and a smile formed at the corners of his mouth. 'Blimey, sis, someone's been busy,' he said approvingly, stamping the snow from his boots.

'There's a room upstairs under the eaves and another one through that door there that are quite dry,' she said, as she took the basket of shopping from him. 'But that room through there can't be used 'til the roof is repaired. But for now, come and sit by the fire and get those wet clothes off. You look frozen through and you'll be ill next if you don't do as you're told.'

Charlie's teeth were chattering and his hands and feet were blue as Opal searched through the cart for a change of clothes for him. Once she'd found them, he turned his back and quickly scrambled into them, then made for the fire as he glanced anxiously towards the two little ones. 'So how are they this morning?'

Opal shrugged helplessly. 'Jack hasn't even woken up and Susie doesn't seem well either, but there's not much we can do apart from try to keep them warm for now.'

'Hm!' He sighed and took a good look around the room. 'Aw well, it looks like we could be here for a while in that case,' he commented. 'But it won't be so bad when I fetch our things from Mrs Kitely's.'

Opal snorted as she glanced at the storm that was raging outside. 'And how are you going to do that in this weather? You'd never be able to drag the cart through this.'

She began to knead the flour and yeast to make some bread on the wooden draining board that was attached to the sink, which she had thoroughly scrubbed. Once it was ready, she wet a cloth to throw over the dough and put the dishes onto the hearth to prove. She'd discovered a pump over the sink that she assumed must lead to a well outside. At first the water it yielded had been brown and rusty looking, but now it was crystal clear, which meant she no longer had to rely on melting snow for their water supply – one blessing at least. She had also found the precious jar of homemade strawberry jam that she had made earlier in the summer, so they were assured of eating – for today at least.

Susie stirred at that moment and raising herself up onto one elbow she croaked, 'Me throat is sore, Opal.'

It was so unlike the placid child to complain that Opal was instantly concerned. 'I'll make you a nice warm cup of tea, that'll help it,' she soothed, pushing the kettle into the heart of the fire again. Jack was stirring too, but one glance into his sunken eyes made Opal's heart sink. His cheeks were rosy red and his clothes were plastered to his thin frame with sweat.

Charlie had also noticed and he chewed on his lip worriedly. 'He's burning up. What can we do for him?'

'Get me a bowl of cool water, I'll try sponging him down,' Opal answered, and he shot away to do as he was asked.

For the next few hours they took turns dripping water into the children's mouths and sponging their feverish brows, but as the afternoon began to darken it was soon clear that their efforts had been in vain. Opal herself was feeling unwell by then and, although she didn't mention it, Charlie had noticed the tell-tale flush in her cheeks.

'Why don't you lie down and have a rest?' he suggested kindly. 'I can see to the children.'

He grew even more concerned when Opal agreed. Usually she would have just kept going, so he knew that she must be feeling ill. Curling up on the blankets next to the children, she drew herself into a ball, and seconds later she had slipped into an exhausted sleep.

Charlie divided his attention between the two children, trying hard to swallow the knot of fear in his throat. What would he do if anything should happen to Opal? How would he cope? She had kept the family together ever since his father had died and somehow they had all come to rely on her. But he tried not to look too far ahead – the future looked bleak at present and it was just too frightening. He knew that he should be out looking for work, any work that would bring a little money in, but how could he leave his family when they were all so ill?

Eventually, as Opal tossed and turned restlessly, he lit the candles and tried to tempt the children with some of the fresh bread Opal had baked – but they both turned their heads away and now he was so worried that even he had no appetite anymore. The snow continued to fall and all he could hear was the spitting of the wood on the fire and the whimpers of the children. He had no way of knowing what time it was, but after what seemed like a lifetime Opal stirred and painfully dragged herself up onto one elbow.

'How are you feeling now?' Even as the words left his lips, he realised how inadequate they were. Any fool could see that his sister was very poorly indeed. Beads of sweat were dripping into her eyes and she was shivering uncontrollably.

Rising hastily, he fetched her a cup of water, but after gulping at it greedily, she leaned over and vomited it back onto the floor.

'I . . . I'm sorry,' she croaked. 'But I . . . I'm not feeling so good. Can you manage if I go back to sleep?'

'Of course I can,' he assured her, but inside he was quaking. Suddenly he had to accept that he could well be about to lose the rest of his family, and it was a terrifying thought.

The night that followed was one of the longest Charlie had ever known, as he ran amongst the invalids, offering cool drinks and whatever comfort he could.

Yet another eerie grey morning finally dawned, and by then Charlie knew what he had to do. It was not going to be easy, and he doubted that Opal would ever forgive him.

If she recovered, that was.

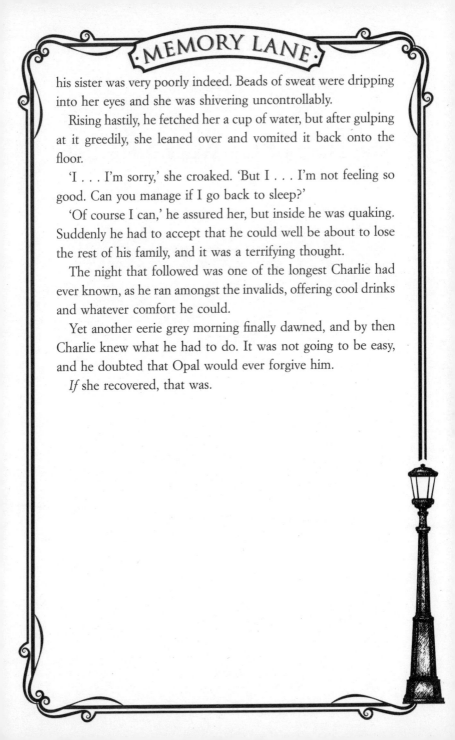

The Days of the Week collection

Time to Say Goodbye is the seventh and final book in
Rosie Goodwin's Days of the Week collection, inspired by
the Victorian 'Days of the Week' rhyme. If you enjoyed this,
why not try the other books in the collection?

Turn over to find out more . . .

Mothering Sunday

The child born on the Sabbath Day,
Is bonny and blithe, and good and gay.

1884, Nuneaton.

Fourteen-year-old Sunday has grown up in the cruelty of the Nuneaton workhouse. When she finally strikes out on her own, she is determined to return for those she left behind, and to find the long-lost mother who gave her away. But she's about to discover that the brutal world of the workhouse will not let her go without a fight.

The Little Angel

Monday's child is fair of face.

1896, Nuneaton.

Left on the doorstep of Treetops Children's Home, young Kitty captures the heart of her guardian, Sunday Branning, and grows into a beguiling and favoured young girl – until she is summoned to live with her birth mother. In London, nothing is what it seems, and her old home begins to feel very far away. If Kitty is to have any chance of happiness, this little angel must protect herself from devils in disguise . . . and before it's too late.

A Mother's Grace

Tuesday's child is full of grace.

1910, Nuneaton.

When her father's threatening behaviour grows worse, pious young Grace Kettle escapes her home to train to be a nun. But when she meets the dashing and devout Father Luke, her world is turned upside down. She is driven to make a scandalous choice – one she may well spend the rest of her days seeking forgiveness for.

The Blessed Child

Wednesday's child is full of woe.

1864, Nuneaton.

After Nessie Carson's mother is brutally murdered and her father abandons them, Nessie knows she will do anything to keep her family safe. As her fragile young brother's health deteriorates and she attracts the attention of her lecherous landlord, soon Nessie finds herself in the darkest of times. But there is light and the promise of happiness if only she is brave enough to fight for it.

A Maiden's Voyage

Thursday's child has far to go.

1912, London.

Eighteen-year-old maid Flora Butler has her life turned upside-down when her mistress's father dies in a tragic accident. Her mistress is forced to move to New York to live with her aunt until she comes of age, and begs Flora to go with her. Flora has never left the country before, and now faces a difficult decision – give up her position, or leave her family behind. Soon, Flora and her mistress head for Southampton to board the RMS *Titanic*.

A Precious Gift

Friday's child is loving and giving.

1911, Nuneaton.

When Holly Farthing's overbearing grand----father tries to force her to marry a widower twice her age, she flees to London, bringing her best friend and maid, Ivy, with her. In the big smoke, Holly begins nurse training in the local hospital. There she meets the dashing Doctor Parkin, everything Holly has ever dreamt of. But soon, she discovers some shocking news that means they can never be together, and her life is suddenly thrown into turmoil. Supporting the war effort, she heads to France and throws herself into volunteering on the front line . . .

Time to Say Goodbye

Saturday's child works hard for their living.

1935, Nuneaton.

Kathy has grown up at Treetops home for children, where Sunday and Tom Branning have always cared for her as one of their own. With her foster sister Livvy at her side, and a future as a nurse ahead of her, she could wish for nothing more. But when Tom dies suddenly in a riding accident, life at Treetops will never be the same again. As their financial difficulties mount, will the women of Treetops be forced to leave their home?